Unconditional Love

SAMSARA-THE FIRST SEASON

Volume One - Book Five

JL Martin

Time Travellers Publishing House PTY LTD

ALSO by JL Martin

FICTION

SAMSARA- The First Season

That Fated Night- A Short Novella of Love and Loss

The Golden Glow

Unexpected Beginnings

Torn in Two

Loss of Innocence

Unconditional Love

Returning Home

Letting go

Soul Connections

Healing the Heart

Legacy and Love

Leo- Back to me!

Lilith- Utopia

SPAWNED OF SIN- Trilogy Series

Through Windows in the Sky I Fall

Tainted Blood, Poisoned Soul

The Ties That Bind Behind Me

Unconditional Love

J. L. MARTIN

Published by Time Travellers Publishing House Pty Ltd 2021

The series is written in British English, as the Author is Australian and the books are based in Australia. My American friends will find U's where they have no right to be, Z replaced with S, and so many double L's you may feel like throwing the book against the wall. I apologise in advance, and hope one day we can all live in harmony...

National Library of Australia

Cataloging-in-Publication data

Martin, J L, 1971-.

Unconditional Love

Samsara-The First Season

ISBN Print: 978-1-925852-30-1

ISBN Ebook: 978-1-925852-29-5

Cover design by Thea Atkinson

Editing and text design by Marianne Delaforce

Printed and bound in Australia by Ingram Sparks

A Note from the Author

IN READING THE SERIES 'Samsara-The First Season', I ask you to consider the era in which this work of fiction is set. In these more enlightened times, elements of this story may be considered homophobic, racist, and outright morally corrupt—along with being barbaric and downright ignorant. However; in 19th century Australia, they were not. Themes throughout the series are reflective of the times and are an accurate account of the attitude, bias and outright hate a large majority of society held towards the LGBTQI+ Community and our First Nations Peoples. In saying this, we no longer consider it appropriate for a fifteen-year-old girl to marry—forced or not—but 130 years ago, it was not uncommon.

The character of Leo is based on a real person. As outrageous, inappropriate and politically incorrect as he is—I love this soul. It is not my intention to stigmatise him or cause offence to anyone—only to remain authentic in my best effort to honour and immortalise a very dear man who left a significant imprint on my life—and who unfortunately was born without a filter and lacks all sensibilities; and can be very, very badly behaved.

Please be aware there are themes of violence, racism, and homophobia throughout this series; however, I have been mindful to write these scenes as sensitively as possible and with the utmost care.

I truly hope you enjoy 'Samsara-The First Season' just as much as I enjoyed writing it.

Dedication

Dear little Makenzie.

You leave sunshine and a little of your sparkle wherever you go — and you've brought your great-grandfather joy beyond words and given him a few more years he wouldn't have had here with us. You are loved. Don't ever hide your light, sweetheart... not for anyone.

Chapter One

THE JOURNEY HOME TO Willow Grove passed in a blur of tears and regret. The image of Aaron standing on the platform alone and broken after we arrived on the afternoon train from Melbourne without our stillborn sons tore at my heart and would be forever etched in my mind as one of the darkest days of my life. Our boys had been transported back to Geelong by an undertaker Aaron had found in Melbourne who had kindly promised to care for them as if they were his own grandchildren. I was hurt. The loss of our weans to the physical violence I had suffered left every part of me from inside to out screaming in pain. Grief had hit me hard and penetrated my very core. The carriage ride to Willow Grove was the longest I had ever experienced. Only the dull, protective shell I had placed around my broken heart kept me outwardly calm while the overwhelming grief numbed my body, allowing me to endure the painful and endlessly bumpy journey home without complaint or care.

Once the undertaker arrived, he had carried them inside and we placed our beautiful boys side-by-side in their tiny, white coffin in the sitting room, their hands intertwined—now resting in a place where we spent so much of our time. Mr Masters felt the parlour would be more appropriate, but to us that room was cold and devoid of feeling—we wanted them in an environment filled with love and warmth, just as they would have been had they lived.

Catherine had made our boys the most beautiful white gowns, which the undertaker had carefully placed on their tiny forms. I sat with them into the evening, touching their little faces, thinking how much like Aaron they were. Staring in wonderment at how alike they were while stroking their wispy blonde hair, I cursed Sister Josephine's God for taking them away. They were identical, in fact, unlike our Thomas and Emmy. Harrison and Jack. Our Harrison and Jack. It would have been so lovely now Thomas and Emmy were growing up to have two miniatures of my husband running around the place and getting up to all sorts of mischief.

Unconsciously, I placed my hands on my belly to feel our unborn child kick, just as I had done every day for months. But I felt nothing. Nothing but my empty abdomen, and the thought caused the shell around my heart to crack. Fresh tears splashed down my cheeks while a strangled sob erupted from my mouth without warning. Within moments, I felt Aaron's kiss on my face. I hadn't realised he was there. I turned to him, my body weak and trembling as I struggled to straighten up to kiss him back.

'How ya travellin', mo anamchara?' His voice was barely above a whisper, his shoulders slumped as he sat down heavily beside me and took my hand.

'I don't know what to do. I'm just so, so sad.' I placed my head on his shoulder and sobbed again, my stomach in knots and my thoughts scrambled.

'I'm bloody sad too, Abi girl. It hit me in the guts.' He swallowed hard, quickly brushing away a stray tear from his red-rimmed eyes before stroking my cheek with his thumb. 'I wanna fix it all for ya, but the truth of the matter is the only thing I can do is to be here for ya in ya grief an' hope we can get through this together.'

He kissed my forehead, then ran his fingers through my loose and unruly hair. He rose to his feet, staring down silently for a long moment at our sons, before pulling me gently to mine and guiding me off to bed. Although the funeral was tomorrow, I needed my strength for what would be a busy and difficult day. Everyone we knew, and many we did not, was expected to attend. I wasn't confident I would sleep. Not tonight, or ever again. Somehow, though, perhaps from emotional as well as physical distress and exhaustion, I drifted off into a fitful slumber, while dreams of a redheaded child called Marigold tormented me into the wee hours and left me regretting closing my eyes at all.

We had been advised we could not hold a funeral mass for the twins in the church—the reason given being they were stillborn and unbaptised. Father Donnelly had kindly offered to perform the ceremony here in the gardens on compassionate grounds. We would then take them out to the island where they would be buried. The kindly young priest had been so supportive since we'd returned to Willow Grove, calling on us each day.

Yesterday, he had visited us with Archbishop Thomas Carr, who had travelled all the way from Melbourne at his request. They had requested to be taken to the island, and Aaron had obliged and rowed them across. They walked from one end to the other, praying while sprinkling holy water on the ground as they went—blessing the place for those who rested there and those who would be entombed in its soil in the future. Father Donnelly declared the ground consecrated, although my understanding was that they had not conducted all the official business or rituals to make it so in the eyes of the Catholic Church—at our request. We wanted those already resting there, and our friends and family who would eventually lay their bones in our small graveyard, to have the blessings of their God around them. No matter what their faith. I had no conviction one way or the other about such blessings, although I appreciated his kindness during this difficult time.

Aaron and I buried Harrison and Jack near our gum tree on the edge of the island, a place that was special to both of us where we could sit and remember them.

I heard the doorknob turn and opened one eye to see little Mary step into the bedchamber with Thomas and Emmy close behind. They ran past her and into my arms, throwing themselves in between us, ready for their morning cuddles and kisses. Aaron stirred, then turned over, smiling sleepily at them before engulfing them in his arms—their squeals of delight piercing my ears and making me cringe. I wasn't in the mood for such closeness, and on the brink of tears, closed my eyes so they wouldn't see my pain.

'Mummy, where are Harrison an' Jack now?' Thomas asked quietly, his head on the pillow next to mine.

'They're in heaven sleeping peacefully in the arms of the angels, sweetheart.' I smiled weakly, kissing the top of his head. We still had these two beautiful children who brought joy to our lives every day, and I needed to hold on to that. Aaron gathered them in his arms to tell them a story, a morning ritual they never missed. I closed my swollen eyes again and listened to the rise and fall of his voice—the narrative gaining momentum and leading to a spectacular ending. Thomas and Emmy clapped their hands as a weak smile touched my lips—a strong desire welling up inside me to be transported to this futuristic land he spoke of where medicine was so advanced no one ever got sick or died from anything other than old age.

'You tell the best stories, Daddy, but get up now. We have to eat breakfast,' Emmy reminded him, tickling his stomach. Aaron lay back on the bed and groaned while trying to shift Thomas and Emmy off him, while they giggled and continued to tickle him. I slowly struggled to my feet just as Bessie stepped into the room. She stopped at the door after closing it behind her, her eyes shining with tears while sadness filled her pretty face.

'My heart breaks for you, Mistress. I couldn't be sicker about it if it happened to me own self.' She crossed the room, her arms wide, and I ran into her embrace, breaking down for the millionth time since we lost them. 'I've been down to pay my respects, bless them. They're perfect little men, so sweet and bonny. I kissed them both and tucked them up under their blankets. It's cold outside.' Her voice broke as she released me, then guided me back to my family, who continued to roughhouse on the heavy quilts.

I lowered myself carefully back onto the bed, grimacing in pain as my bruised body touched the mattress, then patiently waited for her to pick out my dress while the wrestling continued behind me. Pushing everything to the back of my mind for my own sanity—apart from the loss of our sons—I had not thought of what had occurred in Melbourne since the night it happened, repressing it as deep down as I could. Instead, I had focussed what little attention I could on ensuring Aaron and the children were all right, and he did not take the law into his own hands. I knew him better than anyone—I also knew what he was capable of when pushed far enough.

I slowly rose to my feet, the children far too boisterous for my frayed nerves, then made my way over to my large dressing room, limping inside to find Bessie wiping away her tears. She straightened up at the sight of me, then quickly picked up a dark blue housedress and hurried to my side, silently helping me into it before leading me out to my dressing table. I could not hide the unbearable pain I was in from the beating I had suffered from George Maslow, along with the trauma of giving birth, no matter how hard I tried. I sat down dejectedly in front of the gilded mirror for Bessie to do my hair, while Aaron and the children kissed me farewell before running out of the room and down to the kitchen, getting a head start on breakfast. Bessie stood behind me, her hand shaking a little as she picked up the silver hairbrush that once belonged to Sister, but was far older than my beloved nun.

'There's not much I can say that'd help, not being a mother myself and all.' She sniffed loudly, running the brush through my tangled hair until it gleamed. 'I can only imagine what you're both suffering, and I'm sorry for your pain, my sweet girl. You're strong and brave, and you'll come through this, but it'll take time. I know better than anyone how much you love your children, and I can see how sad you are, despite your trying to hide it.'

She wound my hair up and secured it in a chignon, then smiled sadly to herself before touching the back of my head in dismissal. I stood and embraced her, thanking her for everything she did for me daily and all she so generously gave to me, including her loyalty and friendship. I bid her farewell and made my way out of the room, her soft sobs filling my ears as I closed the door behind me.

Leo stood at the stove cooking breakfast, but stopped as soon as I stepped into the warm room, watching silently as I slowly hobbled towards the table on the far side of the bustling kitchen. He hurried to my side and took me by the shoulders, then bent down and gently kissed my lips; his handsome brow creased in concern.

'Didn't expect to see you down here this morning. My servants were just about to make up a tray with all your favourite things. Not that I have to tell you how slowly they move after a night out at the gin house in Geelong.' He took me by the hand and led me over to the large wooden table where my husband and children sat eagerly waiting for their food—the smell of bacon filling the room and causing even my stomach to growl. 'I'm beyond sorry, Abigail. I have no words for you.' I nodded, waiting for him to release my hand so I could sit down next to Aaron. 'But I have words when it comes to myself.' I nodded again, staring up at him in silence and remaining where I was, despite desperately wanting to sit down and trying to slip my hand from his. 'No one here seems to care that I'm grieving the loss of my babies, too. Not one person has offered me condolences, or even a kind word. They've put all the attention on you and have completely ignored my pain and distress. You know how much that upsets me.' He threw back his head and wailed, pulling me roughly into his arms, the room silent other than his sobs. All present stopped to watch—most not without sympathy. I patted his back and nodded my head, making soothing noises until he had calmed, then sat down with my family. He wiped his face before turning on his heel and hurrying away. Aaron smiled sadly across at me before taking my hand in his under the table. 'I'm making you those fluffy buttermilk pancakes you love so much,' Leo called out over his shoulder as he whipped the batter.

Aaron and the children continued eating their hot porridge while I helped myself to a small bowl. It was smooth and sweet, just like I had always wished for as a child, and I was happy my children never got to taste the food they gave me while growing up.

It would be only a few short years until Aaron, the children and I would travel to London to take control of my trust fund so we could plan for our children's futures. After all these years, I still didn't know how much was in my private account where the interest from my Melbourne trust fund went into. I had never needed to access it, although Aaron did when running short.

We constantly replenished the separate farm account with money from the sale of the horses. Aaron used the profits to pay for the feed and supplies we needed around the farm, but as quick as he would spend it, it would build up even more. He bought the best of everything just to keep the money down. If anyone in our village needed money for a funeral, or an unforeseen debt, Aaron would provide it out of the farm account, including paying sick workers their wages until they recovered.

Leo served the pancakes for everyone, and I drowned mine in butter and syrup and started eating.

'Drink your milk, you two, or you won't grow up to be strong like your perfect uncle,' Leo said to the twins, kissing them on the head as he joined us. They obediently finished their glasses, proudly showing him as he patted them on the head. 'You are the most well-behaved chickens I know. There isn't another nine-year-old child I even like, so you are two in a trillion and should feel honoured.' Leo giggled to himself as Thomas smirked at him.

'Uncle Leo, we're not chooks. We don't have feathers or lay eggs out of our bums,' Emmy said, and Leo pretended to be shocked.

'That's not how ladies speak, Emmy,' he gasped, putting his hand to his mouth in mock surprise. Emmy laughed.

'My Mummy talks like that, and even worse sometimes, and people think she is a lady.' She beamed up at me as I shifted in my seat, my cheeks becoming warm.

'Only some people, my sweet Emmy, only some people,' Leo said, poking his tongue out at me. Aaron snorted loudly, shaking his head, while his face agreed with Leo, the traitorous lout.

While I sat with Harrison and Jack for most of the morning alone, Leo ensured I always had a fresh cup of coffee on hand.

'They really are beautiful, Abigail. I'm sorry you lost them. Maybe you can try again?' He sat down next to me and gently stroked the weans' faces.

'No. Dr. Richards examined me last night and gave me bad news. He believes I'm damaged and there will be no more children.' I started to cry, gazing down at the last children I would ever carry, noting again how sweet and perfect they were.

'I don't know what to say. Nothing is going to make you feel better other than time. I'm here to listen whenever you need me, even if you do bore me at times. We can crack open one of Aaron's best bottles of whisky without him knowing. I will sit with you and drink it until we are both too drunk to walk and I will hold your hair back while you vomit.' He smiled at me and I smiled back, and then kissed him on the cheek before he went back to the kitchen. The sitting room soon became busier than Flinders Street Station, many of our staff wanting to pay their respects.

Excusing myself to lie down, I exhaled in relief as I hurried through the vast hallways. Once in our bedchamber, I felt restless and didn't know what to do with myself. Finally, I took out some writing paper and poured my heart out to Sister Josephine. I told her everything, letting my feelings wash out of me into the ink, forming the words she would read and take to her soul. I placed the letter in an envelope with some recent portraits taken of us with the children. Sealing the beautiful paper with wax, I placed it down on my bedside table to take down later.

At that moment, Aaron stepped into the room appearing drawn and sad, his voice gravelly with grief.

'I went to work, but it was the last place I wanted to be. I sat with our sons, but couldn't bear it for a second longer, so came lookin' for ya.'

'Come over here.' I reached my arms out to him. He hurried across the room, then lay with his head on my chest and cried. I was still very sore from being beaten and my face looked a mess—purple bruising obvious on my cheekbones up to my temple, a small gash near my eye, my lips swollen and sore.

Our workers had spoken of my appearance in hushed tones, but no one knew what had happened to me or who had done this—it was all pure speculation. Aaron had told me to tell Leo that a stranger had beaten me and caused the premature birth of the twins, and word would spread like wildfire. Personally, I would have preferred if everyone knew what that terrible man did to me, but it was something I couldn't face yet, so I went along with Aaron's directive.

Bessie came in to get me up, waiting patiently by the bed to assist me.

'Hamish is here to see you. He heard what happened,' she whispered. I wiggled out from underneath Aaron, who had fallen sound asleep. Bessie helped me carefully to my feet. I straightened my dress and went downstairs to find Hamish in the sitting room, leaning over the tiny coffin, his large fingers gently touching their sandy blonde hair.

'I'm deeply sorry fer yer loss, Abigail,' he murmured, kissing their tiny faces before coming to sit with me in the lounge. I told him the truth of the matter from start to finish, leaving out the black aura, or he would have thought me mad. While shielding him from the graphic details, I confided in him how Maslow had beaten and forced himself on me, causing the death of the boys. He sat back in the chair and exhaled loudly, a look of disbelief on his face before it turned to one of fury. 'An' Aaron's naw hunted him down an' killed him yet?' I shook my head, not wanting to think of things like that.

'No, but I'm worried he will, and I need you to talk him out of doing anything stupid. He will listen to you. Please talk to him,' I begged, staring directly into his dark brown eyes that reminded me of chocolate. He sighed loudly, shaking his head in disbelief.

'The problem is if I were in Aaron's position, I'd do the same, Abigail. 'Tis doubtful I'm the best man tae convince him tae restrain himself. I'll speak tae Angus. He's the most level-headed out o' the three o' us. But how are ye feelin'? Are ye in pain? If ye dinnae mind me sayin' so, ye look awful.'

'It looks worse than it feels, and I have powerful medicines to take, although they make me feel sick,' I said, and he nodded sympathetically. We talked a while longer, before he advised me he must return to work. I walked him out, then made my way back to the kitchen and sat down at our familiar table.

I silently watched Leo prepare a sandwich for me, toasting the bread while cooking the fillings separately before melting cheese in the middle. It was delicious. I had little appetite, but sat and ate slowly because of my swollen mouth. Leo had just sat down beside me when Margaret walked in, a medium-sized bag tied tightly at the top held securely under her arm.

'Hello, Abigail. I heard what happened, an' felt I must come right away to see you.' She embraced me before sitting down at the table, placing the bag at her feet. When I invited her to eat and help herself to coffee, she asked if she could talk to me privately. I nodded, finished my sandwich while she got a cup of coffee, and we went to the sitting room. She offered her sympathy for our loss and touched each one on the cheek before sitting down. 'I've heard you're in a lot of pain from bein' beaten an' the doctor has you on the medicine?'

'Yes, it's true, Margaret. It makes me feel really sick, so mostly I refuse to take it, which isn't helping my pain.' Word spread like a raging bushfire around here. In this instance, I was grateful for it. I no longer had to explain anything.

'If you don't mind me sayin', I have somethin' better for you, an' it'll stop you feelin' poorly.' She bent down and untied the bag. A pungent odour came wafting out of it. She took a handful of something from inside and put it up to her nose to sniff. It looked like furry little buds from a tree that hadn't flowered yet. She took out a smoking pipe, a packet of tobacco, some scissors, and a small dish. 'You take one of these buds, then chop it up all small in the dish here like this. Can you see?' I nodded as I watched her swift fingers and took note. 'Then you put some tobacco in, just a small amount, an' mix it up. Pack it into the pipe like this, an' smoke it. It'll take away all your pain an' help you sleep,' she said dreamily. She held the pipe to her lips and lit it.

'What is it and where did you find it?' I asked, my interest piqued. I inhaled the pungent smoke floating in front of me as Margaret exhaled from her pipe.

'It grows wild on the island out on Devils Point, an' no one livin' here knows what it's used for but me. If you don't mind, I'd like to keep this between us. I'm happy to bring you bags of the stuff when you need it. Better to smoke to relax instead of drinkin' alcohol. You don't wake up sick. I use it at night to help me sleep, an' it relieves the pain in me back from liftin' all them bairns all day. It's in all the tonics for pain an' nervous problems.'

She smiled brightly as she spoke of the families in the village. I knew how much she loved caring for other people's children, as well as her own. We chatted as we drank our coffee and she told me of the goings on in the village.

When she bid me farewell, I took the bag and the odds and sods she had left me up to our room. I stepped inside to find Aaron lying on the bed, staring at the ceiling in silence. Crossing the room, I lifted the bag to show him as I explained what Margaret had told me.

'I think I'm going to try it,' I remarked, bringing the pipe to the bed with me.

I took out the small bowl of finely cut green buds and packed the pipe before I lay back on the bed with him. Aaron lit it, inhaling deeply before passing it to me. I drew in the heavy smoke far down into my lungs and held it in like Margaret had told me to. Blowing the white smoke up into the air above me, I watched it dissipate into nothing. I did it again and felt tingles on my forehead as my muscles relaxed. I inhaled several times more, my mind slowing.

'What's it feel like?' Aaron asked me curiously.

'I thought you just said what's it sound like.' I collapsed into giggles, feeling happy and relaxed for the first time since I'd lost my babies.

'What's wrong with ya?' He laughed as I continued to giggle. 'Here, let me try it again.' He took the pipe from me and inhaled a few times, then sat back against the pillows. We took turns until it was finished, my body so heavy I couldn't lift my arm if I tried, not that I was trying. I no longer felt any pain—in body or mind. Margaret had been right about its pain-relieving qualities, and I silently thanked her for the relief, even if only for a time.

'Aaron.'

'Yeah, mo anamchara.'

'I can't feel my face.'

'Whatever this is, they should bag it up an' sell it. It'd bring in a fortune,' Aaron said, chuckling to himself.

'I would definitely buy it,' I murmured. 'Let's hope no one else finds out about it or we'll have to hide the boat. Not to mention the fact Margaret would kill me.'

We lay close, my head on his chest, his arms around me. He became all soft and romantic and whispered sweet words to me as I fell asleep, lost in a world of warmth, happiness, and rainbows.

I opened my eyes, startled by the bushman's clock waking me with his condescending laugh, as if mocking me. I couldn't remember undressing myself and getting into bed, yet here I was without a stitch of clothing on.

'Aaron, wake up for a minute.' I shook him gently as I sat up in bed while attempting to sort out my jumbled thoughts. Besides being disorientated, I felt as though I hadn't moved my muscles in days. He groaned and turned over to look at me, keeping one eye shut.

'What?'

'How did I get here? I don't even know what day it is,' I told him, feeling mildly panicked as he put his arms around me and pulled me down next to him. He kissed me good morning, then settled my head on his shoulder and stroked my back.

'After we smoked that pipe yesterday, ya went to sleep an' stayed that way through the afternoon. When the nippers came home an' ya still wouldn't wake, I left ya to sleep it off. Ya were still sleepin' by tea time so I took ya dress off an' settled ya in. Ya needed the rest after goin' so many nights without sleepin',' he said and kissed me on the nose. 'How do ya feel now?'

'A lot better, actually. That pipe was great for pain, but I will only be able to use it at night until I'm recovered. It makes me sleep too deeply.' I stroked his chest with my hand as he played with my hair.

'That's the best thing for ya right now, so after the funeral, smoke away an' sleep for days if ya need to. Ya seem to forget what ya body has suffered since the attack an' expect to continue like nothin's happened. I know you're worried if ya slow down you'll think more, but ya need to rest an' let ya body recover. Abi, I'm worried about ya 'cause ya won't talk about what happened.'

'I've had no one close to me die, especially not my own flesh and blood. I don't know how to react or feel. I think I'm in shock. I keep touching my stomach and expecting to feel them inside me. I don't know how to explain any of it, even to myself.'

'Me either. It's a feelin' ya can't explain to anyone who hasn't been through it,' Aaron replied, running his fingers across my cheek. 'That's why I can talk to ya.'

He kissed my lips gently, so as not to hurt my bruised and swollen mouth, and I kissed him back.

Before the service, everyone gathered in the sitting room to say their first hellos and final goodbyes to Harrison and Jack. Aaron and I had placed several items into the casket that were special to us, a small family portrait, so we would always watch over them, and some booties Sister Josephine had knitted. Thomas put in a toy train we had given him when he was small and had been saving for a younger brother, and Emmy contributed her favourite teddy bear for them to cuddle. I wrapped them in the woollen blanket they had left me in at the door of the orphanage when I was a newborn, then placed a wooden pair of rosary beads given to me by Mother Hannah not long after we met in their tiny entwined hands. The beads were kept in the drawer of my bedside table, and although only used on the rare occasion up until I conceived Harrison and Jack, I had always felt a sentimental connection to these particular beads as they had come from someone who cared about me. Mother Hannah had made them with love with her own hands especially for me, and that in and of itself meant the world. I had often slept with these beads wrapped around my hands while carrying Harrison and Jack, and now to see their tiny hands holding them took away another small piece of my heart.

'It's time to say goodbye, Abi,' Aaron gently reminded me, yet I found it impossible to step away.

'All right,' I replied, my voice breaking. I leaned down and kissed them both, whispering things from a mother's heart to her sons only another mother would understand. My tears slowly dropped over their bodies as Aaron held Thomas's and Emmy's hands, standing beside me. I touched them for the last time before standing up and allowing Aaron and the children to say their own goodbyes.

I watched silently, my heart breaking as Thomas, who had been brave and not shed a tear, broke down in his father's arms as he said goodbye to the brothers he would never grow old with. Emmy kissed them both gently on the head as tears ran down her face before coming to me for a hug. I embraced her while Aaron said his own goodbye to his two sons, who would never hear his stories or learn from him how to ride a horse. I felt a lump in my throat when he kissed them both before gently stroking them with a shaking hand.

We all stepped back then and allowed our friends and family to say a last goodbye. Aaron led me over to a lounge and pulled me down onto his lap, where I put my head on his shoulder and sobbed as though I would never stop. He, too, cried tears of pain for our two lost boys. Emmy and Thomas sat on each side of us, doing their best to comfort their parents while they dealt with their own loss.

There was much crying and sorrow expressed as the undertaker sealed the top of the tiny coffin. Aaron moved forward and picked up the white casket in his arms, then slowly carried it out to the back garden, where Father Donnelly was waiting. Gavin Cavanaugh came and put his arm around me for support. Outside, I stumbled, and he quickly grabbed me, holding me upright. He escorted me to a chair at the front and set me down. Aaron placed the casket on its stand and joined me, as did Edith Cavanaugh and my brothers-and-sisters-in-law, all broken-hearted and wiping their own tears away.

Once our friends and family seated themselves, the service began. The house staff and the workers and their families were all present, comforting me somewhat to know people truly did care. I sat unmoving, not hearing the words the priest said. Once he'd finished, Aaron picked up the tiny coffin again, holding it close to his chest. I managed to walk under my own strength this time, following him and holding Thomas's and Emmy's hands as he led the funeral procession to the lake. He set the casket down on the boat, tears streaming down his handsome face. Father Donnelly stepped into the boat with us, and Aaron rowed across to the island in silence. Once we disembarked, he rowed back and filled the boat with mourners before his brother, Aiden, took over the rowing.

They had acquitted Aiden of all charges and set him free the day after I was attacked, much to everyone's relief. His family had returned home with mixed feelings—overjoyed the whole mess was over, but deeply distressed over my attack and losing the twins.

After several trips back and forth with the boat, everyone stood on the island gathered around the big gum tree where a small, deep hole had been dug. Father Donnelly committed the babies' bodies to the earth and, instead of throwing in dirt, we asked everyone to take a rose from a bunch Leo had harvested from the garden and place it on the coffin. Once covered in white roses, Aaron and Hamish slowly lowered our sons into the ground to the sounds of my sobbing and much sniffling among our friends. Soon after, the mourners slowly returned to the boat to wait to cross and go up to the main house, while Aaron and I sat down next to the grave under our tree.

'I think the boys will be happy here. I know I always am when I come here,' Aaron said, taking me in his arms before leaning back against the dark bark. So many emotions threatened to explode inside me, but I did not want to burden or upset anyone with my grief, especially Aaron. I kept them all in. Finally, Patrick approached once we were the last left on the island, and we followed him back hand in hand to the boat. He rowed us across while I leaned back on Aaron, feeling his heartbeat against my cheek. After only a few minutes' walk, we were back in the manicured garden. Patrick continued on, stepping inside the back door, while we remained where we were, peering up towards the well lit mansion.

'I could so easily run and hide from everyone, Aaron. I know that's terrible. Our family and friends are the most beautiful people I know, but I just don't feel like seeing anyone. I feel so ungrateful.' Aaron stood behind me, his arms around my waist while his chin rested on the top of my head.

'I know exactly how you feel,' he said, kissing my neck. Reluctantly, we went inside hand in hand to greet and thank our friends for their love and support.

I stretched out in bed; glad today was finally over. We had buried our boys and gotten through the wake before retreating to our bed-chamber, feeling beyond exhausted. Everyone understood we were grieving, recognising we needed time alone with each other and our children. We put Thomas and Emmy to bed, and I read to them as I always did each night. They seemed to cope well with their loss, although they were sad, like all of us. We kissed their sleeping faces before finding our way to our own bed.

'Abi, I haven't wanted to bring anythin' up with ya about Maslow. I know it upsets ya. Now the boys are at rest, I think we need to talk,' Aaron whispered. He held me tightly, my face close to his. I looked into his eyes and felt anxiety rise in me.

'I don't want to talk about that. I can't talk about it,' I replied, starting to cry. He kissed my forehead and wiped the tears that spilled down my face with his fingers.

'All right. Shhh, I understand. I wanna ask ya what ya think he meant by all that past-life rubbish he said to ya—about knowin' ya in another lifetime an' havin' to chastise ya with his fists? I know ya think he's just insane, but what if he's not? What if all this is related to the auras ya see around people? I mean, I know I'm soundin' like a lunatic meself now, but if it's true he shared a past life with ya an' ya see an aura around him, does that mean everyone with the golden aura, like me, also shared a past life with ya? Could it mean that, Abi?' He sounded excited as I shook my head.

'I don't know what any of it means!' I said crossly. 'Please don't put thoughts of that man in my head just before I try to sleep.' I burst into tears. It was all too much for me and I was buckling under the strain. I pushed everything to the back of my mind as Aaron took me in his arms and said no more.

Chapter Two

I WOKE, A HAND stroking me between my legs, and I yawned, a slow smile spreading across my face.

'That's a nice way to wake up.' I stretched and yawned again, luxuriating in the bed.

'Good morning to you, too,' Aaron said, kissing me completely awake.

It had been three-months since we lost the babies and the dark cloud was lifting from both of us. The house was returning to normal and people were becoming cheerful again, including me. Aaron was back at work full time and I had returned to the orphanage while the twins were at school. Although Aaron worried that being around newborn babies would set me back, I found it had given me a sense of purpose and I was feeling better than ever. I had fully recovered from my physical injuries but had not yet dealt with my emotional ones, forever pushing it down and out of my mind every time I would think of what happened in the judge's chambers that day.

All our friends and family had been wonderful, visiting often and keeping us busy. Tamara and Brian still visited once a month to stay overnight for several days at a time, and I now made sure when they were here, I never entered a room without knocking loudly, then waiting for a precise response before opening the door. Tamara was still driving Hamish insane, but then he would give in and sleep with her and she would become worse the next time he rejected her—and he couldn't understand why. I had totally given up on the situation and asked them both to stop talking to me about it.

'Ya day dreamin' again. Kiss me,' Aaron said, and I did. For the longest time.

Thomas and Emmy came bursting through our bedchamber door, waking us both as they stomped towards us.

'Daddy! Mummy! You must come and see the presents we got,' Emmy chortled, pulling at my arm to get me out of bed. I suppressed a sigh and struggled to my feet, as did Aaron, before we slowly made our way down to the sitting room, holding their hands while they talked excitedly. They held up every gift, one by one, and Emmy proudly showed me some new play pants with a feminine shirt that came to the top of her legs. She hated being restricted in long dresses and skirts and loved the playsuits Catherine made for her. I found them pretty and practical, just not something anyone else was wearing, which suited Emmy just fine. She didn't care what anyone thought or said about her, to her face or to others.

If the boys on the property tried to bully her, she would punch them in the nose or kick them in their soft parts, making me so very proud. The majority stayed silent now, and she happily went about her business wearing what she wanted. Catherine was Emmy's strongest ally, convincing us to agree to several outfits she had secretly asked her to make. Once we were confident they suited the young girl she was, we relented. People on the street would stop me and ask where I had Emmy's clothes made, and I would happily refer them to Catherine, who was starting to get orders for similar garments for other young girls. Emmy was not impressed. She viewed them as her designs and hers alone and felt annoyed other children would wear copies of her clothing. Thomas, though, was excited about his new leather saddle for Majestic.

'It's a proper grown-up one, Daddy,' he said, caressing it as Aaron smilingly ruffled his long, sandy-blonde hair.

We soon found ourselves in the kitchen where Leo greeted us excitedly, kissing us all while calling out Merry Christmas, the staff cheerfully wishing us well. None of our guests had arrived, and we preferred to eat in the kitchen where it was cosier rather than at the dining room table. Leo had made a large Christmas cake out of all sorts of dried fruit harvested from the garden, including sultanas, raisins, dates, figs, and apricots soaked in bottles of brandy for months, with glace cherries and nuts. He had also made our plum pudding, which hung over the stoves in a calico bag waiting to be boiled for lunch.

Leo made us a special breakfast of French toast with bacon and freshly squeezed orange juice from our own trees. The twins were ecstatic they didn't have to drink their milk this morning. Aaron and I smiled as they drained their cups, then poured more. Hamish joined us as he usually did, while Leo set a place for him.

'Merry Christmas tae one an' all.' Hamish bent down and kissed the twins on the head, Thomas first, then Emmy. Helping himself to coffee, he sat down heavily at the table. 'Tell me about all yer presents?' The twins chattered excitedly while he silently ate his breakfast, nodding his head or exclaiming when they said something that required an enthusiastic response. Aaron admired the way Hamish treated the twins and how much they adored him. He had said to me recently that you could cite the worst of Hamish based on his past behaviour with women, but when it came to the twins he was devoted and couldn't be faulted. 'I know ye dinnae want tae hear it, Abigail.' I eyed him suspiciously, but he chose to continue. 'I've one question. Possibly two. It'll all depend on how ye answer the first. Are Tamara an' Brian comin' tae stay today?'

'Yes, they are.'

'Weel, here's the second question. How long are they stayin' this time?'

'Only until tomorrow. We will have to guard your virtue until then,' I said. Aaron snorted in amusement as Hamish gave him a dark stare before he stood to leave.

'I only came up tae wish ye a Merry Christmas. An' tae visit with Thomas an' Emmy. An' see all their bonny presents, o' course.' He gazed down at his godchildren and smiled tenderly before reaching out and ruffling their hair. They laughed, and he waved goodbye as he left for the cottage.

Little Mary hurried into the kitchen, her face flushed as she made her way over to the twins, taking their hands in hers, Leo not far behind her. They ushered us back into the sitting room to admire the twins' gifts once again.

'We're goin' back to bed so ya Daddy can get his Christmas present from Mummy,' Aaron called out to Thomas and Emmy, who, busy with their new toys, ignored us. I grunted, shaking my head in disbelief, my face warm, while Leo smirked wickedly as Aaron led me to the door.

'You two are so dirty you make me want to scream in a jealous rage. Go! I can't stand the sight of you!' he shrilled, waving his hand in dismissal before sinking onto the floor to play with the children, their laughter filling my ears as Aaron hastily pulled me down the hallway.

It was a special Christmas day, like so many we had enjoyed before, only there was a lingering sadness that hung over the festivity. We were all still deeply grieving the loss of Harrison and Jack. I hadn't been able to stop thinking we would have had a couple of beautiful three-month-old boys joining us if I had carried them full term. I felt a pang of grief hit my heart so suddenly it took my breath away. How I had longed even before we lost them to hold our babies in my arms, often dreaming of them, to find I would wake sobbing with Aaron trying to comfort me. All I had ever wanted was lots of children and now I was barren—barren now and forever.

Everyone around us had been wonderful and offered unconditional support. I was melancholic and didn't feel like visiting the village, but I looked forward to seeing my friends. Within hours of waking I would find Margaret, Jen or Amelia at my door, ready to brighten my spirits.

Margaret and I would sneak away to smoke a pipe full of green buds over cups of coffee in the back garden with Leo occasionally joining us. He was a hundred-times worse after smoking the stuff, so Aaron had banned him from it. It made no difference, though. As soon as he saw Margaret arrive, he wouldn't let us out of his sight until we relented and allowed him to join us. Aaron hated me smoking the buds, as it made me groggy and silly, and Leo would threaten to tell on me if we didn't give him any.

The other reason Aaron disapproved was Leo would often convince me to do something mischievous and wicked while under the influence of my new 'best friend,' the green bud. Leo always got me caught, with both of us getting into trouble. Margaret would sit back and howl with laughter watching Aaron chastise us when he would catch us in the act. Aaron liked Margaret very much and never berated, even though she was our supplier.

All our friends and family had come to celebrate Christmas with us, bringing their children, who had all enjoyed the day being spoiled with gifts and sweets. They were all staying with nannies or grandparents tonight, so we adults could eat at the dining hall with the staff and the workers, then have a night out at the pub. Except for last year, which we spent at Heavenly Hideaway, it had become a tradition to spend every Christmas evening at the pub. We would get stinking drunk and dance and have fun without our children around. Everyone looked forward to it.

Of course, whenever we could come up with an excuse to gather at the pub for a night out, we would make it a tradition. We celebrated everything from birthdays to weddings. There was hardly a weekend that went by when something exciting wasn't happening there.

We were sitting in the garden after having eaten a huge lunch. All the children had taken off to catch fish in the river with Hamish and Patrick and suddenly, there was quiet. I took a deep breath and relaxed with Aaron sitting behind me. He had given me a beautiful pair of diamond earrings this morning that dangled down my neck, glittering in the sun. The way he was going I would be dripping in diamonds by the time I was thirty.

'Have ya had a good Christmas, mo anamchara?' he asked, kissing my neck.

'Yes, it's been lovely, but as you know, it's one of my favourite days of the year. I hate when it's over.'

'An' what are ya other favourite days of the year?'

'All the ones where I get presents and, of course, yours and the twins' birthdays.' He snorted on my neck in amusement.

'Ya really do love those trinkets. It's probably me own fault for spoilin' ya so much. When we met, ya really hadn't been given many presents in your life.'

'Well, you have certainly made up for that.' I giggled, then turned and kissed him on the lips. I not only received presents from Aaron, but from all his family and our friends, too. They put so much care into what they bought for each other and made sure to buy what they thought I would love, which I did.

I could hear the children in the distance and then saw them come over the hill carrying at least two dozen trout tied to strings. They were all laughing and trying to race each other as Hamish and Patrick strolled along behind. We all admired the fish, then the children handed them proudly to Leo, who went off to cook them. They chatted impatiently at the back door because Leo wouldn't let them all in the kitchen at once. When he was done, Leo brought out a platter with some of the fish cut into chunks and offered it to the adults, making the children wait a little longer.

Hamish sat down next to us and we watched the children sitting in a circle on the grass, as Leo had insisted, before he handed around their plates with a full roasted trout on each. I was amused to see them all eating with their fingers except Tamara and Brian's children, who set their plates in the centre of the circle untouched and quickly returned to their nannies.

'Weel, except fer those four,' Hamish said, nodding towards Tamara and Brian's offspring, 'our adventure was enjoyed by all an' the bounty well worth the effort. When they catch it 'emselves, the bairns can't get enough trout. Seems when you serve it fer dinner without their involvement, they turn up their noses,' Hamish chuckled.

'How did Brian an' Tamara's offsprin' cope around the other nippers, bein' the mere mortals they are in comparison?' Aaron asked Hamish with a smirk. Hamish threw back his head and laughed loudly.

'I'd cut me own balls off with a rusty blade if I spawned obnoxious little shites such as those. Naw tae mention the fact they're so bloody borin'. They dinnae want tae do anythin', an' they rarely speak unless 'tis tae their Nannies or between 'emselves. As ye know, I also thought this was the right way tae raise bairns, but after seein' Willy an' Bella an' Thomas an' Emmy an' what good wee people they are, I've changed me mind. The fact they attend school with the workers' bairns an' count them as friends is an achievement ye should both be proud of. They're all likeable children here at Willow Grove, despite what Leo says.' He stopped for a moment, appearing sheepish. 'I've just realised I've become as bad as Leo fer pickin' on the wee ones.' We laughed aloud before he rose to his feet. He made his way over to the children, picked up the abandoned plates, sat down in the circle and started to eat, making them giggle at how big he was.

Mr and Mrs Cavanaugh got up to leave, taking Patrick, Aiden, and Luke's children with them. Tamara's nannies stood up to collect the four children and take them back to their private wing. We wouldn't see them again until dinner tomorrow night, when they were washed and dressed in their fancy clothes for their parents to inspect.

Little Mary was waiting for everyone else's children, including mine, to finish their trout. After some time, the twins hugged Hamish and then ran to us. Aaron and I hugged them, promising we would come and kiss them goodnight before we left for the dining hall, a smile touching my lips as they happily skipped off with the others.

The adult guests included our family, Patrick and Scarlett, Aiden and Victoria, and Luke and Adele. Brian and Tamara had travelled with Eric and Elizabeth and planned to stay a while. Richard and Jas, Martin and Dana, and Colin and Catherine had also agreed to stay tonight despite living close by. While Tommy and Amelia, Angus and Polly, and Leo and Hamish didn't have far to travel to find their beds. We retreated to our rooms to rest before readying ourselves, agreeing to meet at seven o'clock in the kitchen to leave for the village. My friends who lived there were generously sharing their Christmas dinner and celebrations with us. In the past, Jenny, Margaret and Maisie all found it difficult to attend functions at our house, due to their own responsibilities, although I always made sure they were invited, even knowing they wouldn't come. I had managed to drag them and their families here several times for dinner over the years, which we had thoroughly enjoyed while Mr Masters looked on with disapproval.

Aaron took my hand as we made our way through the wide hallways and up the grand stairs to our bedchamber. He closed the door, then crossed the elegant room to my side.

'What are ya goin' to wear?' he asked, pulling me down on the bed and kissing my face.

'I'm not sure yet. Maybe you can pick one out.' I laughed at the thought, running my fingers through his hair.

'I will then. I know me favourites that'll show off one of ya finest assets.' He smirked and gently squeezed my nipple through my dress, sending tingles throughout my body. He unbuttoned the back of my cumbersome gown so I could slip out of it and I stood up and let it fall to the floor. It was such a relief to be naked. 'Ya wouldn't even know ya gave birth six-months ago lookin' at ya now,' he whispered, a wistfulness touching his eyes for only a moment that made my heart break all over again. I slipped back into bed and took his face in my hands, slowly kissing his cheeks and forehead, then finally his lips.

'It's alright to be sad sometimes, Aaron. As long as you cherish the things you do have, and I know you do,' I said, cuddling into him, tears stinging my eyes.

'That I surely do. More than you'll ever know,' he murmured, giving me a fierce hug and closing his eyes, holding me as if he would never let me go.

We went and kissed the twins and our nieces and nephews goodnight. They were all ready for bed and playing happily with each other in the nursery. Little Mary, who sat in a chair knitting, was watching them like a hawk and waiting to usher them to their rooms once the excitement of being together had worn off.

'Have fun tonight you two. An' Mummy, don't be a dirty little alcoholic,' Thomas yelled as I smirked and kissed him on the top of his head. He was too busy playing bushrangers with his cousins to kiss me back. I could hear Aaron chuckling as he embraced his son then tousled his hair, which hung to his shoulders like his father's. It was shorter at the front and sides, although still shaggy and uncontrollable if let loose from its bindings.

'Don't do anything embarrassing, Mummy. You know Uncle Leo tells everyone everything, the big Luna Park mouth,' Emmy called out after we gave her a kiss and headed for the door. 'Love you to the moon and back.'

I smiled. That was something I had been saying to the twins since they were born, and now she was saying it to us. Aaron looked just as keen as me to leave the nursery. The noise from the children playing was almost deafening. He put his fingers in his ears. I nodded and took his hand, saying goodnight as we closed the door behind us.

'They get out of control when they're all together,' he remarked as we made our way down the stairs.

'Not unlike you and your brothers when your clan gets together. It just runs in the Cavanaugh bloodline.' I giggled, making him laugh.

We stepped into the warm kitchen to find everyone sitting around wearing their most comfortable outfits and chatting loudly—except for Tamara, who always went about in all her Montague dresses. She stood out so much that the workers' wives often made fun of her behind her back. Everyone else knew when they came here, they could dress as casually as they liked.

All the men took their partners' hands, except for Brian and Tamara. Brian chose to walk with Leo while Tamara went straight to Hamish's side. We were all of good cheer, talking, teasing each other and laughing as we headed towards the village. My heart skipped a beat as we stopped at the top of the hill and I saw the lights in the valley below. The village was such a special place for me. I had watched it grow and prosper, and now some of the dearest people to me lived there, just a ten-minute walk from my house. I felt so fortunate to be surrounded not only by family, but by every single person who lived and worked at Willow Grove. The lanterns were brightly lit in every single residence, along with every window of the dining hall and pub. Vicki moved up beside me and took my hand.

'How are you feeling, sister?' she asked, her voice low. 'Abigail, I want you to know you are my closest friend and have been since we met. The friendship you share with my mother, Charlotte, and me, has always been very special. I just wanted to say, my darling sister, I can see you are melancholy today no matter how hard you try to hide it.' She sighed deeply before embracing me. 'I understand why. I know you didn't want to be away from the weans grave for their first Christmas, and that was why we didn't return to Heavenly Hideaway this year. Just know we are all here for you and we haven't forgotten Harrison and Jack. They are our nephews and will always be in our hearts.'

She kissed me, then Aaron, who embraced her tightly. Victoria was such a dedicated friend. Despite having her own young children to care for, she had visited me every day since the death of our boys. Aaron slipped his hand around my waist as we drew closer to the village and spoke to me quietly.

'Abi, I know you're still in so much pain. I wish you'd open up an' talk about what you're feelin'. I'm so worried about ya, mo anamchara. Ya act like nothin's happened when everyone's around an' go about ya day, fixin' their problems an' keepin' busy. I think you're doin' it on purpose, just so ya don't have to think about what happened at the courthouse.' I felt my body tense and my heart started to race as I shook my head.

'Please, Aaron, I'm fine.' I shook my head again and pulled away from him. 'There's nought to talk about. The boys are gone and there is nothing to be done.' He decided not to push me any further and kissed me on the forehead as we passed the brightly lit terraces, then waited outside the dining hall for the others to catch up. Leo and Brian were the first to join us.

'Oh, my lord,' Leo bellowed, his eyebrows raised. 'You cannot get away from the unfortunate-looking snots in this village no matter what time of day or night you come down here. I saw one young girl staring at me from her window, and didn't I get a fright?! She was uglier than Abigail when she wakes after a hard night at the gin house. Do you know who placed a curse on the village to ensure only children with unattractive personalities and frightening faces are born here?' Brian and Aaron burst out laughing, while I wasn't amused in the slightest.

'You are an awful person for constantly picking on the children. They are all lovely and well-behaved, thank you very much. Stop acting their age. I've told you repeatedly to stop teasing them. You're becoming known as the Manster from the main house who isn't the full quid.' He shrieked at the thought of them using one of his own words against him, a smirk touching my lips. 'If you're not careful you'll have some very angry parents at your door, and I won't be defending the terrible person you sometimes are.'

'I am not a very ugly man, nor a very pretty monster. How dare they?' He appeared surprised but could no longer continue due to the others joining us, their laughter drowning out anything further Leo wanted to say. I took the three steps up onto the verandah of the dining hall to join Aaron, who took my hand and led me inside while the others followed.

We found Bessie had set up a table where we could all sit together with her and Danny. I went to line up for my dinner to find the lovely Jenny waiting to serve me.

'Merry Christmas to you and your family. How are Harry and the children, Jen?' I asked as we exchanged pleasantries through the window.

'And to you and yours. They are well, Mistress. All growing up fast, as you know,' she said while dishing my dinner. Harry and Jenny had four children now who were all good looking and strong in character like their parents. I thanked her before agreeing to meet at the pub later, then returned to the table and listened while the others chatted between mouthfuls. It was a magnificent Christmas dinner with all the trimmings, and I ate the whole serving despite not having fully digested lunch. Aaron brought our dessert of plum pudding with brandy custard and cream, which I devoured. I adored plum pudding. It was the only thing we had once a year, which made Christmas even more special. The smell of brandy and dried fruit always made me think of pudding and Christmas cake.

Afterwards, several of our friends thanked Jenny and the kitchen staff for working on Christmas day and doing such a wonderful job. It was obvious they were delighted to be thanked at all, especially by members of the upper class, who only consumed the best in their mind, who raved on and on how our staff could run a world-class restaurant. I knew Jenny was just as talented as Leo, although I would never say it aloud. If he ever suspected I thought so, I was certain his shrieks and tantrums would be heard as far away as the village.

At the pub next door, we pushed some tables together while the boys organised the drinks. The girls and Leo all sat together while the men congregated at the other end of the table. I could see by their eyes that my sisters-in-law were ready to enjoy the night without guilt or regret. Catherine and Polly sat side-by-side, deep in conversation, while Tamara and Elizabeth commiserated with Dana, who had been shunned by upper-class society since her incarceration. Leo listened intently, his eyes twinkling in amusement.

'So, you are left to slum it with us? Those who have absolutely no standing in society? Dana, in all honesty, and I'm telling you as a friend, I knew you were a dirty little criminal when I met you on the boat. It was only a matter of time before you would be forced to face the consequences of your free-natured spirit and criminality. Don't look so cross. It isn't your fault. I believe that psychopathic criminals are born and not made. Can you see now? You couldn't help breaking the law. It was what you were born to do. It's in your blood. That's why I have my servants watch you closely, as we don't want anything going missing in the house, now do we? I've explained it to everyone who works at Willow Grove that you have no control over your unfortunate habits and tend to break the laws of the land without guilt or regret. They are all sympathetic to your plight, so removing the temptation by watching you, we are, in fact, assisting you. You can thank me anytime you like now.' Instead, Dana reached across and smacked him hard across the face.

'Well, I did learn some things in gaol, including that, you fucking brainless imbecile. Shut that fucken mouth of yours or I will strike you again,' Dana stated loudly, her voice surprisingly calm, while her eyes glittered dangerously. Everyone at the table went as silent as Leo. Knowing when he was beaten, he stood and moved a few seats away, holding his face dramatically as I tried to smother a smile. Leo noticed immediately and glared back at me, his eyes bulging.

'Oh, that's right Abigail. Laugh your head off. Literally, I hope. I was only trying to be kind and help Dana understand that it's not her fault she could potentially murder someone in the future. I was only trying to make her understand that anything she does isn't her fault. That is what a good friend does, tries to make those around them feel better about themselves. Well, I've had it with trying to be caring and compassionate to you lot. I'm going back to the old Leo who annoyed you all.'

All the girls smirked, bar Dana, who continued to glare at him while sipping her wine. It was clear Leo had absolutely no idea what he had said to offend her.

Hamish had been right when he warned me many who ran in Dana's circles were fickle and insincere, a reality he had experienced his entire life. I hadn't wanted to believe it at the time; however, in the years since, he had proven to be more than accurate. Dana was no longer invited to any events or galas and had been completely ostracised—the many people she'd once called close friends disappearing from her life the moment she entered the prison gates. She had tried to resume her life as normal, planning dinner parties and inviting all her old friends. When not even one turned up the first time, she realised her life and social standing really had changed forever.

But she rallied, made a symbolically rude gesture at all who had turned their backs on her, and decided she would create a new social life for herself. She made new friends with women who lived in her suburb that didn't care where she sat on the ladder of social status. She was now holding fabulous parties again with people who were much more my style. They might not have been wealthy, but they were funny, outgoing, friendly, and fabulous—as Leo would say. And she always had us, for which she was grateful.

'So, Dana, let's be friends again,' Leo called out. 'I promise I won't call you a dirty little criminal anymore if you don't smack me. We are all you have now since your bum was kicked from your high-society pedestal and you came crashing down, showing your knickers as you landed. You have to learn to open up to your friends now. Tell us some of your prison stories, you wicked little criminal.' I kicked him under the table, connecting with his shin. 'Ow! Who did that? It was you, wasn't it, Dana? I have no doubt you learnt your extreme violence in gaol, as the wallop to my face verified. Come on and tell me a story,' he begged, rubbing his leg dramatically. Dana glanced at me, then rolled her eyes before fixing him with a stare.

'What do you want to know, Leo? How you don't get to wash your body for weeks at a time or how you shiver at night with only one blanket—or the exciting part where you get fed only enough to keep you alive?'

'Oh, those do sound exciting, too, but I want to know what it was really like. Is it true that women turn into normal people while confined without the comfort of men for extended periods of time, and then turn abnormal as soon as they leave? Did you turn into a goal sodomite? Tell us in detail what you did at bedtime with your cell mates.' All present turned to him in silence, their mouths open. I'd heard enough of his scaffy and rose to my feet.

'Stop talking, Leo! Dana, do not answer another thing on the subject, the deviant. You! Stand up and move down with the men before I seriously hurt you!' As he grabbed his drink and stood, he turned to me.

'Abigail, I have no idea why you pick on me constantly for nothing. I am just being friendly as usual, and you cut me off. There is seriously something wrong in that head of yours and I'm going to lag on you to Aaron.' He quickly moved away before I jumped the table to strangle him with my bare hands.

Jugs of beer and bottles of whisky filled the table, and I could already see we were in for a big night. Vicki poured me and everyone else at our end of the table an extra-large shot of whisky.

'Come on, Abi. If you drink that down, I will do the same,' she goaded me. Vicki and I together were not a good combination. We were terribly bad influences on each other, even though we often had the most fun. Scarlett and Adele were just as bad and constantly led me astray. I lifted the glass of whisky to my lips and drank it, feeling it burn my throat as it was going down. I pulled a face and quickly drank some beer, starting to feel warm and heavy almost immediately, like I usually did. Scarlett drank hers, as did Adele, who also pulled a face. I watched Polly, Amelia, and Jenny, along with Margaret, Tamara, and Elizabeth do the same before Dana drank one, quickly followed by another.

Vicki poured more, and we drank it down; it didn't taste as bad as the first shot. We had only been there half-an-hour and all of us girls were more than a little affected. The music started, and I pulled my friends up to dance. Maisie and Bessie had only stepped inside but followed and joined in the line as we danced an Irish jig together, going around in a circle, following each other as we laughed hysterically while getting our feet in a tangle.

A worker from another farm I had never met before approached me on the dance floor, pulling me away from the others and into his arms. Terrified, I immediately froze, and all the fear I felt on that day at the court with Maslow came flooding through my body. My heart was in my throat as he held me by both arms pressed up against his body, leaning down as if he were going to kiss me.

Within seconds Aaron was on him, with Hamish and Angus trying to stop him from beating this man to death. I sobbed as the girls surrounded me and led me back to the table. I hated fighting of any type and it was rare Aaron ever used his fists instead of his mouth. I could see from where I was sitting Aaron had landed several punches to the man's head as he lay on top of him on the floor. Finally, Hamish and Angus managed to restrain him and stand him back up on his feet. Hamish held Aaron with both arms locked around his chest as my husband yelled threats and obscenities while trying to pry Hamish off so he could attack this man again.

Angus calmly escorted the injured farm worker out of the pub and told him to stay away or next time they wouldn't step in. From what I could see, he had a broken nose and his face was covered in blood, his large frame limping away in the direction of the Costello family farm while holding his left arm as if it were broken. Once everything had calmed and the man had left the property, Aaron walked up to our end of the table.

'Come with me for a minute, Abi. I need to talk to ya.' He grabbed my hand and led me to an empty table, where we sat opposite each other. I noticed his knuckles were bleeding, but he didn't seem to care. 'I saw ya reaction to that idiot who grabbed ya. I've only seen ya frightened like that a few times in all the years I've known ya. What's goin' on in ya head, Abi? Ya won't talk to me, an' I know it's 'cause of what Maslow did to ya. You've still never talked about it with me, an' I doubt you've told others. You're keepin' it all inside an' one day you'll explode. I'm so worried about ya I'm losin' sleep over it all.'

He looked so concerned, I felt a lump lodge in my throat. Then the memories of that day started to flood my mind again, my heart pounding hard. I quickly pushed the thoughts back down and swallowed hard while taking his hands in mine.

'I'm fine, Aaron. I'll be fine,' I said, smiling as brightly as I could and kissing him on the mouth. 'Let's get back to our friends. We're being rude.' I stood and walked back to my table with him following thoughtfully behind.

I sat back down with the girls and poured myself another whisky, drinking it in one swallow. I knew he was right, and I hated the thought I was hurting him because I couldn't speak of it, not even to him. I usually told him everything, and it hurt my heart. I didn't understand why I couldn't let myself even think about what Maslow had done and the consequences of that action. I could talk to Aaron about anything else; however, I couldn't let my mind relive that horrific day. Whenever thoughts would come, I would push them to the back of my mind and go on with my daily life. It was the nightmares I couldn't control, when Aaron would hold my shaking body as I sobbed.

I noticed Leo and Brian were missing from the table and I solemnly swore to myself that I would keep my arse on my seat until I saw them back here fully clothed. Soon after, Scarlett and Vicki came and sat next to me, smiling mischievously.

'Come on, sis. Here's another for you,' Scarlett said, handing me a glass. 'You haven't looked happy at all today and we do know why. We are saddened Harrison and Jack aren't here with us, too, celebrating their first Christmas. I can't believe they still haven't found the man who robbed and attacked you on the street that day. He should be strung up.'

I nodded sadly and emptied my glass again. I felt numb all over and the worries and grief I had been holding inside were starting to ease as the alcohol did its job and relaxed my body along with my mind.

Nellie, a kitchen maid who had been working for us for a few years now, approached our table, sat next to Hamish, and shyly started talking to him. I liked Nellie. She was plain, but had a lovely nature—a quality I valued far higher. Her face lit up whenever she saw Hamish. I knew she had liked him for a while now and would be good for him, as she was young and ready to start a family. Hamish, who didn't care about class anymore, had said he was looking for a nice woman to make his wife and have a family with. He wanted to marry for love and decided he would open his heart and allow someone in. The change thrilled me. Tamara, though, instantly became upset and leaned across the table, catching my attention.

'Who is that with Hamish?' she asked coldly, glaring across at Nellie, who continued to chat animatedly with him.

'Just a friend, Tamara. Hamish has a lot of friends here, male and female,' I replied. All at the table went silent, waiting to see what she would do. Although we continued to chat and laugh, it was clear how furious she was, refusing to take her eyes from them.

Soon after, Hamish pulled Nellie onto his lap and began whispering in her ear. She slipped her arms around his neck as they murmured sweet words between themselves. Tamara suddenly stood up from her seat and marched over to them without a backward glance.

'What do you think you're doing? Trying to make me jealous? He's sleeping with me, and wouldn't be interested in a kitchen hand like you, so leave this instant. Get off his lap,' Tamara demanded, her voice dangerously low. Nellie appeared shocked and embarrassed. She hurriedly slipped off his knee and sat next to him, gazing up at him with pure trust. He placed his large arm around her shoulders protectively before narrowing his gaze.

'Tamara, go away before I tell everyone, includin' yer husband, what yer doin' an' how mad yer behavin',' Hamish warned.

'No! Tell her the truth. Tell her you sleep with me every time I come and stay here, which is often,' she spat. I cringed. Tamara was a respectable married woman of high breeding and here she was in the middle of a pub announcing to everyone, including her husband, she was having an affair with Hamish. All the men appeared uncomfortable, but no one more so than Hamish.

Nellie looked as if she would burst into tears at any moment. I quickly went to her side, took her by the hand and led her away from the spectacle now playing out at our table.

'Take nought she says seriously, Nellie. She's drunk and has no clue what she's saying. I'm sure Hamish will come and find you once she leaves him alone. Please don't blame him. He's trying very hard to get his life together now,' I said, not wanting Hamish's chances ruined.

'Thank you, Mistress,' Nellie said. 'I have liked him ever since the first night I met him; however, he was with Angelique and I don't go with married men. He's such a lovely person despite what people say about him. And the women in his past. He is the most handsome man I've ever set eyes on, and the fact he might be interested in me makes my heart race. I don't understand what's going on between your friend and Hamish and it's none of my business. I will wait here and hope he does come and find me. You have been very kind.' She sat with her friends who also worked at Willow Grove, while I returned to our table and drank some more whisky, then beer, then whisky again. Aaron stared at me from across the room, and I returned his stare and smiled. He gave me a worried smile in return and resumed talking with his mates. Tamara sat down heavily near me and silently downed whisky after whisky. She looked miserable, which upset me. I hated it when any of my friends felt down.

By now, I was extremely tipsy, the alcohol spreading its warmth through my body, leaving me feeling relaxed and happy all of a sudden. I didn't have a care in the world after making the bottle of whisky my friend tonight. Catherine sat silently beside me, and I took her hand in mine.

'Emmy loved her pants suit,' I slurred as she beamed at me.

'I knew she would look so sweet in it. She really hates dresses, Abigail. Can you imagine when she's thirteen? She won't wear anything you want her to,' she said with a giggle. 'She is exactly like you. Does things her way or no way.' She laughed aloud, and I hugged her tight.

'I really love and appreciate you. You're my best friend, Catherine. You do so much for me and everyone I know. You're an amazing woman. You have achieved everything and more that you set out to do and I'm so proud of you. Just as I've done everything my own way, so have you. I know how hard it is to go against what everyone expects, and I still get a lot of shit for how we live here.'

'Yes, but that's where we're lucky,' she said, her voice low so no one else could hear. 'We both have so much money we can tell them to shove it up their backsides.'

I was still laughing when Scarlett pulled me up to dance. We were both full as a boot as we twirled each other around the floor. The music quickened, and we moved in time, Scarlett copying the steps from me. We were having so much fun, but when I glanced around the room, I noticed the men had stopped what they were doing and were staring at us, while the women laughed at our silliness. Aaron stood and sipped his beer, watching me intently.

I became self-conscious. Too many eyes were on us. I grabbed Scarlett's hand and left the dance floor. When she sat down again, I made my way over to Aaron and stood on my toes to kiss him. He kissed me back and whispered in my ear, 'Ya have to dance like that for me.' I looked up at him in disbelief, then shook my head.

'We were just having fun. Only playing, really. No different from the bairns,' I replied, wrapping my arms around his waist.

'There are a lot of things about ya, Abi, ya don't mean an' ya can't help. Men see the beauty in ya, inside an' out, an' I'm not jealous, as I see it, too. You've this innocence about ya, an' a vulnerability that makes men just wanna protect ya an' take ya to their bed at the same time. The way ya smile an' talk to people, the way ya walk, an' that body ya own. Well, blokes can't help but admire ya an' want ya for 'emselves. You're oblivious how beautiful ya are an' the effect you have on men. An' women , I'll give ya the drum. It's not ya fault an' I'd never blame ya.' His eyes, the colour of the ocean and usually sparkling, were glazed as I smiled up at him, aware I wasn't the only one who had overindulged.

'What do you mean, effect on women?' I sat on his lap, my arms around his neck as I shifted to make myself more comfortable.

'Some of the women here immediately disliked ya, worried you'll steal their husband's affections. Or they're just envious of ya wealth an' beauty. That's why a few of 'em down in the village are unfriendly towards ya. It's not until they get to know how sweet ya are they give ya a chance an' offer ya their friendship. I can't stand jealous women. It pisses me right off how some of 'em treat ya, but ya just ignore it. I don't know why ya won't stand up for yourself against these bitches.' His face was like thunder, his body tense as I placed my hand on his cheek in an attempt to calm him.

'Stand up to what, Aaron? They are never nasty to my face and only avoid me. I can't say anything awful about that. You just have to let me manage things in my own way. I cannot see the point in arguments and drama if there is a way to avoid it.' He gazed down into my eyes, then kissed me.

'You're the sweetest girl I've ever met. I love bein' ya husband. Ya great-aunt Isabelle sure seemed to know what she was doin' the day she made the arrangements with me Da an' promised ya to me. I couldn't have chosen a better wife to share me life with or to be the mother of me nippers. I know we're both still in pain over losin' the boys an' we can't have any more, but we gotta look to the future an' be thankful for what we do have. The boys will always be in our hearts an' not far from our thoughts, but we've been blessed with not one, but two beautiful children who light up our lives every day. When they're grown, Abi, an' have made their own lives, we're free to travel. Before we make old bones, I'll take ya to every country you've read about in all those books ya love, so we can experience everythin' you've ever dreamed of. I love ya, Abi girl, an' me life is happier havin' ya in it. An' you're the best lookin' wife anyone could wish for.' I scoffed loudly as he smirked down at me.

He was my rock, my anchor, and I wouldn't know what to do if I didn't have him in my life. I wondered for what seemed like the millionth time how great-aunt Isabelle knew he would be the perfect husband for me. She was such a mystery. True, I had all her journals, which I would read one day, although there was something that had stopped me so far. When I picked up the first journal she had ever written and read the first page, I felt like I was intruding on someone's private thoughts and completely invading her privacy. I hadn't been able to read them since, but was hoping the day would come when my curiosity would be stronger than my reservations.

He poured us both another whisky, and I gratefully drank it, feeling a haze of happiness settle on me again. We returned to our friends, where we laughed, drank, and talked for hours. Aaron did have to come and get me off the bar, then help Elizabeth and Dana down at one point, confirming to all that we had drunk far too much. Towards the end of the evening, as people started to filter out to find their beds, Aaron took my hand and helped me to my feet. I staggered, but he caught me in his arms and slipped his arm around my waist while we went outside to meet the others.

There were still people milling around the town square as they finished their conversations and bid each other goodnight. We joined our friends, some of them walking, some being carried on their husband's backs. Their rambunctious voices filled the night, many laughing loudly as we made our way up the street, passing the now dark terraces.

Aaron and I lagged behind as we moved slowly up the hill toward the stables, the only reason I was still upright was a result of his firm and unyielding grip around my waist.

'You're goin' to have to talk about what Maslow did to ya one day, Abi, so it might as well be soon, before it eats ya up inside.' He gently grabbed my arm and brought us to a halt. Suddenly, I felt all the hurt, humiliation, degradation, rage, guilt, and pain explode inside me and I furiously turned on him.

'Why do you keep pushing me? Do you really want to know what he did to me? To have that on your mind. Isn't it bad enough that I have to think about it every day?' I screamed, pushing him away from me. I fell to the ground sobbing as every detail of that day overwhelmed me. 'Fine, Aaron. You want to know everything? Well, I will fucking well tell you!' I shouted through my tears as he came to my side and knelt, gathering me in his arms.

I saw Hamish, who had stayed back to say goodnight to Nellie, standing a bit behind Aaron. He stopped dead when he came up to us and heard my response. I cried and raged and pulled at my hair as I told Aaron of every vile thing that man did to me in graphic detail, and by the time I had screamed it all out of my system, I lay in a ball on the ground, sobbing.

Aaron and Hamish both sat down, appearing shocked by what they had heard. Aaron pulled me up and held me tight against his chest, while Hamish looked on, wiping tears from his eyes. Aaron kept me close, rocking me and whispering into my ear in an attempt to calm me. After what felt like years, he lifted me up, facing him, and I wrapped my legs around his waist and my arms around his neck. I placed my head on his shoulder and he carried me home, while Hamish walked beside us, not saying a word, deep in his own thoughts.

In the kitchen, our friends—including Tamara, whom I was surprised to see—sat around the kitchen table drinking freshly brewed coffee Leo had just prepared. There wasn't a sober person in the room, and I wondered how many people it took to help Leo make the coffee without burning it. Aaron said goodnight, as did I, and he made his way to the stairs. I clung to him, like the koala's I had seen on the property with their mothers. He stopped at the bottom of the stairs, then stared deeply into my eyes, holding me tightly under my backside, my legs still wrapped around his waist.

'I'm more than sorry I brought Maslow up. I should've waited 'till ya were ready to talk. Do ya forgive me?' I tightened my arms around his neck and gazed up into his eyes.

'It's not your fault, so there is nothing to forgive. It was probably for the best. It was obviously ready to burst out of me. I hate the fact you know everything now.' I swallowed hard, trying to focus as everything moved around me. 'I don't want you thinking about it either. It's over and we have to try to find some way to move on. I don't know if I can, but I promise I will try.'

He gave me the sweetest smile as he climbed the grand staircase and through the wide hallways. We stopped in the nursery and kissed Thomas and Emmy, who had their cousins and friends sleeping in the enormous bed with them, before he silently carried me to our bedchamber.

As I tried to stand upright by the bed, Aaron stripped me of my dress, then took his own clothes off before slipping a lace negligee over my head. I staggered and nearly fell, but just in time he grabbed me and helped me into bed, pulling the covers over me.

'I'm so sorry for what ya went through, me darlin' girl, but it changes nothin' for me. You're mine, an' always will be,' he whispered, holding me in his arms and kissing me like he would never let me go. He slowly moved the straps down on my negligee, then began making love to me with a passion and protectiveness he had never shown before. Later, I lay in his arms feeling safe, the burden I had carried alone slowly lifting. I drifted off to sleep, dreaming of a snake, a table, and a rope.

Chapter Three

I WOKE TO FIND Aaron gone, an act in and of itself that was far from unusual. I slipped my hand across the sheet to his side to feel if the warmth of his body was still there, but I found none. I remembered him kissing me during the night and getting up, but fell back into a deep sleep within moments. Assuming he was still down in the kitchen, I snuggled back under the covers to wait for him to return. Soon after, I drifted back to sleep, but woke with a start when I heard someone come through the bedchamber door. Bessie bustled in, her uniform immaculate and her face lit in a bright smile before she started to tidy the room.

'And how are you today, Mistress? I must say your mood has been much brighter since Christmas.'

It was the first week of January and hadn't even been two full weeks since I had broken down and told Aaron everything about Maslow's attack on me. It had made me feel better, and he was relieved I could talk about it with him when I needed to. Ever since, though, I had tried to avoid the subject because it made Aaron furious, despite him trying everything in his power to hide his emotions.

'I'm well, Bessie. Aaron seems to have disappeared from my bed sometime during the night. I know it was dark outside, but I was so sleepy I just kissed him back when he left. I didn't ask where he was going before drifting back to sleep.' She laughed as she moved around the room straightening our things.

'You know what that boy is like. He would've been down in that kitchen for hours before being distracted by some emergency on the property and going to attend to it. I have no doubt you'll easily find that enormous husband of yours as soon as you go looking. He's hard to miss.'

I smiled, got out of bed and slipped on my dressing gown before sitting at my dressing table so Bessie could do my hair. While we chatted about our families, the children came in, confusion crossing their faces as they stared at the empty bed.

'Where's Daddy?' Thomas asked, now appearing even more confused. Aaron was always here every morning to see his children and tell them a story, no matter what was going on in his day.

'He must be in the kitchen. We'll meet him down there,' I replied as they both gave me a hug. They were turning nine in a couple of months, with my own birthday now only a week away. I was turning twenty-six and felt I had aged ten-years since losing my babies. The children kissed us both before racing down to the kitchen.

Bessie helped me into a comfortable house dress that made me look like a gypsy, being off the shoulder with long sleeves flowing down around the skirt. This one had a tight bodice, which minimised my small waist even further and emphasised my breasts, something I had asked Catherine to stop doing. She had refused, saying she believed she knew how to dress my body and wouldn't listen to any of my suggestions when it came to designing my clothes.

In the kitchen, I found Leo and the staff—but no Aaron.

'Where's Aaron?' I asked an indignant looking Leo.

'He came in about five o'clock, inhaled everything I had prepared, then rushed off saying he had something important to do. He is always using and abusing me—not in that way, Abigail. I saw you roll your eyes. I wish he would, by the way. No, what I meant was he thinks he's at a Coffee Palace. He comes in here, tells me what he wants, and then expects it in front of him in five-minutes. I'm a human being who has feelings. He could at least give me a cuddle in appreciation, you know?'

I kissed him good morning as he made our breakfast, then joined Thomas and Emmy at the kitchen table on the far side of the room.

'Hello, our darlin' Mummy,' Thomas called out cheerily. 'Do ya know we were talkin' with our mates at school about who has the best parents, an' we said it's definitely us, 'cause we have you an' Daddy? Some of 'em disagreed, sayin' their parents are the best, but others took our side an' reckon you come out tops. Ya always send us to school with treats for our friends as well as us, an' we never get hit.'

Leo hurried over, then placed our food down on exquisite white-and-gold trays for everyone to help themselves.

'You're the best, Mummy. You never get cross at us, only at Uncle Leo, and then when you do swear, you use flower words,' Emmy said sweetly, making me choke on my toast. Ever since the twins had been born, we all tried to never curse around them, although there were times when we would replace curse words with the names of native trees and flowers. I hadn't realised the children had noticed or even knew what we were talking about at the time.

'Well, then, I have to say that you two are the best children any mother could wish for, and I really mean that. You are both beautiful, independent, intelligent, generous, and loving people, and we are proud of what you have become. You are the sunshine in my day, and I thank the universe every day for giving you to me,' I said as they looked at me adoringly.

'Oh stop it, all of you,' Leo whined. 'How about spreading the love in my direction? I'm the best at things too, you know.' He glanced at Thomas and Emmy, then pouted.

'Well, it's true you are good at some things, but there are lots of things you lack skill in,' Emmy remarked. 'You can't run without tripping yourself or someone else, a bit like Mummy. You're a good cook, but Sally and Jenny are just as good.' I tried not to laugh aloud as Leo's face darkened, Thomas nodding in agreement.

'I know one thing you're the best at. Teasin' the children in the village. No one else is as good at it as you are. Ya make 'em cry almost every time.' I burst into giggles, causing Leo to wave his hands in the air, shriek nonsense, then retreat to the other side of the kitchen.

'Mummy, where's Daddy? He never misses mornings with us. Not one. Ever,' Emmy said, her own face darkening.

'Wherever he is at the moment, I'm sure it's important and he will be back soon,' I assured her.

The children nodded, then filled their plates with toast, eggs, bacon, tomatoes, and mushrooms. I poured large glasses of pear juice for them and for myself. The pears were from our own trees and were delicious. Margaret's husband, Sean, was making pear cider along with the apple cider he made each year for us. It had such a strong alcohol content that all it took was two small bottles, and I would have to go sleep it off.

In truth, I had been worried about Aaron since exploding at him on Christmas night. Ever since, he had been unusually quiet and very protective, to the point of smothering me. He treated me like I would break when he touched me and would stare at me while tenderly stroking my face without speaking. He often brooded and was not his usual self, which everyone noticed.

Hamish joined us, bringing Willy and Bella, who sat beside the twins and happily helped themselves to breakfast, filling their plates as they talked and laughed. I smiled affectionately at the four of them as Hamish sat beside me. He helped himself and I poured him some juice.

'Do you know where Aaron went today?' I asked. 'He seems to tell his mates more than he tells me. I know he does these things when he has a surprise for me or something is happening behind my back, but I generally know what's going on. This time, there was no warning. Maybe he's getting better at hiding his secrets.' Hamish smirked but did look surprised. It was clear he had no knowledge of what Aaron was up to this time.

'I dinnae know he was goin' anywhere. We had work planned fer this mornin' in the north paddock,' he replied, pinching some bacon from Emmy and crunching on it as she rolled her eyes and took another from the tray. If Aaron would have told anyone, he would have told Hamish, but it was far too early to worry yet. He could walk in at any minute as he had done in the past, although never this early in the morning.

Over the years, he had occasionally disappeared during the day and not returned until late at night, usually bringing new livestock of some sort, and always presents for me and the children. He wanted the farm to have as much variety as possible, including goats. He loved the Nepalese goat curry Leo would make for him. We would sit down to beef, lamb, and pork, along with chicken, turkey and goose raised here on the property. I wasn't as fond of the goat meat, or kangaroo the workers would shoot when the opportunity arose, but did enjoy all the fresh seafood we could ever eat, delivered twice a week by my father-in-law himself.

He would come in his large cart drawn by two of our horses with huge orders of lobster, prawns, squid, oysters, mussels, salmon, and fresh fish of all types. It wasn't only for our kitchen, but the dining hall as well, which fed over a hundred people a day. I always ensured the workers had the same food as we did. Jenny was a fabulous cook when it came to seafood. She would serve some fresh and others battered and deep fried along with thickly sliced potatoes that were fried until golden brown and a fresh, crunchy salad.

'How are things going with Nellie?' I asked Hamish in an attempt to stop myself focussing on Aaron or his current whereabouts.

'Good enough, I suppose. She's a nice lass an' all, an' I like her very much, but given me track record when it comes tae women, I'm bein' cautious an' takin' it slow.' A slow grin spread across his face, and I couldn't help but smile back.

'Hamish, she's more than nice. She's lovely and would make a good wife and mother, so don't play with her and then discard her. If you like her and you think it could be serious, follow your heart, but if you're not interested, you will have to tell her. Better a broken heart now than later.'

'Aye, I do like her, an' I plan tae keep meetin' her tae see if we have a future. I've naw intention o' playin' with anyone's heart, or causin' 'em grief. I just need tae be certain this time an' find someone I get along with. I dinnae care about her background. 'Tis naw as though I have tae worry anymore about introducin' her tae me parents tae seek their blessin'.' He took a sip of his coffee then went on. 'Me future wife will naw be forced tae mix with the upper class since I naw longer do, although I'm still welcomed an' invited tae mix in those circles. It bores me now, an' I find the people resemble sheep. Naw one has an original thought in their head. I'd much rather take a wife who'll love me an' treat me kindly. An' live a life like everyone here at Willow Grove. That'd make me happy.' After finishing his coffee, Hamish noticed the children dallying over their pancakes. 'Time fer ye lot tae run off,' he reminded them.

'Yes. Off you go,' I added.

All four embraced Hamish, Leo, and myself, before running out the kitchen door shouting their goodbyes, leaving us smiling. They were like small hurricanes, always busy outside together and riding their horses. We had given Willy and Bella their own so they could ride with Thomas and Emmy—and they did at every opportunity, exploring the property and going on adventures together, as they called it. I took a fresh plate and served Hamish and myself pancakes, drenching them in maple syrup before placing it in front of him.

'I've been worried about ye, Abigail, ever since Christmas night,' Hamish said softly once we were alone at the kitchen table. I sighed deeply, having forgotten he was even witness to what I had told Aaron.

'Please don't fash, Hamish. I'm much better than I was since I spoke of it. I'm making peace with what happened and I'm trying very hard to let myself heal.' He stared into my eyes for just a moment too long, and I saw a flash of pain before he looked away. 'So, what are your plans now Aaron isn't here?' I asked, focusing on my plate as he picked up his fork. He glanced at me again, his face now returned to its usual pleasant expression.

'I'll go work with Angus first, then Harry, 'till Aaron returns from wherever he is. He's probably out lookin' fer a present fer ye an' it's so big he's havin' trouble wrappin' it.' Hamish laughed, as did I. It helped a little. He finished his breakfast, wiping his mouth on a napkin. 'I must be goin'. I cannae be like Aaron an' sit on me arse all day doin' nothin'. The bludger.' He chuckled to himself as he bid me farewell and walked out the kitchen door. I noticed Dingo waiting at the back door, finding this in itself unusual, as Aaron took him everywhere he went. Hamish patted him on the head before Dingo reluctantly followed him to the stables. Leo came over with a full cup of coffee in his hand and sat down next to me.

'It's unlike Aaron to go somewhere and not tell anyone where or how long he will be,' he remarked, settling into the chair opposite me. 'I mean, I know he does this at times; however, he always leaves a secret message with someone. Except me, of course. He says I have a big mouth, which is scaffy. I can keep any secret I'm told if I wanted to. The problem is I don't want to, and I think everyone should have as much enjoyment out of people's secrets and private business as I do.' I smiled across at him but remained silent. 'Now back to Aaron. There are two possibilities we can look at. The first one, which is the one I like so far, he is having a secret affair with a beautiful woman. Let's face it, you're getting a bit long in the tooth for him now given how handsome he is. It was just a matter of time before he found someone better than you. Now, don't feel bad that his Mistress has kept him late in her bed this morning. He will always come home, just like my father eventually does.' I turned towards him, my eyes wide.

'You never told me your father had affairs.' I thought I knew everything about Leo, but he always had something new to add as the years passed.

'Oh, yes. I have at least ten illegitimate siblings I know of, birthed by his many Mistresses, and spread out all across Italy. Can you imagine another ten like me?' He seemed delighted at the thought. I just shook my head, confident they would send the strongest soul to the asylum if all in one room.

'In all honesty, no I can't. What was the second option about Aaron, as I don't like the first?'

'All right. The second option is he was taken from the house in the middle of the night, tortured and killed, and is lying somewhere in a ditch, waiting to be discovered.' I reached across and smacked him across the side of his head, causing him to knock over his coffee. 'Abigail! Look what you've done!' he shrieked, racing to the sink for a dishcloth.

'Well, don't say pig shite like that, you Banksia. I'm already starting to worry about him, and you give me two ridiculous options of what must have happened, neither one better than the other. You're meant to be my friend and act positive, telling me not to worry. Instead you go and put terrible thoughts in my head that I hadn't even considered.' I glared at him as he returned and wiped up the mess before pouring himself more coffee.

'Well, you always bury your head in the sand and pretend you're sleeping. When you do pull it out on the rare occasion, you're wearing rose-coloured glasses. I don't see how a bit of reality can hurt you. I'm sure it's the first scenario and he'll come home soon,' he said, sounding sympathetic as I tried not to smile.

'Well, for his sake, he'd better have a good reason for worrying me like this.'

'I have to say, since you asked Tamara not to come and stay until she's over her crush on Hamish, you've brought my fornicating to a screaming halt. Thank you very much, Abigail. It could be years, or maybe never, before she gets over him.' I chuckled and patted his hand in mock sympathy.

I had been forced to have a difficult conversation with Tamara after Christmas night and her treatment of Nellie and Hamish. She hadn't taken it well. She'd ordered her poor servants to pack up her things, along with her children, and they left the next morning without saying goodbye. With poor Brian reluctantly in tow. I hadn't seen her since or had any communication with her, so had decided to write her a letter now she'd had time to calm down away from Hamish.

'Did Brian get to say goodbye to you before they left?' I asked, thinking how the poor man was required to follow along behind her silently and meet her every demand. I loved Tamara deeply, although I didn't agree with her behaviour at times, just as she didn't agree with how I ran my house and my life. It made no difference to our friendship or the love and connection we shared.

'Why, yes, he certainly did manage to say goodbye to me,' Leo said dreamily—and I closed my ears, preferring not to know.

I left the kitchen with a basket over my arm, a cheesecake Leo had just finished making tucked up securely inside, then headed towards Polly's cottage. It was a beautiful summer morning, the warm air against my skin confirming it was going to get hot today, hurrying me on as I wanted to get the delicate pastry to Polly's as quickly as possible. However, over by a large tree along the path, movement caught my eye. When I set my basket down and looked in the long grass around the base of the tree, I spotted a tiny wombat crawling along. I could tell immediately he needed to be with his mother. If he weren't fed soon, he would die. Picking him up and cradling him in the crook of my arm, I began looking for the missing parent.

There were no wombat holes close by that I could find and no sign of the mother. I knew I couldn't leave the tiny creature out at the mercy of the elements with no food, so I picked up my basket, took out the cheesecake, and placed the tiny marsupial inside.

When I knocked on Polly's door, entered, and hollered out hello, I heard Polly call for me from the kitchen. I found her with her arms covered with flour and dough. She wiped her hands on a towel, we embraced, and I handed her the cheesecake.

'I won't be a minute, Abi. I just need to finish this cake for Angus and Hamish's birthday.' She wiped her brow where beads of sweat had formed from leaning over the hot stove. Forgetting it was their birthday today, I'd said nothing when I saw Hamish at breakfast. I should have remembered his birthday, only a little over a week before my own. I felt awful. Although I had a gift for him, the day had slipped my mind given I was preoccupied and worried about my husband.

I took the tiny wombat out of my basket and showed him to her. After noting how sweet he was, she retrieved a bottle with a glass nipple so I could drip milk into his mouth. I held him like a newborn wean and fed him the milk. He took every drop before I placed him back down in the basket, where he curled up and went to sleep.

I told Polly of the mystery surrounding Aaron's departure this morning. Her brow creased in concern as she stopped what she was doing and gave me her full attention.

'He normally tells someone, even if he doesn't want you to know. Angus didn't mention anything, nor did Hamish, and if anyone would know, it would be them.' Confirming my own thoughts, she noticed the look on my face as she put the last of the icing on the birthday cake and placed it in the pantry. 'Don't worry, Abi. Aaron is a big boy and he can look after himself. I'm sure he has only gone off to do something sweet for you.' Her attempts to cheer me failed. Conversely, the more I talked to people about it, the more worried I became.

'Let's have a birthday dinner for Angus and Hamish tonight at our house with the children. I'll go in a little while and organise it with Leo so you don't have to cook, if you like?' Her face lit up as she cut two large slices of the chocolate cake and placed them on plates. She poured us both a lemonade, put everything on a tray and carried it outside to her back verandah, her favourite place. We sat on comfortable cushioned chairs made of strong bamboo, which we had purchased from a man who imported furniture from Thailand.

'That would be wonderful, and what a generous thought, Abi. You are so lovely to Angus and Hamish, treating them like they are your blood brothers,' Polly said as we started to eat. 'Ever since their parents disowned Hamish, Angus refuses to visit them,' she went on. 'They are being just as stubborn in refusing to visit us or the children, even on special occasions. I know it's not his mother, and she suffers for it. All because their fat headed father has put his foot down. Angus learnt only yesterday Mr Makenzie is furious with you for allowing Hamish to live and work on the property. He wanted to see him on the street after he was disowned, and the fact he is not only doing very well for himself but is happy, kills the old bastard. He has made an enemy of you, so please be careful.' Polly took a sip of her lemonade. 'By the way, Mr Makenzie blames you for sending his son off the rails for all those years that he associated with women of low breeding, as he says. He thinks you are the sole reason Hamish left Angelique at the altar and is spouting off to all who'll listen that you are a cock tease, whatever that means. He has been going around the district saying terrible things about you that I don't wish to repeat. Things that are disgusting and untrue. I wouldn't be surprised if his golden-haired daughter, Jemima, has a hand in all of this.'

'Polly, I would be shocked if Jemima had nothing to do with spreading lies about me. I don't care what they say. I haven't seen them in years and don't wish to. They know nothing of our lives here other than the tiny part we have allowed them to see when they have visited. It's Harriett I feel the most sorry for. She loves her sons, you, and her grandchildren. It must be killing her he's stopped her from visiting. Don't fash, Polly. We will throw Angus and Hamish a lovely dinner tonight and they won't think about their parents once, I guarantee you.' Polly smiled and put a hand on my arm.

'Thanks, Abi. You are such a wonderful friend and sister to me, and looking better than I have seen you look since you lost the boys. You're so strong and brave. I couldn't be like that. I would have crumbled in a heap and not left my bed since. Why haven't the police captured the man who robbed you and caused the death of the boys? Surely they must know something by now?' It was the same question she and just about every other person who knew us had asked me repeatedly.

'I don't know, Polly. They may never catch him, and I don't expect them to. It makes no difference to us whether he is caught or not. Won't change anything that's happened. It cannot bring my weans back,' I replied, bursting into tears. Polly embraced me, and I took a handkerchief from my pocket and wiped my face.

'I'm sorry, Abi. I know you don't like to think about it. Let's talk about something happy,' she said. I blew my nose and pulled myself together as we continued to eat and drink. We chatted about the children, our sex lives, and the birthday dinner tonight. Once we had finished gossiping and laughing, I stood to go.

'Thank you for always being there as my sister and friend, too, Polly. I always feel better after spending time with you.' I embraced her and kissed her cheek.

'I love you, Abi.' Tears glistened in her eyes, and I knew she felt my heartbreak just as strongly as I did without any more words needing to be said.

On our way through the kitchen, I picked up the basket with the wombat. I decided to bring him home and try to nurture him there. Besides, he was so cute I thought the children would love cuddling him when they got home from school.

I sat in my office finishing my letter to Tamara when Amelia walked in looking visibly upset. She closed the door behind her and sat opposite me. She looked as if she had been crying and I wondered what could have happened. It took a lot to upset Amelia; she was usually very calm for a woman who had been brought up with a title.

Since giving it up, she had fit into the village like she had been born into a working-class family and got along with nearly everyone.

'Amelia, what is it? I've never seen you storm into a room like that without being announced first.' Despite her relaxed attitude about class and all the formalities that went with it, she still behaved like a lady, which was ingrained in her.

'I'm sorry for just barging in here, Abigail, but if I don't talk to someone I'll explode,' she said, her face flushed. Mr Masters came in soon after. He too looked flustered.

'I'm sorry, Mistress. Your friend here just rushed by me without a word and I had no chance to come and ask if you were available, knowing how busy you are today,' he said, glancing across disapprovingly at Amelia. I saw her flinch in embarrassment.

'That's fine, Mr Masters. I just finished what I was doing and was about to take tea. Please don't concern yourself. If you wouldn't mind, we would really appreciate something from the kitchen.' He nodded formally, and left to fetch refreshments for us. 'Now tell me what's happened as calmly as you can,' I said. 'I can see how upset you are, Amelia, and if I can help, I will.' She took a deep breath as she stared into my eyes.

'I could kill Mrs McGinty for what she said to my Mathew this morning in front of the whole class. He got his sums wrong and she told him that he will be no better than his father, and will end up as a farm worker because he doesn't have the brains to go to university. He came home crying and now he doesn't want to return to school, ever!' She put her face in her hands and burst into tears. I sighed deeply, then made my way to her side, lowering myself into the chair beside her before taking her hand in mine.

Mrs McGinty was a fine teacher, but she did have the tendency to say what she thought was the truth to the children and parents, whatever that may be. She couldn't see anything wrong with her often tactless delivery and didn't seem to care about the consequences of her words.

'I will talk to her, Amelia. I'm sure once the situation has calmed, you and Tommy can go with Mathew to see her and sort it out. I know how upsetting it must be to see Mathew so hurt.' She nodded, her face brightening as we began talking about the general store and the new stock that had just arrived.

'You must come and take a look. There is so much there you would like,' she said proudly, and I smiled, glad to focus on something other than my concern about what Aaron was doing. We talked about the new products, some we had never heard of, that both of us couldn't wait to try. I loved spending my money on luxuries, especially for the bathroom. I always made sure my children had the best shampoos and soaps. Emmy had a large range of lovely body products she liked to put on after her bath to keep her skin soft and smelling nice. When I would purchase something for myself, I would buy her the same, which she adored and became excited about every time. She was such a dainty little girl who loved bath time as much as I did. She was now very fussy with what she used on her hair and body. If it wasn't something I was using at the time, she didn't want it. Thomas was like his father and happy to use anything I bought him as long as he was clean and didn't smell like a girl.

Mr Masters returned, still looking unhappy. 'Your cook has sent word that luncheon is ready in the kitchen,' he said disdainfully. If Mr Masters could have his way, every meal would be served in the dining room with a bevy of staff, even for one person. While I had formed the belief this was an enormous waste of everyone's time and effort. I hadn't realised it was so late; morning tea time was long past. I thanked him and he returned to his duties.

'Please stay for lunch, Amelia. It's only going to be in the kitchen. Nothing formal.'

She accepted gratefully, and we stood and embraced before walking hand in hand through the hallways to the busiest room in the house. We found Hamish sitting at the kitchen table, the room warm and bustling with staff. He stood politely and greeted Amelia, then pulled out her chair, for which she thanked him profusely. He smiled broadly before returning to his seat.

He was still as handsome as ever, his black, curly hair loose, given he was not working today. He had the most magnificent brown eyes, the colour of chocolate that drew others deep into his soul. There was such kindness and compassion in them now, something that had been lacking when I met him nearly eleven-years ago. He had changed so much. I could see why so many women sought out his acquaintance. It eased my mind and filled my heart with joy. He had finally become serious about life and falling in love with a good woman who would make him happy. He wanted the same as most people—to be loved and have a family he could cherish.

When we met, he freely showed the lovely side of himself to me, while with most others, he appeared distant and cold. As the years passed and he relaxed into the Australian way of life, he had allowed himself to open up more and let his walls down. Now everyone, except Dana, knew what a lovely, kind, and decent person he was.

'Happy birthday, Hamish. I'm sorry I didn't mention it at breakfast. You're getting old now that you have to let go of thirty and add a one,' I said and laughed.

'Ye be careful, Abigail,' he countered. 'Yer five-years an' one-week younger than me, so yer naw that far behind. Although ye bloody well've naw changed much in appearance since we arrived here. Naw wonder most o' the women in the district are jealous an' despise ye fer it on sight.'

I sighed. I didn't understand why people disliked me for how I looked. I wasn't hurting anyone, and I didn't walk around trying to entice other women's husbands. And I certainly didn't flirt. Apparently, I didn't even know how to. Aaron and Hamish had both been clear about that over and over and over through the passing years.

Deep down, though, it did hurt my feelings, despite people telling me not to worry about it. I hated being judged solely on my appearance, something that had occurred constantly since I was fifteen. Once I left the shelter of the orphanage and was no longer protected, I found out the hard way that many people were unkind, not just a scattering of the nuns I'd had to put up with. I would look back and shake my head at how naïve I had been; not knowing just how nasty some people could be for no reason at all. I also hadn't known the extent of the evil that permeated the world then, either, or just how it would touch me without warning.

Leo placed an oversized tray of seafood in front of us for lunch. This morning Luke had delivered prawns, abalone, oysters and mussels, along with six lobsters. Leo, who had made a secret seafood sauce to accompany it all, passed around the claw crushers, as I called them, that cracked open the lobster shells. He had thoughtfully peeled the large prawns, as he knew I hated doing it. If I had to pull their tiny heads off while their beady black eyes glared at me hatefully, then strip their little legs off, I couldn't eat the poor things. I dipped a prawn into the sauce and found it delicious. Amelia ate the mussels simmered in red wine and tomatoes with garlic and onions, while Hamish attacked a lobster with vigour.

'It's such a luxury to have fresh seafood delivered whenever we like.' Leo sighed contentedly, swallowing an oyster from a tray that held at least six dozen, freshly shucked and ready to eat au naturel.

'I know. When Polly and I were growing up, we were rarely given good seafood like salmon or langoustines like everyone around us in Scotland. And never fresh like this. To this day I hate stinky haddock because of it,' I replied, finishing my prawns and then squeezing some lemon onto a few oysters and beginning on them.

'You rarely got anything when you were growing up,' Leo complained. 'My family wasn't rich, but being Italian, we always had good food. And a lot of it. At every meal. That's where my passion for food came from. My grandfather made everything himself. He pickled the vegetables, made the sauce from the tomatoes, and bottled all the fruits from the trees. He had a magnificent vegetable garden with everything you can think of, like here. That's how I know how to cook all the vegetables that you had never seen or heard of before we arrived here.' Leo glanced across at Hamish and smirked. 'See, Adonis?' Hamish returned Leo's stare, a slow smile touching his lips as he nodded, waiting for him to go on. 'I would be a far better wife to you than any of the slappers currently chasing you around town. I have never seen so many spinsters come to our pub just to see you. You must understand that if you hitch your wagon to a nagging minger, you'll only have a few years of happiness, if at all. Should you choose to hitch yourself to my frilly handsome cab, I'd look after you like no other.' Leo studied his face for a long moment, then his muscular body. I attempted to smother a smile as Hamish stared back at him, his face void of emotion.

'Aye, ye think me a fool, Leonardo? Yer sittin' here tryin' tae convince me ye'd naw be a naggin' wife when every man an' his dog knows ye tae be the worst complainer that's ever walked the soil of

Willow Grove. Yer the biggest nagger I've ever met, man or woman.' Hamish took a sip of wine as Leo's eyes widened. 'Thank ye kindly fer yer ridiculous offer, but I'll take me chances with an abnormal person rather than hitch meself tae yer wee handsome cab an' never get a moment's peace again. At least I can get away from ye. Livin' in the cottage an' all that allows me some privacy, but I dinnae know how Aaron can stand it.'

'Stand what?' Leo snapped, his arms crossed against his chest.

'Och, he's told me ye still sneak in tae bed with 'em an' get in on the other side o' Abigail thinkin' he'll naw notice. Aaron also mentioned how ye wrap yer arms around her so tightly while she's sleepin', the poor bloke cannae get ye out o' the bed 'till she wakes on her own. Yer as cunnin' as a dunny rat, I'll give ye that.' I choked on an oyster. I wished Hamish hadn't divulged that bit of information with Amelia present.

Lately, at least once a week, I would wake in the early hours to find Aaron sleeping on one side of me and Leo on the other, holding onto me for dear life. He knew the moment he let go, Aaron would push him out and onto the floor. Hard. True, he had gotten better about it over the years. It had been several times a week at the start of our marriage when he felt Aaron had stolen me from him. Now it was never more than once a week, which I didn't mind, but Aaron hated it still.

'You're just jealous because it's not you,' Leo replied wickedly. Hamish raised an eyebrow at him.

'I cannae say the thought o' ye in bed with me, naw matter with whom, sounds like a good time, Leo. Aaron can have it, ye pain in the arse. I'm glad 'tis him havin' tae deal with ye, ye wee shite. He's a patient man. I personally would've strangled ye with me bare hands by now.' Hamish chuckled, while Leo appeared offended and turned away to watch the staff efficiently tend to their duties. 'How's Tommy an' the bairns, Amelia?' Hamish asked, grinning widely. He liked Tommy and included him as a friend.

'They are all well, Hamish, thank you for asking. And many happy returns of the day,' she said, smiling brightly back at him.

I took a lobster and placed it on my plate, but didn't know where to begin. Aaron always sorted out the lobster for me so that all I had to do was eat it. Hamish noticed my dilemma, reached over, and took my plate. He split the body lengthwise, removed something that looked disgusting, and then passed it back. The sweet, white meat was delightful, and I enjoyed every bite.

'Watch me, Abigail,' Hamish said, cracking open the legs and the claws. I felt stupid; Aaron always did this for me, or Leo often prepared them ahead, so I had never had to get my fingers dirty. I appreciated Hamish's thoughtfulness in trying to limit my embarrassment. 'I saw yer wee wombat in the basket by the stove. Where'd ye find him? Are ye keepin' him? He's maybe a week or two old, an' is unlikely tae survive without his mother. Dinnae get too attached.'

'It's all right, Hamish. I looked for ages for his mother and found no evidence she had even been around the area. I'm just going to feed him and care for him until he's old enough to release back onto the property. You don't keep native animals as pets. It's cruel.'

'Aye, ye wee hypocrite. How quickly ye ferget about yer four-legged friend named Dingo.' A slow smile spread across his face as I shook my head at him.

'That was all Aaron's doing. I wanted to release him back to the bush but Aaron couldn't part with him. His reasoning is Dingo isn't kept locked up, and can return to the other dingoes on the property at any time; however, he chooses to stay here. It's actually true, though. I saw a pack of dingoes close to the house last week and Dingo showed no interest in joining them despite some of the females being in heat. He must have very high morals and be of strong character.' I giggled, and he laughed aloud, his eyes twinkling in amusement.

'Has anyone heard from Aaron yet?' Leo suddenly chimed in, and we shook our heads. My errant husband would be hearing a few stern words from me when he got home, that much was certain.

It was coming on dinner time, or tea time as Aaron liked to say, and he still hadn't returned. I was beyond worried. He had never been gone this long before without leaving word for me. Angus and Polly had arrived with Willy and Bella, who chatted with Thomas and Emmy as we all waited in the sitting room to be called for the birthday dinner. Soon after, Hamish arrived and sat in a lounge next to Thomas and Emmy, ruffling their hair. He was such a wonderful godfather to them. Whenever he had spare time, he would take them riding or fishing or on some adventure they would excitedly tell us about when they returned home. They adored him as much as they loved their godmother, Catherine, although it was a different relationship. Both were close, but Hamish was the one they saw every day.

I handed Emmy and Thomas their presents for Angus and Hamish. My twins hugged the elder twins as they gave them each their gift. Angus opened his first and his face lit up. It was a large fishing pole made out of strong wood that he could use in the ocean and he thanked me and the children. It had been extremely hard to disguise, so I hadn't even tried, just wrapping the pole as best I could and leaving the long, bulky thing in the sitting room. Hamish's was smaller. When he opened it and found a solid gold watch, he appeared emotional, swallowing hard several times before he was able to speak.

'Thank ye, Emmy an' Thomas.' He kissed them on the forehead before turning his attention back to the gleaming timepiece.

'Do ya like it, Uncle Hamish? Mummy helped me pick it out for ya,' Thomas said proudly as he strapped it on Hamish's large wrist. Hamish glanced over at me, a smile on his face.

'Thank ye, Abigail. An' Aaron. If he were here, the bludger. I'll always treasure it,' he said, studying the timepiece, an odd expression on his tanned face. At least I knew he liked it. Besides, anything he received from his godchildren, he treasured. He still had a leaf from a gumtree they had collected and given to him when they were not quite three—still pressed in between the pages of a bible left to him by his long dead grandfather to this day.

Just then, Mr Masters came in and bowed, causing me to roll my eyes. 'Dinner is served,' he announced formally. Polly noticed my reaction and smiled to herself before rising to her feet and hurrying us along.

Stepping into the dining room, we found a large birthday cake on the table, which excited me no end. Everyone knew I would rather eat cake than anything else in the world—except for chocolate. The children chose to sit together at the far end of the long table, leaving me between Polly and Hamish. He kept looking at his gift, his large fingers caressing the band.

'How did ye know? I've really missed havin' one o' these. Me father repossessed me grandfather's timepiece when I was disinherited. An' I dinnae feel like buyin' just any old bauble fer meself like a dandy. Thank ye, again.'

'We knew about your grandfather's timepiece,' I remarked, my mouth full. 'Although you only showed it to me once, I remembered how much you loved it. So we tried to find one similar.' He nodded before I continued. 'And failed. But given Thomas and Emmy told me your gift had to be perfect, I took them to Melbourne to our jeweller, Mr Dawson. We provided him with a sketch of your grandfather's watch I did from memory. We hope it's at least similar to what you once had.'

'Similar? 'Tis exactly the same. Only this is crafted far better an' is o' a quality rarely seen these days. Ye have a memory like an elephant, Abigail. The only difference I can see is this is far superior an' has diamonds on the face. Why so heavy, though?' He held his arm out in front of him as if to estimate the weight of it.

'That's because it's solid gold, Uncle Hamish. Mr Dawson said it was the best watch he's ever made and that you are a very lucky godfather to have me and Thomas,' Emmy called from the end of the table, making us laugh. It didn't matter that the children were chatting animatedly among themselves. They always seemed to have one ear on our conversations.

'Thank ye, me darlin' wee Emmy. 'Tis also the best watch I've ever seen,' he called back, much to their satisfaction. The twins took after me and loved giving special presents to people. I had always encouraged them to buy what the person would like, and not what they themselves would prefer.

They had asked me why we no longer saw Mrs Makenzie like we used to, leaving me to explain as best I could what had happened between them and Hamish. I had spared them most of the details; however, they understood what it meant to be disowned, and that was the reason we no longer saw his mother up to five-times a week.

Bella and Willy loved their Grandmother and were extremely upset at being cut off from her.

Leo joined us, and we all ate our entrées while we chatted about the day and joined in with the children's conversations.

'Did you hear what Mrs McGinty said to poor Mathew today?' Emmy asked, her eyes wide, the children surrounding her nodding enthusiastically. 'To be told that you will never go to university is cruel. Everyone can go to university if they set their mind to it and work hard enough. Daddy and Mummy say you can achieve anything you want, even if you are a girl.'

'Mummy, ya didn't go to university an' you're the smartest person I know,' Thomas said. I smiled at him affectionately. Naturally, I was one of the smartest people he knew—he didn't know all that many people.

'That's true, Thomas, about university, anyway. I didn't go, but if I'd been raised by my parents and had the opportunity to attend, I would have been grateful and made the most of it.'

He nodded approvingly. The twins favoured me in their love of the written word, and were both good at school, often coming at the top of the class in English and arithmetic. The fact they would be educated would make things so much easier for them in the future. I wasn't concerned with what they chose to do with their lives, as long as they were happy and true to themselves.

'I know what I'm doin' tomorrow,' Angus teased the children.

'What are you doin'?' Willy asked curiously as Bella jumped up and down, begging her father to tell.

'I'm goin' to get up early in the mornin' when it's still dark, hours before the bushman's clock calls. I may take a horse an' ride down to the beach an' go fishin'. Who'd like to come?' he asked, a mischievous grin spreading across his face. They all screamed out they wanted to go, then loudly clapped their hands. Hamish looked across at Angus, his face darkening as he continued to eat.

'I suppose that means I'm goin' fishin', too, then? An' at that ungodly hour?'

'O' course you are, brother. How else will I manage four wild bairns like these? Two are your own niece an' nephew, an' the other two your godchildren. You're obligated up to your neck, mate.' Angus chuckled as Hamish stared back at him in silence, then shook his head.

'Aye, I knew the hook was in when ye invited all o' 'em an' dinnae flinch. Naw a twitch,' Hamish replied sarcastically.

Angus, Polly, Leo, and I howled in laughter until tears ran down our faces. After we had contained ourselves, we finished dinner and retired to the sitting room, where we drank coffee and pretended we weren't waiting for Aaron.

As the minutes turned into hours, it came time for the children to retire for the night. I suggested to Polly that Willy and Bella sleep here with Thomas and Emmy. They could all get up together and have breakfast before leaving for their fishing trip in the wee hours of the morning. The children hugged Angus and Hamish goodnight before Polly and I escorted them up to their bedchambers.

Little Mary followed us in to prepare nightclothes for all of them, and Polly and I helped them wash and dress for bed. Bella joined Emmy in her ornate four-poster bed, while Willy and Thomas threw themselves down on the end of the bed and made themselves comfortable, much to the irritation of their sisters. Willy would remain with Thomas in the room next door, where he often chose to sleep in the large lounge when he stayed over. Only a few weeks apart in age and thicker than thieves, they were the best of mates and, in fact, more like brothers.

Polly and I settled down to read them a chapter from Seven Little Australians, written by Ethel Turner in 1894, a story of seven lively and very naughty children who lived with their father and young stepmother in a house on the banks of the Parramatta River in New South Wales in the 1890s—a story I could well relate to living at Willow Grove with so many children. We kissed them all goodnight, turning back to wish little Mary luck, their rambunctious voices filtering out into the hallway as we closed their doors.

'Yes, they're fair wee fiends when they're together and it comes to bedtime. No different from the Woolcot children,' Polly said with a smile, while trying to look annoyed but failing miserably. We soon returned to the sitting room where Hamish and Angus relaxed and sat sipping Aaron's whisky, while Leo had a glass of wine in hand.

'You better not overdo it if you're planning to be sharp for your early morning adventure,' Polly said, imagining her children lost at sea due to the neglect of their father and uncle.

'Aye, we'll stop after this. We only had a few while waitin' for Aaron,' Angus said, kissing her. They were still like young lovers, with Angus unable to keep his hands off her. And her, him. It warmed my heart to see it after all their years together. They knew from the day they met they would be together, and despite all the naysayers, they still were. I stifled a yawn. It was getting late and Angus had already decided it was time to go to bed, hauling his enormous frame upright and encouraging Polly to do the same.

'I'll wait up a wee bit longer with Abigail,' Hamish said. He knew I would get no sleep until Aaron was home. Polly and Angus kissed us goodnight, then quickly left for their cottage. Hamish and I sat in silence for a time while he made himself comfortable on the couch opposite mine as I lay snuggled under a blanket. 'How's yer wee wombat?' His eyes twinkled in amusement and I smothered a smile.

'Oh, he's so very sweet. He's eating well enough, so far. Every man and his aunt Flo wants to help me feed and care for him. The only downfall of finding the poor wretch abandoned. He's sleeping in his basket by the stove as we speak.' He chuckled to himself before silence again hung over us.

'Do ye think I'll ever find someone an' have what ye an' Aaron share between ye?' Hamish remarked, his hands behind his head. He lay on the opposite lounge staring up at the ceiling, while I curled my legs up under me and gazed across at the door.

'Yes, I do. I think you just have to wait for the right one to come along, and you will know right away. You have the pick of any woman, Hamish. There are so many lovely girls who would snap you up in a second.'

'What if ye only get given one chance? What if ye mess it up an' once ye've lost that perfect person, ye dinnae get another chance at a love like that again?' I could hear the sadness in his voice as I gazed across at him thoughtfully.

'I don't believe it works like that, Hamish. I think there are many people in this world we could each be happy with. You'll find your match. I'm certain of it as you deserve every happiness in the world.'

We waited and waited, the time passing quickly into the early hours of the morning. 'You should go find your bed since you have to rise from it so early,' I reminded him. 'I'll be fine. I'm sure Aaron will be home soon.'

'Aye. If he's naw back by tomorrow, I'll go an' report him missin' tae the coppers.' Hamish sat up, yawning widely. He stretched, then stood to prepare himself to return to the cottage. Accompanying him to the kitchen, I collected my pipe, filled it, then walked him to the back door. Lowering myself down onto a seat outside on the verandah, I struck a match and inhaled deeply while he pulled on his boots and grabbed his hat from a hook on the sandstone wall. Usually, I only smoked my green buds when in pain, and that was rare these days, but I knew I wouldn't get a wink of sleep tonight without it. Feeling far more relaxed by the time I finished and said goodnight to Hamish, who had kindly kept me company under the stars, I slowly and very carefully made my way upstairs. Once in bed, albeit fully clothed, I allowed myself to float away into vivid dreams of thunderstorms, a dozen men in chains, and Heavenly Hideaway.

Chapter Four

'**A**BI, WAKE UP.'

Aaron. The sound of his voice jolted me from a deep sleep, and I sat bolt upright in my bed, my body trembling. It was still dark outside, and long before the bushman's clock started his morning song. When I reached over to light the lamp, I was horrified to see blood stains on his clothes and hands and cried out in fright.

'Are you hurt?' I gasped as he sat down gingerly on the edge of the bed.

'Nah, it's not me own blood, but I've done somethin' an' I have to go an' hide so as not to bring police attention to ya an' the nippers. I want ya all kept out of this,' he said, hurrying into his dressing room, where he began stuffing some clothing into a sack.

'What? You're leaving me and the children?' I asked, my voice barely audible. He soon returned, placed the bag on the floor, and kissed me.

'It's the last thing I wanna do, but I have to. The coppers could be here within hours.'

Tears filled his eyes as he took me in his arms. I didn't ask him what he had done. I could only guess, but I wasn't prepared to hear it. All I knew for certain was whatever he had done, it was very bad.

'Where are you going to go?' I asked, my body shaking with fear. He grabbed my hands to stop them from trembling.

'It'll have to be far away from Australia. I can't stay here. Once I'm settled, I'll send for ya.'

'No! I'm not letting you go, Aaron. You are not leaving. I don't care what you've done, but you vowed before God you would always stay with me! 'I cried. He held me again while I sobbed, stroking my head.

'What about under the house?' I had found a section down there a few months ago when I was poking around that appeared to have been set up as a living space. I hadn't looked closely, so I wasn't sure, but maybe he could hide there instead of fleeing abroad.

'Let's go an' look. I didn't even think about the cellar. No one knows it's there except for you an' me. We don't have a lot of time, though, Abi. We must move quickly.'

He helped me put on my dressing gown, took my hand, and hurried me down the stairs and into the office. I locked the door behind us, going to the fireplace and feeling down the side until I found the tiny lever and heard it click. Aaron pulled it open, exposing the door that led to the stairs. We both carried lamps, while I pulled the fireplace closed behind us. I led Aaron through the hallways that had rooms off them we hadn't even looked in, and tried to remember where I had seen that particular room.

I finally found it and opened the door to a large space with a fireplace. I set the lamp down on the table, brightly illuminating the windowless room. There was furniture still in here covered in sheets, while another two rooms led off this one.

I nearly fell over when I walked into the first of the two to find a bed, along with more furniture, all covered in sheets. I placed the lamp on a table, then climbed up onto the bed. It was surprisingly comfortable and only seemed to require fresh bedding and for the room to be cleaned. Aaron appeared impressed, but slightly confused.

'It's like someone has lived down here before, Abi. But that's not possible when the house was only a year old an' had never been lived in when ya moved here. Just think about it. How did all that money get down here, an' all your great-aunt Isabelle's things, when she wasn't even alive? Someone she trusted had to have moved it all here from the cottage where she lived twenty-years before you arrived. It has to be someone who was in her employ and could now be in ours.'

'That could be many people,' I replied. 'Harry and Sean were here then, as were about six others who still work here today. But who would prove so trustworthy as to not filch some, if not all, of that money? Or keep the secret of the underground space?' The fact Harry Black had been my great-aunt's lover and confidant made him the most likely candidate, but I kept that thought to myself as I entered the second room to find a privy closet and an old bath.

'This is the perfect place for you to hide, Aaron,' I called out over my shoulder as he stood in the doorway staring at me. Until that very moment, Aaron and I were of the opinion this secret cellar was a ridiculous waste of space and effort. We had never used it, and I rarely came down here except to withdraw money from the mountain of cash held in the locked room. 'It's only until we can sort out whatever mess you are in.' I kissed him before leaving him there and hurrying upstairs to get Bessie. It was still dark, but I could see daybreak would arrive soon as I raced past the stables, over the hill, and down to the village, my boots wet and slippery. I knocked on Bessie's door, feeling terrible for waking her and Danny at this time. Within moments she stood before me in a nightcap and dressing gown, her eyes still half closed.

'Has something happened, Mistress? Are the children well?'

'Yes, yes, Bessie. It's something else. My bloody husband,' I replied, rubbing my hands together in an attempt to warm them. I told her of what I knew, which wasn't much. 'I am so sorry for calling at this time, but I need you to come to the main house as soon as you can to help me.' I confided in her, speaking of the underground space in hushed tones so as not to wake Danny or her neighbours, going on to tell her how Aaron would be forced to hide there for a while, but not disclosing why as I didn't know myself.

'Your secret is safe with me, Mistress. Now if you don't mind, I will get myself ready and be up at the house shortly. We must make sure he has everything he needs for the full day in case the police do arrive and we can't get back down there. Lord have mercy on him, whatever the silly boy has gone and done to get himself covered in blood. Let's hope it's from a beast he's brought home to hang.' I nodded, impressed by her matter-of-fact tone and efficiency in a crisis, all the while feeling heavy knots of apprehension clenching in my stomach.

I quickly left her and ran all the way back to the house, where I stood for a time at the back door to catch my breath. The kitchen was bustling with staff getting their breakfast, while Sally and Leo were cooking at the stoves, which was a relief. Finding them busy and preoccupied meant I didn't have to explain my quietness or dour countenance this morning, as none of them had time to take much notice of me. I poured a cup of hot coffee and waited for Bessie to join me, which she did twenty-minutes later.

Once in my office, I locked the door behind us, then turned to find she had already placed her tools in a bucket ready to clean the rooms below, leaving it by the hearth.

'Oh, Mistress, I feel sick with worry. Something terrible has happened for Mr Aaron to be needing to hide away like this.' I placed my hand on her shoulder and lowered my voice.

'I'm sure it's just a misunderstanding and nothing for us to get worked up about.' She nodded silently before picking up the bucket, her eyes wide as I opened the door to the secret passage. We carefully descended and soon found ourselves in the dark hallway. I carried fresh linen for the bed over one arm and held the lamp up to light the way. Bessie followed close behind, her mouth wide. We finally arrived at the main room to find Aaron sitting quietly on a chair, a single candle dimly lighting the room. Bessie took my lamp and marched off to explore the other rooms before coming back and standing in front of us with her hands on her hips.

'It looks like this was set up to live in and has everything here,' she said. 'It just needs a bit of a clean here and there and I'll have it sparkling. Now I want you two gone for a couple of hours while I sort things out down here. Is it safe for him to go up to the bedchamber for a time?' I turned to Aaron, as I still didn't know what had actually occurred.

'Yeah, if it's still dark outside. I should be safe 'till mornin' at the earliest, mid-mornin' at the latest,' he replied, taking my hand and leading me upstairs. Once in our bedchamber, he stripped off his bloodied clothes and got into the bath drawn by the maids at my request. He went to wash while I got back into bed.

I pondered if he'd killed someone, while praying it wasn't who I thought it was. I knew Aaron could hand out swift and often brutal punishments to anyone he believed had wronged him, as was the case with Leroy and George in years gone by. Both times, he had remained calm when dispensing his own form of justice. I lay silent and alone, thinking of a million scenarios, all frightening, until he got into bed beside me and pulled me into his arms, his forehead creased in concern.

'Abi, I will not apologise for what I've done, an' I'm not sorry I did it, but I do apologise to ya an' Thomas an' Emmy for makin' ya a part of me actions in this sorry business,' he said, gently kissing me. He looked as if he hadn't slept in days, yet he had only been gone for a little more than twenty-four-hours.

'Aaron, please tell me what you did. I can't stand not knowing. I'm scared, and you aren't telling me anything,' I said, frustrated and desperately worried. He slipped in beside me, lay on his back, then took a deep breath.

'I went to Melbourne yesterday mornin' an' waited outside the courthouse all day for George Maslow,' he murmured as fear overwhelmed me. 'I followed him back to Moray Street in South Melbourne when he left for the day, an' waited across the street opposite his terrace at Freers Tavern 'till he'd gone to bed. Then I broke in an' went to his room, where I punched him several times an' dragged him downstairs by his hair to the dinin' room.' He stopped for a moment and loudly cleared his throat. 'I tied him to a chair with rope. He knew who I was an' what I was there for, an' begged for his life.' I sat up abruptly and turned to him, horror filling me.

'Oh, Aaron! What have you done?' My body started to shake, and I felt I would be sick. I could sense life as we knew it was about to fall to pieces around us and I was unable to do a thing to change it. He grabbed my shoulders and pulled me back into his side.

'He went on about the same things he told ya. Past lives an' all that. Said he knew me, too, but I wasn't an evolved soul like you an' he are, an' have no memory of it. He reckons he didn't have a black aura in his past life when ya were with him. Vows an' declares he had no aura at all 'cause he only met ya in that life Says that the golden aura can only be seen by someone who has lived before an' achieved great things here on earth. An' on a planet called Hiriarni. He said you're able to recognise the souls of people who've lived before with ya, an' whom ya love very deeply. Reckons they love ya back just as fiercely without knowin' why.' I tried to dislodge the lump that had lodged in my throat as he continued. 'Those without auras are new souls who've crossed ya path only in this life cycle an' not before. He didn't explain to me what the grey an' black auras mean, but I don't imagine them to be a good thing if you can believe anythin' that comes out of that criminal's gob.' Aaron sighed and paused for a time to gather his thoughts. 'I really dunno what to believe anymore after hearin' what he had to say to me,' he went on. 'Maslow admitted everythin' he did to ya an' said he couldn't help himself an' that he was like a man possessed when he saw ya again. He told me he loved ya very much durin' his last life, which could have been five-hundred-years ago if it's true 'cause he told me when he died he was taken to a very dark planet where he was held for what was meant to be eternity. He told me in all seriousness he somehow escaped an' reincarnated back as George Maslow. That souls who've a connection always have a way to find each other again in the next life. An' what seems like coincidence is far from it. He did say the strangest thing, though. He told me if you reincarnate into the same bloodline an' ya parents have known ya before, you're often given the same name as the one you had in your previous life. Despite 'em havin' no conscious knowledge or memory of ya.' He blinked quickly as he shook his head in disbelief.

'None of it makes sense to me.'

'He didn't make a lot of sense, Abi. I was beatin' an' hurtin' him while he begged for his life. He thought if he could explain his actions to me, I'd let him go, which was never gunna happen. I threatened him an' hurt him for the pain he inflicted on ya 'till he was cryin' like a wean. I couldn't stop meself. I was so full of rage an' thinkin' of ways to make him suffer. I took a sharp knife an' carved into one side of his face the word rapist, then on the other the word killer. For our boys. I sat for a time an' just stared at him snivellin' at me before I cut off his dick an' balls, then left 'em on the table. He's probably dead by now from the bleedin', but I'm sure he won't be found 'till mornin' when he doesn't turn up for court.' He was surprisingly calm, while I lay beside him, unable to breathe. My body trembled, and I could feel my heart racing. My throat tightened, my mind filled with regret. This was my fault. If I hadn't gone and gotten myself drunk Christmas night and told him what Maslow did to me, this never would have happened.

'Aaron, I'm so sorry,' I whispered, then promptly burst into tears.

'Ya have nothin' to be sorry for, Abi. That yellow bellied bastard does.' I held him tightly around the neck and kissed his face, sobbing uncontrollably. I certainly knew I had plenty to feel sorry about. 'Ya don't have to think about it anymore, or have bad dreams in the night about him. He'll never hurt ya again. He doesn't have the equipment, an' after this, if he does survive, he'll never have the courage to come near ya while I'm beside ya.'

He grabbed me and kissed me forcefully, desire pulsating through him. He then pulled me on top of him and slipped off my negligee, and I didn't stop him.

We fell asleep in each other's arms, my dreams tormenting me until Bessie came in just after daybreak.

'Come on, downstairs with you. I will move your things later this morning, Mr Aaron,' Bessie said, hurrying us along. I slipped on my dressing gown and followed them downstairs, parting in the hallway so Aaron and Bessie could hurry underground while I went to the kitchen, my heart racing as I stepped into the cosy room.

'Leo, I need to speak with you.' My voice was barely above a whisper, yet I wondered if the staff had heard me. Dropping his work immediately without question, a rare occurrence, he pranced along behind me from the kitchen to the sitting room. We sat down next to each other on a lounge and I let out a deep sigh. I told him everything I knew about the situation while he remained motionless, listening intently without interruption.

'I can't believe Goliath is a killer and will go to gaol. He will do at least thirty-years of hard labour, maybe even more. You will never see him again. Who is going to protect me from you? Hold on, though. We don't know for certain this man is dead, do we?' I shook my head.

'No, we don't. I don't think anyone would survive that though, do you?' He looked at me thoughtfully.

'Hmmm, I'm not sure. I know when I get a stiffy, every pint of blood goes directly to my cock-a-doodle-do, given it is so large and needs to be filled. It takes every drop from my body to maintain my erection, yet I still survive, and the blood isn't technically in my body anymore. Do you understand what I mean? He may survive without any blood in him just as I have to. Do you understand now, thicko?' As quick as a flash, I grabbed his ear.

'Stop being a cock face! How dare you call me a thicko, whatever that means? I'm trying to be serious and you're talking about six-foot penises, which you don't have by the way, so just stop it. I need to make sure you know exactly how serious this is and that you'll keep your mouth shut until I know more. Are you comfortable serving Aaron his meals in secret, even from the other staff? Do you understand you cannot utter a word to another soul, you twit?' I let go of him as he nodded, then moved his dark hair away from his eyes, his other hand on his ear. He nodded again as I rose to my feet, hurrying him down the hallway. I led him into my office, then showed him how to lock the door with the key I provided, reminding him how important it was that he followed our instructions. He nodded silently as I opened the fireplace, a gasp omitting from his lips as I stepped aside.

'This is imaginative. How clever would you have to be to think of something like that? Better than you and I put together, and we are the two smartest people I know, Abigail.' He followed me inside, and I turned to show him how he must close the fireplace behind himself every single time.

I held the lamp high as he followed me down the stairs and into the labyrinth of hallways, his hand on my backside until we arrived at Aaron's room. I carefully opened the door, then stepped inside, gasping to myself. The room was a comfortable extension of the house, with two large couches surrounding the fireplace, a low table in the middle, and a small kitchen table off to the side. The furniture was of high quality and the décor luxurious. Once cleaned, it was almost as good as a hotel—and certainly better than a prison cell.

Aaron greeted Leo warmly, then sat down to tell him in detail what had happened and why he had done what he'd done. Leo appeared surprised. I hadn't told him or anyone of the rape, but I said nothing. I went to look at the bedchamber again and was pleased by what I found. Bessie had done a marvellous job of sprucing up the place. Aaron's suspicions that someone was living here in the year before I took over the house and knew about this underground space through great-aunt Isabelle seemed to be more accurate than I had first thought. I was just grateful she had had the forethought to build the house like this in case we ever needed to hide. I again thanked her, wherever she was, for all she had done for me. Leo left to prepare a breakfast tray for Aaron and me and Bessie followed him, leaving us alone.

'So, you're not mad at me, Abi?' he asked, closing his red-rimmed eyes for a moment, clearly emotional and exhausted.

'No, Aaron. Deep down I knew something would eventually happen, but I made it worse by telling you what Maslow did. I'm sorry. I'm the cause of this,' I said, bursting into tears again.

'Please stop sayin' you're sorry. I was glad ya told me, instead of me spendin' every night since it happened wonderin' what he put ya through. Once I knew for certain, I had to do somethin' to make him pay for makin' ya suffer so terribly,' he said, pulling me towards him on the lounge and wrapping his arms around me as I lay my head on his chest. His voice broke as he held me tight. 'I promised to protect ya always, an' I take that very seriously. I feel like I failed ya that day, an' I needed to make it right. I don't expect ya to understand, but I pray it doesn't change ya love for me.'

'Aaron, nothing could ever do that,' I replied, and kissed him. He stroked my back as we quietly talked. 'What do you think of his ramblings about past lives and having known both of us?' I mused. 'I still believe he's insane and it's just a coincidence that he talks about auras. There have been others in the past talking about similar things that have been institutionalised for their entire lives. I've read about it in medical books. Maybe he has the same disorder they had.'

'I'm not sure what to believe, Abi. He didn't sound insane, an' he spoke like he knew both of us well. One thing he did say, which I've heard ya say also, is that people with the golden glow who've lived in a past life with ya are strongly connected an' don't understand why they feel so drawn to one another. He spoke to me as though I was a peasant an' he was me master, sayin' that I, like the majority of souls on this earth, cannot see the golden glow, but when we come across someone who has lived with us before, we feel that inexplicable pull towards them an' become friends or lovers—an' we're closer to family members who have reincarnated.' He paused and ran his fingers through his hair before continuing. 'Maslow told me that no matter how hard ya try to break the connection, it's never been done. Whatever that's meant to mean. I think this has actually happened to me. Me bein' friends with Hamish. Who would've thought that could ever happen? Here we were, ready to hate each other forever, an' neither of us could do it 'cause we have some sort of connection or soul contact that piece of shit mentioned. The whole thing is odd an' too difficult to comprehend. I stand by me first thought, though. I dunno what to believe.' Aaron fell silent as he gently stroked my head, still pressed to his chest while we waited for Leo to return with our breakfast trays.

After we had eaten an enormous breakfast, we made our way into the bedchamber. Aaron hadn't slept properly for over forty-hours and it was starting to show.

'Are you all right, my love?' I asked as he stripped off his clothes while I sat on the bed, watching him.

'Yeah, I am now I'm home with ya. Where's Thomas an' Emmy? They don't have school today.' I explained about the fishing trip and how they were unlikely to return before lunchtime at the earliest. He nodded before getting into bed naked and pulling the fresh covers over himself as I stood to let him sleep. 'This bed is as comfortable as ours. What? Ya think I'm stayin' in here alone?' he asked, sitting up and slowly undoing my dressing gown as I moved closer to him.

Shouts and laughter filtered into the kitchen where I sat waiting at the table for the children to return with Angus and Hamish. The four of them came rushing through the back door, my twins holding up their fish proudly for me and Leo to admire. Leo quickly showed them how to clean and fillet them to cook for lunch. I was amazed how growing up on a farm had left the children unfazed by blood and guts.

I grabbed a carafe of coffee as Hamish and Angus, appearing quite sunburned, followed me to the sitting room, where I filled them in on the situation, leaving the graphic details for Aaron to tell. Soon after, they silently followed me to my office, where I showed them how everything worked, then led them down through the labyrinth of hallways to Aaron's room. He was still sleeping, but I kissed him awake and told him who was here. He sleepily got up and joined them in the lounge room.

'I can't believe this has been under the house the whole time and you never told us. I thought you were our mate?' Angus said, his eyes wide as he gazed around the brightly lit room.

'We rarely come down here ourselves, an' never really explored it properly until today,' Aaron said, yawning while pouring himself a large mug of the fresh coffee I'd brought for him.

'Aaron, whatever ye need us tae do 'till this is sorted, we're willin',' Hamish said, lowering his large frame onto the couch, then making himself comfortable next to his brother.

'Thanks, cobber. You're a good mate an' I appreciate everythin' you blokes do. Just keep things runnin' as they are. I'm not goin' anywhere soon, so ya can come an' visit me. As a matter o' fact, I'll go completely mad bein' locked up down here if ya don't come an' see me at least once a day.' Aaron's handsome face broke into a grin and they chuckled. I saw the pity in their eyes as they commiserated with him, despite agreeing far too enthusiastically they would have done the same thing, if not worse, if in his position.

Other than worry, I didn't know what I was feeling about it all. I hadn't had time to stop and think about anything since he woke me this morning. I knew for certain Maslow was insane and everything he said was simply unbelievable. I had heard of people who claimed they could read other people's minds, and maybe he could, too, and that was how he knew I saw auras. It was the only way I could explain it to myself.

I didn't believe at all that I had lived before, alongside all my friends who had golden auras, and several others who had crossed my path possessing grey or black auras. If I did, I would then be forced to consider these souls I supposedly loved in another lifetime had somehow turned on me and come back to inflict their revenge in this one. It was all too fantastic, no different from the stories Aaron would tell our children about the future and what the world would be like in a hundred-years. My husband was sharp witted, and had a grand imagination, but this wasn't something fanciful or fun—it was pure madness.

I left the three of them to talk and returned upstairs to Leo and the children, who were enthusiastically eating their freshly cooked battered fish. I nibbled at some of the fish while they described the exciting things they had done since they'd left this morning. Soon after when they went upstairs to change, Leo joined me at the table.

'So, I take it all this is purely on a need-to-know basis? I'm not even allowed to gossip about the most exciting crime that has ever been committed in Victoria, even when it could make me famous by pure association?'

'No, you're bloody well not,' I replied, narrowing my gaze at him. 'It's vital that you say nothing to anyone. Bessie will take over most of the tasks associated with looking after him and will be taking down his meals each day, then collecting the trays when he's finished. She will be responsible for cleaning the rooms and ensuring he has all he needs. For now, only you and I, along with Hamish, Angus, and Bessie, and soon, our children will know he's down there.'

I slowly ate a piece of cheesecake Leo had made this morning when Hamish and Angus came into the kitchen and sat down.

'At least he's in good spirits, Abigail,' Hamish remarked, noticing the strain and worry in my eyes.

'For how long, Hamish? If Maslow is dead, Aaron will swing,' I told him, a lump lodging in my throat. As soon as the words left my lips, Mr Masters entered the room, and I cringed as he bowed low before me.

'I'm sorry to disturb you, Mistress. There are a number of police officers out front wishing to speak to you,' he said, appearing nervous, his hand trembling slightly by his side as he straightened his tall frame.

I hurried to the front door with Angus and Hamish following close behind, and found more than thirty police constables standing outside our grand entrance.

'I'm Mrs Cavanaugh. What's this about?' I nodded politely at the two men who had more stripes and medals pinned to their uniforms than the other, younger police officers, many of whom appeared uncomfortable in such elaborate surroundings.

'I am Detective Paul O'Neill from Geelong and we have a warrant to search your home, the surrounding buildings, and your property. Do you understand? We are looking for your husband, Mr Aaron Cavanaugh,' he said far too loudly, as if I had lost my hearing or any understanding of the English language.

'Yes, I do understand what you are saying, but please let me get my children out of the house first. I don't want them to see this or know anything about you storming into my house like an army ready to invade and take over a small country,' I spat at him. He looked uncertain for a moment as he stood unmoving in the doorway. 'You can bloody well come with me to the kitchen and see for yourself,' I continued. 'Fuckin' bastard coppers! You think you can just walk over everyone because you have a badge made out of some cheap metal, you poor excuses for human beings,' I snapped as he followed me inside. After what the police had done to me at the hospital the night I lost my babies, I despised them and didn't even try to hide my contempt.

He glanced suspiciously at Hamish and Angus, who stayed close by my side as if they were guarding me as I hurried down the wide hallway and into the warm, bustling kitchen. I turned and introduced them to the Detective and explained that they worked and lived here while Hamish and Angus made themselves comfortable back at the large table.

'So, do you know the whereabouts of Aaron Cavanaugh?' he asked, giving them a piercing stare.

'Naw,' Hamish said. 'That's why we're here an' not out in the paddocks workin'. He left yesterday an' no one knows where he is. We were comin' in tae Geelong town this arvo to report him missin' if he'd naw returned by then.'

'Would you please take Thomas and Emmy from here with Willy and Bella? I don't want them seeing any of this. Thank Mary, Jesus and Joseph they're playing in the larder and are blissfully unaware of this intrusion.' They both nodded silently, then rose to their feet.

'Aye. We'll be goin' so you can get on with your work,' Angus said, nodding to the Detective as they left. He waved a hand in dismissal, then stood in front of me, a little too close.

'Mrs Cavanaugh, may I please speak to you somewhere more private?' I reluctantly showed him through to the sitting room, where I could hear the officers going from room to room looking for Aaron. He made himself comfortable opposite me as I settled into a chair near the fire. 'Do you know why we are here, Mrs Cavanaugh?'

'I do not. Only that you are looking for my husband who has been missing since yesterday,' I said, outwardly upset while dramatically reaching for a handkerchief.

'You are obviously a woman of high breeding.' He nodded to himself, his gaze dropping from my face to my chest. 'I understand the wealth you so obviously display here is yours and not your husband's. You're the sole heiress to the late Lady Isabelle Delmont, aren't you?' He nodded again as he gazed around the room, while I remained silent. 'My family is connected to yours going back many generations, so I am well aware of your aristocratic ties to the Howard family. I believe your husband comes from a working-class family, who we will also be visiting later in the day. I am here because your husband committed a serious assault on a Judge last night. He was found close to death early this morning by his housekeeper.' I swallowed hard, unable to move while summoning all my strength to hide my emotions. 'Judge George Maslow has identified your husband as the perpetrator of this attack on his person while in his own home, the poor man. I will save you from the details, though needless to say the crimes your husband has committed are sickening even to a hardened police officer. I'm very sorry for you and your children, Mrs Cavanaugh. Very sorry indeed.' His eyes hadn't left my breasts and I shifted in my seat, loudly clearing my throat. He straightened up in his seat, then gazed once again into my eyes.

'I don't believe my husband would do any such thing, but I have been told this morning by a maid he was having an affair and has fled the country with his Mistress,' I said bitterly, trying to look angry.

'If I didn't know any better, I would think you were trying to send us on a wild goose chase, Mrs Cavanaugh,' he said with a smile. I looked across at him, confusion crossing my face.

'I don't know what you mean,' I replied, returning his stare.

'Oh, I think you do, Mrs Cavanaugh. I think you do. I have been told of your husband's reputation, and his love for you, and I have also been made aware that you made a false rape charge against Judge Maslow over six-months ago. It sounds to me like your husband has gone to defend your honour. Why else would he cut... ' He paused, his eyes shimmering dangerously. 'I must stop there. I would hate for you to faint dead away on the floor if you truly knew what injuries your beloved husband has caused a respectable member of our community.'

'Respectable? That's a barefaced lie. I was attacked and raped by Maslow, and it was you swines who covered it up!' I spat at him. 'Don't expect me to cooperate or have any respect for you corrupt pieces of pig shit. Fuckin' leave my house and never step foot in here again. I don't know how I will get the stink of you lot out of here.' He sat back in his seat, surprised as I rose to my feet.

'Ahh, looks like a lady but speaks like a trollop. It is somehow very attractive on you. We have a detailed statement from Judge Maslow identifying Mr Aaron Cavanaugh as the perpetrator of the crime against him. Along with what Mr Cavanaugh threatened him with before leaving. The only thing that I have to do now is find your husband, because as far as I'm concerned, he has already been tried and convicted.' He stood up, while I remained seated, knowing if I moved, I would punch him hard in the face.

'Fuck off, Detective O'Neill,' I snarled as he smiled.

'I will go and supervise my officers, but this will not be the last you will see of me, Mrs Cavanaugh. No, I think you and I will become closely acquainted,' he said, directing his words at my breasts.

I followed him out, then made my way to the kitchen, while these strangers continued to go through my house, looking in every room and cupboard, through the servant's quarters and down into the separate cellar where we kept wine, root vegetables and preserves. I felt invaded and knew I would be forced to ask the maids to give the house an extra thorough clean tomorrow to get their stench out while straightening the mess they would no doubt leave behind. The only thing that brought me some comfort was knowing Aaron was safe downstairs and wouldn't come up.

I knew I would have to find someone to devise a signal system to warn anyone visiting Aaron not to come up if the police were here. I knew many of the workers here at Willow Grove were inventive when it came to things like that. I expected many more visits like this after today, and I didn't want Aaron caught over some silly mistake made by one of us. I stood silently at the back door and watched the coppers leave the house to search the stables and Polly's cottage, and then the village. Two-hours later, Mr Masters escorted Detective O'Neill into the sitting room, where I was waiting alone for him.

'We haven't found him or his horse, so we do believe he's not here. That doesn't mean you don't know where he is, Mrs Cavanaugh, and I expect in time the more I visit you, the more inclined you will be to tell me.' He smiled pleasantly while undressing me with his eyes.

'Goodbye, Detective. Take your corrupt arse out of my house and off my property. If you would like anything else from me, contact my barrister, Richard Malcolm, in Geelong. I have no desire to seek out your company or set eyes on you again,' I replied coldly, standing and pointing to the door, where Mr Masters waited to escort him out.

'Not goodbye, Mrs Cavanaugh, but see you again. Soon,' he called out over his shoulder before tipping his hat, his eyes twinkling, then disappearing through the doorway.

Goliath had been put out to pasture with the herd in the south paddock by Harry this morning, so I was confident the police would not find Aaron's horse amongst them. Bessie had burned Aaron's bloody clothes in the early hours, leaving no evidence Aaron was here now, or had been here, since he left yesterday morning.

I hurried to the office, locked the door behind me, and made my way downstairs to tell Aaron what had happened. He kissed me when I sat down, then I explained what the Detective had told me.

'He's not dead, Aaron, so at least you won't be charged with murder.' He appeared thoughtful for a moment as he lay on the lounge with me settled comfortably on top of him, my head on his shoulder.

'Maybe I should just turn meself in, Abi, an' do the time in prison. At least there wouldn't be raids on the house, an' I wouldn't be hidden away like a rat. Once I've done me time, I'm free to live in the open again.'

'Absolutely not,' I said a little too loudly, and he looked at me surprised. 'Do you honestly think you would get a fair trial in Victoria before any Judge in any court in this state after what you did to Maslow? They look after their own, remember? He's one of theirs, and you are now just a criminal. You will end up with double the amount of years you would have been sentenced to had it been a regular person. Knowing what happened to me, do you still think you would be dealt with without prejudice or favour?'

'Yeah, nah, now ya say it like that,' he said, leaning away to stare into my eyes. 'I can't stay down here forever though, Abi. We'll have to come up with a plan when they stop lookin' for me.'

I nodded and poured us some of the coffee I'd brought with me. We sat back to drink it, not saying much. I promised I would bring the children to eat dinner with him, and when I had put them to bed, I would return to stay with him. He kissed me and pulled me onto his lap. I could see already how he planned to fill in a lot of his time down here, and it involved my participation.

After asking Leo to prepare dinner for our small family, and for it to be served in the underground hideout, I went to the nursery and found Thomas building an elaborate castle from notched dowels he had invented and Emmy copying and colouring steel engravings from a book about ancient Greece.

'Such creative children,' I remarked affectionately. They ran to me, embracing me in a tight hug. 'I need to talk to you,' I said as calmly as possible. 'Would you please come with me to my bedchamber?' They both excitedly agreed, each taking one of my hands in theirs before we made our way down the hallway. We stepped into my room, and I kicked the door closed behind us, then sat down on the bed with them. 'I have to tell you a secret and you can't tell anyone. Not your friends or any other adults, not even Daddy and Mummy's friends.' They stared up at me wide eyed, while Emmy's face had paled.

'What will happen if we do? Will someone come and kill us?' she asked.

'No, sweetheart, no one is getting killed. It's just that the police will come and take Daddy away and we won't see him for a long time.' I explained as honestly as I could how their father had returned to us, but he was in trouble with the police, who were looking for him. I told them of the secret place where he was hiding, and that we could see him every day, but we were not allowed to tell anyone. They both nodded, appearing to understand how important this was.

I took them down to the office and unlocked the hidden door, stepping back to watch their reaction. Their eyes widened again and Emmy gasped before they followed me in, and I shut the fireplace behind us. We carefully stepped down the wide, marble stairs and hurried through the hallways to where Aaron was. The moment I opened the door, the twins ran screaming into his arms, where he kissed them and held them tight. We snuggled on the lounge together until Bessie, with Leo's help, brought our dinner down.

'So, how does it feel, my little angels, to have a criminal for a father?' Leo asked as he placed the tray down on the table. 'I always knew your mother would turn him stark, raving mad, and now it's happened. Don't worry, my little chickens. Uncle Leo will be here to look after you while your father spends the next fifty-years in prison. Emmy, are you crying? Don't cry, Emmy! You know how I hate it when people cry. It makes me cry. Why are you crying? Please stop crying!' Leo sobbed, tears running down his face, while Aaron held Emmy in his arms as she wept softly against his chest. Bessie walked up behind

Leo and smacked him across the ear with such force, his lobe turned a dark red almost instantly.

'Get out of here, you little shite,' she roared. 'Don't open that mouth of yours again. No. Stop right now and shut it. I can't believe the scaffy that comes out of your mouth. Now it's not just the village children you are upsetting, it's my babies, so you'll now have to deal with me. Get your mischief making bum back upstairs and quit your crying. You're acting like an obtuse bairn. Stop it this instant and move.' He looked at her wide eyed, then promptly ran out of the room, crying loudly with the occasional shriek as he got farther away from us. He had no lamp with him, and it would be pitch black as he tried to find his way back to the stairs. I worried for a moment, then realised he would just have to wait for Bessie to come along and save him. 'Right. Now that's been sorted, there is no need to cry, little Emmy. Your Daddy won't be going to gaol for long and it won't happen for a while yet, so you have nothing to worry about for now, cherub,' Bessie told her, which eased my mind. I didn't want anyone lying to them and telling them that Aaron would be fine and wouldn't go to gaol; however, I didn't need idiots telling them he would be gone for decades, either.

'Thank you, Bessie. I think we just need time now to think about what's happened,' I told her, and she smiled kindly at us.

'Of course you do. You have hours until the children have to go to bed. Plenty of time to explain and put their minds at rest. I need to get upstairs and finish something that Leo started.' She closed the door far louder than usual and hurried away.

We ate at the kitchen table; the children telling Aaron all about their fishing trip and how Uncle Leo cooked their catch for lunch. They went on and on about how much they loved seafood as he grinned widely at his offspring, offering an encouraging nod here and there while he continued to eat. I was not surprised, given they were Cavanaughs' and had been eating it since their teeth came in.

Once we had eaten our fill, we led them to the bed where we lay together while their father attempted to explain the situation from the start, hoping they would understand. They both listened intently as Aaron and I took turns explaining as simply as we could what Maslow had done to me and what Aaron had since gone and done to him. At first, they were angry, but soon seemed much more at ease knowing the truth than if we had tried to hide it from them. Since they were intelligent children who were constantly around adult talk, they understood how serious the situation was. After Aaron told them a story, they kissed and hugged him goodnight, and I took them up to bed. I tucked them both in, Thomas first into his large four-poster bed in his blue room, then Emmy in her purple room.

'I'm sorry that man hurt you, Mummy,' Emmy said as she wrapped her arms around my neck. 'He did the right thing, making him suffer like that. I'm glad Daddy is still here and not in gaol. I promise I will never tell anyone.'

'I'm glad he's still here too, Emmy,' I said, then kissed her good-night and shut her door, leaving her to her dreams, while hoping they were only good and darker thoughts would not torment her—as they would me.

Aaron lay in bed, watching me undress. 'Do ya still have any of the dresses ya wore when I first met ya?' he asked, looking me up and down while I slipped on a negligee.

'Yes, I have them in the storage area under the other part of the house. I have every dress I've ever owned, including the two I left the orphanage with.' I slipped into bed beside him then leaned over to extinguish the lamp, not before noticing the surprise flickering in his eyes for a moment.

'I knew ya had a lot of clothes, Abi, an' I often wondered where they all went when Catherine brings ya over a whole new wardrobe each season. I had no idea they were stored away. I thought for some reason ya donated them to the poor.' I sighed and turned to face him. Bessie had put fresh linen and new covers on Aaron's bed, and it was cosy and comfortable.

'I had planned to, but Bessie pointed out that since I'm so tall and slender, most of my dresses wouldn't fit the average woman. Not to mention the size of my breasts,yet she did. She always has to bring up, very rudely I must add. The most valid point she made was she doubted a woman who was struggling to feed her family would appreciate walking around in a Montague gown while peeling the potatoes and changing shitty bums—something I used to say about Tamara at the mere thought of her cast offs being dropped at the benevolent societies around St Kilda through to South Melbourne. Oh my, have I really turned into that woman?' He chuckled, and I smiled at him.

'I want ya to put on the orange dress ya wore the day I met ya. I bet it still fits,' he said, running his hand down my body. I already knew he was right. Catherine had told me recently my measurements had hardly changed, other than when I was pregnant—my heart heavy at the thought.

'It will take me a day to find it. I have that many in there.' I laughed aloud, burying my grief once again as he smiled brightly at me.

'I love ya, Abi. Thank you for always standin' by me, no matter what I do,' he said, pulling me close and holding me tight against his chest.

'There is no one I would rather be with, or stand beside, my love,' I replied, kissing him passionately. Much later, as I slipped into slumber, I dreamt of the moon, a gun, and a black bird with beady little eyes.

Chapter Five

IT WAS THE BEGINNING of April 1901; the middle of a beautiful Australian autumn totally ruined by the constant presence of the damned police. Their raids, carried out at all hours of the day and night over the three-months since Aaron had been in hiding, were unpredictable and violent. He had remained under the house for the entire time, never seeing daylight, but the police were determined to catch him for inflicting injuries to the corrupt Judge George Maslow, who was one of their own.

Detective Paul O'Neill was a regular visitor to the house and was becoming a big, fat pain in my arse. He would arrive for morning or afternoon tea each day on the pretence of ensuring Aaron hadn't returned while enquiring if I had heard from him or knew his location. He would flirt shamelessly with me and undress me with his eyes, always remaining courteous even as I sat glaring at him and treating him with disdain.

There had been another police search of the house at midnight, jolting me from my sleep. I had run to the children and placed them in one bed, where we stayed for the rest of the night while the police tore through our home. I couldn't feel my arms, as I had Thomas snuggled into one shoulder and Emmy the other, snoring softly like their father. Finally, after the police had left, I pried my arms out from under them and left them sleeping while I went down to see Aaron before they woke for school.

Once underground, I went to his room and found him awake, still in bed and staring at the ceiling.

'Good mornin', mo anamchara. I saw there was another raid durin' the night. Are ya all right?'

Angus had installed a system, at my request, where we could push a button near the front door when the police arrived, alerting anyone downstairs with Aaron that the police were here. Angus hadn't known how to make this contraption, but we had a farm hand in our employ whom we referred to as Scientist Sam, who was always inventing things. He didn't know why he had been asked to make it; however, he was so excited that someone was interested in his abilities, it motivated him to let his imagination run wild. Angus had taken him into Geelong, where they had purchased fine wire and a number of items I was unfamiliar with, and within a week, Scientist Sam had completed the project. He then showed Angus how it worked and how to install it.

Once the button at the entrance of the house was activated, it switched on a small light in Aaron's sitting room and at the top of the stairs to warn anyone down there with him before they exited through the fireplace. We had all been in awe how he had made this work when the house didn't have electricity as yet. He told us it was something to do with catching energy from the sun and storing it for future use. None of us had any idea what he was talking about, but we were extremely grateful to him. It had saved Aaron from being discovered on many occasions, and for that I would be eternally grateful to the young man.

All the staff knew to push the button when the police arrived, although they didn't know the reason. We had kept it between Leo, Polly, Angus and Hamish, along with Bessie and the Cavanaugh family, that Aaron was hiding below the house. Aaron would have visitors all throughout the day and into the evening, keeping him busy. Everyone knew we had family time every night with Thomas and Emmy, eating dinner down there with him and spending hours together before I put them to bed. I would then return to spend some alone time with him before reluctantly going back to my bed, most times in the early hours of the morning.

I had to make sure I was there in case we were raided and the children became frightened. The police didn't give a shit if they scared them or not, and would even tear their bedchambers apart in the most aggressive way while shouting obscenities at us. I would hold my hands over their ears as they lay their heads on my chest and cried in fear each time the police decided to terrorise us.

'Yes, we're fine, my love,' I said, climbing into bed with him and into his arms.

'I miss ya when ya leave durin' the night,' he said, kissing me firmly on the mouth.

'I know. I hate it, too, but the last two night-time raids I was down here, little Mary told the Detective I was away. I think three-times would have been suspicious, which he has always been. Plus, the children get frightened if I'm not with them when they come.'

He nodded angrily, then took a deep breath. Infuriated at how we were being treated by the police, he'd asked Hamish to come to the house each time they were here to ensure they did us no harm without him there to protect us.

During a recent raid, Hamish had been outraged and said exactly what he thought to the Detectives, who threatened to take him into custody. It was only because I intervened and distracted them with my own foul language and threw a crystal vase at an officer's head they forgot their threats and left without him, keeping a great distance away from me. Luckily, I missed my target and wasn't charged with assault on an agent of the crown.

'I know I'm bein' selfish, but I miss the time we used to spend together before all this happened,' he said, sitting me on top of him and slipping my nightgown off over my head. I continued talking to him while he gazed up at me and caressed my body with his hands.

'You have a lot of support from the public since those articles were published in the newspaper. I'm getting hundreds of letters a week from strangers, offering their assistance,' I told him and smiled encouragingly.

When Aaron had first gone into hiding, the newspapers printed terrible things about him. There were strongly worded articles saying how dangerous he was, and the government had placed a bounty on his head. I contacted an editor at the Geelong Advertiser to tell

Aaron's side of the story. He assigned me to Cain Stephenson, a young journalist who seemed disinterested when I attended his office in person to seek his help. After talking to him for some time, he finally agreed to come to Willow Grove to hear our story and look at the evidence I told him I held in safekeeping.

When Stephenson met with me at the house the next morning, I told him of the assault and rape in the chambers after court that day and how the entire courtroom had witnessed Maslow ask to meet with me. I went on to explain that my boys were born dead as a consequence and my treatment at the hospital. I told him how I was pressured to sign a second police statement, withdrawing the charges when they realised who the perpetrator was, and how the doctor had been threatened to change his first report and had admitted it to us.

He had immediately asked to see the documents, so I produced the police and hospital reports, with the second reports clearly altered. I then provided him with the report on the injuries I had sustained, including the loss of the boys and evidence I had been brutalised sexually. His demeanour changed as he read them, and he glanced at me with pity before continuing to read. Once finished, he sat back in his chair and stared at me for a long time. I had seen true empathy in his eyes and decided I really liked this man. I hoped I could trust him to write a fair article in Aaron's favour.

Stephenson first apologised for what I had suffered with true emotion in his voice and told me he believed there had been a police cover-up due to Maslow being a Judge. I breathed a sigh of relief when he said he was willing to write our side of the story, as he believed it was something the public had a right to know.

He asked me several times if I was comfortable with publicising what had happened to me, as rape was not something that was talked about. Often women were blamed for the attack, and there was an immense amount of shame forced on them. He was concerned the article would humiliate me and cause me a great deal of pain. I had made it clear that if it helped Aaron's case, I didn't care what anyone thought of me. I knew I had done nothing to cause what had happened and the guilt should remain with the offending party, but also knew more often than not, it didn't.

He asked me question after questions about my life with Aaron and our relationship. He wanted to know what kind of man Aaron was, which impressed me that he was thorough and actually interested in righting a wrong. As he was leaving, I gave him a picture of Aaron and me on our wedding day, looking so happy and in love, with his arm wrapped protectively around me. I also provided him with a casual family portrait of Aaron holding Thomas and Emmy with me beside him in the garden.

Stephenson was given approval from his editor to submit the article and the newspaper ran our story that week to a huge outcry against the police from readers in Geelong and surrounding districts, and within a day, The Sun in Melbourne picked up the story and ran it for all of Victoria to read. I was now being recognised on the street and often had people approach me to tell me how unjust the situation was, many angry how the rich and powerful so easily avoided justice compared to the average Joe Blow. Many were of the opinion they would have done the same thing in Aaron's situation; although, I had been told to my face more than once when out in Geelong running errands that I was a sinful woman and had seduced Maslow and brought the attack on myself, but people like that were few and far between.

We started to receive letters of support from Geelong residents within a week of the article running, and more began pouring in from all over Victoria after The Sun article. There were only a few letters saying I was a wanton woman who should be ashamed of herself for talking about such things, and some stating Aaron was a criminal who should be caught and severely punished. The rest were supportive, caring, and compassionate, with some writers so moved by emotion they wanted George Maslow charged and punished for his crimes against me. Stephenson told me people were writing in to the newspapers, enraged by what had happened to me, and they saw Aaron as a hero for defending his family and rising up against the justice system.

After the newspaper article, the police raids became more frequent and thorough, with them now destroying our property inside and outside of the house as they went about their search. Hamish had marched into the police station in Geelong and filed an official complaint within days of it going to print. The Superintendent of Geelong town came out on the next raid and was horrified at how we were being treated. He quickly put a stop to the brutality and fear mongering. It didn't stop the raids, but now they didn't break my things every time they were here. The searches had become more about finding the reports I had released to the newspapers and less about finding Aaron. They believed he was long gone, either interstate or overseas by now. That didn't matter, as Detective Paul O'Neill was determined to make my life, and everyone else's at Willow Grove, a misery from dawn 'till dusk through to dawn again.

The police would spend hours going through our things and searching my office, leaving the house dishevelled on purpose to show their contempt for bringing negative attention to them. They even disrupted the files in Mr Masters' office, causing him a great deal of consternation at being disorganised in his attempt to run an efficient household. Little did they know, I had the reports safely hidden under the house where they would never find them.

I continued talking, still sitting on Aaron as he rested against his pillows, when he pulled me down and kissed me.

'Be quiet,' he said, rolling me onto my back and shifting his body onto mine. 'It's my time with ya now.'

I sat in between Thomas and Emmy at the kitchen table, the room bustling and warm thanks to the stoves already baking bread and cakes for later in the morning and the cheerful staff, many I had grown to love as my own kith and kin over the years. Hamish strolled into the room, greeting us warmly before sitting down to a hearty breakfast prepared by Leo.

Hamish was still stepping out with Nellie, and all seemed to be well, which delighted me. Nellie was a lovely girl in her late twenties who had never married. She came from an impoverished background and went into service at the age of sixteen. She was timid and shy when in my presence; however, I was certain she was a kind soul who cared about Hamish as deeply as he did about her. Although plain of face and considered a spinster by most, he treated Nellie like she was the most beautiful woman in the world, and she had blossomed because of him. I could see they would be happy together and he would finally have the love and family he had desired for so long.

Hamish had been running the farm in Aaron's place, meeting with him each day to discuss any problems or issues that arose. They would spend hours talking of the week's plans and Aaron's future dreams for the property. Working alongside Angus and Harry just like Aaron did, despite not having to, as the de facto manager of Willow Grove. From what Aaron told me, he was doing a wonderful job.

'How's the behaviour o' those coppers?' Hamish asked incredulously. 'They stormed the cottage an' tossed me out o' bed in the naw long after midnight. Took four o' 'em, the weedy wee pricks. Aye, it took all me strength tae keep from strikin' 'em this time. They're only doin' it now tae piss us off.' I agreed, nodding silently, and continued eating my toast and drinking my coffee. The children finished their breakfasts, kissed me goodbye, hugged Hamish and Leo, then ran out of the door to meet Willy and Bella to walk to school.

'The police think they are a law unto themselves,' I spat, rolling my eyes. 'What do they imagine they'll find under us in our beds? Aaron? He's far too large to hide in most of the places they decide to look. I don't care how often they come, though, as long as I know he's here and safe.'

'I dinnae like how that Detective acts around ye, Abigail. He looks at ye with lust in his eye. 'Tis why he comes here so often. He thinks he has a chance tae warm yer bed now Aaron is out o' the picture.'

'I can't stand him either, but he can legally come here whenever he likes. What can I do?'

'Nought! That's the whole point o' it. He knows very well he can do as he pleases.' He paused and took a sip of his coffee as Leo pranced over and slid into the chair beside him.

'Abigail, why don't you just give him a sympathy shag? Take one for the team like they do in that Australian game called football. It would save us all having to go through this. Aaron is the only one in the house who gets a full night's sleep, yet he's the cause of us all being terrorised by those big, handsome brutes. I wish I had four of them putting their hands on me when I'm in bed. But no, I get the fatty, the unfortunate looking one who walks in and shouts at me to get my fancy boy backside up. I often ask him what position he would like, but he tries to smack me. I've learned to close my mouth after last night, just as you always wished for.' He rubbed the side of his head as I tried not to smile. We talked about what the police had done and said to us all at different times during the night while we finished our meal, before Hamish rose to his feet and grinned.

'Thank ye fer breakfast, Leo. It was bonny, yet again,' Hamish said before thumping Leo on the back. They had been getting along much better of late. Leo had started to warm to Hamish since he had taken over Aaron's role running the property and ensuring the children and I were protected. Taking notice of what a good friend he was to Aaron and myself, Leo had recently shown him far more respect than he ever had. 'Aye, I must be off. Work tae do an' all that. If ye or Aaron need me, I'll be in the stables tae day workin' on the bloodlines. We're lookin' tae mate Goliath with as many o' the mares as we can, but 'tis complex. Aaron only wants the best mares, 'cause Goliath is the best sire we have on the property.'

Leo blew him a kiss and I noticed Hamish start to flush. He quickly left the kitchen and exited through the back door, making me giggle. Leo and I were alone now, the staff going about their duties organising and collecting what they needed for the day from the root cellar, pantry and the small bluestone dairy at the end of the garden.

'How are you coping, my little butterball?' Leo asked, taking my hand in his then raising it to his lips before kissing my palm.

'I'm fine, Leo. I'm getting used to living this way now, and although it's upsetting, I would rather have him here than in a prison cell. I won't let him give himself up. Well, not until we're sure he will get a fair trial. With the public behind us and gaining momentum, I am confident now he won't have to stay there forever like I thought he would when he told me he had killed Maslow. Thank God the evil bastard survived,' I said as I felt my stomach knot up.

'Well, at least he now walks around without his little sausage and quail eggs dangling between his legs. Ahhh, I just can't imagine myself without my beloved Abel,' he told me, confusion crossing my face. 'You know? My cock-a-doodle-do?' I rolled my eyes but nodded anyway, knowing nothing I could say would stop him at this point. 'I decided to change his name from Cannon to Abel. Cain and Abel from the bible? Why do you stare at me like you don't understand the English language? Well, anyway, Abel is ready and able at any time. I wouldn't mind introducing him to his long-lost brother.' He collapsed into giggles as I smothered a smile.

'I know you want me to ask. All right, I'll step inside your rabbit trap. Who is his brother?'

'Your friend, the reporter, Cain. I would be very happy to show him Abel and let him shake hands with him so they can make up,' he replied wickedly as I giggled.

'Do you ever have a single thought where fornicating and the male appendage don't eventually come up in conversation, Leo?'

'Well, they can't help but come up, can they?' I yawned widely, forgetting to place my hand over my mouth as he looked across at me and wrinkled his nose. 'You'll never be a lady, I'm sorry to say, you tavern troll. Go and have a sleep. I'm sure whatever plans you have you can put off for this morning. No doubt you and Goliath will be going at it like horny horses. I certainly would with that big stallion. Not the four-legged one either. The police won't be back for a while now and if anyone comes, I'll tell them you're running errands,' he said kindly as he took my hand in his.

'All right. I will go down to Aaron to keep him company, but can you delay anyone who wants to visit him until I wake up please, honey?' I asked as I yawned again. After the police had decided to conduct their midnight raid, I hadn't been able to go back to sleep once they finally left at four o'clock in the morning. What annoyed me the most was they would get the kitchen staff out of bed and have them cook and provide refreshments for all of them as they tore our house apart. Sally was the one they forced to cook, given Leo had threatened them to their faces he would poison anything he made them, including putting in the contents of his chamber pot, causing me to laugh so hard the police thought I had lost my mind.

'Of course,' he said, smacking my bum as I was leaving.

I left the kitchen and made my way into my office, locking the large, heavy wooden door behind me. Looking around, no one would ever have guessed what lay beyond this room or what it opened up to.

Whatever reason great-aunt Isabelle had to even think of building something like this, caused me to idolise the woman a little. She had obviously experienced things in her own life that had caused her to believe something like this was a necessity, a way to protect all who resided within its walls and the valuable possessions it held. I walked over to the fireplace, placing my lantern down on the floor before feeling down the side of the fireplace until I heard a small click. I pulled back the front of the entire fireplace, the wall coming away in its entirety like a large door. I picked up my lamp and stepped inside, pulling it closed beside me, then made my way down the stairs and into the hallway that led to Aaron's room.

I found him in the small, comfortable sitting room, lying on the couch and reading a book I had brought down to him last night about the breeding and bloodlines of Martarinos.

'Whatcha doin' back? Ya never pop in 'till much later,' he remarked, appearing pleasantly surprised as he closed the book and placed it down on the side table.

'Do you mind if I sleep down here? I'm so tired and I only need a few hours. Those bloody fuckin' pigs are making me insane and will put me in the Asylum in Ararat, just like Leo has predicted for a decade.' I shook my head bitterly as I sat down beside him.

'The pigs in the pen, or the pigs, as in the coppers?' he asked, his blue eyes twinkling.

'The coppers that belong in my pig pen. I would make Leo responsible for feeding them.' I kissed him as he lay with his hands behind his head, appearing relaxed, his laughter filling the room.

'I'll let ya sleep here if ya let me come with ya.' I smiled as I stood and made my way into his bedchamber. Bessie had been down already and made the bed, along with tidying the rooms, I noticed as I slipped off my dress and got into bed. Catherine had made me some gowns recently that were so easy to get on and off, I was able to dress and undress myself without assistance. I was just starting to relax and doze off when Aaron came in and joined me. He lay behind me and started to bother me, playing with my hair and poking me awake.

'Aaron, let me sleep. I was awake all night trying to keep the children away from the coppers.' I yawned as he kissed my forehead, then placed his hand on my breast.

'I can't. I have to touch ya when you're next to me,' he said, stroking my arm with his other hand.

'Aaron, I'm scared for you. I don't want to lose you, even for a short time. I couldn't bear being away from you if you have to go to prison,' I whispered, tears running down my cheeks. He gathered me into his arms and quietened me.

'Abi, listen to me. I'm not goin' anywhere for the moment. Like ya newspaper friend has told ya, I'll tell ya again, me love. Within the next month, even people abroad will have heard about our plight, includin' those in England. It gives me a much better chance of things goin' me way the more support from the public we have. Ya don't need to worry, mo anamchara. I'm stayin' right here.' He soothed me gently, stroking my head until I was asleep and dreaming of envelopes, a cloud and an enormous steam ship.

Chapter Six

RICHARD WAS SHOWN INTO my drawing room where I sat at my desk, writing to Sister Josephine about what had occurred over the last two-days. He greeted me warmly before embracing me in a bear hug, then placed me back down on my feet.

'How are you, Abigail? Are you and the children well?' he asked, smiling brightly at me.

'Yes, we are, thank you, Richard. I called on Jas the day before yesterday. You were at work of course; however, I did spend a couple of hours with her and the children. She tells me your practice is so busy you have taken on another barrister and two solicitors to cope with all the work. You will be wealthier than me soon.' I collapsed in a fit of giggles, and he smiled.

'Yes, my family is very proud. My parents were overjoyed seeing you, as they love you like their own daughter. They were so delighted to meet Aaron, even though it was under difficult circumstances.'

The Malcolms had come to visit Richard and Jas four-months ago, and had planned to stay for two, but had enjoyed themselves so much they stayed on, leaving only a week ago to return to England. I had been overwhelmed with happiness at being reunited with Mr Malcolm and Jenny, and had spent as much time as I could with them. They had even stayed a week with us, riding around the property with Hamish as their guide and staying up until all hours of the night talking with Aaron and me under the house. They were delighted at the life I had here and so relieved things had worked out well for me. They were obviously concerned about Aaron's plight; however, Mr Malcolm believed he would only serve a few years in gaol for serious assault.

Aaron had been hiding under the house for nearly twelve-months now, and Richard would come to see him as often as his work and family duties would allow. All of our close friends knew where Aaron was, and everyone would visit with him when they could, so he rarely got bored, despite his confined living quarters. He missed riding Goliath and being out on the property, and especially our Sunday lunches in the dining room, but he was safe. I would always make sure I took his lunch down to him and occasionally we would sneak him up to the main house, for an hour at most. This seemed to help him as he always had that sparkle back in his eye after seeing everyone on a Sunday.

Hamish would take Dingo down every night before dinner to keep Aaron company and come and get him in the morning to go to work with him. Poor dingo was missing Aaron during the day, but had taken to Hamish as his second best friend. Richard let himself into my office to go and see Aaron, while I went to ask Leo to bring refreshments and food down to them, finding him at the workbench in the middle of the kitchen.

'Wombles has been looking for you this morning,' he told me casually as he finished piling fresh raspberries on a raspberry and white chocolate cheesecake he had just made.

'Oh, he shouldn't be coming here like he does. He is meant to be acting like a proper wombat on the property along with the others,' I said, rolling my eyes as Leo giggled.

I had found Wombles, the wombat, when he was only a few weeks old and had lost his mother. I hand raised him and once he was used to finding his own food outside, I had released him back onto the property, a long way from the house. Within a day he had found his way back to the back verandah where he had slept in a basket since he was born. I hadn't wanted to name him, believing that native animals shouldn't be kept as pets; however, Thomas and Emmy had overruled me and called him Wombles.

He really was the most gorgeous thing and I had given up on trying to make him behave as a wombat should, and not like a puppy dog. I had placed a large basket, piled with blankets, back out on the verandah for him. He would follow me around when I was in the garden and was growing quite big and strong. The children loved him, and their friends who would come to play would look at Wombles in disbelief as he would meander over to them and place his head in their lap.

'I will try my best with the food, Abigail. You always ask for something delicious; however, to this day, you fail to understand that everything my hand touches is delicious. Hmmm, that sounds rude. My hands touch many things that are long and firm.' He collapsed into a fit of giggles, making me laugh. I waited for him as he placed the cheesecake on a tray along with bottles of beer, sandwiches, savouries and apple juice.

He followed me as we made our way downstairs, talking and laughing. Halfway down the staircase, I nearly lost my grip on the lamp, causing us to both jump in fright.

'I would hate to be caught down here without a light. It's pitch black in these hallways.' He nodded as we continued on. 'Have you noticed, it's not as dark in the rooms Aaron's living in. Light filters in through vents just above the side of the house, causing it to be dim, but not gloomy.' He nodded again, still following closely behind so he could see where he was going.

'I think I am starting to like Brian a little. He really is a beautiful person inside. It's such a shame he wasn't born beautiful on the outside as I was; however, I am overlooking that due to his other, should I say, larger and more interesting qualities.' He laughed aloud as we rounded a corner and the light from Aaron's room came into view, casting a soft, golden glow from under the door into the hallway.

I knocked once before pushing open the door to find Richard and Aaron deep in conversation. I made my way to Aaron's side and sat beside him before he slipped his arm around my shoulder. Leo placed the refreshments on the table and walked over and kissed Aaron on the lips before he had an opportunity to greet his own wife.

'What are ya doin', ya bloody idiot?' Aaron whined as he wiped his mouth with the back of his large hand.

'I was just passing on everyone's love to you. That kiss wasn't from me, so you can't go getting all angry about it. Your friends and family who do know you're down here are always saying to make sure you kiss him for us, so I was forced to. Just pretend my lips are Abigail's and we will get along fine,' he told him as he picked up a lamp and promptly left. Richard chuckled to himself as Aaron looked across at him and grimaced.

'Yeah, it's funny for you lot. Stop laughin', Abi. Why does he have to kiss me? He could pick on Angus, Hamish, or Harry. I know he thinks they are all gorgeous, as he says,' he told us, his voice high as he attempted to imitate Leo, while we laughed harder.

Richard attempted to contain himself, straightening his shoulders while his face became serious.

'Let's get back to the business of what I'm here for.' He cleared his throat before continuing. 'When you hand yourself in, I believe you would only serve a few years at most, under the circumstances. If they allow Abigail to testify regarding what Maslow did to her, you may even get less time than I anticipate. They will not find a jury in the land who would be unsympathetic to your plight now that it has been all over the papers Australia wide for nearly a year now.' Richard let out a deep sigh as I reminded myself to breathe. I listened in silence, feeling my stomach knot up at the thought of him going to gaol at all. I knew deep down the day would come when he could no longer live like this and would give himself up. However, I hoped that wouldn't be for a long time, if ever. I knew I was being selfish, wanting him here when he felt like a caged animal, but I couldn't bring myself to let him go. Richard was now a Barrister and highly regarded in criminal law, and I trusted him completely, knowing without doubt he would do what was best for Aaron in the end. 'If he had died, I would be advising you to leave the country and start again somewhere else. The fact that you will be imprisoned for only a few years, rather than decades, results in less disruption for Abigail and the children. I know it's not the best option; however, I do believe it's the only one you have, if you ever wish your life to return to normal,' he told him as Aaron gazed across at him, silent while deep in thought.

We ate and talked comfortably until it was time for Richard to leave. I stood to walk him out, picking up the lamp near the door where I had left it, while Richard thumped Aaron on the back in farewell. They were all becoming more Australian the longer they lived here, and I couldn't help but smile to myself as I waited for him by the door.

'Abi, can ya come back after you've seen Richard out? There's somethin' important I need to discuss with ya.' Aaron smiled reassuringly as I nodded, knowing if I spoke aloud, I would lose control of my emotions. Richard followed me out of the room after bidding Aaron goodbye, and we walked side-by-side down the dark hallway, the small lamp illuminating the way.

'You realise you will have to let him go at some point to face the courts and whatever consequence they hand down?' he said gently, stopping and embracing me. He knew more than anyone how much I loved Aaron and how difficult I was finding the situation, often breaking down for no apparent reason as I tried to go about my day.

'I know, but just not yet.' He smiled sadly before I pushed it to the back of my mind, as I so often did when unable to cope. We continued walking until we found ourselves standing at the bottom of the stairs. Reaching over in silence, he took my hand in his before leading me up and into the office, closing the secret passage behind us. I opened the office door, slipping the key back into my pocket, then saw him out to his carriage.

'I will be here for you in any way while Aaron faces what he must. It will happen, Abigail. I think it's best you start getting used to it now,' he advised, not without sympathy, before kissing me goodbye and getting into the fancy, two-seat carriage he drove himself. I stood in the driveway and waved until he was gone from my sight. I remained where I was, all alone, and cried tears of sorrow, knowing that soon, one day in the future, I would be parted from my beloved.

Aaron was still sitting on the lounge when I arrived back half-an-hour later, drinking his coffee.

'Tell me, what's so important you needed me back here right away?'
I crossed the room and sat down again, making myself comfortable
next to him.

'You're as slow as a wet week if ya think ya returned right away.' He
threw back his head and howled with laughter. 'I wanted to spend
time with ya, that's all. Have there been any more articles in the
papers?'

'There seems to be a lot of people writing in, and general debates
about your guilt or innocence, without any further articles written
or published. Cain is coming next week to do another and wants
more photos of you as the family man you are.' I tried to smile and he
nodded, seemingly distracted. He finished his coffee and pulled me
into his arms, kissing my lips gently.

'How is everythin' in the village? Ya seem to spend an enormous
amount of time there due to various problems arisin', forcin' ya to be
the peacemaker.' A smile touched his lips as he relaxed back and held
me against his chest. I sighed deeply, nodding slightly, as that was all
I seemed to be doing at the moment. Trying to bring peace, despite
my inability to find it for myself.

There had been an ongoing feud between the wives in the village,
with half against the other. I was relieved my close friends were all on
the same team. It had begun over an argument between two children
from families that didn't get along to begin with, then had escalated
quickly, with many taking sides, despite it being a school yard fight
that should have stayed between the children. The two mothers
couldn't stand the sight of each other and would yell obscenities in
front of the community, children included. I planned to sit down
with both of them tomorrow morning after school began, to try
and at least come to a point where they ignored the other instead of
involving everyone at Willow Grove.

'Honestly, Aaron, it is a nightmare. It shouldn't have happened.
Can you imagine how many people we would be arguing with if
we fought with every family whose child had a fight with Emmy?'
I asked exasperatedly as he chuckled. Emmy was known to stand up
for herself with the boys who picked on her. I had tried to explain
to her that many believed this was what boys did if they liked a
girl, which left her astonished at what stupid creatures they truly

were. Emmy felt highly offended that their parents dismissed their aggressive behaviour with such a pathetic and untrue excuse and no consequence for their actions. I did not disagree.

'Hamish told me from the beginnin' he was happy to take over from me, as long as he didn't have to have anythin' to do with the women in the village an' the problems they create,' he told me as we both laughed.

'Well, I've decided I wouldn't swap places with Edmund Barton for any reason. Being the first Prime Minister of Australia, he has nothing to compare his performance to. I feel sorry for him that he has to find his own way and make it up as he goes along. Did you know, they did a census a few months ago and there are 3,788,123 people living in Australia right at this very moment? Well, except for the bairns born since, I suppose.' He chuckled to himself before I continued. 'What I find disgusting is that the Aboriginals were left out as though they don't exist. Not one was counted. I wrote him a letter, I was so appalled. It's such a large population. It's too many people to comprehend, isn't it?' I asked in awe, and he smirked.

'So, ya obviously believe yer the Prime Minister of Willow Grove, an' can empathise with him havin' to deal with trivial bullshit,' he teased. 'I can't say whether I like or dislike his political views yet. I think the Immigration Restriction Policy that was just passed, the one they're referrin' to as the White Australia Policy, may leave out people who'd contribute to this country. There's plenty of room.'

'You could fit a billion convicts here, Leo believes,' I chimed in as he chucked again.

'Any bloke who chooses to immigrate here should be given the opportunity to assimilate and become an Australian, just like we did. It just bothers me, Abi, as we're all immigrants, except for our Aboriginal friends, an' if we hadn't been given the chance to start a new life here, who knows where we'd be,' he said as he kissed me on the neck. He loved discussing politics and world events that would affect us all, which I enjoyed debating with him.

'Hey, you didn't say why you wanted to see me,' I said, suddenly remembering as he stroked my hair and continued to kiss me.

'What's wrong with me wantin' to make love to me wife?' he asked innocently, kissing me again.

'I thought you had something important to tell me, you wee shite.' I ran my fingers through his shaggy hair and relaxed into him.

'I do. I love ya an' I'm takin' ya to bed,' he said succinctly before rising to his feet and gathering me in his arms.

Thomas, Emmy and I ate our dinner every night with Aaron, and stayed with him until the children would retire to their beds in the evening. Tonight, Thomas had shown him his drawing of the new Australian flag that had been chosen to represent our country. When the six separate colonies merged to become one country at the start of the year, the Prime Minister announced a unique, nationwide competition; to design a flag for the newly minted federation, the Commonwealth of Australia. When they chose the winning flag from 32,823 entries, settling on a beautiful design that included the Southern Aurora, with a navy blue background and the union jack on the top left-hand corner, they found five people submitted almost identical designs. Declared joint winners, Annie Dorrington, an up and coming artist from Perth, Ivor Evans, a fourteen year old schoolboy whose father owned a flag making business in Melbourne, Lesley Hawkins, an eighteen year old from Sydney, Egbert Nutall, an architect from Melbourne, and William Stevens, a first officer with the Union Steamship Company, all shared the prize money of £200, receiving £40 each when the winners were announced by Edmund Barton in Melbourne on the 3rd of September, 1901.

I was impressed with Thomas's drawing, gazing across at the vibrant colours while Aaron proudly hung it next to his bed. After putting the twins down for the night, I would always return to him and stay until he was asleep, then find my way back to my bedchamber. I had left him several hours ago and was in a deep sleep when I was startled awake.

'What are you doing? What if the police come?' I asked, my heart pounding as I looked up and tried to focus. It was still dark outside, and I quickly glanced at the clock on the mantel, the room dimly lit by the lamp Aaron carried allowing me to see it was just before midnight.

'It's all right, mo anamchara. I'm gunna risk it. Get up an' come with me.' He pulled the covers back and helped me to my feet. I quickly slipped on the dress I had worn yesterday, then took my cloak from the dressing room. Aaron placed it around my shoulders, taking my hand and leading me downstairs and through the empty, dim kitchen. He led me out the backdoor to find Delly waiting, all saddled up. He lifted me on top of her, then swung up behind me.

'Aaron, what are we doing?' I asked as I yawned loudly.

'I wanna make a memory with ya. It won't be long now, Abi, an' I'll have to face what I've done. I wanna feel the cold sea air on me face, an' have ya all to meself in our cottage. I just need a few hours of freedom.' He kissed me deeply, taking my breath away. Soon we were racing across the paddocks towards the sea. We arrived at the honeymoon cottage and he lifted me down. This place was so special to both of us, and we had so many happy memories here. I felt tears sting my eyes at the thought of not coming here with him for who knew how long, once imprisoned. I followed Aaron inside, the rooms chilly and dark, the single candle I carried barely lighting the way. He grabbed me in the kitchen and kissed me hard while roughly taking my dress off, then carried me into the bedchamber, kissing my neck before placing me down on the bed. He lowered himself gracefully onto the bed and stared into my eyes. 'This could be the last time we're here together for a few years at least, so let's make the most of it. No worryin' or thinkin' of what's to come, all right?' I nodded my head as he kissed me deeply, then melted into his arms as I had a thousand-times before.

Before daylight broke, we dressed to return home. We hadn't slept, and although it had been wonderful spending time here with Aaron, I was looking forward to my bed as I was exhausted from yet another sleepless night.

'I wanna stay here with ya forever, me sweet girl.' I nodded silently as he stroked my face, holding me close while standing in the kitchen.

'And me too, my darling man. I don't want you handing yourself in without telling me first. I sense you plan to give yourself up any time now, and I'm not ready.' I lowered my head and promptly burst into tears.

'I know, mo anamchara, an' that's the only thing keepin' me here. I can't bear the thought of partin' from ya either. I know I'm bein' a coward, but we haven't spent a day apart since we were courtin'. I know in me head it's somethin' I have to do, but me heart won't let me 'cause of you an' the nippers.' He held me tightly and stroked my back until my tears stopped. I turned and slipped my arms around his neck, then kissed his mouth as he gently wiped away my tears. He took my hand and led me to the front door, locking it behind us.

Delly was already saddled and waiting. She walked straight over to me and nuzzled her head into my stomach, making me laugh as I gently stroked her forehead. Aaron checked he had secured the windows of the cottage before striding over to my side, then gently lifting me on top of her before swinging up behind me. He took a deep breath, staring out over the ocean for several minutes before turning Delly's head for home.

Aaron walked her the entire way, clearly enjoying being outside in the fresh air for the first time in so long. He held me around the waist as he whispered dirty things into my ear, making me giggle. There was only a week until Christmas and we would be in 1902, the first week of January being the anniversary of Aaron's attack on Maslow. We planned to celebrate Christmas underground this year, as I could not even consider celebrating such a special time of year without my darling husband present.

I had found a room earlier in the year when exploring the underground space, confirming it was perfect when lit up with candles to hold a family gathering. I had also discovered a large dining table, amongst many other pieces of furniture, stored in the adjoining room. Angus, Hamish and Aaron had shifted the heavy furniture, then moved the table and twenty matching chairs into the empty room where we would now hold Christmas. The furniture was nowhere near as elaborate as our dining table upstairs; however, it was crafted from solid red gum, and was polished nicely, causing the deep, red wood and its grain to show through. The seats of the chairs were covered in fine leather, but there were no intricate carvings on the wood, much to my surprise. Little Mary had been taken into our confidence, and cleaned the rooms underground every day now, while Bessie maintained Aaron's private rooms. We were finding items we never expected to find as she fastidiously cleaned one room after another, putting everything in order so we knew just what we had.

We arrived home just as the sun started to rise, Aaron quickly guiding Delly into the stables. Harry stood by his work bench, his body jerking violently as he caught sight of us, the blood draining from his face. He had no idea Aaron was still on the property, as we had only told those who needed to know. Despite trusting Harry, we felt if we told him we would feel obligated to reassure others Aaron was safe here at Willow Grove.

'It's bloody good to see ya, mate,' Aaron called out as he swung down, then strode over to Harry and embraced him. He slowly, and very awkwardly, put his arms around Aaron, then thumped him several times in greeting on his broad back.

'It's good to see you, my friend. I won't ask any questions. I see you're in a hurry. If you don't mind, I'll speak with the Mistress later today an' find out what's been happenin' for you, mate,' he called out as Aaron lifted me down and handed the rope to Harry, who swiftly led Delly to her stall. We said goodbye before hurrying up to the house and quietly entering through the front door. We quickly walked towards my office, and I only let out the breath I didn't know I was holding when I closed and locked the door behind me.

'It's all right, me sweet Abi. Harry won't say anythin'. At least he can come an' see me now as I've missed him. I don't want ya bein' worried for nothin'. No one else saw us, mo anamchara. It's all fine, I promise.'

'I hope so. You never know who would betray us if they saw you, given there is a price on your head. Especially the newer workers who are not as loyal as Harry, Sean and all our old workers who were here when the property first started. They are as steadfast to us as they were to great-aunt Isabelle.' I kissed him goodnight in the office while he held me like he would never let me go. I watched him go through the entrance and I gently closed it behind him before going and unlocking the door. I made my way up to our bedchamber and slipped off my dress, pulling on my nightgown before falling into bed exhausted. I fell into a restless sleep dreaming of a large steamship, a pink diamond and a large, bluestone building.

Bessie came rushing into my room, startling me from a deep sleep.

'Wake up. Quickly, Mistress. That Detective is here to see you. The tall one who seems to have his eye on you,' she said disapprovingly, hurrying off to get my clothes ready. I reluctantly got out of bed and stretched, then took off my nightgown to dress. It had been two-days since I had been with Aaron at the honeymoon cottage and I wished we were still there. The last thing I felt like dealing with was that bloody Detective. It was still very early in the morning, far too early to expect a warm welcome if calling unannounced. The children hadn't yet come into my room so I could take them downstairs to visit with their father and say good morning.

'Leave my hair, Bessie. I don't have time! I'd like to get him out of this house as soon as possible. I hate having those pigs here when my children are present, breathing the same air,' I spat as she quickly ran the brush through my hair in an attempt to tame it.

'You can't go down with your hair all loose and hanging down like that. He will think you are not a lady and may try to misbehave with you,' she warned, her eyes wide as she shook her head in disbelief.

'Well, I am going like this and I don't give a fat rat's arse what Detective Paul O'Neill thinks. I don't give two shits what his opinion is of me, lady or tart.' She gasped and smacked me lightly on the arm before I continued, jutting out my chin. 'As for misbehaving with me. He'll never get the chance as I don't let him get close enough. I always have Mr Masters with me when I have to meet with the funt face.' She narrowed her gaze and smacked me on the backside with the hairbrush as I stood unmoving, waiting to put my clothes on.

'Stop cursing like a filthy heathen. I get your meaning, and I know you don't like the man either.' Her face softened to a smile as she gazed at me affectionately, then helped me into an emerald green day dress. Catherine had informed me I wasn't to call them housedresses anymore, as they looked as good as what any fine lady would wear to an expensive restaurant. I didn't care about that at all. They were so comfortable, along with the fact she designed them so I didn't have to wear a corset, and had won me over the first time I had slipped one on.

I looked in the mirror before leaving to find the dick head. Indeed, I did look like a lady going out to socialise for the day—all except for my hair, left loose and flowing in waves down to my waist. My hair shone as a result of the new hair products I had been buying from Amelia, containing coconut oil in the conditioner. I narrowed my gaze, my face hard and void of emotion, turned on my heel, and marched out of the room after saying my goodbyes to Bessie.

I found him in the sitting room waiting for me. Leo pushed past me carrying a pot of steaming coffee, along with warm pumpkin scones just out of the oven smothered in butter, placing them down on the table between us with a flourish. Leo glanced at me for a moment, his eyebrows raised, before casting his eyes over Detective O'Neill, whom he thought delicious, in his own words. Mr Masters stood at the door of the sitting room as he usually did if Hamish wasn't available to sit with me. Leo pranced out of the room while the Detective stared after him suspiciously before turning his attention to me.

'How are you today, Mrs Cavanaugh? You do look lovely this fine morning.' His handsome face broke into a wide smile as he studied my hair intently. I returned his gaze, my eyes glinting dangerously.

'What is your business here this time, Detective? What could you have possibly come up with now? You have tried nearly everything to break me and crush my spirit, along with my family and staff, waking us at all hours, damaging my possessions, terrorising my young chil-dren and delighting in it. Go on, tell me? What now?' I hissed as Mr

Masters took a half step back, clearly surprised by my tone—concern crossing his stern face as he eyed me warily, then fixed his gaze on the Detective.

Detective O'Neill always ignored the presence of my staff, treating them as if they were invisible and only acknowledging the people who lived here like Polly, Angus, and Hamish. I suspected he had come from money, as he appeared comfortable in his surroundings when he visited Willow Grove. Most people who visited initially spent the first hour gazing around in wonder, but not him. He had never been overwhelmed by my wealth, nor did he seem to notice my disgust when he blatantly cast his eyes over my body from top to bottom.

'I've called on you today because I believe we can come to some sort of arrangement that would benefit us both,' he said, his big, brown eyes staring into mine intently. Bessie was right. He was an extremely handsome man. Not in the same category as my Aaron, but certainly attractive, and charming to boot. I could see he would rarely sleep alone, unless by choice.

'And what sort of arrangement would I need to be making with the police? That would be no different from signing a contract with the devil,' I spat, his eyes twinkling in amusement.

'You are a very beautiful woman and stir something deep within a man, no matter how hard he tries to fight it—just like your late aunt Isabelle, from what I know of her. It was said she also had a way with men, and had many of them flocking to her right up until her death, never being one to sleep alone. You, my dear Mrs Cavanaugh, have been alone without your husband for more than a year now. I'm sure you have certain, ah, needs, shall we say, that require attention? I wanted to let you know I would be prepared to do that, and in return, make your path with the police easier.' He leaned back and placed his hands behind his head as he relaxed back into the chair. I couldn't believe the nerve of this man, invading my home, then trying to seduce me. I stared back silently for a time before running my tongue along my lips, my mouth suddenly dry.

'Fuck off, Detective. I am not a common whore you can call on at any time for your own pleasure,' I said through gritted teeth, an overwhelming urge to jump over the coffee table and strangle the perverted bastard taking hold of me.

'No, you're not. You are far from it, thus the reason for my offer. I wouldn't lower myself to sleep with a whore. As I said, I've found you to be a woman of strong character and high morals, as I've seen for myself during the past twelve-months we have been getting to know each other. You are an exquisite woman who every man in the district wants to bed. The only reason you don't have men calling on you constantly is the fact they are frightened of what would happen, with your husband still being on the loose. He has earned himself quite the reputation from all the articles in the paper. People seem to have turned him into some kind of hero. I will bed you, Abigail, if it's the last thing I do.' He shifted comfortably in his chair, his grin wide.

'I wouldn't let you touch me with someone else's cock,' I spat at him, my hands starting to shake. Ever since I had been attacked by Maslow, I had a morbid fear of men I wasn't familiar with. This fear became even more extreme if a man flirted or tried to seduce me in some way. My body would freeze up and my heart would race at a thousand beats a minute.

'Now, now, Mrs Cavanaugh. You've only seen one side of me, which unfortunately has been my role as a police officer enforcing the law of the land. If you gave me a chance and got to know me away from work, I'm confident you would have a different opinion and would change your mind.' I watched him closely, prepared to scream if he made any move towards me.

'No, my mind won't be changed by anyone or anything, and especially not by a bloody corrupt pig,' I said defiantly as I clasped my hands together on my lap so he wouldn't see them shaking.

'I must say, I have never seen your hair down before and you are magnificent.' A smile touched his lips, while he ignored my contempt. 'I can understand why your husband did what he did. If I had a woman like you and someone hurt her as you were hurt, I would have tortured him, too, but finished the job. Unlike your husband.' He sighed as I stared across at him, confusion crossing my face. He had always been polite to me no matter how rude or coarse I was towards him, but I was taken aback the man had the arrogance to even consider I would be his friend, let alone his Mistress.

'Leave now, Detective. I have things to do. You may not realise or care, but your raids disturb my children and cause them much distress. They have school today and spent half the night terrified while their rooms were being pulled apart without care or concern by you and your men.' I clenched my teeth and leaned forward in my chair, raising my hand to point my finger at him. 'I'm warning you now, copper. My children and their bedchambers are off limits from this day forward. Not unlike my husband, I am very good with a knife.' He flinched for a moment, sitting back in his chair as if I had struck him as I rose to my feet and straightened my skirt. 'Go now, Detective. Oh, and by the way—fuck you, and your mother,' I called out over my shoulder succinctly, leaving him alone in the room as I marched out, but not before pausing in the doorway and turning back towards him to use my right hand, lifting it several times in the rudest of gestures my Leo had so kindly taught me. Mr Masters shook his head in disapproval and sighed as he silently watched me storm down the hallway, the Detective's loud laughter still filling my ears.

I stomped into the busy kitchen, leaving Mr Masters to see him out. I felt furious, so furious I wanted to punch someone; however, my babies were at the kitchen table with Hamish and Leo. I sat down in between them, kissing Emmy, then Thomas.

'Are you too tired to go to school today? A day off wouldn't hurt,' I remarked as they smiled up at me.

'No, Mummy, we're used to it now. We only woke up when the pigs got here because they were so excited and loud, as usual, but once you came into our rooms and put us into bed with you, I went straight back to sleep. I don't feel scared anymore if you are with us,' Emmy said, and I felt tears prick my eyes. They shouldn't have to get used to anything like this in their young lives.

'I'm right, too, Ma. I was the same an' went back to sleep. Doesn't matter how loud they are, I sleep through it. I only woke 'cause ya came an' got me outta bed,' he told me as I kissed the top of his head. They continued eating their breakfast while Hamish watched over them, appearing unimpressed. He had taken them down this morning to see their father while I was being harangued by Detective Drongo, as Aaron liked to say.

'Was it O'Neill here again?' Hamish enquired, screwing up his nose in disdain.

'Yes. I will tell you about it when we have coffee,' I replied, glancing at Thomas and Emmy and raising my eyebrows. He nodded and continued to eat.

'That Detective is one good looking man. It's unfortunate he is such a golden wattle,' Leo commented as he ate his chicken sausages with his eggs, fried tomatoes, and toast. Leo and I had decided when the twins were born that when we wanted to say a really bad word around them, which was often between the two of us, we would pick the name of a flower and use that instead. Hamish nearly choked on his breakfast and I thumped his back and handed him a glass of apple juice. He sat back, gasping for air while trying to contain his laughter.

'Between the two o' ye, I've learned more names o' native trees an' flowers than I ever knew existed,' Hamish teased after catching his breath. Thomas and Emmy stood to kiss me goodbye, then Hamish and Leo, turning to wave as they ran to meet their cousins at the back door to walk to school.

'Aye, so what happened, then?' Hamish asked as Leo put the coffee on the table and sat down again with us.

'He made me an offer. If I was to make my body available to him, he would make my path easier with the police,' I told them as I sat back and sipped my coffee. Hamish's face darkened while Leo collapsed into a fit of giggles.

'He dinnae? I cannae believe how some think. As far as he knows, Aaron's in hidin'. Naw dead. What an immoral bastard. From now on, I'll stay with ye when ye meet with the filthy sleekit. Maybe that'll deter him, an' at the very least, force him tae keep his hands off ye,' he growled, startling me.

'Oh, what's the harm, Hamish? If Abigail shagged that delicious looking man it would make our lives so much easier. No more being woken in the night and thrown around by those handsome men with backsides you could bounce a penny off. You need to do it for your children's sake, Abigail. Stop being so selfish and put them first for a change. The only effort on your part is to lay back, open your legs and think of England, as they say,' Leo told me as I raised my hand as quick as a flash, grabbed his ear and twisted it, his shrieks filling the room.

'Don't you dare use my children to manipulate me, you fat headed idjit. I won't be shagging anyone but my husband,' I spat as I let go and he grabbed his ear, grimacing while Hamish chuckled. 'Do not mention this to Aaron, as he will only get angry. Given there is nothing he can do about it, I think it's best he doesn't know.'

'Aye. Otherwise, the next time O'Neill feels the need tae visit, 'tis likely Aaron will come up an' belt him. 'Tis Leo you have tae watch. He cannae stop himself from teasin' his Goliath about the blokes chasin' his missus,' Hamish remarked pointedly. I turned my attention back to Leo, who appeared extremely frightened as he held his purple ear, still moaning in pain.

'You know how much your ear just hurt? Imagine it was your balls, but they were twisted so hard they came off in my hand. That's what will happen to you if you dare open your mouth to anyone about this,' I threatened as Hamish threw back his head and howled with laughter. Leo merely nodded in silence, eyeing me suspiciously as he drank his coffee.

Hamish had proven to be a steadfast and dedicated friend to Aaron, even more so now he was in hiding, always available to him while running the farm in his place,while spending time with him downstairs each day. He was still seeing Nellie and I had high hopes for them, as they seemed to get along well. Although I was uncertain if Hamish was in love, I knew he liked her a great deal. Tamara had returned as our guest, causing no problems, as she had taken a new lover in Melbourne with whom she was infatuated. Much to everyone's relief, but none more than Hamish. Leo was overjoyed now he had his Brian back with him once a month.

'Well, I have to get down to the village before Trixie is hung by the feet on the gumtree by the other wives,' I said as they both rolled their eyes. Although Hamish hated anything to do with gossip and petty fighting, Leo thrived on it and I knew he would want a blow by blow account of every word, action and my thoughts on the matter when I returned. I planned to see my friends while I was down there, and possibly sit outside with Margaret and smoke her pipe with her while we chatted. She tended to hear the most, given the mothers of the bairns she cared for would tell her at the first opportunity. Jenny also knew a lot about the comings and goings of the village, despite not being a gossip herself. I rose to my feet and bid them farewell, then made my way to the door, deciding to take my time and enjoy the walk, while knowing whatever the outcome this morning, it would end in tears for someone.

Chapter Seven

I STRETCHED, YAWNING AS I woke to find Aaron's arms still around me, his face serene as he softly snored beside me. It was the middle of winter of 1902, and Aaron had been living under the house for eighteen-months. The police raids had lessened, and when they did occur now, they weren't as hostile in their treatment of us or our possessions. I felt these intrusions were being instigated by Detective O'Neill, who still called on me in his own time several times a week in an attempt to win me over.

I had come face to face with him last year when many of us from Willow Grove travelled into town to watch electricity come to Geelong for the first time. We had seen history in the making, an event Aaron unfortunately was forced to miss. On the 4th of June 1900, the first power pole was erected in Geelong on the corner of McKillop and Yarra Streets, opposite the Jewish Synagogue. We had been forced to wait until the 3rd of May, 1901, when they held the ceremony to officially switch on the electricity to Geelong.

I had tried to ensure as many people from Willow Grove as possible had the opportunity to attend, and every child was there to witness the event, requesting Mrs McGinty accompany them as part of their school lessons. I clapped and cheered along with everyone else as the light flickered at first, then shone brightly as the ceremony concluded—all feeling privileged to be a part of history in the town we loved and appreciated so much.

Geelong was a beautiful city and had everything anyone could want. The people were friendly and would do you a good turn before a bad one. I was starting to feel I belonged here, and was finding the locals so supportive towards me since Aaron went into hiding and everyone had read his side of the story. Aaron had remained under the house, terribly upset he missed such an important event in the history of the town he too loved so much.

Detective O'Neill had approached me on the street after the ceremony. He propositioned me, and I had again rejected his advances, much to his chagrin. He was a stubborn man, which worried me when it came to my Aaron. I was well aware Detective O'Neill had a reputation of being like a rabid dog with a bone, and wouldn't give up until he had Aaron in handcuffs and behind prison bars.

Our routine had not altered much, with Aaron having visitors most of the day and family time with us at night. I slept with him every night downstairs now, and if the police did turn up, the staff told them I was away. The children now slept through any visits from the police, as Detective O'Neill had instructed his constables that the children's bedchambers were off limits. In the raids that had occurred, the staff had been able to easily explain my absence. The police couldn't prove any different, although Detective O'Neill was still very suspicious of me.

He had stopped propositioning me in secret, changing his tact and seeking to court me publicly. Hamish would sit in on the meetings I took with him and despite him being there, the Detective didn't care. He would flirt shamelessly, complimenting me while not taking his eyes from me the entire time, along with bringing flowers and chocolates with small trinkets that I would reject immediately. Hamish had been tempted on several occasions to tell Aaron, but had promised me he wouldn't due to how my husband would react, and had kept his word so far.

'Good mornin', mo anamchara,' he whispered, kissing me gently on the lips. 'Ya don't have to rush off anywhere 'till it's time for ya to go to me parents, so I have ya all to meself for a while.'

'Yes, you do.' I laughed at him as he pulled me tightly against his body, then slowly ran his hand down my back, settling on my backside.

Thomas and Emmy were staying with Patrick and Scarlett, so as to be close to their Grandmother. Edith had taken ill with pneumonia and had been confined to her bed for several days now, causing us to worry greatly for her. Aaron felt helpless and frustrated he couldn't go to her and help her in some way. The only thing that cheered her were visits from her grandchildren, particularly Thomas and Emmy, who were her eldest. They would take it in turns to read her the romance novels she loved so much, for hours at a time, despite finding them sickening and boring—in their words, much to my amusement. They made me so proud how lovely and respectful they were towards everyone, not just their family and elders.

I planned to visit late in the morning to see her, and spend time with the twins and the rest of the family, especially all my nieces and nephews. Patrick and Scarlett had four children now, as did Aiden and Victoria, and Luke and Adele were the proud parents of two.

'I'm a bit worried about me Ma,' Aaron said. I caught the note of concern in his voice and raised my head to look into his eyes.

'I know, my love, but she is being well taken care of. The doctor visits every day, so there is no point worrying. One of your brothers will be straight over here if she deteriorates. You know you can't go there as the police are still watching the houses at times,' I reminded him before kissing his cheek.

'I know ya right. Let's talk about somethin' more pleasant,' he said as he pulled me to his side. He lay on his back, my head on his shoulder and my arm across his chest. He played with my hair and stroked my back as we lay and enjoyed just being together.

We talked about how much progress had been made with the farm, and how he had recently drawn up his plans for the next twenty-years. He wanted to turn Willow Grove into the largest Martarinos horse stud in Australia, and possibly the world, given the breed was so rare and in great demand.

We talked about the family trip that we would take to Paris, London and New York for my thirtieth birthday, in just over two-years from now, and the things we would see and do with the children, exposing them to sights and places we never had the opportunity to see. We dreamed about all the things we would do once this was over and how we thought our lives would be as we grew old. I snuggled into his arms and drifted back to sleep as I listened to his voice reveal his hopes and dreams and his heart's desires. All of which were so very similar to mine, we could have been the one heart, mind and soul.

Bessie woke us, cheerfully bustling into the room. She placed her bright lantern down on the bedside table, illuminating the pitch-black room, before carrying over the breakfast tray.

'Good morning to you both. Leo has spoilt you today and made you a large breakfast with buttermilk pancakes to follow, which I know you love, Mistress,' she said brightly, placing the tray down on the side table.

'Why? What's he wanting from me now?' I asked suspiciously as I heard Aaron chuckle.

'Who knows, but knowing him as I do, it is likely something ridiculous,' Bessie replied darkly and I giggled.

'Bessie, do you mind letting Leo know we don't wish to be disturbed until eleven o'clock, please?' Aaron asked as he rubbed the sleep from his eyes and yawned, the smell of bacon filling the room.

'As you wish, Mr Aaron. I will pass on the message,' she said, patiently waiting for us to sit up before placing the tray on the bed between us. I rearranged the pillows so they supported my back, leaned back and watched as Aaron did the same.

'What's this? It's delicious,' Aaron remarked as he drank his coffee milk.

'It's coffee with really cold milk mixed in. It's my new favourite thing,' I told him happily as he chuckled.

'Everything is ya favourite, me darlin' Abi. I can't believe ya body hasn't changed one bit since we first married with the amount ya eat. Ya belly is so flat no one would ever know ya carried twins in there. Twice. Not that I plan for anyone else to see ya stomach except me,' he said smugly as he ran his hand over it, then returned to eating.

I drank the ice cold coffee that Leo had made me, finding it delicious. I had watched on intently when he first made the beverage for me a few days ago. He would pour strong coffee on the bottom of a glass, adding a little sugar, then fill it with cold milk. I had become addicted and now it seemed Aaron also had a liking for it. He poured himself another large glass from the jug while eating his eggs. I had focussed my attention on the buttered mushrooms, thoroughly enjoying them and his company.

'It's nice to have ya here beside me. I know it's hard for ya in the mornin's gettin' the nippers ready an' fed then bringin' 'em down to me. I love eatin' breakfast in bed with ya,' he said, kissing me with crumbs on his mouth. We finished our meal and sat back in bed drinking the hot, creamy coffee. 'It's only the thought of havin' ya with me that's kept me sane down here for all this time. I'd have handed meself into the coppers a week after I did it,' he admitted as he held my hand and I felt knots in my stomach. I knew he had only stayed for me and the children. It was unbearable for him living down here and not being outdoors everyday doing something he loved, and I knew he hated it. I was being selfish, but I couldn't help it. I could not stand the thought of being parted from him, even for a moment.

'Aaron, do you think it's time we leave here? Take ship somewhere and start again so we can have a normal life?' I asked, knowing this was the only way we would get our lives back.

'Soon, but not yet. I can't bear to be apart from ya or the nippers for long. I'd have to organise Hamish to run the property on his own 'till we're able to come back. If ever,' he said sadly. I knew how much he loved Willow Grove and its people, and the lifestyle we had here before he went into hiding. It would be a wrench for all of us to leave and be apart from our family and friends for an unknown period; however, we had no other choice. The time was coming upon us where we would have to make a decision and agree on where we were going to go. We had narrowed it down between Paris and New York. I wanted to go and live in France, but Aaron had his heart set on America. 'Now, how are we gunna spend the next few hours?' he asked, a grin on his face.

'Well, I think we should go out to a restaurant or go dancing some-where. We could always ask the coppers to meet us at the Barwon Heads Coffee Palace,' I teased, and he laughed, grabbing me in a hug.

'You're not goin' anywhere one minute earlier than you have to,' he said, pinning me down with his body so I couldn't move and kissing me like he would never let me go.

I slowly rode Delly through the paddocks towards the far side of the property where the Cavanaughs lived, taking my time while enjoying the crisp winter air while pondering over what we were going to do. I didn't want to return to England, although I did want to see Sister Josephine. Richard was completely against us running away, and had continued to try and convince Aaron to hand himself in. He advised us if he was caught running, he would endure a heavier sentence. My mind was going in a thousand different directions, as I didn't know what the best thing to do was, no matter how much I tried to find a solution.

I could see the four large homes from a fair distance away and I kicked Delly into a canter. We soon arrived at Patrick and Scarlett's home, far larger than the others that stood nearby and considered a mansion by the average blokes standard. I dismounted and tied Delly to a rail at the front, inhaling eucalyptus as I climbed the stairs. Before I could even get to the door, it was thrown wide open.

'Hello, my darling sister,' Scarlett called out, greeting me with a warm embrace. 'The twins have been perfect, as usual. They've been helping me around the house and caring for the younger children. Ma has really benefited from them being here, let me tell you. Emmy sits with her and wipes her face with a cold cloth while Thomas reads to her, then they swap. They really are the loveliest children, and so grown up now. I know they hate those romance novels with a passion. They despise the love scenes they are forced to read out loud to their Grandmother, often shocking the both of them,' she said, smirking at me as I collapsed into giggles.

Thomas and Emmy were a few houses away with their Grandmother, so I decided to take tea with Scarlett when she insisted. I followed her inside and through the enormous house until we were in the kitchen. All the Cavanaughs' used the kitchen for their family meals unless they were entertaining.

'You can't leave now, you only just arrived,' she said, putting the water on to boil.

'Is your cook sick?' I was concerned, as I liked Mrs Grist.

'Yes. I think she is getting a bit beyond it, actually. Her legs give her a lot of trouble. She did tell me she is considering moving in with her daughter, so I have no doubt I will have to replace her. It's a shame really, as she is such a lovely lady and works so hard. A very good cook too. Remind me before you go to give you the New Idea I saved. I've read it from cover to cover. This week, it's your turn to buy it,' she reminded me. New Idea was a magazine only published for the first time this year. We had become addicted to it already, being an Australian magazine, finding between its pages many interesting articles and fashion pictures. Amelia had made sure she stocked them every week since, and Scarlett and I took turns buying them, and then swapping. 'I miss going out together with you and getting way too drunk and dancing, then watching you and Aaron have so much fun and be so sweet to each other. I can't stand that he is locked up under the house.' Her eyes welled up with tears as I patted her hand until she composed herself, then drank my tea while chatting with her about Patrick and the children.

We had held some wild parties with our friends and family underground with Aaron over the time he had spent down there, with too much whisky, beer and dancing until it was daybreak. We would then crawl into our beds, having had a wonderful night together. I felt confused and didn't understand what Scarlett was missing. I suspected what she really meant was she missed the freedom we all had before, not having a care in the world before all this happened.

I said my goodbyes to Scarlett and walked Delly down the road towards Aaron's parent's house. The children came running to me when they heard me arrive. They kissed and embraced me as I hugged them tightly.

'Where is Grandma?' I asked them as they held onto me tightly.

'In her bed. Grandpa said she's a whinger, but she really is sick this time, Mummy. We have been looking after her and she told us we make her very happy. No one else will read those terrible books to her. Mummy, do you know there are rude parts in it? Lily white breasts, thrusting of hard lengths, throbbing knobs, nubs, nipples, and slippery slits,' Emmy remarked as she led me to the bedchamber, while I choked on my own saliva. It took me several moments to pull myself together, while I had every intention of telling Aaron what his mother was exposing our eleven-year-old children to when I arrived home.

I knocked softly on the door, then stepped inside with Thomas and Emmy following behind. Edith looked pale and sickly, her skin bathed in sweat, the large bed making her appear so tiny.

'Hello, my darling daughter,' she croaked, then coughed, reaching her hand out towards me and motioning me to the bed as she coughed again into her handkerchief. I sat down beside her on a lovely tapestry chair and took her hand in mine, tears stinging my eyes. 'I must tell you before news of anything else distracts my fuddled mind. I am so proud of you and Aaron and how you have raised Thomas and Emmy. They could have turned out so spoiled and disconnected from family should you have left their sole care to a team of nannies.' She coughed again, before continuing. 'You could have easily palmed them off, but you haven't even to this day, choosing to raise them yourselves. They're the most caring, sensible, well-behaved children I have ever come across.' She coughed louder, unable to stop as her body heaved while I patted her back to no avail. I quickly passed her a glass of water, supporting her by the shoulders as she sat up to drink. 'Thank you, my dear. How is my wayward son?' I lay her back on the pillow as she smiled weakly, wiping her forehead with a wet cloth before I sat back down.

'He is well, Ma. He sends his love and apologises he can't be with you. He feels quite helpless, and is very upset. He said to tell you that you better be up on your feet by tomorrow, or he will personally come here and drag you out of bed,' I teased and she smiled again, brighter this time.

'That son of mine is a cheeky little shite. You know, Abigail, he hasn't changed since he was a small boy. Always easy to get along with, and always very advanced. He talked and walked very early, and seemed to understand things years beyond what's considered normal. He took it very seriously when told at a young age he was betrothed. I will never forget the day he came home and told me he met you for the first time and he was in love, struck instantly as though by lightning. Personally, I think it was lust from the moment he set eyes on you, then love came later; however, he disputes that to this day, the lying little fiend. I still find it quite unbelievable your great-aunt Isabelle befriended my husband one day for no apparent reason. He'd brought the boat back in and she saw him and the boys on the dock and approached them. I will never know why she chose my son to be your intended husband, Abigail; however, it is the best thing that could have happened to the both of you. You have made him an honest, loving, generous wife with the patience of a saint having to put up with his recklessness. I cannot believe how he has been collecting those new horseless buggies, as well as the carriages, in secret, mind you. The carriages I understand, but who wants to be sitting in a buggy with no horses to draw it? You would look ridiculous on the street. People would stare at you and laugh. I cannot understand that son of mine at all. I heard from his brothers that he has ordered more recently. My dear daughter, you must listen to me. You are a very sweet girl, and lovely to my boy, but you need to be firmer with him. You have to learn to say no and that's that,' she snapped, her eyes giving away how much she loved him.

'I can't, Ma. Aaron has his own money from the income he generates through Willow Grove. As I don't do the work to make that money and he does, I can't stop him from buying anything he likes. His partner in crime, Hamish, does all the legwork for him.' I sighed as she took my hand in hers and smiled sweetly at me.

'You are a wonderful girl with the heart of a lion. The way you have helped my family, well, we could never repay you for your kindness. You are, and always have been, my favourite daughter-in-law. Just don't tell the other girls,' she confided, and I laughed aloud, leaning over to embrace her.

I stayed with her for a time before going and heating some broth, then fed her slowly between coughing fits. The twins had gone back to Scarlett's for lunch and to play with their cousins. I waited until Mr Cavanaugh got home before preparing to leave.

'How is she?' he whispered, stepping into the room with Thomas and Emmy behind him. He went to her side and kissed her pale, sweaty face, then took her hand in his before sitting down on the chair beside her bed.

'No better. When is the doctor due back?' I asked quietly as I stood to go.

'Tomorrow mornin',' he replied, kissing me goodbye. I embraced the twins before Thomas left us to get Delly ready for me, while Emmy and I walked downstairs, hand in hand.

'Is Grandmother going to die, Mummy?' Her little brows drew together as tears filled her eyes.

'Sweetheart, no one can answer that. Not honestly, anyway. None of us know when our time here will be over, and that's why you have to make sure that every day you live is fun and exciting, and you do no harm. I think your grandmother will be alright, as she has a very good doctor. They are giving her all the medicines she needs to try to make her better. Don't think too far ahead, little one. It is a waste of energy to worry about the future when in actuality, we have very little control over it, if any at all.' She turned and hugged me tightly before we walked down the front steps of the house. I embraced them both again before mounting Delly, taking the reins in my hands and thanking my Thomas. Mr Cavanaugh had come to see me off, and I raised my hand and waved goodbye to the three of them as they stood on the front verandah.

'See ya round, Mummy. Don't fall off ya horse. We all know ya aren't the best rider at Willow Grove,' Thomas called out and they all laughed.

'I heard Uncle Leo say Mummy was the worst rider, not just at Willow Grove, but in the world,' Emmy said to her grandfather, wide eyed as I giggled and trotted out of the driveway.

My riding skills were often the subject of much teasing from my naturally gifted, horse loving children. I smiled to myself as I rode through the paddocks, thinking of how they teased me constantly now they were getting older. Delly and I had an agreement. I was nice to her as long as she didn't do anything stupid to hurt me. All had been working out well until recently. I had agreed to go riding with Thomas and Emmy, and once we were cantering through the paddocks towards the sea without a care in the world, Delly decided she wasn't having fun and came to a complete stop, sending me flying over her head and into a pile of horse shit—much to the twins' amusement. It had been the subject of much laughter as Emmy and Thomas recounted the story to Aaron during dinner that night.

I arrived in the village and went to see Amelia at the store, quickly tethering Delly to the post out the front where a large trough of water stood for the horses, before making my way inside.

'How are you, lovely?' I called out as the bell chimed over my head and I stepped inside. She beamed at me, welcoming me in before hurrying out the back to make coffee. I strolled around the immaculate shop, selecting a number of luxury items from her fully stocked shelves for myself and the children, along with some sweeties for Aaron, leaving them on the counter. Amelia soon returned with our coffee, hurrying up the hallway as I went behind the counter and sat down at the small table, the chair far more comfortable than it looked.

'How have you been, Abigail? It must be so hard for you with Aaron gone so long, and still no word from him. I know he is safe, as I would feel it if he wasn't and something had happened to him. I don't know why, but I can't shake the feeling he is somewhere close by.' She shook her head as if to clear her muddled mind as she sat down.

'I'm coping, Amelia. How are you and your family? The business seems to be busy every time I visit you,' I replied sincerely, changing the subject.

'Busy as usual. It doesn't stop here during the day, especially when I have new stock from Paris.' She yawned, the dark circles under her eyes prominent against her porcelain skin as she sipped her tea.

'Amelia, you have that much money now, you can afford to get someone in to help with the children. Four is a lot to take care of when you're working as much as you do.' It was difficult enough to raise children when your husband worked from morning 'till night, let alone running a thriving business, and I felt she was far too hard on herself.

'I know, but can you imagine the gossip if I got help? They would say I thought myself better than them, and slander me as an unfit mother. Most in the village have three to four children. They believe if they can look after theirs, I should be able to look after mine without complaint,' she whispered, promptly bursting into tears.

'Who gives a furry wombat's arse what other people think? They are not running a busy general store. You have to do what's best for you, Amelia, and what you're doing now isn't working. You have to try something different,' I told her, not without sympathy. The bell tinkled and she unsteadily rose to her feet to serve a customer, while I waited in silence, worried for her. No sooner had she sat down than two more ladies entered. I sipped my tea, then took a slice of chocolate cake while I waited again.

'Do you have this in a larger size?' A well-dressed lady asked, holding up a lace corset that wouldn't have fitted her leg.

'I'm sorry, I do not. That's the largest size we have in stock,' Amelia replied, nodding her head apologetically.

'How do you expect to run a business if you don't cater to your most important customers? Can you order me one in?' she snapped, looking down her nose at Amelia, then glancing across at me.

'I'm sorry, but that particular corset doesn't come in a larger size. I can order you one in a different style if you wish?' The woman grimaced, then slammed her hand down on the counter.

'I don't want a different style. I want that one. Are you suggesting I am fat because your largest corset won't fit me?' she asked, narrowing her gaze.

'Not at all, Madam, and I apologise if you believe that was implied.' Amelie's voice was gentle, her tone polite, while only I was aware the smile on her face was not genuine. The woman slammed down the items she had wanted to purchase on the wooden countertop, promptly turned on her heel as quick as her rotund body would allow, then stormed out of the shop empty-handed without another word.

'Another satisfied customer, I see.' I collapsed into giggles as she slid back into her chair beside me. 'You should have told her the truth.'

'Oh, if I were to tell the truth it would be that no corset here, or in the State of Victoria, will fit because you're a butterball, and have a close resemblance to one of those camels running wild in the outback of central Australia. And they have no need for corsets.

That's what should have come from my lips to her ears and I'd have been done with it.' She threw back her head and laughed aloud before composing herself and pouring our tea. 'I hate being so hateful, but in my own defense, that woman did resemble a camel with her hair the same colour, brown eyes and that stumpy nose.' She laughed again before continuing. 'You have no idea, Abigail. This is what I put up with day in, day out. I have never had a problem with anyone from Willow Grove, but these outside people make me want to run screaming down the street, pulling my hair out.'

We finished up soon after so she could return to her work. We said our goodbyes before I walked out onto the street. As I strolled across to Delly, I waved to Margaret across the road. She waved back from her front garden, surrounded by several children left in her care, watching them play on the grass. I wondered if she had been sucking on her pipe today, as she appeared very relaxed and carefree, reclining back in her chair, her eyes closed now, while the children played happily around her. I mounted Delly and blew a kiss to a snoring Margaret and her energetic charges as I rode past and headed for home.

Leo stood near the sink as I stepped into the kitchen. I called out my greetings to him and the staff, working hard as usual, before quietly making my way over to the table to sit down while he prepared a jug of iced tea. He pranced across the room to join me, jug in hand and a cheerful grin on his handsome face. His backside had barely touched the chair when Hamish walked in and hurried towards us.

'G'day, Abigail. I've naw seen ye around tae day.' Hamish pulled out a chair and made himself comfortable beside Leo before pouring himself a drink. 'How's Mrs Cavanaugh farin'?'

'No better, but the twins are helping to care for her, and that brings her much joy.' He nodded as he took a deep drink, finished his glass, then poured another.

'Aye, I've missed our mornin's together these past few days. When are they back?' Hamish cut himself a large piece of banoffee pie Sally had brought to the table. He was still stepping out with Nellie, and I believed he would soon ask her to marry him.

'Who cares if you haven't seen her all day?' Leo interrupted. 'What is of concern is Abigail has been so distracted lately, her attention is not on me. Given I am so fabulous, and delicious to boot, I don't know what the hell has gotten into her. She's my best friend, and I have to put up with her running around after every Tom, Dick, and Harry on this property. Well, she doesn't really chase Harry, and Tom is fairly quiet and well behaved, but Dick wants her attention constantly. Yes, Dick is the one she is partial to and spends a lot of time with. I think Dick's her favourite around here. Why aren't I a Dick?' Hamish returned his stare, his face blank, while I snorted with laughter.

'Do ye even know what yer talkin' about? Half the time ye make naw bloody sense, then go an' get all offended when we point it out tae ye. Who the hell are ye referrin' tae when ye say Tom, Dick an' Harry? Abigail has naw dealin's with the farm workers. Only their wives an' children,' Hamish muttered, confusion crossing his face. Leo grinned wickedly, and while I knew he was being sarcastic, Hamish was not as familiar with Leo or his eccentricities as Aaron and I were.

'Just ignore him. To answer your question before we were so rudely interrupted, Thomas and Emmy will be home soon. I asked them today if they were ready to come back, but they wanted to stay a bit longer to make sure their grandmother will be alright. At a guess, they will be home sometime tomorrow,' I told him, and he nodded.

'Och, sweet bairns they are fer helpin' their Granny,' he said proudly. Chewing thoughtfully, he fixed his gaze on me. 'Ye look well rested today, Abigail,' he remarked as he reached for another glass of iced tea.

'I am, actually,' I replied, suddenly feeling guilty over how much time I had spent in bed with Aaron today. Although most of it wasn't restful at all. I blushed slightly, unable to stop myself fidgeting in my seat.

'What's wrong with ye? Ye look like yer sittin' on a bullant nest?' Hamish remarked, narrowing his gaze.

'Nothing. Why?' I replied, my face becoming warmer.

'I can tell on yer face yer thinkin' o' somethin' embarrassin'. I'm tellin' ye now, if ye an' Leo are goin' tae do yer dirty talkin' that I'm forced tae listen tae at least five-times a day, I'm leavin' the now,' he growled as Leo and I laughed, teasing him relentlessly. Once I finished my cheesecake and drained the last of my tea from the glass, I stood to leave.

'I'm off underground. It makes me feel like a wombat.'

'Aye, yer wombat. I saw him eatin' yer roses as I was comin' in,' Hamish remarked, his eyes twinkling in amusement as I sighed deeply, my shoulders slumped.

'Wombles is not my wombat. He is free to go and dig his own hole underground and make it his home, but chooses not to,' I snapped, gathering my things before picking up my bag.

'Aye, o' course he is. Problem is, he prefers his large basket with its warm blankets. Why would he go? Wombles, as ye call him, has everythin' here, naw tae mention how he gets fed all the vegetable scraps from the staff. He could naw rough it out bush now even if he wanted tae. He's used tae livin' the good life at Willow Grove these days. I've noticed he's very attached tae ye an' follows ye around like a wee dog. Have ye seen how big these wombats are when fully grown? They'd weigh three-times as much as ye.' Hamish threw back his head and howled with laughter as Leo collapsed into a fit of giggles.

'All right, all right. I seem to be the only adult in the room. I'm going and won't return 'till after,' I called out over my shoulder as I walked to the door.

'After what? After you have attended to Dick again?' Leo called back, giggling madly as Hamish sat beside him, again appearing confused. I grabbed the tray I had made up for Aaron and made a rude gesture with one of my fingers, walked out, and refused to look back. Bastards.

I found Angus sitting with Aaron discussing business, so I busied myself serving the refreshments I had brought with me, including two bottles of beer. I placed them on the table before sitting down next to Aaron and poured their drinks.

'How's Polly? I haven't had a moment to myself to visit with her today,' I remarked while Angus grinned broadly at me.

'She was busy herself today. She invited my mother over for lunch to discuss tryin' to heal the rift in the family. I haven't seen her myself as yet, so I don't know how it all went,' he said, his good cheer now gone and concern crossing his face. Polly was desperate to see Hamish and Angus reconcile with their parents again so the children could see the only grandparents they had. She knew it was upsetting the boys not having contact with their parents, who were getting on in years now.

The only good thing that had come from it was that Polly was no longer forced to exchange pleasantries with Jemima through gritted teeth. She was now on to her second husband, with her first having died of the influenza. She had inherited a small fortune and married Mr Gavin Macdonald after being widowed for four-months. They built a large house on her parent's property, twice as grand as theirs, making the Makenzie mansion look like a workers cottage. I had seen it shortly after it was finished when we drove past on our way to Shelford to visit with my friend, Janet Russell, and her new husband. We had attended their wedding on the 7th July 1900 at Scots Church, Melbourne, when Janet married John Biddlecombe, an English-born naval officer, and had a grand time.

I found Jemima's home to be an offensive monstrosity, just as ugly as its owner. She had no children as yet, and Polly hoped and prayed it would stay that way. She was of the firm belief Jemima would make a terrible mother given how selfish and malicious her disposition. She showed no interest in her own niece and nephew, and hadn't from the moment they were born. Polly was civil when forced to see her in the past, but ensured she avoided her company at all costs when possible.

Angus excused himself and quickly departed, calling out his farewells long after he had disappeared into the hallway, leaving Aaron and I alone.

'How's me Ma? Has she gotten any better?' He gently pulled me into his arms, and we lay down together on the lounge. I began to tell him, and then became distracted with stories of the twins and how I had spent my day. 'Do ya think she's gettin' any worse, Abi?'

'No, my love. She's the same from what your father told me. He doesn't seem overly worried, though, and he talks to the doctor every day.' I stroked his face gently as he nodded, then turned to stare into my eyes.

'I love ya, Abi. I always have, an' always will. You're the wife every bloke wants when they're a lad thinkin' ahead of makin' a home an' family. A best friend, me lover, an' a lovin' mother. It sounds simple, but it's hard to find. You an' the nippers are me life, an' I'll stay down here as long as ya want me to.' I felt tears prick my eyes. I was such a selfish bitch keeping him locked up here. I knew I would never be able to let him go. Not now. Not ever.

We chatted until our dinner arrived, then sat at the table to eat together. Aaron lit a candle, then placed it in the middle of the table.

'This is romantic,' I remarked, smiling across at him, his handsome face even more so in the candlelight.

'Only the best for you, mo anamchara.' He chuckled to himself before pouring us both a glass of wine.

Much later, as I lay in his arms naked, I dreamt of an iron gate, a planet named Hiriarni, and a newspaper with my face on the front page.

I could hear someone calling Aaron's name, bringing me up from the depths of slumber. I sleepily opened one eye, yawning loudly, to find his brother, Luke, gently shaking him awake.

'Aaron, ya have to wake up. Ma has taken a turn for the worst, an' the quack doesn't know if she'll last the night,' he whispered, his voice hoarse. Aaron sat bolt upright, shaking his head vigorously, attempting to wake as he rubbed the sleep from his eyes.

'Give me a quarter of an hour, an' I'll meet ya out at the stables, mate.' He yawned again before rising to his feet and stretching, his loud groans filling the room. Luke quickly departed and Aaron leaned down and kissed me on the forehead. 'I should be safe enough, mo anamchara. It's the middle of the night. I promise I'll be home before daylight.' He gathered me in his arms, then kissed me again. 'Luke can wait a bit longer.' He lowered himself back down on the bed, then kissed me like he would never stop.

Chapter Eight

I OPENED MY EYES to find Scarlett gently shaking me by the arm. I gasped aloud and sat bolt upright, my heart racing.

'What's wrong? Why are you both here? Oh, God in heaven, it's mother. She's passed, hasn't she?' Scarlett placed her hand on my shoulder, then helped me to my feet.

'Come to the sitting room, Abigail. We need to speak with you.' I hurriedly slipped on my dressing gown and followed her out, feeling sick to my stomach.

I made my way across the small room, noticing they had freshly brewed coffee waiting on the table. I leaned over and poured myself a cup, adding milk and sugar before settling back on the lounge. They stared at me in silence, both seated opposite me holding hands tightly. Scarlett appeared to have been crying; however, had calmed and seemed in control of her emotions, whatever they were.

I let out a deep breath as I waited; knowing in my heart they were here to tell me Aaron's mother had died. I had been trying to prepare myself ever since seeing her yesterday and seeing for myself how poorly she was. She was more than just a mother to me—she was my friend and confidante, and I loved her.

'Abigail, something bad has happened,' Patrick finally said, appearing as if he would be sick, but I waited to hear him say it before I let myself cry. I tried to swallow the lump in my throat, wanting to hear the actual words that she was gone. 'The coppers captured

Aaron this mornin', he growled, his voice barely above a whisper, his face white. I was overwhelmed with fear and grief within moments, my vision turning grey. I felt faint as I sat back in the chair, the room spinning, shocked to the core as this was not the news I had been expecting to hear.

'Abigail, are you alright?' Scarlett asked, hurrying to my side and taking me by the shoulders.

'What happened?' I shook her off and attempted to compose myself.

'Aaron made it home safe an' spent time with Ma. The twins were awake, an' 'cause he hadn't seen 'em for a few days, he spent several hours on his own with 'em, then put 'em to bed.' He smiled sadly, leaning back in his chair before continuing at my request. 'After spendin' more time with Ma, he decided to leave before dawn, an' we saw him out the front to say goodbye. As he got on his horse, those bloody coppers came from everywhere with guns, an' as the bastards pulled him from his horse, a gun went off an' shot him through the arm. There was nothin' we could do, Abigail, an' I'm sorry for it,' Patrick said, tears in his eyes.

My poor, darling husband. He was now with the pigs who had been trying to get their hands on him for the last eighteen-months—and now they had him. I doubted very much the gun that had shot him misfired accidentally. This had been my biggest fear, only I had always worried they would kill him rather than take him alive.

'Where is he now? I need to go to him.' I broke down, sobbing uncontrollably as Scarlett passed me a handkerchief, obviously distraught herself.

'They took him to the prison hospital in Myers street to have his wounds taken care of. He'll be transported to Melbourne Gaol as soon as he's fit, 'cause the crime was committed in Melbourne. One of the coppers was kind enough to tell me that much.' Patrick shook his head bitterly. 'Ya must get ready now, Abigail. The carriage will be waitin'. I sent word to Harry you had to go to Geelong, post haste.' My legs had turned to jelly, and it took me a few moments to get them to obey me while I waited for them to stop shaking.

I stood and readied myself to go and dress upstairs. Patrick hurried off to the kitchen, while Scarlett followed me up to my bedchamber. I felt I was no longer in my body as I quickly organised myself and went to the bathroom to wash. I came out soon after and made my way over to my dressing table where I placed all my hair up on the top of my head, then pinned it securely. I hurried to my dressing room and selected a purple dress and a hat, quickly returning to my room so Scarlett could assist me. Within minutes I was ready.

'I don't know how you've stayed so calm, Abigail. It's as if you aren't worried at all. I think you're in shock,' Scarlett commented as she pinned the matching hat to the crown of my head, then gently took me by the arm, leading me downstairs to the kitchen.

We found Patrick sitting at the kitchen table enjoying a cup of coffee as he waited for us. He and Leo were deep in conversation over this morning's events, ignoring our presence. Scarlett and I remained standing while we waited for Patrick to finish.

'I warned you a thousand-times, Abigail, but did you take notice of one word I said? No. Having one criminal friend in your life tends to turn those around them into criminals too. Now there are two of them. Who will be next? I should start up a book among the farm workers and take bets. I would have to put low odds on you, my little butterface. It's only a matter of time before you're on the wrong side of those prison walls,' Leo chastised me, shaking his head in disappointment. I raised my arm as quick as a flash and grabbed him by the ear.

'You are a fat headed moron. Do not vex me when I am already upset. My tolerance for your pigshit at this time is extremely low. I would put low odds on me becoming the next criminal too, you imbecile. Not just a crim, a fuckin' murderer, actually. I will take you up on it and put a hundred quid on myself because, when I have time, I am going to fuckin' strangle the shit out of you,' I yelled as I twisted his ear so hard, he collapsed onto his knees, while I continued to hold on tight. His agonised screams filled the room as I heard Patrick come up behind me.

'Carn, Abigail. I know you're upset, but killin' Leo isn't gunna help Aaron today. If ya don't stop twistin', that ear is gunna come off.

It's already startin' to bleed,' he said, still standing behind me while looking down at Leo with pity.

'Let me go, you vindictive troll. You heard Patrick, you're pulling my ear off. Stop it now or I will tell Goliath on you.' He stopped screaming for a moment, then closed his eyes as if in prayer. 'Oh, he's not here to protect me anymore. He's a criminal now. Alright, I'll give in then.' He held up his hands in defeat before narrowing his gaze at me. 'I'm sorry for whatever I did wrong, even though it was probably nothing and you are just being your usual insane self,' he snapped. I continued to hold him by the ear, although I had stopped twisting.

'Well, don't speak to me—and they're called lunatics, you lunatic. I'm sending you to Coventry.' I roughly let go, and he stumbled to his feet, clutching his lobe as if it would fall off.

'No. I'm not going there. Not again, under any circumstance. You all have to keep talking to me. I won't be ignored. Listen to me when I speak. Stop ignoring me, you pack of funts,' he shrieked as he stomped away, throwing a spatula and bowl into the sink before continuing out the door and into the kitchen garden.

Patrick took me by the shoulders and led me outside, while Scarlett followed closely behind. Harry was waiting with the carriage, attending to a stone in one of the horses hooves. Given he and Aaron were close, I felt he should be one of the first to know. Patrick and Scarlett climbed up into the carriage and closed the door, while I stayed where I was and spoke quietly with Harry. I was surprised I hadn't fallen into a heap or a screaming mess, and was actually quite calm as I told him what I knew. I saw the colour drain from his face, and sadness filled his eyes.

'I'm sure he'll come out of this fairly unscathed. He certainly has the public behind him, which can make a huge difference during a trial,' he reassured me as he helped me up into the carriage. He closed the door and I settled myself across from Patrick and Scarlett.

'Maybe it's for the best, Abigail. Not that he got hurt. The fact he can now live openly, whatever that may mean. Livin' under the house was drivin' him mad. He only stayed this long for the sake of you an' the children. I'm not sayin' it to make ya feel guilty, as he wouldn't swap a minute of havin' you, Thomas and little Emmy with him, but we all knew it couldn't continue. So, did you, Abigail, but ya never wanted to admit it. I know this is breakin' ya heart at the thought of being away from him for a time, but this too shall pass,' he told me as I silently sobbed.

We arrived at Richard's law practice soon after. Patrick left the carriage to go inside and talk to him, as my legs wouldn't carry me. I couldn't think straight, and doubted I could have an articulate conversation with anyone. Scarlett sat across from me, tears rolling down her face.

'I'm so sorry, Abigail. You and Aaron are the last people that deserve this. When you did the interviews with the papers, it was the first we knew you had been attacked by this Maslow creature. I cried for days when I read the articles about how Aaron went to seek vengeance for your honour. That's why the people of Victoria love him, and you. I know that no one but you and Aaron know the graphic details of the attack on you, as the papers didn't say. People have their own minds, and can read in between the lines of how badly you were hurt because of those hospital reports they published, including what you endured and the injuries you sustained. I saw you shortly after the attack, and remember how badly beaten you were; however, at the time we believed you had been robbed in the street and beaten by an unknown assailant. I wish you had been able to talk to one of us. We could have supported you so much better.' She sighed deeply as she wiped away her tears. I leaned across and took her hand in mine.

'You have all supported us through everything. I am privileged to be a part of this family, and I love each of you deeply. It wasn't that I didn't trust any of you. It's only I cannot talk about it without breaking down and becoming a complete mess. I find it's better to leave it in the past,' I explained as she nodded sadly.

I glanced out of the carriage window to see Richard and Patrick walking towards us, chatting between themselves. They had stopped by the time they got in, Richard sitting down next to me and embracing me tightly.

'I'm sorry it has come to this, Abigail. You know Jas and I are here for you and will support you through this,' he said sincerely as he took my hand in his.

'I know you are, Richard. I'm beside myself with worry about his bullet wound. What if it gets infected? They won't provide him with the right medical treatment there. God knows, they treat them worse than animals. Dana has told me. You virtually have to be dying to see a doctor when you are behind bars. Please promise me you will make them let our own doctor treat him while in Geelong, then we will find another when he is transferred to Melbourne. People die from these kinds of wounds. Not from the bullet itself, but from the consequences of infection,' I said as I burst into tears.

'There, there, Abigail. I will ensure he has the best medical care you can afford. One thing I know for certain is if you have money to grease a few palms, it makes life much easier, not only for the prisoner, but for the family and friends visiting.' I looked up at him, confused as I wiped my face with my handkerchief. Scarlett and Patrick had stopped talking and were listening intently. 'You know what I mean. Bribery. You pay the guards, and they turn a blind eye to anything, depending how much you pay. You must remember these men are on very low wages.' Patrick smirked as he glanced across at Richard admiringly.

'Well, you can only imagine what kind of person would aspire to be a prison officer, Richard. You certainly wouldn't do it for the money. It's for the power. To have that superiority over another human being. Having the permission of the government to hand out humiliating punishments and inflict pain on another human being would be quite empowering and would take a special person to carry it out, don't you think? They are no different to the fuckin' coppers. Give them a little power, and they'll abuse it,' I spat bitterly as Richard put his arm around my shoulders.

'It's alright, Abigail. He will be okay there. He is a big, strong lad, and no one will be game to try him. I would be terrified if faced with him, especially when angry. No, you don't need to worry about Aaron. He can take good care of himself. I will do everything I can to get him a lighter sentence. He will be up on a serious assault charge, and he could spend a number of years in gaol. Given who he assaulted, he's likely to get the maximum penalty. Wait. Stop sobbing. I haven't finished what I was saying. Now here, wipe your face and blow your nose.' He passed me his clean handkerchief, and

I blew into it loudly. 'What I was going to say is with the enormous amount of public support his case has generated, and the fact we have your testimony and evidence from the hospital the police acted fraudulently, he is likely to get a much lighter sentence. If one at all; however, I do not wish to raise your hopes. You must remember who he attacked. Aaron will be sitting before one of Maslow's mates who he probably attended university with. They all belong to the same Gentlemen's club in Melbourne, so they definitely know each other. What does go in his favour is he will also sit before a jury of his peers. Men and women who have wives and husbands. They will have a strong reaction to your testimony, Abigail, and not one will be unsympathetic toward Aaron for doing what he did. You must look at the worst-case scenario. He will be convicted and serve a prison term. Get used to the fact, and if it doesn't happen, you won't be disappointed.'

'So, he may get off, he may not? He may spend a short time there, or possibly years and years? It's all too much for me to think about,' I said, pushing it all to the back of my mind. My heart pounded so hard, I worried it would burst out of my chest. My hands trembled as I tried to slow down my breathing. I couldn't be without my Aaron for years. It would kill him as much as it would me. He was my best friend, my safety, and the person I went to for everything. We saw each other ten-times a day, and spent every night in each other's arms. Thomas and Emmy wouldn't cope without their Daddy, who was so involved with their lives in every possible way. I couldn't face the thought of any of it.

'Maybe it's better this has happened now, Abigail. He couldn't stay under the house much longer. It was driving him mad. He told me many times. The only thing keeping him there was you and the children. At least now we can concentrate on getting him acquitted, based on the circumstances surrounding the case,' Richard said sympathetically, patting my hand. I remained silent, thinking a million thoughts, all involving Aaron, while tears poured down my face.

We arrived at 202 Myers Street, where Richard believed Aaron was being held, and waited in the carriage while he made his way to the front gate of the prison to speak with an officer.

'There is hope, Abigail. You heard what Richard said,' Patrick told me, smiling kindly as he held his wife's hand. After only a few minutes, Richard returned looking grim. He pulled himself up into the carriage and settled himself back down next to me.

'Aaron is here. They will let me see him for a few minutes as his legal representative, but that is it. I'm sorry, Abigail. The officers will not let you visit with him. You will have to write to the Chief Secretary's Department for permission before they will allow you entry,' Richard said apologetically. I sobbed harder than I ever had as Scarlett came to sit next to me, attempting to comfort me.

'This is not fair, Richard. It could be weeks before I get a reply. I have never gone that long without seeing him. Never!' I sobbed into Scarlett's shoulder as she embraced me.

'Let me go inside and see him. I may be able to find out what is going on, and will have more to tell you when I return,' he said reassuringly, patting my back before making his way back to the gate, his leather bag in hand.

'It will be alright, Abigail, you'll see,' Scarlett said, her confidence irritating me now.

'How, Scarlett? Do you really think he will get a fair trial or sentence when he attacked a Judge in his own home? Don't forget, it will be one of his brothers in arms who will hold Aaron's future in their hands. They want him to suffer and to make an example of him, to send a message to the people that they are untouchable. They will give him the maximum penalty. I know it.' I sobbed, my body shaking uncontrollably as I thought of what torture I would endure to be separated from my beloved Aaron, no matter how long, was not something I had ever foreseen or expected.

'I have known Aaron all my life, as you know, and he always comes out of situations unscathed in the end,' Patrick remarked, appearing to not even believe his own words. I pulled myself together, wiped the tears from my face and sat up, turning to gaze out of the carriage window. I sat silently waiting for Richard and news of Aaron, while Patrick and Scarlett spoke of other things between themselves. After what felt like hours, Richard returned and joined us in the carriage. He appeared perturbed as he relaxed back into his seat.

'I have seen him, and he is alright, except for his arm where he was shot. The doctor has treated the wound and bound it up in a sling. The dressing will be changed once a day with sterile material as I slipped the doctor a significant amount of money to treat him as a priority, to which he agreed. They have remanded him to Melbourne gaol to await his committal hearing, which will be held in the next twenty-four-hours. They plan to transport him there this morning. Now this will upset you, Abigail, and I want you to understand before I tell you there isn't a problem that can't be fixed, and we will fix this one.' I felt sick to my stomach, and swallowed several times in an attempt to dislodge the lump in my throat. 'The police have not charged him with serious assault as I expected. They have charged him with attempted murder and classified him as a dangerous prisoner,' he explained. I felt like someone had hit me in the stomach and gasped aloud. 'There's something going on that doesn't feel right, and I can't put my finger on it yet, but I will. Everything seems to be getting rushed through.' Richard appeared thoughtful as the carriage stopped abruptly in front of his office, picking up his bag and preparing to leave.

'Richard, what does that even mean? It is obviously much more serious than we first thought. I can see it in your eyes.' I held the carriage door closed so he couldn't leave and avoid my question.

'Yes, Abigail. It is significantly more serious. The penalty for attempted murder is up to twenty-five-years imprisonment. There are also other forms of punishment dealt by the court for this crime if found guilty.' His face was grim as he shifted in his seat, anxious to leave.

'I will go home now and organise everything so I can be in Melbourne with the children by tomorrow night. I can't leave him there alone,' I said, bursting into tears again.

'Abigail, there is no point going to Melbourne with the children. You could wait weeks before they allow you to see him. You are far better to stay where you are, surrounded by your friends and family until the time comes when he does need you. I will leave for Melbourne today and stay there to work on his case, and I'll visit him every day until the trial. I will send word to you as soon as you have permission to see him. Please listen to me. If not as your barrister, as your friend and brother. You and the children will be going through enough without sitting alone for weeks in a hotel room waiting.' Richard gazed across at me, pity in his eyes before he said his farewells and stepped down from the carriage. I knew he was right; however, I felt so helpless. I didn't know how I was going to cope without him for a few weeks, let alone a few years, or even twenty-years. I wiped my face as I looked across at Patrick and Scarlett.

'How is mother? With all the shock of this morning, I forgot to ask, and I feel awful about it.' I gazed across at Patrick, who nodded slightly before clearing his throat.

'We thought we'd lose her durin' the night. Her fever was the highest it's been since she became poorly. We sent word for the doctor to come, an' after seein' her, he wasn't confident she'd last 'till mornin'. It was by God's own intervention her fever broke not an hour after Aaron was arrested, an' when we left to come to ya, she was restin' comfortably.' Patrick smiled at me half-heartedly. I knew she would blame herself that Aaron had been caught because he visited her. She was my biggest supporter, the only one who agreed he should remain under the house indefinitely, something we both knew deep down was an impossibility. I stared out the window silently for the remainder of the journey home.

On our return, I went straight to the kitchen where Leo, Angus and Hamish were waiting expectantly. Leo stood up and came to the door, then embraced me.

'Please pay for my return voyage back from Coventry. I promise I won't do anything else wrong now that I know how hard this is for you. Hamish and Angus had a long talk with me. They weren't very nice about it either, bossing and bullying me. Please, please, please, Abigail, do the right thing. You know I won't be able to bear it if I'm not part of the conversation about Goliath. I love you, sugar lips, and I wouldn't do anything to hurt you on purpose,' he pleaded. I softened towards him immediately. He was my best friend, and I needed him now.

'Oh, all right. Fine. But open your mouth, Leo, one wrong word, and I will pack your bags myself so you can spend a month in Coventry, and I mean it,' I threatened him as he flashed me his beautiful smile.

'All right, then. See boys, I told you she would forgive me. You both owe me five pounds each,' Leo called out to Angus and Hamish, his face smug. He turned to them before collapsing in a fit of giggles as they grinned, Angus chuckling to himself.

'Oh, you pig of a man. You only did that to make money off me. How dare you, you little... ' I went to say as Hamish cut me off, distracting me completely.

'Abigail, would ye just ignore the wee idjit? An' please sit down an' tell us what happened? We're all mad with worry,' Hamish called out across the room. I hurried over to the table and sat down next to Angus, Leo joining us soon after and making himself comfortable beside Hamish.

'They're trying to stitch him up,' I snapped, telling them all I knew, and what Richard had explained to me about the charges they had laid, while Leo poured me a coffee.

'Those filthy, corrupt coppers. Even the newspapers said 'twas naw more than assault, albeit a serious one. Naw excuse fer the coppers treatin' Aaron like a murderer. They said that over a year ago, an' I read it again somewhere recently. They've an entire page o' The Sun dedicated tae the correspondence they receive about his case. Ninety percent o' 'em support Aaron an' what he did. I never realised how much the Aussies distrust the coppers an' the judicial system 'till this happened. If ye read some of the letters, they're extremely interestin' an' make some great points,' Hamish told me, and I nodded tiredly.

'I get enough letters here every week. I was replying to every single one up until recently, but it's become too overwhelming. There are so many, some of our staff have kindly offered to read them and pass on anything they think I should know about and reply to. I have so many letters from women who have themselves given birth to a stillborn, then others who have been raped and were too frightened to report it to the police because of how they would be treated. I make sure I reply to each of those as a priority, then go through the others and reply to as many as I can. It's lucky I am a fast writer. I'm storing the letters in boxes under the house because there are literally thousands and thousands of them.' I sighed deeply, then listened to them talk of Aaron, the police, and the impending trial as I silently drank my coffee, thinking a thousand things.

My poor Aaron, taken from us to sit in a tiny gaol cell while he awaited his fate. I would have to be strong for him and the children, as that would be his main worry right now, knowing him like I did. The children and I were his whole life, and his world revolved around us. We hadn't been apart since we met, and he was rarely away from the twins unless they were at his parents' home. I took a deep breath and let it out slowly. I had a lot to do, and many important decisions to make. I would spend the next couple of weeks preparing for an indefinite stay in Melbourne where the children and I could be close to him. Only we could help him through what I was sure would be just a bump in the road. I knew that in many years to come, we would look back on it and wonder why there was such a fuss—bringing me hope that in the future, whatever was to come, we would face it together.

Chapter Nine

WE ARRIVED AT THE Delmont and were given the family suite, consisting of four bedchambers, all with their own bathrooms, a small dining room, along with an enormous sitting room. Filled with comfortable looking lounges and low, ornate tables, it was more than adequate. A small, well-equipped kitchen hid away behind the dining room—rarely used but handy when you wanted to brew your own coffee or a pot of tea rather than bothering anyone. Bessie and little Mary had accompanied us, determined to look after me and the children while we were here in Melbourne. I could have used the hotel's ladies maid, but Bessie insisted she was by my side to ensure I was eating well and taking care of myself.

Aaron had been in custody for two-weeks and had been committed for trial in a week. I hadn't seen him yet as I had only now been granted permission, receiving a formal letter yesterday from the Chief Secretary's Department. I intended to visit the gaol as soon as I had settled everyone here, and not a moment longer.

'When are your friends and family arriving?' Bessie asked, bustling about my bedchamber, ensuring all was up to her standard.

'Before the trial starts next week. I have made reservations for them all here, so we are close to the courthouse,' I replied, fixing my hair as I prepared to leave. Bessie went to unpack our trunks while I hugged Thomas and Emmy, then took the picture they had drawn for me to give to their father, breaking my heart for the millionth time.

The carriage arrived at the Melbourne Gaol, a dreary bluestone building on Russell Street. I stepped down from the Delmont carriage with the driver's help, then tipped him as he smiled brightly and thanked me. I stood as straight as I could before smoothing down my skirt, then raised my hand to touch my hair to ensure it was in place. I had worn half of it down, just how Aaron liked it, and placed the rest up at the back of my head, several strands now loose and falling down my back.

I hadn't brought Thomas and Emmy with me today, not knowing what conditions I would find. I also knew there would be things we would need to discuss that the twins wouldn't benefit from hearing. I had promised them I would bring them in tomorrow to see him, which had excited them both so much they had simultaneously burst into tears.

I took a deep breath and marched up to the entrance, took a deep breath, then walked inside to the small foyer. An officer standing behind a desk beckoned me over within moments, taking my name then turning away to check his records. After several minutes, he asked me to follow him to a small, empty room, then silently pointed at a table and two chairs, the only furniture present. I obediently took my seat while he disappeared back into the hallway. The room was grimy and sparse, with nothing attractive to draw the eye. Seeing my Aaron after being apart for the longest time caused my heart to race and my hands to tremble at the thought of being near him, and to be able to speak with him again eased my heart.

The door opened and he stumbled in followed by a guard I hadn't seen before. He was still in the same clothes he had been taken in, and was filthy and unkempt. He stood at the door in chains, running from his ankles up to his hands, then wrapped around his waist, providing minimal movement. His face lit up at the sight of me and I ran to him, throwing my arms around him. We kissed for the longest time before I was pushed away by the guard.

'No touching the prisoner, Misses,' he snapped as he sat Aaron down opposite me, then walked away to stand by the closed door.

'You're a sight for sore eyes, mo anamchara. Are you an' the nippers all right, Abi? I've been so bloody worried about ya. You're all I can think of,' he whispered as I gazed into his beautiful blue eyes, the colour of the ocean on a sunny day.

'Aaron, I'm not the one locked up like an animal. How are you, my love? Are you safe?' I asked, my voice shaking.

'I'm safe. Ya mustn't worry yourself about me. I'm copin', but I desperately miss ya an' the twins.' He smiled, and my heart fluttered. 'They keep ya locked up in ya cell, except for an hour a day when they take ya outside to exercise. It's not as bad as it sounds, so please stop cryin', mo anamchara. I have a memory like an elephant, an' can remember back to when I was a small child in Ireland before we moved to Scotland an' settled in Edinburgh. I've a lifetime of memories to keep me busy, but I mostly focus me mind on the ones that include you an' the nippers. I lie in me cell an' relive every detail of the days an' nights we've spent together, alone an' as a family. Ya need not worry about me, me love. Me mind is strong, an' I'll not let them break me. I stand by what I did to Maslow, an' I feel no remorse. An' anyway, I'm a hero in here, Abi. Come on, give me a smile. Surely that deserves it. Me, a hero?' He chuckled to himself as I dried my face and tried to smile at him. I failed miserably and bent down to take the drawing from my handbag that the twins had sent for him. I held it up to the guard to get his attention.

'Excuse me, Mister?' I paused, waiting for his response.

'Me name's Stuart. Stuart Milne.'

'Thank you, Mr Milne. Is Aaron allowed to keep a picture drawn for him by his children? I doubt very much he could kill you with it, and it's not a map describing how to tunnel out of this hell hole,' I called out, my voice dripping in venom.

'It'll cost ya,' he replied, glancing across at me, then quickly looking outside the door before closing it again.

'Ha. Why doesn't that surprise me? You bastards are no better than the mutton shunters who pull your strings. Pieces of pig shit the lot of you,' I spat as he took a step back, arching his eyebrows in surprise.

'I thought ya were meant to be a lady, with all that stuff said about ya in the papers. You're the prettiest one I've seen in person, though. I even told me Missus that the other day when she was reading an article about ya an' ya husband here. At risk of bein' flogged, mind ya. I'm not a bad man, Miss, but I have to live. With what they pay me here, it's barely enough to keep food on the table. I like ya husband very much, an' support his cause, no word of a lie. So does most of Australia,' he told me wearily as he leaned back against the wall near the door.

'I don't want to hear your sad story, or how hard-done-by you are. Just tell me what it will cost for me to be able to come every day with the children, and again on my own later in the day. I want to bring in items that will make him comfortable, like blankets, clothing and books, including writing material. I only want you to supervise our visits, and you're to let Aaron touch his children by removing his chains when we visit. I want to bring in extra food too. I won't pay a penny until you give me your word,' I said as an afterthought, while Aaron looked at me amused, his eyes twinkling. The guard appeared flustered as he tried to put a figure on what he believed it was worth to me. When he finally made up his mind, he told me an amount, looking hopeful. I picked up my handbag and opened my purse, taking out double the amount of what he had asked for. 'You had better keep your side of this arrangement or I will go to the police commissioner and the papers and tell them you are corrupt and accept bribes,' I threatened, watching the blood drain from his face.

'I give ya me word.' I stood up and went to him, handing over the money in ten-pound notes. He looked up at me wide eyed as he counted it, before thanking me and putting it away in his pocket.

I returned to Aaron, feeling at ease now, knowing we would have at least some freedom when we saw each other, and he would be comfortable while he was here. After his chains were removed, he held the drawing in his large, calloused hands, tears in his eyes as he looked at the family portrait they had drawn of the four of us with our horses at Willow Grove. I handed him the last portrait taken of us as a family, and one of me alone in the garden taken at close range.

He took them and tucked them under his shirt, next to his heart. I stood and made my way around the table to sit on his lap.

'I told ya, no touchin',' the guard called out weakly as I glared back.

'And I just paid you as much as you earn in a year, so shut that fuckin' mouth of yours and look the other way,' I snapped, and he flushed red but remained quiet. I held Aaron's face in my hands and stared into his eyes for a long time, silently communicating my deepest feelings, then kissed him on the mouth. He slipped his hands around my waist and kissed me desperately, and I him. After what seemed like only minutes, the guard told me our time was finished and I had to leave. 'I love you more than life itself, my love. I will bring the children in tomorrow, then come back alone to spend some time with you. I have no doubt your guard Stuart here won't mind supervising two visits of two-hours each, every single day, at all. He will even have a smile on his face tomorrow so he doesn't scare the children. He needs to practice for the cameras on the chance someone may tell the papers he's corrupt. The people of Australia seem to have a bit of a grudge towards anyone who works in the criminal justice system, just from what I can gather from the letters I read in The Sun today,' I said, glaring across at the guard for a moment, who looked away. 'Anyway, my love, enough of that. You are my heart and my one true love. I vowed to stand by you through better or worse, and I always will. This is the worst part they talk of, I suppose. Life throws things our way that are unexpected, and all the money in the world doesn't help or fix it. I love you, my darling man,' I said softly, stroking his brow as he stared into my eyes.

'I love ya back, an' that's what keeps me strong. I hang on to the thought of one day bein' back with ya at Willow Grove, an' bein' free again. Ya must prepare yourself that I may be away for a time. That'll never change how I feel about ya, Abi. I know we'll get through this, an' life will return to how we once knew it. Never forget how much I love ya, an' how you're constantly in me thoughts, me beautiful girl,' he said as I stood to leave. Stuart stood behind me, waiting to escort me out before returning to lock Aaron back up in his tiny cell. I held my arms around his neck and held him close, kissing him deeply.

'I'll see you tomorrow. Rest your mind, as well as your body. Only think pleasant thoughts,' I whispered, smiling as he kissed me goodbye. I stood and stroked his hair before walking out the door with the guard beside me. He escorted me down the hallway, silently walking by my side, but keeping his hands to himself. 'I will be back tomorrow with the children. I don't care what you have to do to make it happen, and I really don't care if it bites you on the arse, as it is no longer my problem. Make sure you are the one supervising us at every visit. Or one of your cohorts you pay off to do the same,' I said with an air of authority, jutting out my chin. He appeared flustered, but nodded his head as he showed me out into the foyer. I could see he had never been spoken to like that by a woman before, and a so-called lady at that, and it pleased me no end.

The morning of the first day of the trial had come quickly, and I was beside myself with nerves. The children and I had been visiting Aaron every day since arriving, and I had quickly figured out which officers were open to a bit of extra money on the side. In return for allowing me to bring food and bottles of ale, and spend extra time together without the guard watching too closely. Stuart was the one who normally supervised us, allowing me to bring whatever I liked to Aaron and removing his chains during our visits. He had quietly informed me of who else was open to bribes if he were unavailable to supervise us. Everything had gone to plan, with me taking the children to visit him for two-hours every morning, then I would return in the afternoon and spend another two-hours with him.

The children would bring him sweeties, which he would share with them while holding them on his knees. Now they had allowed him to be unrestrained by his chains when we visited, he was able to touch and hold us, something he did constantly. No one challenged the extra privileges Aaron received, with many of them sympathetic to his plight. They had been keeping Aaron locked in his cell, except when he received visitors, due to his classification as a dangerous prisoner, which made me furious. I knew he was being treated well because of the media attention it would bring if he wasn't, as they all knew I had formed close relationships with several reporters since Aaron went into hiding.

It seemed this special treatment was also a result of our wealth. It still surprised and disappointed me how differently people were treated if they had money or power. The privileged few could buy whatever and whomever they chose. Except in Aaron's case. If he had attacked a regular person, he would have been charged with serious assault and more than likely would have been acquitted had we paid the right person the right amount of money. Maslow's appointment as a judge complicated everything, and there were far too many people in the judicial system who wanted to see Aaron punished severely.

Richard felt he was being blocked at every turn by the police, and the wardens at the gaol would often turn him away, preventing him from seeing Aaron to prepare his defence without reason. Richard truly believed the orders came from high up, and many were trying to ensure Aaron lost his case and was sentenced to the maximum penalty. I had heard whispers of corruption constantly from people around me, causing me to be absolutely terrified. If Maslow had all of these powerful people looking after his interests, it would be like us trying to protect ourselves with a feather from someone holding a gun to our head. Useless and very dangerous.

Aaron had decided to plead not guilty from the start, as he felt he was justified in what he had done. Richard believed the attempted murder charge should have been a serious assault charge, and the police had come up with the harshest charge they could think of due to who Aaron attacked. Richard completely supported Aaron's decision to plead not guilty, as he didn't believe Aaron meant to kill him, only maim him.

I was extremely anxious as I was being called first to give evidence today. Richard wanted to set the tone as to why Aaron acted as he did and have me testify as to what George Maslow did to me. The thought of seeing Maslow again made me physically ill, and I pushed it to the back of my mind, as I often did to protect myself. Bessie had dressed me in a conservative dark green dress, and styled my hair to perfection. I looked in the mirror and noticed dark circles under my eyes, which Bessie had tried to disguise with makeup.

'There, you look like the lady I know you are deep down when you're not up to mischief with that Leonardo. If I was on the jury and heard your story, I would be congratulating Mr Aaron instead of trying to put him in gaol,' she said gently, then touched me on the back of my head, indicating I was finished. I stood before the mirror and gazed at the dress Catherine had made for me. It was truly beautiful, the boat neckline and fitted bodice conservative and plain, the wide skirt falling elegantly around me to the ground. It had a small matching headpiece, now clipped into the side of my hair, my long curls gathered and bound tightly at the nape of my neck. I decided I was presentable enough and walked out into the sitting room to wait for the twins, while Bessie busied herself, trying to distract me from my own thoughts.

'You are the strongest woman I know, Mistress. Do not let any of these monsters break you again. Remember this man, Maslow, has no power over you. He cannot harm you again after what the papers have said about him. He wouldn't dare come close to you. I know what you will be forced to relive, and I know how painful it will be for you, especially with the loss of the bairns. I truly believe that justice will prevail for not only Aaron, but yourself too. This man has been exposed for the evil soul he is, and despite not getting his just rewards so far, it is as rare as hen's teeth to hear anyone say they believe him to be innocent. You only have to read the papers to know that. You'll make me proud today, and I will be here to comfort you on your return. Be strong there, but let yourself fall to pieces with your friends around you to care and love you in your grief,' she told me, tears in her eyes as she embraced me tightly.

'Thank you, Bessie, my dear friend. I don't know what I would have done without you since this horrible mess started. I don't thank you enough for everything you do. Not just your work, but your friendship and how you have looked after me for so long now. Thank you. I do love and appreciate you more than you know. I will be strong today for Aaron, and because I want people to hear the truth from my own lips. It's time I faced it myself and talked about what he did, as I now realise, I did nothing wrong to have caused it. He is a lunatic who suffers delusions about past lives, and he is of the firm opinion that everyone is connected in some way. If I even tried to explain to you some of the things that bastard believes, you would need your smelling salts. You think Aaron has a wild imagination? Maslow's goes far beyond. He is simply a madman and needs to be sent to Ararat,' I spat as I sat back down on the settee.

Thomas and Emmy came running to me shortly after, looking immaculate. Little Mary had taken extra care readying them today. She was taking them to the Melbourne Zoo to spend the day while we were at court. There was a knock on the door and Hamish entered, dressed in a dark suit like a gentleman.

'I've come tae take ye all tae breakfast. We cannae go breakin' our daily breakfast tradition, can we, Thomas an' Emmy?' He laughed, bending down slightly and opening his arms wide before they ran and embraced him. They ate breakfast together every day, now, and called it their new tradition. Emmy cuddled into his lap until it was nearly time for us to meet everyone in the restaurant for breakfast. 'How are ye holdin' up, Abigail?' he enquired, concern crossing his handsome face.

'Not well, Hamish, and thank you for asking. I'm terrified of having to go through my testimony in front of everyone, but I'm trying to be strong and do this for Aaron,' I replied, feeling my hands start to shake at the mere thought of giving evidence.

'I cannae imagine how hard today'll be fer ye, but ye ferget that I know ye better than most. Yer one o' the strongest women I know, an' yer intelligent an' articulate. Just tell the jury everythin' that happened. Look at 'em when ye tell 'em the facts o' the matter, an' watch their reaction. 'Tis them ye need tae reach, naw the judge or the prosecutor. Never ferget ye have yer friends an' family all around tae love an' support ye an' the twins, whatever the outcome.' He smiled sympathetically as he stood with Emmy in his arms before placing her back down on her feet, kissing the top of her head.

'Thank you, Hamish. Your friendship means a lot to me. Who would have thought twelve-years ago you and I would go on to have such a strong and lovely friendship? I truly appreciate everything you do for Aaron and the twins,' I said sincerely, and tried to smile back at him, but failed miserably.

We met with our friends and family in the hotel restaurant. Hamish sat down with the twins on each side of him, while I made myself comfortable opposite them next to Leo. Angus had left the care of Willow Grove to the very capable Harry and had arrived last night with Polly and the children to stay until the trial was over. The entire Cavanaugh family were here, as were Richard and Jas and Dana and Martin. Amelia and Tommy and Catherine and Colin had travelled to Melbourne together, while Leo had been forced to catch the train alone as a result of his bad behaviour. Tamara and Elizabeth planned to meet us at the court this morning, and I was grateful to each and every one of them. No one said much through breakfast, choosing to listen to the children chatter and laugh. I was becoming used to being recognised in public, and today was no different, with the other guests staring and whispering between each other.

'Abigail, ye look pale. Please eat somethin' before we leave,' Hamish insisted. I relented and took the plate he had ordered for me. I picked at it like a bird, not tasting any of it, my thoughts completely filled with Aaron.

'Excuse me. My name is Agatha. I just wanted to meet you, and wish your husband all the luck in the world. We are all so sorry for what you are going through, and it breaks my heart to see your little kiddies in the newspapers without their Daddy. The journalists are saying the courts are so corrupt, he could spend twenty-years behind bars,' a woman I had never met before said to me as she stood beside our table. I burst into tears, and she gasped in surprise.

'Step away from the table, butterball? Can't you see you made it worse by sticking your warty nose into someone else's business? Look at her now? How are we to take her before a court looking ghastly as she does, even worse now since you decided to grace us with your presence? Be away with you. Fly high on your broomstick, you old troll. My goodness, the fact we have to even set eyes on your unfortunate looking face astounds me. Why can't the frightful creatures just accept the fact and keep themselves hidden away so as not to offend the eyes of normal people? Go on, waddle off, fatty. We don't need your good luck or best wishes, either. I know you only came over here to see what you could find out, you gossip. Fly away and return to Salem,' Leo told her, shooing her away with his hands as the woman gasped again, so offended she looked as if she would faint. I heard my brothers-in-law snort with laughter as the woman slowly backed away and returned to her table without another word.

'Yer an evil wee man sayin' things like that tae a lady. She dinnae mean any harm. Abigail is highly emotional an' rightly so. Anythin' an' everythin' is settin' her off,' Hamish remarked as he handed me a clean handkerchief.

'I'm just defending my best friend, a kind act on my behalf that has nothing to do with you. You may be her friend, but not her best one. I am, and as her one and only, I will not sit back and let people we don't even know upset my precious little Abigail. I will give them my famous slap if they annoy me,' Leo told him, some at the table attempting to hold back their laughter.

It was soon time to leave, and we gathered our things and made our way out to the front of the hotel, finding the carriages already waiting. Hamish said his goodbyes to the twins and hugged them both, telling them to look closely at the giraffes. He went on to explain it was the first exotic animal I had ever seen up close at the London Zoo. It amazed me at times some of the things he remembered from when we were together so many years ago now.

Thomas and Emmy had become even closer to Hamish since their father's incarceration, so close they barely let him out of their sight when he was around. He cherished his time with them, just as he always had since they were born. They hugged me, jumping up and down excitedly, before little Mary wished me luck as she waited for Emmy to stop skipping around the small fountain. Richard helped me up into the carriage as I waved goodbye to them, then made myself comfortable.

Richard and Jas rode with Patrick, Scarlett, Hamish and I to the Supreme Court at the corner of William and Lonsdale Street, an exquisite building, I noted as we entered. It also held the County court, with the newly formed High Court convening in the building until their own was completed.

'Now, Abigail. You must remain out here until you are called. It shouldn't be too long. I know you are terrified, but I need your mind to be clear. You must recall every detail and tell the court what Maslow did to you. I'm sorry to be putting you through this; however, it will make such a difference to the outcome for Aaron.' Richard squeezed my shoulder before we walked down the enormous corridor towards the courtroom where Aaron would appear.

'I know, Richard. I have been awake half the night thinking about it. You need not worry for me. I will recall every single thing he did and said to me. I am a very private person, as you know, and wouldn't speak of this to anyone under normal circumstances. Because of the love I have for my husband, I don't care about my privacy, or what people will think of me. You and I both know rape victims are viewed as women of low morals who brought the attack on themselves. I understand that, and I really don't care as long as it keeps Aaron out of prison. I couldn't bear it if we were separated much longer, Richard. These past few weeks have been hell for me, and an absolute nightmare for our children. They sleep with me every night because they wake up crying for their father. You must get him off. I don't care what it costs, or who you have to bribe. Just do something,' I said, breaking down as he embraced me.

'Abigail, it will not come to that. They will have to prove he intentionally went there to kill Maslow, and he had every opportunity to do so, but he chose to leave the man alive. It will be extremely hard for them to prove their charge, and if the jury isn't convinced, he will be acquitted.' He slipped his arm around my shoulders reassuringly as I tried to pull myself together and clear my mind.

'All right. I will do my best to have the same faith you do. Thank you, my dear, dear friend. Aaron and I both appreciate how very much you are doing for him. I know for a fact you haven't worked on anything but his case since he was arrested. Thank God you spent so much time with him before his capture, discussing court strategies and how you would defend him, given they have restricted your access to him. Do you still believe something strange is happening, in comparison to other cases you know of that are similar to his?' I asked as he nodded thoughtfully.

'Oh, yes. I'm certain someone at the top is pulling the strings of the puppets down below in relation to Aaron. From the beginning, correct procedures were not followed, and the charges have been trumped up by the police, but accepted by the court, are strange to say the least. The coppers do this all the time, laying more serious charges than required, and are often told in no uncertain terms to go back and rethink those charges and compare them to the evidence they have regarding the case. It didn't happen in Aaron's situation, and was the first sign something was amiss. I am not the only one in legal circles who is of the firm belief this is a farce, and the judicial system they are a part of is corrupt. The problem is, you can't go around pointing the finger. I have my suspicions given I'm aware who Maslow is close to in private; however, I have no evidence at this time I can use, and we must proceed with what we have.' He smiled in silent apology before leaning down to kiss my cheek, then excused himself and entered the courtroom, our friends and family following.

I sat outside the closed door as the court session started, unable to hear a word. I knew the courtroom was packed to capacity, and there were journalists from The Sun and The Geelong Advertiser. Cain was here somewhere: however, I hadn't seen him yet. There were people everywhere, and a large protest was happening at the front of the courthouse. Hundreds of people were outside with large placards making various demands—from asking for Aaron to be pardoned, to calling the police crude names, several causing me to smile as we walked past them this morning, amidst much cheering and clapping.

I was approached by a court officer shortly after Richard left me, my stomach in knots at the sight of him.

'Mrs Abigail Cavanaugh?' I nodded once, remaining silent. 'You have been formally called to give evidence in the matter of the crown versus Mr Aaron Cavanaugh.' He bowed slightly to me before I stood and followed him to the large doors leading to the courtroom where my darling man was being held prisoner like an animal. I felt tears prick my eyes as he opened the door for me. I walked inside to see a crowd of people sitting in each row, squashed up like sardines.

I glanced over at Cain, who smiled encouragingly from where he sat in the back, paper and pencil in hand. Our family and friends sat to the left of the courtroom behind Richard, who had made himself comfortable at the front table, his opposing counsel to his right. I held my head up high as I was escorted by the arm towards the front of the room, aware every eye was on me, while their whispers felt like shouts to my ear. Strangers who I had never met seemed to believe they knew me and were entitled to an opinion based on what they read in the papers. Despite the crowd of people in the room, the only person I could see was Aaron standing in the prisoner's box in chains, staring back at me with such love I felt my heart would burst.

I was taken to the witness box, and stepped inside, my legs trembling, before being sworn in. I again held my right hand over the bible just as I did the day Maslow attacked me, repeating the words I was told to say that really meant if I lied, God would punish me in the cruellest and most terrible ways imaginable. The court officer glanced at me, pity in his eyes, as he placed the bible under his arm and returned to his chair at the side of the courtroom.

The presiding Judge, James Murray, stared across at Aaron, his cold, hard eyes causing my stomach to knot up again. Judge Murray, a handsome man for his age, called the court to order before all present went silent, waiting with bated breath to hear what I would say. The police prosecutor appeared to be a kindly man, despite being one of them, giving me some hope he would not be too cruel to me. I had already been advised by Richard that some of the questions I would be asked would be intrusive, personal and downright offensive at times, as it was the prosecutor's job to trivialise, confuse, and throw doubt on my testimony. I sat down and waited, my nerves already frayed as the prosecutor approached me. He was a short man with greying hair, and he looked to me like a family man. I hoped he was and sent a prayer above for Sister's God to give him at least some compassion for even those he was trying to have gaoled.

'You are Mrs Abigail Cavanaugh, married to the accused, Mr Aaron Cavanaugh?' the prosecution, Mr Edward Strahan, asked me, and I replied in the affirmative. He questioned me for over an hour and a half, asking if I was aware of Aaron's intention to kill Judge Maslow, where he was for nearly two-years, and enquiring if I was part of his murderous plan. He attempted to paint Aaron as a violent man who would kill you as quick as look at you. I argued every question he put to me, and he was becoming frustrated, rolling his eyes at my answers, his face deepening to a mottled scarlet when I would continue to finish what I was saying, despite he and the Judge telling me to answer with only a yes or no. I refused to be boxed in like that, so when I was asked a question, I answered it fully, despite the amount of times the judge banged his hammer down, calling for order. Of most importance, I had the full attention of the jury, who were hanging on every word I said, even when told by the judge to disregard what they had just heard.

'I have no further questions at this time, Your Honour. I believe this witness is unreliable given she would say anything to save her husband.' Mr Strahan sat back down at the front table where Richard was sitting in his gown and wig. I smiled sweetly at the prosecutor who shook his head in disbelief. Aaron hadn't taken his eyes from me the entire time I was giving evidence, and I held his gaze as he mouthed the words I love you across the courtroom where he stood with a large guard beside him. He appeared tired and fearful, worrying me greatly, as he was never one to be too concerned about anything until it happened.

Richard rose to his feet to address me, then slowly walked over and stood a few feet away, enabling the jury to have a clear view of me.

'Good morning, Mrs Cavanaugh. Can you tell us here today what caused your husband, Mr Aaron Cavanaugh, to assault Mr George Maslow?' Not one person in the room misunderstood his question or tone, his refusal to refer to Maslow as a Judge causing several loud gasps to rise above the silent room as I tried to maintain my composure.

I answered, telling the court in graphic detail of the attack on me, leaving out no aspect. I glanced over at the spectators to see revulsion and disgust on their faces as they stared up at me, most not without pity. I then told of the heartbreaking loss of our sons, caused by the brutal punch to my stomach, further gasps and shocked whispers filling my ears as I continued on and relived that day. Women openly sobbed as I told them what Maslow had done to my body and my mind, exposing his insanity and the content of what he had said to me. Our family and friends appeared shocked, with Aaron's mother breaking down in tears. My sisters-in-law and female friends had tears pouring down their faces, all discreetly wiping them away with their handkerchiefs, as until now they never knew the full truth.

I stared across at Maslow sitting behind Mr Strahan, appearing pleased with himself. His aura hadn't changed—not that I expected it to turn gold at any time. He was truly an evil man, and what he had done to us had destroyed our lives. He gazed back at me, a smug smile settling on his lips, his demeanour calm as he stared into my eyes. I felt my throat start to close up and my legs start to shake, and I quickly looked away. I couldn't lose my composure now. Not when I was so close to finishing my testimony. I found if I focused on the jury, I was less anxious; however, I would often look over at Aaron and smile as brightly as I could—if only to reassure myself all would be well after this was over.

I told the court how the police had intimidated the hospital doctor, and me, into changing the reports. Richard held up the documents to submit into evidence for the jury to examine.

'Are these the said hospital and police reports?' He held them up and I nodded before he handed them over to the court officer to pass to the judge. I could see the reporters at the back of the court writing madly in their notebooks, and knew without doubt Aaron's story would be front page news again tomorrow—not just in Victoria, but nationwide. It seemed all of Australia were aware Aaron's trial was currently being held, and many had made their way to Melbourne to show their support by demonstrating in the street against the police. This had caused chaos in the central business district of Melbourne, the police barely able to contain the crowds that lined the streets from the gaol to the Supreme Court.

Richard questioned me for what seemed like hours, while George Maslow tried to intimidate me, not taking his eyes from me from the time I had first stepped into the courtroom. I took great pleasure in the bright letters carved into his cheeks, identifying him to the world for what he was. A rapist and a murderer. The scars would fade in time, no doubt; however, it was obvious to all they would never go away. Marked for life—with no sausage or eggs, as Leo would say. I looked away, not giving him the satisfaction of upsetting me further. Judge Murray turned to the jury.

'I would like to inform you that the allegations this witness had made against Judge George Maslow have been investigated by the police, and they have established without doubt these said allegations are unfounded,' he announced, before turning to glance coldly in my direction. I held my head high and stared back at him.

'They are only unfounded because the police refused to do their job and bring a rapist to trial. You all look after each other, don't you?' I jutted out my chin defiantly and crossed my arms against my chest, the sounds of several people clapping and cheering causing the judge to scowl, then furiously bang his gavel down over and over as he called for silence.

'Have you finished with this witness, as she is standing on my last nerve?' Judge Murray asked impatiently before grimacing at me. I pulled a face at him, causing him to reel back in his chair, turn back to Richard, while stabbing his fat finger in the air in my direction.

'I will not be disrespected in my own courtroom. Did you see what your client's wife just did to me? She poked out her tongue and mocked me like an obtuse five-year-old lass throwing a tantrum. I am in complete disbelief that a grown woman would behave this way towards an upstanding member of the judicial system. I am warning you. Keep the woman in line, or she may find herself locked up in a cell just like her husband.' Richard sighed deeply, knowing my temper far too well, and wisely told the Judge he had indeed finished with me before he sat back down, then gave me a look—one I recognised he often gave his children when they were in trouble. I narrowed my gaze at Leo, who was bent forward in a fit of giggles, while Angus roared with laughter beside him. I watched in amusement as Polly reached over and smacked them both to the back of the head—a short, sharp slap that instantly made them sit up and take notice of her as she whispered furiously at them.

I was excused immediately, and rose to my feet, then stepped out of the witness box. I looked across at Aaron, who smiled at me, then blew him a kiss as I walked towards the seats behind Richard, finding Hamish and Catherine and making myself comfortable in between them. Catherine took my hand in hers and moved closer, lowering her voice to a whisper.

'Abigail, why didn't you tell me what you went through?' I could hear the anguish in her voice, and I tried several times to swallow the lump in my throat that had been there since I woke.

'I didn't tell anyone, Catherine. Only Aaron knew the details, and Hamish found out by accident,' I whispered back, squeezing her hand.

We sat together the entire day, hearing testimony from Detective Paul O'Neill, along with the many and varied officers who had raided our home so often. By late afternoon, the court was adjourned for the day, and I was relieved. I watched several guards take Aaron to the holding cell, and my heart felt like it would break. Catherine slipped her arm through mine, leading me from the court and through the crowd to the waiting carriage. Catherine and Dana climbed in behind me, along with Polly and my dear friends, Margaret and Jenny, who had come without their husbands to show their support.

'I have to ask this, as I'm sure everyone else is just as confused as me. What was all that nonsense he was talking about, referring to past lives and knowing you from another time?' Jenny asked, and I smiled wearily at her before exhaling loudly.

'He is of the firm belief we have all lived before. Some, hundreds of times, and somehow that's where he thinks knows me from. He is a lunatic and nothing he says makes sense.' I shook my head in frustration as Dana took my hand in hers and straightened my dress for me.

'What does he mean about auras? I don't even know what they are. I have never heard of them,' Polly mused quietly as she gazed out the window at the busy streets.

'All I know is he believes souls live on from one life to the next. He told me a soul can choose whether to reincarnate back to earth as a newborn wean, or stay at a place called Hiriarni. He says souls recognise each other from a past life by an aura surrounding their body most cannot see—like a soft glow that illuminates several inches around their physical body. He said souls are strongly connected to each other, and when they reincarnate back to earth, they are drawn back to those who they loved or had some relationship with, not always good. He told Aaron that only extremely evolved souls can see these auras radiating from the bodies of souls they are connected to from a previous life,' I explained as they all stared back at me in silence, their faces blank. I tried again. 'An evolved soul is apparently someone who has lived many lives, and achieved many things. Both here on earth and at this so-called place, Hiriarni.' Polly and Catherine gasped, while Dana gave me a knowing look. I gave up and shook my head. 'It's all pigshit, and I wouldn't pay attention to one word that comes out of his mouth. He is as mad as a cut snake and should be admitted to the Ararat Asylum. Who could make up such fanciful stories unless their mind was not right, or they are a writer of fiction?' I asked, rolling my eyes, and they nodded, still silent as relief washed over them. As the carriage made its way back to the hotel, I opened my heart to my friends and told them everything about Maslow, and how much it had affected me. They all sat and cried, as did I, while they comforted me. I knew at that very moment, I had been given the best friends and sisters that anyone could ever ask for—and I was grateful.

Chapter Ten

I RECLINED ON A sun-lounge, the children playing beside me in the small swimming pool only recently installed by a friend of Elizabeth's husband, Eric—who seemed to know every man and his dog that worked in the construction industry these days. My friends and family had decided after sitting in the courtroom all day, they needed some fresh air and sunshine, but refused to walk to one of the nearby gardens. I had suggested the refurbished courtyard on the ground floor of the hotel, aware they had not opened it to the guests as yet and we would have privacy. The smell of manure from the nearby streets filled my nose, along with rotting food scraps and rubbish piled up in the alley behind us. Richard strolled over, greeting me warmly before making himself comfortable on the chair beside me.

'You did well today, Abigail. You held your head up and told your story without shame. I saw several members of the jury were emotional when you told it, which will only go in our favour. I know how hard it must have been for you.' He stopped abruptly and placed his hand on mine. 'Well, actually, in all honesty, I don't. I have never experienced anything like you have endured, and to then have to talk about a very private matter with the world listening? I cannot think of anything more soul destroying. And we mustn't forget I am a man, living in a world run by men. It would be offensive for me to compare my experience to any women, even one of my own class.' I smothered a smile as I waited for him to continue. He relaxed

163

back in his lounge and closed his eyes, a deep sigh filling my ears as I turned to look at him. 'Did you know Aaron's story has gone around the world? The London papers picked it up a few months ago before he was caught, then sent a reporter out here to cover his case. It's pure luck he's here for the trial. I saw him in court today, and I must say, I'm thrilled—and you should be too. The attention and support Aaron has received is beyond anything I have ever seen, and I'm stunned by the outpouring of emotion from the people of Australia. I receive hundreds of letters every week offering to pay for my services on Aaron's behalf. Then there are others contacting me to enquire if there is anything they can do to help in a practical way. I must tell you, I have received several letters that were in very poor taste, asking me to introduce you to them if Aaron goes to gaol. They seemed to want to court you. Those went into the fire, unanswered.' He paused for a time, staring up at the darkening sky. 'I know it took a great deal of strength to get up there today and relive such an unspeakable attack. I'm sorry for it, Abigail. No woman should ever be treated in this manner. Only an animal would behave in such a way. I too was unaware of the details as we heard them today. You are a brave woman, and I'm proud to call you my sister.' He reached across and gently patted my hand as I wiped tears from my face, then moved to his side and placed my head on his broad shoulder. 'Be prepared. They will use tactics that are not only immoral, they are pure evil. All in an attempt to paint Aaron as a monster. You must keep your temper in check, no matter what is said. Pulling that face at the judge could have damaged our case today, and I have no doubt your contempt for the law and those that carry it out will be described in every detail in tomorrow's newspaper. Just keep your head. Can you promise me at least that, Abigail?' I nodded, rolling my eyes as relief washed over him.

'All right. I'm sorry. I know it was juvenile; however, they just infuriate me to a point I lose control. I promise I will behave myself for Aaron's sake,' I replied as he embraced me. I knew how fortunate I was to have such special people surrounding me at what was the worst time of my life. I would forever treasure every one of them.

The trial had continued for weeks now, stirring up the people of Victoria into a frenzy of emotion. The Sun had been following the trial closely, ensuring they sent a reporter to the Supreme Court every day, printing their story the following morning. Aaron was spoken of with affection in nearly every article, his courage in rising up against the establishment and fighting injustice himself admired by most. My own story, no matter how humiliating, had resonated with many people, both in Australia and many far-off countries. It still felt surreal that Aaron's life, along with my own private matters, were being relayed across the world via newspapers.

People from all classes came to witness the trial from the public gallery, often spilling out into the street, the courtroom proper filled to capacity every single day. Maslow had given his evidence; however, refused to speak on the rape and assault allegations, stubbornly stating over and over that he was not the man on trial. I assumed he did not want to perjure himself, but didn't understand why given he was of the firm opinion he was accountable to no one—even God. As far as the public were concerned, Maslow didn't need a trial. They had tried and convicted him in their own court of law, believing him to be a sadistic rapist, while branding him insane due to his very public rantings about past lives—Madman Maslow, and Lunatic Lawman, a common catch cry of the protesters lining the streets day after day.

Aaron had remained calm when giving his testimony, stating he was enraged when he saw what Maslow had done to me, but did not seek revenge on that very day for my own sake. He told them with tears in his eyes that when our sons were born dead as a direct result of Maslow's attack, the grief he carried over the loss of our children, while watching his wife barely able to function and in much distress, caused him to go mad over a period of months. Finally seeking revenge only when he realised the police would not act to bring Maslow to justice for his crimes.

Doctor Brown testified, quietly stating he had been pressured by the police to change his report, confirming the first report was indeed accurate. He looked down at his trousers wherever he saw me watching him, his embarrassment and shame obvious to all present. Inspector Peter Cahill was unwavering in his testimony and again stated I had called the police back to the hospital several hours after making the first statement to withdraw my allegations willingly. He denied any knowledge of the hospital report being changed, or that he placed any pressure of any kind on Doctor Brown to do so.

We had attended court every day, while Hamish and Angus caught the train back to Geelong each Friday afternoon to oversee Willow Grove, both making the trip back to Melbourne on Sunday night to be present for the trial. The jury had finally retired this afternoon after closing arguments, and now we were forced to sit back and wait while Aaron's fate was left in their hands. I was doing my best to prepare for a period of separation from my beloved, well aware he would spend some time in gaol for the simple fact he had inflicted serious injuries on another person—no matter the reason or justification. I would have to be outwardly strong, as I knew once he was incarcerated, it would make it even harder for him if he thought I wasn't coping.

I sat alone in the darkened sitting room on a comfortable chair, the children in their beds hours ago, a small glass of whisky in my hand, hoping it would help me relax before I went to bed. I had hardly slept since Aaron had been arrested; however, every time I lay down to close my eyes, all I could think of was him. My mind would not rest, and sleep barely found me anymore. When it did, my dreams were filled with evil, and I would wake screaming. I was avoiding my bed for that very reason when there was a knock on the door.

'Oh, what now?' I sighed deeply before rising to my feet and crossing the room, mumbling to myself as I reached across and opened the door to find Hamish standing in the hallway. I welcomed him in before returning to my seat, placing my finger up to my lips in warning while pointing to the children's bedchamber.

'Aye, I know 'tis late an' the bairns are sleepin', but I brought ye somethin' at Leo's request. He's worried about ye. Weel, we've all been worried about ye, lass, an' haven't known how tae help ye. Leonardo told me where tae find it when I returned tae Willow Grove. I hope ye dinnae mind, though, or get the devil in ye over it.' He stood over me, a small leather bag in his hand. 'I was forced tae go through some o' yer personal items. His instructions were far from helpful.' A slight smile touched his lips before he took my pipe and a small container of green buds from the bag, already mixed with tobacco, then handed it over to me. I laughed aloud, thanking him.

'I've not used it for that long. I'd forgotten where I put it. Leo seems to have found it and put it away for me. No doubt he smoked half of it himself beforehand.' He chuckled as I ran a suspicious gaze over the content.

'Aye. Naw doubt. 'Tis the only thing that'd explain his outrageous behaviour. Do ye want me tae stay while ye smoke it afore ye ready yerself fer yer bed?' I nodded before he made himself comfortable in the chair opposite mine.

'Thank you for your kindness, Hamish. I didn't think to bring it with me. Margaret only smokes it when at home, and even then, only at night. Well, most of the time. I should have remembered to bring it with me, knowing how much it helped when Harrison and Jack were born. It not only eased my mind, it eased my body. I have smoked it a few times with Aaron just for fun, but I always fall asleep almost immediately. He doesn't find it fun at all.' Hamish laughed quietly to himself as I filled the pipe, feeling much brighter already.

'Aye, I've heard the stories. Me favourite is the one where ye an' Leo, an' possibly Margaret, got out o' yer minds before lunch, an' Aaron could naw control the three o' ye at once. An' there was gossip fer weeks about the pigs in the pen havin' painted lips.' He leaned across and lit the pipe, his eyes sparkling in amusement.

'I had nothing to do with that, and I will say no more on the matter, other than it was years ago. Aaron forbade us from smoking it from that day forward. Other than for medicinal purposes.' I frowned, thinking back to what Leo had forced Margaret and I to do, and the resulting wrath of Bessie when she found every single lip paint I owned was nowhere to be found.

Hamish talked of Thomas and Emmy while I smoked, trying to distract me from my own thoughts. I inhaled again, leaning back into my chair, the heavy burden I carried starting to lift, while sadly aware the relief it brought would only last a short time. I breathed in the pungent smoke filling the room, my eyes closed as I listened to him speak of the goings on at Willow Grove, his voice low and deep, comforting me.

'Seems yer ready fer yer bed.' I opened my heavy eyes and smiled, nodding slightly as he rose to his feet. 'I'll leave ye be. See ye in the mornin', old friend. Bessie will soon attend ye. I'll let her know yer waitin'. Sleep well.' I grunted as he waved before stepping outside into the hall, closing the door behind him. I soon stumbled into my bedchamber and lay on top of the heavy quilt. Closing my eyes once again, peace settled on me for the first time in years just as Bessie came bustling into the room.

'I see they brought your green buds down for you. Very kind and thoughtful since you haven't complained to any of them, or said you're not sleeping. I never thought I would say this, but you and Mister Aaron have a loyal and steadfast friend in Hamish. He's a good mate to Aaron, closer than kin. Who would have thought he'd straighten himself up after all these years and find himself a decent woman like he has in Nellie? Not me.' She disappeared into the wardrobe to find my nightgown. 'I believe they'll be happy together. She thinks the sun rises and sets only for him, and it seems he loves her too. Maybe not how he once loved you, but at least it's a start. I really don't know how Willow Grove would have survived like it has without Hamish. He's been Aaron's legs and arms, so to say. He's earned admiration and respect in his own right for his loyalty and hard work. No, Mistress. You have a very dear friend indeed when it comes to Hamish. All of your women friends are wonderful, as well. They just surround you with their love, don't they?' She soon finished undressing me, then slipped a white nightgown over my head, her arm around my waist to steady me.

'Yes, they are all wonderful. All of you have been wonderfully wonderful, and I love each of you. Wonderful. Just wonderful,' I murmured as she helped me into bed, giggling to herself. I called out my farewells as she quietly left the room, closing the door quietly behind her. Within moments, I fell into a deep sleep—dreams of a ship, an orange, and a carriage with four black horses filling my head and tormenting me until dawn.

Richard had received word yesterday the jury had reached a decision, and would announce their verdict today when they reconvened. I sat behind Richard, unable to stop fidgeting, as we waited for Judge Murry to enter the courtroom. Within moments, the door behind the high bench where he sat day after day for weeks opened and he stepped inside, his long gown swishing behind him, the horsehair wig on his head slightly askew. I quickly stood as expected, those around me doing the same, only sitting back down once he was seated on his throne, calling the court to order, then banging his grovel and loudly stating the court was now in session. We had waited for this day for what seemed like years, now. My heart pounded hard, thumping so hard I couldn't hear a thing, my hands clasped in my lap in an attempt to stop them trembling. Dear Catherine sat to one side of me, Jenny on the other, while the entire Cavanaugh family surrounded me and my friends—all refusing to leave my side since arriving in Melbourne a week before the trial even began.

Aaron and I had made the decision to not allow our children in the courtroom. We did not consider it in their best interest to be exposed to the evidence given against their father, or witness him in chains. Or guarded by a man who didn't look as if he could protect himself from a woman, let alone a man as imposing as Aaron. I gazed across at him shifting from foot to foot, his chains rattling as he too fidgeted, nervously awaiting his fate. He hadn't taken his eyes from me, both silently praying this would all go away so we could resume our lives back at Willow Grove and put this chapter of our lives in the past where it belonged. I blew him a kiss, and he raised his hand as high as his shackles would allow, catching it then placing his hand flat on his stomach, closing his eyes for a moment as I smiled across at him.

'Have you, the jury, reached a decision?' Judge Murry asked, turning to the jury. The foreman, a small, well dressed man, rose to his feet, a folded piece of paper in his hand. He appeared nervous, his hand noticeably shaking, while he refused to look at anyone, even the Judge.

'Yes, we have, Your Honour.' He paused for a moment, swallowing hard, the silence in the room almost deafening. 'We, the jury, find the defendant, Aaron Cavanaugh, guilty of attempted murder.' His voice broke as he collapsed back into his chair, tears in his eyes as I glanced around the room, shaking my head in confusion. I felt nothing but disappointment, but deep down had expected this and prepared myself accordingly. I gazed across at Aaron and tried to smile reassuringly; however, his attention was fixed on the jury, his face void of emotion. My heart ached at the thought we were likely to be separated for a time as I continued to stare at my beautiful husband—who now, even after hearing the verdict, finally turned to me and grinned widely as if we were the only ones in the grand room, bringing tears to my eyes. Bloody man! He had to go and administer his own punishment, no longer prepared to wait for the law to avenge my honour. Stupid, sweet, bastard of a bloody man whom I adored more than anything or anyone in the world. Judge Murray raised his eyebrows before slowly turning to Aaron and narrowing his gaze, a slight smile on his lips.

'I have considered all the evidence put before this court, Mr Cavanaugh, and I find the alleged assault on your wife as an unsubstantiated excuse to inflict violence on an upstanding and respected member of our community and the judicial system . A system we are all bound to live within and abide by, I am here to remind you. You have shown no remorse for the attack, or the sickening injuries you inflicted on your victim—injuries he will carry for the rest of his life. There is no reason or excuse I can find that even slightly defends the violent and sadistic nature you possess. The community deserves to be protected from people born with a defective character—the same character you so obviously possess—while ensuring this atrocity can never be repeated. I cannot hold out any hope that the sentence I am about to pass down will be minimised or dismissed in the future. Therefore, I advise you to accept your fate,' Judge Murry stated, then bent forward and picked something up from his desk. A woman coughed, interrupting the silence for only a moment before rising to her feet and running from the room. Not a soul present moved or spoke as they waited for the Judge to continue.

He placed a square, black cloth over his wig, the blood draining from Aaron's face as Richard gasped, pushing his chair back from the table before springing to his feet. I had no idea what any of it meant, and did not want to. I leaned forward slightly, clutching my stomach as I tried not to retch.

'I have now to pronounce your sentence, Mr Cavanaugh. You will be taken from here to the place from whence you came, and thence on a day appointed by the Executive Council to a place of execution, and there you will be hanged by the neck until you be dead. May the Lord have mercy on your soul,' Judge Murry announced without emotion. Angry howls filled my ears, those around me yelling abuse and jeering, many rising to their feet while shouting obscenities at him before the Judge disappeared through the back door as quickly as he arrived. I could hear women sobbing all around me. Above that, I could hear screaming so loud I couldn't hear myself think. It was only when I dropped to the floor as my vision turned from grey to black, I realised it was me.

Chapter Eleven

AARON'S EXECUTION HAD BEEN scheduled ten-days from sentencing on Monday the 6th October, 1902. Richard had been frantically writing letters to anyone and everyone who was in a position to help plead Aaron's case. The newspapers were in an uproar, demanding an inquiry into what they believed was a biased and corrupt police investigation that led to Aaron's unjust sentence. They were encouraging Victorians to show their fury by attending the gaol where Aaron was being held, resulting in thousands of people protesting out the front of the Melbourne Gaol each day, demanding his freedom.

I hadn't given up all hope, as Richard was waiting to hear the outcome of the fourth and final appeal he had lodged. He expected to know the outcome the day before Aaron's execution, at the very latest, leaving all who knew and loved him on edge, not knowing what to prepare for. Richard felt positive he would win on appeal and have the death sentence commuted to twenty-years in gaol—a reality I was still unable to accept. However, I preferred he was alive and breathing and held somewhere we could visit, no matter how terrible.

Only two full days and nights remained until Aaron was due to hang at ten o'clock on the Monday morning. I had continued to take the twins to him for two-hours every morning since he had been sentenced, then would return in the afternoon to visit by myself. The guards were treating him well, as they all seemed to genuinely like him. There were no longer any problems during our visits, and they allowed me to bring him anything he asked for.

They would take his chains off to allow him as much privacy as they could give when we were present. Not a great deal given they were obligated to remain in the room. Often Stuart would bring the newspaper with him and read while we chatted to him, trying to ignore us. Aaron and I had sat down together yesterday and told Thomas and Emmy the truth of the matter, wanting to prepare them in case the appeal failed. Both were understandably inconsolable at the thought of their father being taken from them. They were old enough to understand death, having experienced not only the loss of their infant brothers, but workers and members of their families who had died suddenly and tragically at Willow Grove over the years. I didn't know what to say or do to comfort them when we returned to the hotel, and had held them both in my arms all night as they cried for their father.

I kissed Emmy's sleeping face as she snuggled her head into my shoulder, while Thomas slept on the far side of the large bed, holding my hand tightly as he snored. They turned twelve in six-months' time and were so grown up for their age. They seemed to get along with everyone who crossed their path—much like the man who sired them. They were far more extraverted than me, a trait I was thankful they took from their father who could talk the leg off a chair, his mother often remarked.

'Good morning, Mummy,' Emmy murmured, yawning widely as she opened her large, emerald eyes, already glistening with tears. I pulled her closer and wrapped my arms around her as she broke down and sobbed. I spoke soothingly to her, stroking her back in a futile attempt to calm her. Thomas woke soon after due to her howls, and quickly sat up, his hair a mess as he yawned and moved over next to us. He put his arm over Emmy who lay on top of me, cuddling into my side as he too tried to calm her.

'It's gunna be alright, Emmy. Uncle Hamish said all hope is not lost. Mummy an' Daddy just wanted to prepare us for the worst. He told me himself last night. He says there's no point worryin' an' cryin' 'till it actually happens, an' we need to enjoy our time with Daddy when we see him 'till we know for certain what they're gunna do.' He patted her hand soothingly, my tears now overflowing and sliding down my face as I slipped my arm around him.

'Your Uncle Hamish is exactly right. We're going to spend all morning with him,' I explained soothingly, kissing Emmy's tear-stained cheek before Thomas took a handkerchief and wiped his sister's face.

'How'd ya get 'em to agree to that? Are they givin' us much longer?' He shook his head in disbelief before screwing up his nose in disdain, Emmy now silent other than the occasional hiccup as I patted her back.

'I spoke to the guard when I saw Daddy last night, and he said that for today and tomorrow you can have three-hours with him.' They brightened immediately, hugging me as I exhaled slowly. I heard someone at my door, and turned, waiting for Bessie to come rushing into the room as was her usual habit. Instead, I found Leo running towards us at great speed, his heavy frame landing on the bed beside me without warning, almost throwing us out.

'Hello, my little mince tarts with brandy custard. I have come to put the sunshine back into your rain filled day. I am a ray of light shining through the darkness, guiding all the lost souls, just like you three little butterballs. I seriously don't know what any of you would do without me. I am your rock of Gibraltar, your anchor in a stormy sea, your... ' he went to say.

'Oh, all right, Banjo Paterson. We understand what you are trying to say.' I hugged him, then kissed his handsome face before continuing. 'How are you after yesterday? I've never seen you so distressed.' He had gone to visit with Aaron in the late afternoon for what was possibly the last time and hadn't coped at all. He had exited the prison screaming hysterically while leaving Hamish to carry him from the front gate, through the crowd and into the waiting carriage. Unable to walk under his own strength, poor Leo was carried back to the room next to mine, where I heard him sobbing throughout the night. Our family and friends were only allowed one last visit each, and Aaron's parents planned to attend the gaol today to visit with him for the permitted two-hours in between the children and my own.

'Oh, Abigail. I don't know how I'm feeling. I know we all must be positive and think of only the best outcome; however, I found yesterday one of the most miserable of my life. Goliath and I talked for a long time, and I even made him laugh sometimes, which pleases me.' He paused, sniffing loudly. 'I listened to everything he told me, which is secret between us, so do not ask.' He narrowed his gaze at me then leaned closer, lowering his voice so only I could hear. 'Do not turn green, but he allowed me to kiss him on the lips before I left. He refused to open his mouth, though, but at least I got that. My hand did slip down to his derriere for a moment, and he certainly didn't take that in a loving way. Thinking back, I was fortunate a guard was present.' I collapsed into giggles, glancing over at Thomas and Emmy lying beside each other now, talking softly between themselves and ignoring us as Leo moved up from the bottom of the bed and slipped under the quilt beside, embracing me before kissing my forehead. 'How are you, my dear? You are still my favourite friend in the world, even if you are quite unfortunate looking these days. There is no excuse not to look your best, and you're certainly not setting a good example for your children, who do know the most important thing in life is how you look on the outside.' I composed myself, now wiping tears of amusement rather than sorrow from my face.

'I don't even know how I am. It all feels like a bad dream I am trying to wake from. In my mind, I know I must be prepared for the worst, but I cannot imagine losing him. I can't lose him. He is so important to so many people, He can't be taken away from us at the age of thirty-two. He has far too much left to do here. My heart tells me he will come out of this with only a few scratches, just as he usually does, but my mind is filled with a thousand thoughts, and I cannot accept one of them.' My voice faltered, my heart hurting as he held me tighter and stroked my back.

'I'm certain he will come through this just as you said. Unscathed, as usual. He has gotten himself into trouble in the past, and always managed to get out of it. I cannot accept that he could die the day after tomorrow. I just can't believe anyone could do that to my Goliath. I have loved him too for more than twelve-years now. Who will come and nag me every morning for food, then come and sit with me for hours while I make the anniversary cupcakes he eats most of? Is anyone even thinking of my suffering and grief? No. Not one person has asked me how I'm coping, except for you. They all told me I need to be strong for you, but as I told them, what about me? Patrick, Aiden and Luke threatened to kick me in the behind if I upset you in any way or say anything stupid. They are all as big as Aaron and could really hurt me, you know? I tried to tell them if I knew what I was going to say was stupid, I wouldn't say it, would I? They couldn't answer that, let me give you the tip. Some men are thick as two bricks. Anyway, back to me. You're the only one who cares about my feelings. You are being so brave and strong, I think the time has come for you to support me. It cannot always be a one-sided friendship, Abigail. It wouldn't make you a good friend at all,' he shrieked before bursting into tears. The twins casually looked over at him then returned to their conversation, ignoring his dramatics as they called it, now so used to him and his various emotions constantly on display, they no longer took notice.

'There, there, Leo. I know you love him too, and of course I will support you. Don't fash, nothing has happened yet, and we will just have to wait and see where the cards fall. The public support is enormous now. There are thousands of people descending on Melbourne as we speak. Some are camping in the botanical gardens, well, until the coppers move them along, and all the public houses are full. The point is, they are committed to Aaron's case and seeing justice, and will set up camp elsewhere until they are moved on again. I was told it is now impossible to get any accommodation in the Melbourne central business district. Even the most expensive of lodgings are full. All the hotels are booked, including the Delmont, which has never happened before. Even when we are busy here, we always have spare rooms for those who don't send word ahead of their arrival. I don't know if you realise how significant that is. Richard told me having the public behind him could swing the appeal in Aaron's favour,' I reassured him, gently patting his back.

'You shouldn't say swing, Abigail. It's in poor taste. The important thing is you believe he will be all right.' He wiped the tears from his face, then sat up and stared at me for a moment.

'I don't know for certain, but I do know he still has a chance. That's better than nothing.' He nodded, swinging his legs out of the bed.

'Do you want to eat breakfast in the restaurant, or here in the suite?'

'Here. I want to leave straight after breakfast and get the twins to Aaron, as I don't want to waste a minute of the extra time they are giving us.' He nodded again as he rose to his feet, pulling his robe back on over his pink silk pyjamas.

'I will go and order a banquet fit for a King. Who is our King, by the way, and why doesn't Australia have their own King?' He paused at the door, turning back to await my response.

'Because England still thinks it owns Australia, as she does with every other country she has invaded. We are the poor cousins to England. Their King is our King, Edward the seventh, by the way.' I could still hear his laughter after he had stepped into the sitting room to order our breakfast from the maid who had brought fresh coffee and juice for the children. I lay in bed hugging the twins as we listened to Leo ordering enough food to feed fifty people.

'I enjoyed the story Daddy told us about heaven yesterday very much. I don't want him to go there yet, but it sounds like such a beautiful place. Pathways of gold, and beautiful rivers and mountains. He said there is nothing but happiness there, and you get to be with people who love you that have already died,' Emmy told Thomas as I felt tears prick my eyes. I couldn't bear to listen sometimes to Aaron speak to the twins, as it broke my heart hearing him attempting to prepare them for his own death. It was something I didn't want to think about at this moment and pushed it to the back of my mind.

'Yeah, it sounded beaut, especially 'cause there are Martarinos there. Dad said when ya pass over the green divide, ya can be around those ya love that are still here. He told me if he does have to die, he'll be by our sides as we grow into adults, even though we won't be able to see him,' Thomas remarked thoughtfully. I felt my heart leap into my throat. I couldn't listen to my children talk of death so calmly, not understanding they really could lose their father in a few days. I wiped the tears that had escaped from my eyes and stood up, putting on my dressing gown.

'What are you two lazy tykes going to do? Are you staying in here, or joining us for breakfast, my little Prince and Princess?' I gazed down at them, my hands on my hips as they lay back in the enormous bed, their hands behind their heads, exactly like their father.

'We're comin' now. I'm starvin', an' could eat the crotch out of a low flyin' duck. I hope Uncle Leo ordered enough food,' Thomas said as he got out of bed and put his robe on, while Emmy did the same.

'You won't have to worry about a food shortage—and mind your language, my beautiful boy. It's considered uncivilised when amongst strangers to speak of a duck's private parts,' I replied, smiling to myself as I kissed them both.

'Mummy. Tamara's children say we are uncivilised because we eat in the kitchen at home, and sometimes in our dressing gowns, like this morning. What do they mean? Doesn't everyone eat in their dressing gowns sometimes? I know they are lying about the kitchen, as everyone has to eat in a kitchen or they would fade away to nothing,' Emmy asked, confusion crossing her little face.

'What they really mean is there are different ways of living your life. Some people do things a certain way because that's what they were taught as children, while others may do things differently. The world would be a very boring place if we all acted the same way and did exactly the same thing now, wouldn't it?' She nodded slightly, still looking muddled. 'It means there is no right or wrong way, Emmy. You do what makes you happy, and don't worry about what other people think—as long as you cause no harm to another. Never judge anyone for how they choose to live their lives, and you will be less likely to be judged yourself, my darling girl. There are people in the world that say things to be mean and hurt others feelings on purpose, and others who say things without realising they are being cruel.'

'Like Uncle Leo?'

'Let's not use him as an example today. We're likely to go round in circles given his uniqueness—and very bad behaviour. Tamara's children have been brought up in a very different way compared to you and Thomas. That's not to say one is better than the other. You are different because your parents have taught you different things that don't match with what Tamara's children are taught. You don't have to dislike them because of it. Always be kind and friendly, but don't expect them to become close friends, sweetheart. They don't like visiting Willow Grove, or doing any of the things you and Thomas enjoy. All you can do is continue to invite them along when you go to play with your friends in the village, and if they don't want to go, leave them be.' She nodded, rising from the bed and taking my hand in hers.

We walked into the sitting room to find Leo and Hamish chatting as they sat on the lounge. Jenny and Margaret had also joined us and were sitting comfortably on a lounge together drinking coffee. I went and sat with them while the twins went to Hamish, sliding on to the lounge beside him before he handed them a glass of orange juice each. I poured myself a coffee and settled back in between the girls.

'How are you feeling today, Abigail? You look as if you haven't slept for days,' Jenny enquired, taking my hand in hers.

'I'm fine. There is still hope, and I am holding onto that. Someone with some power will take notice of the public's reaction, surely?' I asked as they nodded in agreement. If it wasn't for the fact that even the newspapers were saying something odd was going on in relation to Aaron's trial and heavy sentence, I would think myself biased. I knew this wasn't the case, given the sheer volume of angry Australians who had contacted me, the papers, and government officials. And then there were those who had chosen to hold demonstrations and protests against the government and its police and judicial system. The closer it came to Aaron's execution date, the more desperate and violent the protests were becoming, with many being arrested yesterday while protesting outside Parliament House. I was concerned someone would be hurt. Some present were children at risk of being crushed or trampled when the police went in to break up the demonstration and make arrests for being a public nuisance. 'I want to thank you both for staying here with me for this length of time. It's going on two-months now. How are your families coping without you? I feel terrible to have taken you away from them,' I told Jen and Margaret as I drank my coffee.

'Our families are right as rain. My own mother has come to stay and is driving Sean to drink, or so he tells me. Other than that, and me Ma's advancing years, they're coping fine. I'm sure they're all happy to see the back of us,' Margaret teased as Jen laughed.

'Yes, my lot are the same. They are fine without me. My staff have taken over and they're doing an impressive job by all accounts. There haven't been any complaints about the food at least. As long as they all have full stomachs, they don't care where I am.' Jenny laughed aloud as I smiled at her. Soon after, there was a knock on the door and Leo went to open it. Half a dozen maids walked in, all carrying heavy trays laden with food.

'How many people do ye think yer feedin' here, Leo?' Hamish asked, not taking his eyes from them for a moment as he watched them place the food on the large dining room table in the adjoining room.

'Just us, and anyone else who may turn up. I ordered a crème brulee especially for my darling Abigail. I wanted to cheer her up, and I know she just adores dessert for breakfast. You must eat a hot meal first before I hand it over to you,' Leo warned as I smiled up at him, then nodded. I rose to my feet, as did the others, then followed them to the dining room overlooking Flinders Street Station—a special place that held special memories, all imprinted on my heart where they would remain for eternity.

Chapter Twelve

I JOINED SCARLETT AND Vicki, along with Adele and Dana, for a late lunch at the Delmont restaurant. I had taken Thomas and Emmy to see Aaron as soon as they had finished breakfast, arriving at the Melbourne gaol just after eight o'clock. They had let us in discreetly, allowing Thomas and Emmy to carry an assortment of food they had ordered for their father from the Delmont kitchen. Stuart had supervised us today, sitting quietly the entire time in the corner reading New Idea while we spent time together as a family. He had even placed a small stretcher in the room so the four of us could sit together comfortably and talk as the hours passed far too quickly. I saw a kindness in the guard I hadn't seen before, allowing us to stay until one o'clock, which had surprised me; however, the twins were thrilled to be in their father's company for five-hours—the longest they had spent with him since the night before he was arrested. He had told them stories and spoken to them as gently as he could about the possibility of his own death. They seemed to accept what he said without question, breaking my heart yet again. They both believed he would be all right, and would be returned to them soon.

The waiter stood beside me, a small notepad in his hand, a pencil perched behind his ear. I assumed he was new as I had never seen him before, and Aaron and I made a point of meeting all who worked for us no matter what position they were employed. He cleared his throat while waiting for my friends to stop gossipping, then turned his attention to me.

'Good morning, Mrs Cavanaugh. Are you ready to order?' He took the pencil from behind his ear as I nodded, scanning the menu within moments before handing it back to him while taking notice of the small badge pinned to his shirt with his name.

'Good morning to you, Timothy.' I cast my eyes over his new uniform and curly dark hair while smiling up at him. He looked no older than our Thomas, only smaller in height and weight, saddening me once again how poverty turned children into adults years before their time. I closed my eyes for a moment and sent a message to the angels above, asking them to take extra care of my aunt and thank her for all she had provided to us. 'I would like the Mulligatawny soup to start, with a basket of freshly buttered bread for the table, please.' He nodded politely as he wrote it down, then turned to Dana. I raised my hand to get his attention, my face starting to flush. 'I do apologise, but I haven't finished. I would also like the Chicken Fricassee with rice, and I will finish off with a slice of treacle tart with extra clotted cream on the side—oh, and a serve of brown bread ice cream.' He stared down at me in silence, his eyes wide.

'Is that all for you alone, Mrs Cavanaugh?' He swallowed several times as Dana snorted, making no attempt to hide her amusement. I nodded slightly, placing my palms on my cheeks to cool them.

'Yes. Is there a law against a woman eating in public?' He shook his head, his face a slight shade of pink. 'I am acutely aware I eat as much as a man. And yes, I know my backside should be the size of this hotel. Give it a few years and no doubt it will.' He flushed deeper, averting his eyes as I turned to my friends. 'When entertaining or dining in a restaurant, twelve to thirteen courses are served at the very least, and six courses when eating alone is common, yet women are expected to take a few bites and push the rest around their plate. I refuse to apologise for being hungry and choosing to rectify that.' They erupted into giggles, my sisters-in-law behaving worse than their own bairns, while Dana wasn't much better. I watched in amusement as they placed their orders with poor Timothy, who I believed was unlikely to return tomorrow, then followed him to the kitchen to apologise on behalf of our table. We stood in the small hallway and talked for a time, and I found him to be a polite child with a strong work ethic and big dreams. After leaving him to his work, I made my way back to the table, relieved the other guests seemed to have forgotten our rambunctiousness already and had returned to their meals.

'I'm so glad I no longer have to eat like a bird in public when I'm starving inside. Now I'm married and Aiden is stuck with me until death separates us, I can eat whatever I like. Makes no difference now if I turn into a fatty, as your Leonardo likes to say.' Vicki giggled to herself as I smirked at her. She hadn't changed a bit since we had met on the ship all those years ago. Tall and slender, she had kept her figure despite bearing four children, and she possessed the loveliest face, her bright orange hair falling down her back and skimming her waist when loose, just like her mother. They had been proper ladies when we met; however, they had relaxed over the years and didn't seem to care what anyone thought anymore.

Dana had been shunned by her upper-class friends, just as Hamish had predicted, which had devastated her at the time. However, she had picked herself up and formed new friendships with women from a different class who were far more genuine, and I was proud of her. I had always enjoyed socialising with Dana and her family no matter who was present, but now I never turned down an invitation to a gathering at their home. Their change in circumstance gave me the opportunity to mix with many new and interesting people. Now she was free from the elitist snobbery that came with her position, she appeared much more at peace. And far happier.

'How was your visit this morning with Aaron?' Dana enquired, her eyes on Timothy as he placed our drinks on the table. I had ordered something called a Dapper Pineapple Slapper, a creamy concoction with a heavy handed splash of vodka. I felt the need for something to take the edge off and ease not only my mind, but my body, unable to stop myself shaking at the thought of what they planned to do to my love, my best friend, my everything.

'It was lovely to spend more than a couple of hours with him, but I try not to interfere or say too much during the morning visits as it's his time with Thomas and Emmy. I find it so terribly hard to watch and listen to him talk to them about death. It's breaking my heart.'

I promptly burst into tears, not only surprising my companions, but myself and the other patrons looking on. Scarlett handed me a handkerchief, then took my hand in hers.

'Don't go losing hope now, Abigail. I saw Aaron just two-days ago, and he confided he is worried you'll fall in a heap before we reach the finish line. leaving you unable to care for the children. You are the strongest woman I know—and the most sensible. You know it's not over yet, our dear sister. You have an excellent Barrister in Richard, who is doing everything he can to get the sentence commuted to a gaol term. No country is going to allow a man to hang for an assault—I admit, a serious one—but an assault was what it was. The public would lose their minds and turn against their own government if they carry out such a harsh and unjust sentence. Who knows how people would react in the heat of the moment.' She paused for a moment, our companions silently nodding while Vicki wiped away a stray tear sliding down her cheek. 'No.' Scarlett shook her head before continuing. 'I think Edmund Barton is far smarter than he looks. He'd be reading the papers along with the rest of us and wondering what the hell is going on. I've no doubt in my mind that if the appeal is unsuccessful, he will step in. If they execute him, they'll look like barbarians. And in the twentieth century too. Who would believe things like this could still happen?' I nodded before lifting my glass to my lips and taking a long drink.

'The Prime Minister hasn't done or said a bloody thing up until now. Do you really think he gives a fat rat's arse about any of it?' I shook my head in frustration, then lifted my glass again and took another long drink, wiping my mouth with a napkin before continuing. 'I know for a fact Aaron has written to Alfred Deakin pleading for him to intervene, but has received no response.

'Aren't they acquainted?' Adele asked and I nodded sadly.

'Yes, they met many years ago, but it seems Mr Deakin has a short memory, along with questionable morals.' I was beyond disappointed with a number of people Aaron and I had once considered friends, including Alfred, a barrister and journalist in addition to his political position. He had been elected to the Victorian Legislative Assembly in 1879 at the age of twenty three, a decade before I arrived in Geelong. Serving twice as Attorney General of Victoria in the following decades, he had been one of the leading figures in the movement for the federation of the Australian colonies, and I felt betrayed by his silence.

'You must be strong, no matter what happens. Try not to focus on those who have let you down,' Scarlett reminded me again.

'I know, Scarlett. It's hard not to when his life hangs in the balance and they are in the position to help. I'm just so bloody worried for him. Everyone is telling me over and over that he will be fine, but no one knows that for certain. My mind won't rest until I know the death penalty has been taken from him.' I finished my drink, then ordered another as our first course was brought to the table by our enthusiastic server, Timothy. I noticed Mr and Mrs Cavanaugh standing at the entrance to the restaurant, patiently waiting to be seated at a table. I caught Mr Cavanaugh's eye and waved them over, his handsome face breaking into a wide grin.

'Hello, me dear girl. We didn't know ya were down here. We saw the twins just before they ran off with their favourite uncle, so assumed ya were takin' some time to yourself after the visit. I know how much it takes out of ya.' He bent down to kiss my cheek before lowering himself into the chair next to me, while Mrs Cavanaugh embraced me warmly then sat down beside her weary husband. They both appeared distracted, although my dear mother-in-law seemed better equipped in the art of hiding her feelings. striking up a cheerful conversation with Dana. I continued to eat my soup, enjoying every bite. The Cavanaugh and Sons Seafood Company supplied and delivered to the Delmont, along with a number of the hotels and restaurants; therefore, it was no surprise when they placed their order with Timothy when he stopped at our table.

'Abigail. Abigail. Our server is talking to you,' Adele informed me, jolting me from my daydream.

'Oh, I'm sorry. What did you say?' I asked, turning to gaze up at him.

'Here is your crayfish, Mrs Cavanaugh. I hope it is to your liking. We only serve the best seafood here, all caught fresh daily in Bass Strait.' He grinned to himself as he placed the large tray in front of me, while Mr and Mrs Cavanaugh looked on proudly at their produce. I didn't have the heart or the ill manners to tell him I had ordered chicken. The crayfish, cut in half and smothered in a creamy sauce, piled with prawns, oysters and scallops, the smell wafting up my nostrils and reminding me of home. I smiled weakly as I began to eat, finding it far more delicious than I expected the chicken would have been. We enjoyed our meals while I listened to them discuss everything bar what was happening to my Aaron.

I planned to return to him as soon as the luncheon concluded. If I was lucky, they could allow me to stay with him until dinner, but only if the right guards were on duty, something we could not rely on due to illness or restraints within the gaol due to staff shortages. All I knew was I needed to get back to him, the desire to spend every minute possible by his side until he was released back into my arms overwhelming me. I ate quickly now, leaving Mr Cavanaugh to crack open the legs for me so I could suck the meat out, saving the claws for last.

'Abigail, slow down. You will choke, my dear. Ten-minutes won't make a difference as Aaron will be eating his own lunch now. The children told me they took him a basket with everything they could think to order from the kitchen,' Mrs Cavanaugh remarked, reaching over and placing her hand on mine, her eyes twinkling.

'I'm sorry, Mother. I need to get back to him. He is all alone in there, while here I am surrounded by everyone who loves us. It hurts my heart to think of him locked up by himself in that tiny cell, his only relief being when he receives visitors. I'm sorry I haven't been contributing to the conversation. I really don't know where my head is. I can't think straight and I'm muddling everything up,' I tried to explain as dessert was placed in front of me, the dirty dishes quickly removed and taken to the kitchen.

'Abigail, please don't be silly. We understand, and that's why we're here. To support you. You go as soon as you are ready. If you feel you must be with him, then you must go. We don't expect you to sit here and entertain us given what you are going through. We know why you're so quiet at the moment, and we are here when you are ready to talk,' Victoria said kindly. I nodded, the tart I ordered half eaten already.

'Thank you, dear Vicki. I really mean that. You have all been won- derful to stop your lives for this long now to support Aaron and me so lovingly, along with the children. We will never forget your kindness and generosity for as long as we live.' I finished my dessert, wiped my mouth, then rose to my feet, groaning as I bent down to pick up my handbag from the table, realising I had again eaten far too much and my digestion would benefit from a sleep, rather than rushing around.

'Godspeed, daughter.' Mrs Cavanaugh blew me a kiss and I smiled, discreetly sending one back to her.

'Thank you for understanding. I will see you all tonight.' I made my way around the table, kissing each of them goodbye. I turned, almost running from the restaurant in my haste to get to the front desk to collect my basket, then increased my pace and sprinted out to the Delmont carriage, opening the door and yelling out the address before the driver had even seen me. Within moments, I felt the carriage pull away and turn towards the place they were holding my love, my heart, and my everything.

I stepped into our suite and closed the door behind me, pausing for a moment with my back to the door as voices from the next room filled my ears, satisfied and in good spirits after spending the afternoon, and a good part of the evening, with Aaron. I had taken a large basket of food from the Delmont kitchen, as I did religiously to ensure he had a good dinner in the evenings, and not the pig swill they expected the inmates to be grateful for. When I took the twins to see him in the mornings, I brought along his breakfast and lunch, including extra to share if he so chose. When I returned in the afternoons, I brought him his dinner and an assortment of cakes and desserts.

He was still in good spirits, holding onto the hope that Richard's most recent appeal would be successful. The prison guards would take The Sun to him each day so he could read about his case, along with what the public were saying and doing in their attempts to have him released. He had been overwhelmed with emotion, and humbled that people cared so much they were willing to risk losing their own freedom in their mission to gain his. Aaron was treated like a member of the royal family by the guards and other prisoners, many drawn to him because of the easy way about him, along with the fact he treated everyone he met with respect, showing genuine interest and concern, no matter what their class—until they showed him it wasn't deserved.

I silently entered the sitting room to find Leo, Catherine and Hamish relaxing on the lounge near the fireplace, while Angus, Polly, and Margaret sat together around the large coffee table. Jenny stood motionless by the window, gazing down onto the Yarra River.

'Finally, you've decided to grace us with your presence. I have been waiting all day for your return.' Leo glanced down at his timepiece, tapping the glass before turning his attention back to me, widening his eyes dramatically before continuing. 'Polly Wolly has been irritating me all day and trying to be the boss of me. I won't stand for it. You have to do something about her, Abigail. Why did you have to choose her as your sister? There were hundreds of orphans raised with you that were far more deserving. You had the pick of the litter, and you chose the fattest runt you could find without a brain in its head.' He turned up his nose in disdain as he sat leaned back on the lounge, his legs crossed and his arms folded across his chest. I heard a grunt and turned to see Polly glaring across the room at him from her chair beside Angus.

'Oh, you lying wee cockhead. Abi, he has done nought but get under everyone's feet today while whining like a five-year-old lass about anything and everything. He tried to touch Margaret's breast only two-hours ago. Even I cannae believe it, and I know how badly behaved he is and expect this shite from him.' She shook her head, then waved her fist in his direction, a smile touching his lips despite refusing to acknowledge she was in the room. 'I feel like taking to him with a belt. I was so embarrassed. And still am. To be standing in the middle of Swanston Street when he did it. Well, I wanted the ground to open up and swallow him,' Polly spat, her face bright red, while her eyes glinted dangerously. I looked across at Margaret, and much to my relief, found she didn't appear to be damaged or upset, her attempts to hide her amusement failing miserably.

'Aren't you meant to hope the ground swallows you?' Angus enquired as he reached for her hand and she slapped him away.

'No. I was definitely praying it swallowed him. We all know if that miracle occurred and my prayers were answered, even the ground wouldn't tolerate him and would spit him back out.' I heard someone snort, while Polly screamed in frustration, causing me to jump. 'Anyone else would be arrested, but of course there wasn't one copper around to see it. I'm still tempted to go and report him myself.'

'Oh, stop talking, Pollyanna. You are making no sense, even to yourself, and have gone even softer in the head that you were when I was unfortunate to meet you on that ship of shattered dreams.' He paused, Polly's screams filling the room, while Angus's large arms were now wrapped around her as she fought against him. 'I will explain it one last time for you, butterball. Slower so you can understand this time. I only placed my hand there to establish if Margaret's breasts were as big and firm as Abigail's. She was not harmed, and to the contrary, appeared to enjoy the examination more than she should have.' Leo glanced at Margaret and smiled, winking suggestively at her, setting her off in a fit of giggles, before turning to me. 'I would have thought twice if I'd known Polly now qualifies for admission to Ararat. The lunatic turned on me, then slapped me to the ground until I was begging for my life. Abigail, she refused to stop and behaved no better than that mad trollop in Little Lon' who threatens to kill anyone who passes by her corner without paying. No different to how you react to the silly things in life that annoy you, Abigail. Bad tempered the both of you, I will add.' I narrowed my gaze at him, aware Polly could break free at any moment and strike him dead where he sat.

'You are generally the only silly thing flapping around my feet,' I mumbled to myself, debating if I should go to him on Polly's behalf. 'And her name is Mabel,' I called out. He raised his hand and dismissed me, focussing his attention on Margaret.

'I was more embarrassed than the lot of them when Margaret decided to call attention to herself by screaming like that in public. I was horrified, and only then realised, not one of your friends has the ability to behave like a lady. Not even the real ones, like Amelia, who has clearly forgotten where she came from. You have corrupted them all over the years, Abigail, and should be ashamed of yourself. The way Margaret behaved on the street in front of everyone was shameful. People from everywhere came and watched her and Pollyanna beating me. Not one of them stopped to help, despite my screams. I am never going out in public with any of them again if you aren't there to protect me. Even Hamish was no help. I thought Adonis and I had come to an arrangement. I refrain from gazing upon and/or touching his backside, and he won't beat me to death or allow anyone else to beat me to death.' I collapsed into a fit of giggles, the thought of Margaret losing her temper too much to bear. Usually calm and sensible, I knew it would have taken a lot to upset her enough to go on to commit common assault in the street in front of hundreds of people. Margaret laughed the loudest, the others joining her, except for Leo and Polly.

'That's the thing, Leonardo. I am yer friend. Which is why I let ye take that hidin' from wee Margaret here. If yer stupid enough tae stick yer hand down a woman's dress without bein' invited, then ye deserve whatever punishment is handed out. An' she did. Punish ye, I mean. 'Twas bonny, by the way, Margy. I'm impressed with the arm ye have on ye, an' could hear each an' every smack ringin' like a bell as ye belted him tae the ground. An' kept him down there. I'd hate tae be one o' the bairns ye look after, though. Me arse'd be sore fer a month if ye walloped me with half the force.' A slow grin spread across Hamish's face as the room erupted into laughter.

Leo rose to his feet, and on seeing no one was on his side, stomped off to bed, slamming his bedchamber door behind him. Collapsing again into hysterical laughter, I realised just how good it felt to laugh out loud. I hadn't laughed like this since Aaron had been arrested. Choosing to remain with my dearest friends a little longer as they talked and teased each other, they spoke of things other than Aaron in an attempt to distract my mind. I couldn't have wished for better people to share this life with me. They had surrounded me with their love and care, never once letting me down.

As the night wore on, my eyes became heavy, my yawning more frequent. Since Aaron's arrest, I was exhausted by the end of the day. Every situation I faced was highly emotive—dealing with guards, the newspapers, journalists, well wishers, and hateful people. All while watching our precious children with their father, who they could lose any day. Even my time alone with him drained my strength, forced to talk of things I didn't want to think about, let alone discuss.

Bessie came bustling into the sitting room, kicking the door shut behind Little Mary. They had dined together at the hotel restaurant, and it was obvious they hadn't been drinking tea. Thomas and Emmy were asleep hours ago in Patrick and Scarlett's suite with their cousins, and I would be sleeping alone tonight for the first time since we arrived in Melbourne.

'Come now, Mistress. You look tired. Let's get you into bed,' Bessie said kindly, covering her mouth as she yawned. I stood and embraced my friends, bidding them goodnight before following her to my bedchamber.

Much later, as I lay in the enormous bed all alone, the night sky even darker than usual, I wondered if this was what my future held. It was a life I couldn't bear to think about, and I pushed it to the back of my mind. As I drifted off into a tormented sleep, I dreamed of a gum tree, a birthday cake, and a black lamb.

Chapter Thirteen

I HAD WOKEN EARLY from a dream I had no recollection of. I knew it hadn't been pleasant, finding myself sitting bolt upright, cold sweat dripping from every part of me, my heart racing and panic engulfing me, though I didn't know why, taking me several moments to realise where I was and catch my breath. Bessie had come in soon after to help me dress for the day, leaving me only minutes ago. The twins were still sleeping as I kissed their foreheads and left them in my bed. I stepped into the sitting room to find Richard reading the paper while sipping his morning coffee.

'Good morning, Abigail. I must say, Catherine does an incredible job with your clothes. Even as a man who has absolutely no interest in fashion, I have even noticed I can pick a Montague gown on the street.' He threw back his head and howled with laughter as I slowly crossed the room, a smile touching my lips. 'Jas is getting all her clothes made by Catherine now, and I will only go to Colin. He's the best I have found, and I speak for the time I lived in London. They charge like a wounded bull, but it makes Jas so happy that I don't mind paying. She looks stunning in them too.' He smiled to himself as I sat down opposite him and poured myself a coffee.

'She is extremely talented. Even more so than her father, believe it or not, and he is famous. I'm so proud of her. When we met on the train, she told me exactly what she was going to do with her life, and she went out into the world and made it happen through pure hard work, just as she said she would. She is one of my dearest friends, and I'm so grateful to her and everyone else who is here to support us. Have you heard anything yet?' I asked hopefully as I sipped my smooth, creamy coffee, cheering me immensely.

'No, not yet. It could be anytime between now and tomorrow. He is set to be hanged at ten o'clock, so it will be early morning at the latest.' He nodded reassuringly, then smiled at me again. Richard had made a final attempt to have Aaron's sentence commuted to life by appealing to the Executive Council for the fourth time. This was the last appeal Aaron had open to him. If he lost this, he would be executed.

'Do you believe he has a chance, Richard? Please be honest with me. I need to know because it affects what happens today during the children's visit. If you believe he will hang, please tell me, as this morning will be the last time that he will see the children. I need to know so I can prepare Thomas, Emmy and myself,' I said softly, a lump lodged in my throat. He nodded, such deep sympathy in his eyes as he fixed me with a stare.

'I know this is difficult for you, Abigail, but yes, I think he has a very good chance. There is always the possibility his appeal won't be successful, though, and that's why I am of the firm opinion you need to treat today as if it is the last time you will see him. That way, when he is set free, you will have no regrets. I am only suggesting this for your own sake and for that of the children on the off chance things do not go as I expect.' Tears filled my eyes, and I quickly brushed them away with the back of my hand as Hamish strolled into the suite, greeting us warmly then sitting down next to Richard, thumping him on the back. I poured him a cup of coffee, handing it over as he made himself comfortable.

'I had the strangest dream last night. 'Twas like watchin' a play from up above the stage. Ye were there, Abigail, an' so were Bessie an' Polly. We were somewhere in England in a tiny village, an' ye'd re-turned after a long voyage. Even Leonardo was present, still throwin' tantrums like a two-year-old bairn. Seems I cannae escape him even when I sleep,' Hamish teased, and I smiled weakly. He had been wonderful since we had been here, relieving little Mary of her duties for most of the day and taking the twins on adventures around

Melbourne. He knew my afternoons were filled with Aaron, and he didn't approve of them being left from midday until after dinner in the care of a Nanny—any Nanny—despite little Mary being family to us all.

Catherine would spend the day with Hamish and the children when her schedule allowed. She was incredibly close to them, and had been a pillar of strength for all of us in recent times. Aaron and I had made a wise decision when we had chosen them as godparents. Not only did they love them dearly, they gave their time to them without measure and ensured they were available to them unconditionally. Hamish had taken the guilt that lay heavy on my heart from me by caring for Thomas and Emmy in the afternoons, and I was grateful. I knew they enjoyed every moment with him no matter where they were or what they were doing, confident in the knowledge they would have fun because their godfather insisted on it. He had taken them to the museum a few days ago to expose their minds to history, and the world outside Willow Grove, and they had embraced it all with unmitigated excitement.

'That is strange because Aaron has experienced similar dreams over the years, only he said he was in Tasmania. He recognised the place because when he was younger, his father took them there for a fortnight on the boat. Everything else you said sounds the same. Only Aaron saw Catherine and Dana walking the streets of Hobart in my company. Once in poorly made clothes like a vagrant, and several times dressed in the finest gowns in the land. He also mentioned Leonardo was there, and expressed similar feelings to you regarding never being able to escape him.' I laughed aloud as he slapped his knee and chuckled to himself, while Richard shook his head.

'Ye lot an' yer dreams. The amount o' strange, an' may I say, quite disturbin' dreams I've heard ye all talk about over the years are ridiculous. Some o' 'em are beyond entertainin', I will add.' He chuckled as the twins came running out of their room, their faces washed and shining, their hair brushed, both dressed in their play clothes ready for breakfast. They came and sat on each side of me before I kissed them, slipping my arms around their shoulders and pulling them into a tight embrace.

'Are we seeing Daddy today? Thomas told me last night that if Uncle Richard doesn't save him, they plan to kill him tomorrow and we will never see him again.' Emmy's eyes filled with tears, and I pulled her back to me, holding her tightly against my chest. I saw Hamish discreetly wipe a tear from his own eye as he watched his sweet goddaughter break her heart.

'Yes, sweetheart. I am taking you in to see him this morning.' I swallowed hard, brushing several stray hairs from her eyes. 'It is true that if the court doesn't change its mind, Daddy will go to heaven tomorrow. That's why we are going to have to make today as special as we can. We can have a think about what you would like to take in to him, and I will accompany you and Thomas to your favourite department store to choose a beautiful gift. Maybe we could buy him a special blanket just from you and your brother to wrap himself up in tonight and dream of you both,' I suggested as she looked up at me and smiled.

'It's called Paterson, Laing and Bruce, Mummy, and that would be lovely. I know Daddy would appreciate a new blanket. It must get so cold in there, but he'll never admit it. I will kiss it all over before we give it to him so he will be wrapped in my love while he sleeps.' I felt a familiar lump lodge in my throat, leaving me unable to speak as I hugged her again and stroked her back.

'That's touchin', Emmy, an' I'm sure yer Daddy will treasure that blanket. How about I order us all a big breakfast so ye can be on yer way tae buy that special present? Ye can then spend the mornin' with yer father. 'Tis still very early, but I think the quicker we eat, the sooner ye'll be havin' fun with yer old man,' Hamish said soothingly. She stood and made her way to his side, hugging him tightly before kissing his cheek in greeting. Thomas slid into the chair beside Hamish, who placed his large hand comfortingly on his godson's shoulder. Thomas had been trying so hard in recent days to act like a man and be strong, masking his emotions, and I was concerned. Hamish had attempted to reassure me it was all a normal part of growing into a man and believed we should be treating Thomas as he wanted to be treated—but ever so gently.

The twins were truly blessed. Not only were they close to Catherine and Hamish, but all their Cavanaugh aunties and uncles—our brothers and sisters—who were always available to them and loved them deeply. They opened their homes every weekend for them to sleep over, allowing them to spend time with their cousins and grandparents. Whatever happened, I knew my children were loved by so many and would be supported and cared for the rest of their lives by their family. They were close in age to their ten Cavanaugh cousins, all of whom attended the village school with them. As did Willy and Bella, who they considered cousins and treated no different from the rest. Despite being aware they were not connected by blood. They had many close friends at school who lived in the village, and I was comforted in the knowledge that they were surrounded by people who cared deeply for them.

Hamish had left us to order breakfast only moments before when Polly and Angus walked in to join us. Willy and Bella immediately went to Thomas and Emmy, their voices low before deciding they needed privacy from the adults, soon retreating into Emmy's bed-chamber, where the four of them lay on the large bed deep in discussion. I watched fondly as Bessie closed their door, smiling to herself. Shaking her head at how grown up they were all becoming, she made her way into the kitchen to sit at the small table with little Mary to have tea while waiting for breakfast to be delivered.

Little Mary had found it difficult to adjust to eating at the dining table with us since we had been in Melbourne. Bessie had convinced her it was best everyone ate together, and not to concern herself with all the scaffiness that came with class and social status. Going on to explain to Mary that I didn't care about any of it, I was welcoming her to my table. Little Mary knew it would be rude to not accept and, over time, got used to sitting down to meals with us in the evening and helping herself from the large platters we would order.

She was a bundle of nerves and beside herself with worry over Aaron. The thought that her beloved babies could lose their adoring father at the age of eleven was breaking her heart. I knew if this did happen, little Mary would be there for both of them. They were so close to her and loved her like an aunty. Even though they were getting too old for a Nannie, they had insisted they still needed her around for the little things she liked to do for them. I believed they enjoyed it far more than her, if I were honest. She still liked to prepare their baths for them each night, setting out their night clothes so they could then ready themselves for bed. They were of an age now where they liked to bathe privately, which I understood, although I missed giving my children their bath at night. They had become used to sleeping with me in the few short months since Aaron was arrested, and I enjoyed them being with me.

There was a knock on the door, and Angus rose to his feet, strolling across the room to answer. Four maids soon entered pushing trolleys, the noise of them akin to the carts on the street down below, carrying platters and jugs. I watched as they set down trays of bacon, eggs cooked in several ways, and roasted tomatoes, along with mushrooms cooked in butter, sausages, and hot toast on the dining table in the other room. They put out jugs of fresh orange juice, along with freshly brewed coffee, and a large jug of hot chocolate Hamish had ordered for the children. There was also a pot of sweet, creamy porridge. and trays of fresh fruit sliced up, ready to eat.

I followed my dear friends into the dining room, Bella and Emmy, followed by Thomas and Willy, running ahead and seating themselves first, all eager to fill their empty stomachs. I sat down in between Polly and Bessie, the children's excited chatter filling the room. The mood was cheerful, all present discussing anything other than Aaron and our present situation, and I was grateful.

'How about after lunch today, I take ye all on an adventure down tae the St. Kilda foreshore? We can buy ice cream, an' watch all the passin' strangers go about their day. Ye'll even be able tae swim if yer game. It's a nice day fer spring but I doubt the water is warm. If ye want tae risk it, bring yer swimming gear, an' we'll see who's the bravest out o' the lot o' ya,' Hamish called out, and they all roared in delight.

'Are we taking the tram, Uncle Hamish? I love the trams in Melbourne. It is so much better than having to go around in a carriage. You can see everything as you pass and all the different people in the world we're yet to meet,' Emmy said cheerfully, sounding exactly like me when I was her age. She was genuinely interested in others, just as Thomas was. They loved meeting people who were different from themselves, and were fascinated by members of the Yaawangi tribe who occasionally roamed our property, sometimes staying for weeks.

These gentle souls gave not only our children, but all the children of Willow Grove, an opportunity to learn about the culture and traditions of the natives, a proud clan who had their land cruelly and brutally taken from them by force, and were still suffering and being treated worse than the pigs in our pen.

'Aye, if ye like. I'll speak with yer Aunty Catherine this mornin' while yer visitin' with yer father. I'm sure she'll want tae come along with us when she finds out there's ice cream involved,' Hamish told her, a wicked glint in his eyes, and I smiled. Catherine possessed a sweet tooth like me, and Hamish was constantly teasing her, informing her at every opportunity she would have no teeth of her own by the time she turned thirty. They had always been friends; however, since being anointed as godparents and guardians to our children, they had become even closer over the years, as had Hamish and Colin, who made all of his clothes.

'I'll be swimmin'. I'm not scared of a bit of cold water,' Willy said bravely as the others laughed.

'Aye, really? Well, me boy, I wish I was there to see it when yer balls hit the icy water an' ye shriek like a wee lass,' Angus called back, chuckling to himself.

'Da, you can't say balls at the dining table. It's very rude. Mama says she is trying to bring us up as a gentleman and lady, but you are ruining us. I heard her complaining the other day to old Mr Hinkle that you don't set a good example, despite being well bred yourself. I can't even picture it in my own head that you were once a gentleman. Or your brother sitting there beside you.' Angus and Hamish threw back their heads at the same moment, then howled with laughter. 'The last time I saw Aunt Jemima she said she was the only one in your family who turned out respectable, and if I decide I want to be brought up in the correct manner, I can live with her. She said you and Uncle Hamish have turned out to be the biggest let downs in the history of the Makenzie line. I really don't understand a lot of what she says 'cause she uses words that are very posh, and she talks like she has something stuck in her teeth. I can't even imagine how she's your sister 'cause she's so different from you. Why did you and Uncle Hamish decide to be useless disappointments?' Bella asked, Angus now bent forward and holding his stomach, tears streaming down his face, while Hamish laughed harder. I couldn't help but smile as I ate my breakfast, sipping my juice while listening to them all.

'Ah, Bella, you bring us joy with that mind God gave you. You haven't seen yer Aunt Jemima for so long now, I cannae even remember when it was. How you can repeat conversations word-for-word impresses me, you bright little darlin'. Yer Uncle Hamish an' I are disappointments to yer Grandparents 'cause we didn't choose to live our lives the way they wanted us to. I've explained to you many times before, you have to make a happy life for yerself an' not worry about what others think. You lot never have to worry about disappointin' yer parents. It doesn't matter to any of us what the four of you choose to do. We'll always love you an' have a bed in our home for you, no matter how old,' Angus told them. His words melted my heart, and I smiled lovingly at my brother-in-law as the children continued eating, talking and teasing each other—and I pushed what Richard had said this morning to the back of my mind.

I had accompanied Thomas and Emmy to Paterson, Laing and Bruce of London on the corner of Russell Street and Flinders Lane. I had shopped here since arriving in Melbourne, and had been thrilled to find once settled in Geelong they had a store there, too. In 1850, Mr John Charles Young took a chance and opened a clothing wholesale business in Geelong with only a small stock and four assistants. When gold was discovered at Ballarat in 1852, Mr Young, said to be quick to avail himself of an opportunity, opened a branch in the town and secured the services of Mr John Paterson as manager. In 1856, a large building on Russell Street was purchased and their Melbourne store was opened, and had been there ever since, much to my delight. In 1879, John Monro Bruce became a partner and by 1887 the firm was styled as Paterson, Laing and Bruce, Merchants and Soft-Goods Warehousemen, also of London.

A decade ago when shopping there with Catherine, we had been given a tour by Mr Bruce himself, taking us down to the basement of the building that was used as a receiving and despatching room for bulk packages. We were shown through the ground floor, where woollens, clothing, hats, and caps were displayed beautifully. Catherine appeared to have died and gone to heaven when escorted to the first floor—the entire level devoted to the storage of silks and silk-mixed goods of every description, along with ribbons of every hue. I much preferred the second floor filled with French and English millinery, gloves, feathers, plumes, hats, and other requisites for ladies. The third level was used as a package floor for bulk and bonded goods for trade, a stern Customs Officer always in attendance. And nothing had changed.

There were blankets made from angora, alpaca and merino wool, some so soft they felt like silk mixed with feathers to the touch. Thomas and Emmy had chosen a pale blue blanket that was thick and soft, made from Australian merino wool. They held it carefully, wrapped in a large linen bag, while I carried the basket containing Aaron's breakfast and lunch, along with food for the children to eat while we visited. We hurried through reception and stepped outside to find a carriage waiting. The driver stepped down and helped the twins in first, then taking the basket from me, assisted me up before handing the basket back and smiling warmly at us.

'Are you off to the gaol, Mrs Cavanaugh? I must warn you there are hundreds of people, possibly more, lining the streets to the gaol. Protests are going on everywhere, and the streets are in chaos. It may take us a little longer to get there, that's all,' he said kindly, and I returned his smile.

'Thank you. That will be perfectly fine,' I replied as he gently closed the carriage door. I still wasn't used to the fact that wherever I went, people recognised me and knew everything there was to know about what Maslow had done to me. I was touched that people we'd never met cared so much; however, I was getting sick of the pitiful stares and glances I received constantly. I felt people had given up hope that Aaron would live. I too had doubts at times that settled on me and clouded my mind, but I knew without doubt if anyone could survive this, and come out of it even stronger, it would be him. I sat back and relaxed as the carriage slowly made its way through the streets towards the gaol, and closer to the only man I would ever love.

The carriage came to an abrupt halt, and I gathered my things as we waited for the driver to assist us. I wouldn't normally bother anyone; however, today we had far too much to carry, and there were people surrounding the carriage. It had taken twice as long as usual to get to the gaol from the hotel, the streets overflowing with protesters the closer we came, causing the carriages, carts and trams to stop, many unable to continue their journey until they moved on. I witnessed several drivers jump down from their seats, yelling and waving their whips around as they forced people off the road.

Our driver soon came to the door, moving people away and shouting at them to step back from the carriage. He had managed to pull up directly in front of the entrance to the bluestone building, and quickly reached out to help me down. Once I had straightened my dress, I helped Thomas and Emmy, picking up the large bag that held the blanket, then passed it to them with a reassuring smile. The driver took the basket and closed the carriage door, making way for me and the twins to pass through the crowd.

'Oi, it's Abigail, Thomas, and Emmy. Look everyone. It's Abigail Cavanaugh,' someone called out and the crowd erupted in cheers, deafening me.

'Oh, you poor woman. We're all here fighting for you and your husband. We love him and our hearts are with you. He will be released. They cannot kill a man when all he did was seek justice when no one else would. Good luck, Mrs Cavanaugh, and to your sweet little ones. Give Aaron all our love,' a well-dressed lady called out. She seemed to be the one in charge of the protest currently underway, as everyone had stopped to listen to her. I thanked her as I passed and entered the gaol, the guard closing the large door behind us as they all roared and clapped outside.

We were escorted to the cell where our visits took place to find Aaron already waiting with his guard, Stuart. Once the door was closed, he removed Aaron's chains so he could embrace his children, who ran into his arms the moment he was free.

'How are you, Mrs Cavanaugh? We are all still holdin' out hope for Aaron here. I wanted you to know that. Not all of us workin' here are heartless men. You'd be surprised just how many people are on your husband's side.' He nodded sympathetically before strolling over to the door, lowering himself heavily onto the chair to read the New Idea I had brought along especially for him.

'Thank you, Stuart. You have been very kind, despite the fact we were forced to pay you to do so. Don't look at me like that. I don't hold it against you. Everyone takes opportunities where they find them. I do appreciate your kindness, and the lengths you've gone to. How you convinced the other guards to turn a blind eye to our visits, given he has someone with him from morning into the night, has been a feat in itself. One we will always be grateful to you for. I know you have been allowing visitors after I leave at night, which we appreciate more than you will ever know. I am aware we would have been restricted to seeing my husband and the children's father once a week at most if it hadn't been for you. We will never forget your kindness. I brought in some lunch for you, too. It's from the Delmont kitchen, so I hope you enjoy it. This is just to start,' I replied, taking a bowl of sliced fruit over to him, then stopping to pour him a mug full of beer before returning to my family, our privacy now ensured.

Aaron sat down heavily on the bed, the metal stretcher pushed up against the wall, the thin mattress providing no comfort at all. He gathered Thomas and Emmy in his arms and embraced them tightly before pulling them onto his lap.

'Now, it's time for a story. Do ya know that I've told ya a story every mornin' since the day ya were born? Ya were only an hour old the first time I held ya both against me chest an' told ya the fable of a pirate an' his wife who had two little nippers, an' they went sailin' around the world to find the treasure,' he roared, his fist in the air as they giggled, their heads resting against his broad chest. I sat down next to them while he told them one of his famous stories about the Min Min, one they knew by heart; however, this didn't stop them asking countless questions, which he answered in good humour before continuing.

I felt tears prick my eyes, thinking how this could be the last time they would ever hear any words from their fathers' lips, or be held by him, or hear him laugh. I watched the three of them together, and I couldn't stop the tears running down my face, his arm around my shoulders while we held our children tightly on our laps. We spoke quietly between ourselves for a time, before sitting up at the table while the twins stayed on the bed, drawing pictures for Aaron and writing letters to him with the paper and pencils I had provided him with. They had also allowed me to bring Aaron ink and a quill, enabling him to write letters in his own hand to all the people who were important—those he loved without measure, along with others who had made a difference in his life, no matter how small.

I placed his porridge in front of him while I poured him a fresh apple juice, then took out his omelette that was wrapped on a large plate. I unwrapped another filled with fried bacon, eggs, tomatoes and mushrooms and placed it down in front of him. He had already started to eat, and I was confident he would finish the lot given time. I reached back into the basket and took out a plate containing another omelette, along with bacon, tomatoes and mushrooms. I walked over to Stuart and handed it to him, along with solid silver cutlery, a linen napkin and a glass of juice.

'Thank you very much, Mrs Cavanaugh. It's more than decent of you. I hope there is no outstandin' business between us that you would feel the need to poison me food.' His eyes twinkled in amusement, a smile touching his lips as he took the plate from me and placed it on the small table beside him. I smothered a smile as I returned to Aaron, who appeared deep in thought.

'I need to speak to you, my love. Richard advised me this morning that he believes you need to say your goodbyes to the children today, just on the slight chance your appeal fails.' I felt my heart break once again as tears stung my eyes. We had tried to avoid all talk of failure with them, choosing to focus on a positive outcome and keep their spirits up.

'I think he's right, Abi. I'd hate to leave this world without sayin' the things I need to say to them. I've been thinkin' a great deal about this, an' been preparin' meself if it comes to this. I've written me letters to everyone, includin' you, mo anamchara, tellin' them all what they've meant to me, an' me dreams for them for the future. It doesn't mean I've lost hope, so don't look at me that way, Abi. It's just that I wanna be prepared. Just in case.' I nodded sadly, my hand clasped tightly in his across the table, the twins paying us no mind as they lay side-by-side drawing.

We spent the morning surrounded by our beloved children, talking about their memories they had of their lives with us as their parents during the short time they'd been here. We laughed until our faces hurt, and shed tears at others, while we cuddled together on the rickety bed. They gave their father his new blanket, which thrilled him. He gave them his word he would go to sleep tonight wrapped up in it, thanking them for their thoughtfulness. Emmy did as she promised and kissed the blanket all over as Aaron watched her, his eyes twinkling in amusement, while filled with tears of sorrow at the thought of parting from them so soon. Even Thomas kissed the blanket several times, causing the tears to spill over and slide down his handsome cheeks. The morning had passed far too quickly, and It was time for us to leave so Aaron could have his lunch and see other members of his family. I felt his body tense as he pulled Thomas and Emmy into his strong arms and sat them on his lap.

'Now, I have somethin' very serious to talk to you both about.' He gazed into their eyes, holding them close to his chest just as he had done every day since they took their first breath. 'Do ya remember the times we talked about what happens when animals an' people's bodies die?' They nodded, both silent as they waited for him to continue. He swallowed several times, then ran his fingers over their faces, committing everything to memory. 'An' how their soul, which is ya heart an' ya mind filled with all that ya love combined into one, goes to a better place where they're happy all the time? There comes a time when everythin' must die one day.' They nodded their heads, staring back into his beautiful blue eyes, so much like the ocean on a sunny day.

'Yeah. Michael's Grandma died the winter just gone, an' he told me she was in heaven with the angels,' Thomas replied as he touched his father's face gently, tracing the outline of his eyes.

'Yeah, well, it's my turn to go there. I want ya to know that wherever I am, I'll be lookin' after ya, an' I'll watch ya grow. Ya just won't be able to see me anymore.' Tears filled his eyes as he kissed them, holding them tighter before realising Emmy couldn't breathe, and he quickly loosened his grip.

'Why do you want to go to that place away from us, Daddy? Isn't Willow Grove a happy place? Why do you need a better one? Don't you love us anymore?' Emmy asked, her lip quivering.

'Of course I do, Emmy. I love Mummy, you an' Thomas with all me heart. You're the most important people in the world to me. I'd do anythin' to stay with ya, but Daddy doesn't have a choice. If I'd only one wish in this world, it'd be that I am together with ya all forever. Ya must remember that. I'll be with ya always, 'cause inside each of you is a very big part of me that'll never die.' He pointed to his own heart before placing a hand on theirs. I sat beside him watching, silently choking on tears I knew would never stop. My heart ached as I looked at my beautiful man trying to say goodbye to his children. I took a silent photograph of the three of them together in my mind for the last time so I would always remember this moment.

'Are the coppers gunna kill ya, Daddy?' Thomas asked quietly, his face darkening. We had tried to protect them from the graphic details of Aaron's case, particularly since he had gone to trial and all the sordid details had been revealed. Unfortunately, they were of an age where they were completely aware of their surroundings, and could pick up a newspaper and read it anyway. We had done our best and told them the truth about what had happened to me, and what Aaron had done to Maslow.

'Yeah, Thomas, they are, an' I'm sorry for it. I want ya both to know I loved ya from the time you were in ya Mummy's belly, long before I ever saw ya. I used to touch ya an' talk to ya before ya were even born, pokin' ya to wake ya up so ya would kick me hand. We didn't know then there were two of ya in there. When I saw ya both for the first time, I felt like the luckiest bloke alive to be ya father. I'd never experienced such instant love for anythin' in me life like I did when I saw ya, other than the day I met ya mother. Ya were so tiny an' precious, an' I couldn't believe ya were mine. I fell in love with ya that day, an' every day since, me love for ya has grown even more, somethin' I thought impossible. All I ever wanted was for ya both to be happy an' have wonderful lives full of love an' laughter, an' I know for certain that's what you'll have. You're the most beautiful souls I've ever had the pleasure of knowin' an' lovin'. It doesn't matter what happens now, as long as ya know I'll always be ya Daddy, even when me feet no longer walk on the red soil of Willow Grove, an' me bones rest beneath it. I know me soul will find ya both again. You'll only have to think of me, an' I'll be by ya side. Ya may not see me, but I'll make sure ya know I'm there. Ya may feel a soft touch or a slight breeze on ya face when the air is still. or find a feather blowin' by unexpectedly that touches ya face. That'll be me kissin' ya, me darlin' nippers. I know you'll both grow into wonderful people 'cause ya have ya Mummy here to love an' guide ya like she does. When ya think of me, remember how much I love ya an' all the memories we made. I'll always be proud of ya, whatever choices ya make in ya lives.' His voice broke as tears poured down his face. He held Thomas and Emmy fiercely to his chest, and they clung to him, sobbing inconsolably.

'We don't want you to die, Daddy. We need you with us. Who is going to look after Mummy? You have always looked after her even when she gets into trouble with Uncle Leo. Without you there to stop them, he will kill her one day. I need you to stay, Daddy. Nothing will be alright without you here,' Emmy sobbed as Aaron broke down again and cried out in anguish.

'I know, sweetheart. I don't wanna leave ya either. I want ya both to listen to me an' always remember what I have said to ya not only to-day, but every day we've spent together. You've made me the happiest man in the world havin' two beautiful children like you to call me own. I've had the best life a bloke could have with ya Grandparent's an' Uncles, an' then when I grew to be a man, ya Mother an' both of you. I'll take that love an' happiness with me. That part of someone never dies. I hope you'll remember me often as you grow, an' know I'll be around ya, even though that's hard to believe. I'll be lookin' after ya brothers, Jack an' Harrison, as they need me now. I'll find some way to show ya I'm all right. I promise ya, an' ya know I never break a promise. Live ya lives exactly how ya want to. Always be kind an' generous to those around ya an' always, always be honest. If you stick to those few things, you'll always be happy, me darlin's. I love ya to the moon an' back a million-times.' He made no attempt to hide his tears, holding them in his arms as they continued to cling to him, crying hysterically.

Another guard entered the room and spoke quietly with Stuart, before he turned to tell us our time was up. He saw the children crying, and pity flashed in his eyes for a moment before he glanced across at Stuart, who looked as if he too would break down.

'Just a few more minutes, then you will have to leave, Mrs Cavanaugh. As you know, we allow you as much time as we are able, but it's coming up time for lunch now. I'm not trying to be callous, but you're able to come back this afternoon and stay until tea. We are trying our best to be accommodating,' the guard told us, and I nodded as I wiped my tear-stained face.

'We know ya are, an' we thank ya for it an' how you've treated me an' me family. It was kind of ya to allow me wife to arrange dinner for every prisoner here from the Delmont kitchens. They enjoyed it very much, just as I did. You've been more than accommodatin', an' we thank ya for the extra few minutes you're providin' us,' Aaron said politely as I wiped the tears from his face with a clean handkerchief, the bright yellow and brown honey bees embroidered on the fine white linen standing out against his ashen face. The guard nodded politely before turning on his heel and walking out, leaving Stuart staring at us sympathetically.

Thomas sat quietly with his arms around his father's neck and his face buried into him as he silently cried, while Emmy was becoming hysterical.

'Don't they know you're our Daddy and we need you here? Let me talk to them and change their minds. I hate the police, and I am going to hate them forever for taking my Daddy from me. Fucking pig bastards,' she screamed, her voice piercing not only my ears but my heart. She clung to him, her face bright red as she released all her fury, lashing out. Aaron sobbed unashamedly now as he held them against his chest for one last time, while he stared at me with such deep sadness I too burst into tears, despite my efforts to stay strong for our children. The officer entered again and waited at the door, while Aaron rose gracefully to his feet, Thomas in one arm and Emmy in the other.

'I love ya, Daddy, an' thank ya for bein' the best father anyone could have. I'll never forget one minute of the time we had together. I'll be as strong as I can be an' look after Mummy, but I know I'll cry every night for ya, an' will always miss ya 'till the day I die meself. I want to be exactly the kind of man you are. You've taught me everythin' an' I know everyone thinks I'm still a bairn, but I'm not, Daddy. I know what's goin' to happen to ya, an' if I could kill them coppers an' that Maslow meself, I would. I'll wait for a sign from ya to tell me you're safe, 'cause I believe ya when ya say you'll be around us. I promise, I'll make ya proud of me, Daddy,' Thomas said, kissing him as Aaron broke down again, sobbing loudly. He held his son in his arms as Emmy clung to his side, his body shaking as he kissed and touched them for what would be the last time if the police got their way. I moved over to them and stood for the last time as a family, hugging the three of them as I sobbed.

'You really must go now,' the officer reminded us gently. Aaron took Thomas on his knee and whispered in his ear for a few minutes, his voice so low, I couldn't hear a word that passed between them. He then did the same to Emmy, cradling her on his lap as he spoke quietly in her ear. I watched her face as she silently cried while listening intently to him. He took them both in his arms for a final time, kissing them all over their faces. He placed Thomas down on his feet, and I took his hand, pulling my darling son into my arms and kissing the top of his head. Aaron tried to put Emmy down, but she held him tightly, screaming and begging him to stay, while he looked at me then shrugged his broad shoulders helplessly.

'Come on, sweetheart, we must leave now,' I said gently, prying her from her father's arms to the sounds of her violent shrieks.

'I'll see ya later today, mo anamchara,' Aaron murmured as I kissed him goodbye. I carried Emmy towards the door as she struggled against me, trying to get back to her father. Thomas kissed his Daddy one last time, turning to thump him on the back, causing Aaron to break down again as he returned the favour and thumped his son on the back in farewell. He stood at the door watching us walk away, and as we rounded the corner, I heard a strangled sob from the man I would love for an eternity as they closed the door behind us.

Chapter Fourteen

THE DRIVER FROM THE Delmont was waiting for me exactly where I had left him, and I wondered if he had even bothered to return to the hotel during this time. The carriage was surrounded by protesters, some holding candles and praying for Aaron's soul, while others were angry and looking for trouble. I made my way through the crowd as the driver went before me, creating a clear path as he waved his stock-whip around, shouting for people to move. Emmy was screaming at the top of her lungs and lashing out as Thomas walked bravely beside me, his head lowered. A man with a large camera took several photographs of us as we struggled through the crowd, finally arriving at the carriage. I placed Emmy up inside and climbed up behind her, trying to calm her while Thomas got in after us, closing the door. I kept my eye on him as he sat next to me, his head pressed against my upper arm. I wrapped my arm around him in an attempt to comfort him, while holding Emmy on my lap with the other.

'I want my Daddy! I need him here alive with us! Not in some heavenly place! Make the driver take us back to the gaol! I will go inside and bring him out myself!' I held her to my chest, her shrieks piercing my ears, and shredding my heart into pieces. I embraced them both tightly as the carriage turned into Swanston Street, Thomas burying his head deeper into my side crying silently, while Emmy's screaming turned to shrieks of desperation, her attempts to break free of me so she could jump out and run back to her father becoming increasingly violent.

The carriage turned into the driveway of the hotel, and within moments stopped outside the front doors. Thomas wiped his face with my handkerchief before climbing down, leaving me to struggle with Emmy, still screaming hysterically as she tried to kick me. People had stopped in the street, some scowling at me as if I were trying to kill the poor child. I fought against the urge to scream, and fought even harder not to snarl at these strangers standing around watching as if they were at the theatre reviewing a play. Emmy had more right to scream than anyone I knew. She was doing exactly what I myself felt like doing. I managed to lift her down from the carriage, holding her against my chest, her tiny body shaking. I stood outside the hotel, our driver nowhere to be found as people started gathering around us, blocking our path to the door.

'Oh, my goodness. It's that poor Abigail Cavanaugh. You know, her husband is Aaron? The one who is being strung up tomorrow at the gaol? Jesus, Nigel, you don't notice a thing. Sometimes I wonder if that brain of yours retains anything at all. It's been all over the papers for months. Look at the poor woman trying to console that little red-haired angel. She must have seen her father for the last time today. Oh, does it not just break your heart. Taking a man like that away from his family when all he did was try and protect his poor wife. I believe what the papers are saying, and that something corrupt is going on. The punishment doesn't fit the crime, and the most he should have got was a few months hard labour in Pentridge for taking the law into his own hands. Someone up high wants the man dead is all I can say,' a well dressed woman informed her husband, and he nodded before turning towards the sound of heavy footsteps running towards us. Within moments, I saw Hamish step through the crowd, his jaw set as he approached us, pushing several people out of his way without a backward glance or apology.

'Shhh, little one. Calm yerself or ye'll be sick.' His voice soothing, Hamish took her from my arms, placing her head on his shoulder, his large hand stroking her tear-stained face. 'I was two doors down buyin' ye some sweeties, an' could hear ye from there.' She clung to him like a wee koala to its mother, burying her head into his chest as she sobbed and screamed for her father, his hand now stroking her back. 'Naw matter what happens, Emmy, an' life knocks ya down as it so often does, I'll always be around tae pick ya back up an' set ye on yer feet.' He turned, growling at several people to back up, while Thomas stood at his side staring up at him, his hand on his godfather's sleeve. He tugged several times to get his attention, his eyes so much like his father's.

'Uncle Hamish, the coppers are gunna kill our Daddy. Please, ya have to stop 'em. Remember when ya said you'd do anythin' for us? If ya do this, we'll never ask another favour of ya as long as we live.' Hamish glanced across at me, unable to speak as tears filled his eyes. Emmy's screams were all I could hear; however, she had stopped thrashing about, much to my relief. Hamish bent down, Emmy still clinging to him, and murmured in Thomas's ear for the longest time. Placing his large hand on his godson's small shoulder, Thomas nodded as he listened intently, the tears he couldn't stop now drying up. I held the back of Hamish's coat as he pushed through the crowd, many backing away when they saw the size of him, Thomas still close by his side.

'You must stop them, Uncle Hamish! You must! We will die without our Daddy! We will die!'

'Shhh, wee Emmy. Let's take ye up tae yer room tae see Mary. Ye can have a warm bath an' somethin' tae eat. That should help tae settle ye down a wee bit. If ye still want tae go tae St. Kilda on the tram, then me an' yer Aunty Catherine will take ye. An' Thomas, along with yer cousins. I'll even let ye all have chocolate, as well as the ice cream I promised.' He carried her into the hotel, stroking the back of her head as she sobbed into his chest. I followed behind, holding my brave boy's hand. We walked through reception, a number of guests stopping to stare, recognising us from the papers. I had no doubt the picture that had been taken this morning would be in The Sun tomorrow.

We stepped into the suite to find Bessie and little Mary waiting for us. Bessie gasped aloud when she saw the state of me and the children, hurrying off to make a pot of tea, while little Mary ran a bath for Emmy, still sobbing in Hamish's arms.

'Mummy, I'm gunna go an' lie down for a while in ya bed. I need some time to meself to think about what Daddy told me. He can talk the leg off a chair, an' said a lot, an' I don't wanna forget a word of it. I'd be all right about ya comin' in later if ya needed me to hug ya, 'cause I know ya just as sad as I am.' Thomas embraced me, then Hamish, before making his way to my bedchamber. He was such a beautiful boy. I understood exactly what he meant, and I would go and hold him as soon as Emmy was settled. Little Mary came and took Emmy, who was starting to calm a little, from Hamish's arms. She buried her face into little Mary's shoulder as she carried her to the bathroom, murmuring soothingly before closing the door behind them.

'Abigail, that was the most heartbreakin' experience o' me life.' He sniffed loudly, then hung his head and cried.

I was seated comfortably at the small dining table, eating my lunch with Jenny. I had told her about this morning, and how Aaron had seen the children for what could be the last time. She had cried and cried, so broken-hearted for me and the children, her pain obvious when she told me she would do anything in the world to make all this go away. Jenny was a wonderful friend, and had supported me in every way since Aaron was taken into custody. The fact she hadn't left my side since my arrival in Melbourne had shown me just how deeply she cared, and I valued our friendship just as much. Under no circumstances would she have considered leaving her kitchen for this amount of time, always very protective over her work area. She held my hand in hers, speaking words of encouragement, when Richard walked in. He sat down heavily on the seat next to mine, exhaling loudly.

'Where are Thomas and Emmy? Has Mary taken them out somewhere?' he enquired, pausing as I chewed the steak in my mouth, finding it hard to swallow.

'No.' I took a sip of water before continuing. 'They've gone to the St. Kilda foreshore with Hamish and Catherine. They only just left,' I explained, and he nodded.

'I bring news with me, Abigail, and none of it is good. Certainly not what any of us want to hear. The Executive Council met this morning for the fourth time, and decided for the fourth time, unanimously, that the law should take its course. I'm so sorry, Abigail, but there are no further options available to us. Not legally, anyway. We now must accept Aaron's fate. He will hang in the morning.' His voice faltered as Jenny gasped, then closed her eyes in silent prayer. Richard leaned forward and placed his head in his hands, his body shaking as he silently sobbed. I remained where I was, motionless, my heart in my throat. He couldn't be right. All along I knew there was the possibility Aaron may not be pardoned; however, not for a moment did I actually expect he would be murdered by the government of Victoria. I always believed he would come through in the end as he usually did—victorious in every difficult situation he had ever faced in his life. I felt the blood drain from my face as the reality of Richard's words started to sink in. I would be a widow, and my children fatherless. I couldn't imagine my life without him by my side. Taking a deep breath, I summoned all the strength left in me, and pushed it to the back of my mind.

'Surely there has to be some way, Richard. If you can't win this legally, then find a way to get him out illegally. I don't care who you have to bribe, or how much it costs. I would give every penny I have. Please go and find some way to save him,' I said before lowering my head and bursting into tears. Jenny hurried to my side and placed her hands on my shoulders, helping me to my feet, then guiding me to the sitting room while Richard followed, unable to stop the tears spilling down his handsome face. I sat down beside Jenny, moving over slightly so Richard could join us.

'I'm more than sorry I failed you. I was certain the sentence would at least be commuted to a prison term, as was everyone else. I don't know one legal expert who doesn't believe Aaron's case was tainted somehow and filled with police corruption. I plan to spend the rest of the day at The Melbourne Club in Collins Street to see what I can find out. Since we have been here, I have made some excellent contacts in the legal profession, as well as amongst the police. I've become friendly with several Detectives recently, who are kind enough to tell me what goes on behind closed doors. They would know the chaff from the wheat, along with the best person to approach who is open to a bit of quid pro quo.' I turned and embraced him, relief washing over me.

'Thank you, dear Richard. You have my consent to give it all away if someone is willing and able to save him from the gallows.' Tears streamed down my cheeks, but I no longer noticed, or cared. Deep inside I knew it was over. There was no one left to bribe, no court willing to hear another appeal, and no matter how much money we had, I was powerless and unable to save my beloved Aaron. He was going to die, and I was the cause of it. If I hadn't told him what Maslow had done to me, we would still be happily living together as a family at Willow Grove, getting on with the wonderful life we had been blessed with. Instead, we were here in Melbourne, waiting, while knowing every minute that passed brought my love closer to taking his final breath here on this earth.

Aaron had been able to say his final goodbyes to his family and our friends over the past few days, and I would now be the last he would see of those he loved when I returned to the gaol after lunch. I wiped my face and straightened myself up before walking back to the dining table, slowly lowering myself down onto the chair to finish my lunch, much to Richard and Jenny's surprise. I glanced over at them through the arched doorway as I bit into a roasted potato.

'I know you all are expecting me to fall apart, and believe me, I feel like I am on the inside. I have two children who are relying on me to be strong, and. I can't go and see Aaron if I'm crying and fashing. It would make him feel even worse than he already does.' Jenny smiled as she made her way across the room to finish her own lunch, taking the seat beside me.

'You're being extremely brave. I don't know how I'd be if it was my Harry. He'll be devastated, as he's great mates with your Aaron. Please do not lose all hope, my dear, dear friend. You never know what Richard may find out later today.' I nodded as she turned to Richard, pulling his chair in opposite me before making himself comfortable. 'Does Aaron know about the decision?' My eyes widened, my head snapping up to stare at him, my heart racing. I hadn't thought to ask if Aaron did know, or how he was coping if he did, and felt an enormous wave of guilt wash over me.

'Yes, he knows. I've come straight from the gaol. There are so many people on the street, and now news of the appeal being rejected will spread like a bushfire at Hanging Rock. I have no doubt there will be violence between the protesters and police. The tension is palpable when you're walking amongst them. Only a spark is all it will take for a firestorm to erupt that will be impossible to put out once burning.' I nodded, attempting to hide my frustration with him as I chewed my tender eye fillet, cooked to perfection.

'Please tell me how Aaron reacted to the news. Is he all right in himself?' I asked, wiping tears from my face again with a fresh handkerchief, one of many I kept close these days.

'Yes, Abigail. He is taking this better than you or me. Aaron has accepted his fate and feels he has prepared himself. He told me he said goodbye to the children this morning, and for that alone, he is grateful. Devastated at the thought of leaving you alone to raise the children, though, and that is his only concern now. He isn't frightened to die, but he is suffering at the thought of being parted from you.' His voice faltered as I burst into tears again.

Bloody man. He should have thought about that before slicing off Maslow's equipment. He wouldn't have though, would he? He was raised to protect what he loved and had formed his own beliefs as he grew regarding revenge,and meting out his own justice to anyone who threatened or harmed those he loved. He wouldn't have given it a second thought at the time, or even considered he could end up being taken from us forever, only wanting to punish Maslow in the same way he had harmed me. It didn't change my love for him, despite often wishing he weren't so quick to seek vengeance, and in such a brutal way. He hadn't thought twice about killing Leroy all those years ago. Or beating George until his bones were broken. I knew Aaron better than anyone, and understood him even better than that. I would never resent him for what he had done, knowing always that he only did it for me out of love—despite the consequences.

I sat at my dressing table staring into the looking glass while Bessie silently styled my hair. She had been crying since finding out Aaron's appeal had been rejected. Assisting me to dress earlier, she now fussed about unnecessarily with my hair, taking the longest time.

'I just wanted to say I'm more than sorry for it. Not for a minute did I think the law would go through with killing him.' She paused for a moment, her cheeks now matching the colour of her swollen, red-rimmed eyes. 'I know I must be strong for you and the bairns, but it's hit me like a ton of bricks, as they say. I don't have any words left, other than to say my heart is breaking for you, Mistress—and I'm not talking to the heavenly Father, Jesus, or Mary and Joseph at the moment. They've ignored me and failed to hear our prayers, and I'm furious with them and their angels,' she called out angrily to the ceiling as she finished my hair, touching me on the back of the head. I stood and embraced her.

'I do not know what to say anymore myself, Bessie. The emotions we are all feeling must be normal in these circumstances. I don't really know how I am meant to feel or behave as I have never had the threat of my husband being killed and losing him forever to face.' She nodded sadly, watching me bend down and pick up my handbag from the dressing table before bidding me farewell as I turned to make my way downstairs. The basket I ordered last night was waiting for me at reception, the staff smiling as they greeted me, all maintaining a cheerful demeanor despite their sympathetic glances. I thanked them before making my way out to the carriage, avoiding eye contact with the guests standing around in reception. The Delmont driver helped me up, then handed the basket to me with a gentle smile and a reassuring nod. I was no longer required to advise the drivers of where I was going. They all knew.

Placing the heavy basket down beside me, I closed my eyes for a moment, resting my head back against the seat. I had ensured the Delmont chef prepared his favourite food, and included several large desserts, along with a bottle of the finest whisky I could find, several bottles of beer and wine. Leo had given me a bottle of lemonade he made especially for his Goliath, taking over the Delmon kitchen for an hour yesterday, much to the staff's chagrin. The whisky was for Aaron to drink tonight before he went to bed. I doubted very much he would sleep, knowing the man as I did, and all that knew and loved him were well aware how much he enjoyed his whisky. He would need it tonight, I thought, as I tried to swallow the lump lodged in my throat.

The carriage stopped in front of the dreary bluestone building in Russell Street, a large crowd starting to form around the gaol and surrounding streets. I had never witnessed so many people together in one place, some holding signs and loudly demanding to be heard, while others knelt on the ground praying quietly for Aaron. It touched my heart how many people, all strangers to us, had made an effort to support him like they had. He was all every man, woman and child in Australia could talk about at the moment. I knew there was interest from countries far and wide as I had started to get letters from people around the world, the support from Ireland and Scotland strong given they viewed him as one of their own.

I followed the driver to the main entrance, impressed by his strength as he roughly pushed several people out of the way who were calling out to me. I knew they were only being kind; however, the drivers from the Delmont were sick of trying to get me in and out of the gaol safely without their disruption. He left me inside the front door of the gaol to return to his carriage, now surrounded by a large mob. I turned back to watch them patting the horses and touching the luxurious exterior of the carriage, enraging him. He pulled out his stock-whip and I turned back to the door, a smile touching my lips, his roars filling my ears as the door closed behind me.

A senior guard, Bill, a kindly man of advanced years, accompanied me to the cell they allocated to supervise the prisoners' visits, a room I had unfortunately come to know well, where Aaron waited with his guard, Stuart. His face lit up when he saw me standing in the doorway, and he stretched his arms out wide ready to embrace me. They didn't bother keeping him in chains anymore, and hadn't for weeks. I had insisted on wearing the dress I wore the first time I met him, all those years ago. He had asked me to come for this last visit alone, sending word through Richard today, saying there were things unsaid between us.

He stood, and I ran into his arms and tight embrace, his passionate kiss on my lips. He led me over to the rickety bed and we made ourselves comfortable, his face close to mine as he wrapped his arms around me and whispered his secrets in my ear. Stuart ignored us, pretending we were not in the room as he read the New Idea I had brought him recently, kindly trying to give us some privacy in a place where there was none. We lay together for hours talking of all the memories we had made together, and how blessed we were to have found each other in such a big world. Our joy, our sorrow, our life, yet no talk of the future. We laughed, and cried often, as the hours passed far too quickly.

The light was starting to dim outside when I rose to my feet to pour us both a glass of wine. He joined me at the table, then lowered himself down onto the chair, picked up his glass and drank the entire thing without taking a breath. I poured him another as he sat me on his knee, then turned me around to face him. He placed his finger under my chin, tilting my face up towards his own to stare into my eyes.

'My business here is nearly done. Except for you. Once that's been sorted, I can die in peace.' I started to cry, burying my face in his neck as I held him tightly by his enormous shoulders.

'What business? I don't know what you mean?' I said through my tears, placing my cheek against his.

'Well, mo anamchara, the first is this.' He reached into his pocket and pulled out my golden locket he had given me as a wedding gift. I had never taken it off in all those years; however, it had gone missing a few weeks ago after I had left it on the handbasin after bathing one evening. I hadn't wanted to tell him I had lost it, and here he was with it in his hand.

'How did you get it?' My eyes widened as he held it up so I could look closely.

'I asked Bessie to take it to Colin Dawson to have six small diamonds embedded into the gold. They represent us and our four children. I want you to wear it, Abi, with all my love. Never forget what we had or how much I adore you. Or the memories we made.

Hold all of it close to your heart, just as I will.' He placed the locket around my neck as I sobbed, louder now. I pushed myself deeper into his lap, my arms tightly around his neck as I screamed into his chest while he stroked my back. 'Now, I want ya to listen to me now, mo anamchara. There's nothin' left unspoken between us and what we feel for each other, but there are things we need to discuss. It's very important ya listen to me now, Abigail. Ya need to stay strong an' calm yaself, just so I know you've heard what I have to say.' He stroked my head soothingly, patiently waiting for my screams to subside. I lifted my head, feeling my heart would explode into a million pieces.

'I cannot talk of you dying. I cannot and will not accept they will murder you tomorrow, or consider a life without you in it.' I sniffed loudly before blowing my nose into my handkerchief, aware Stuart was staring across at me with pity in his eyes. He averted his gaze when Aaron smiled weakly back at him, tears in his eyes.

'I know you'll grieve me deeply, an' that's acceptable for a time. I'd be offended if ya didn't, to tell ya the truth, but ya then need to stop an' let me go. I want ya to move on an' live the life ya deserve an' are here on this earth to live. An' be happy. Just as ya were with me.' He gently stroked my face, a loud hiccup emerging from my lips without warning.

'I will never be happy again without you by my side.' I lowered my head and burst into tears, my body trembling as he held me close.

'Abi, look at me. You're young an' beautiful, an' there will come a time when you're ready to love again—an' be loved. There's only one man who'll love ya as much as I do, an' treat ya how ya deserve to be treated, an' that's Hamish. There's no other bloke on this earth who loves our nippers as much as he does, other than us, of course. He's still deeply in love with ya, an' he's never stopped lovin' ya, an' I know he'll take care of the three of ya, just as I would if able to stay. There are goin' to be many eligible blokes tryin' to court ya once I'm gone, somethin' I don't think ya realise,' he murmured, his large hands around my waist as I stared up into his eyes, the colour of the ocean on a bright day.

'I cannot and will not consider this ridiculous request, Aaron. I will never love anyone other than you. Hamish and I will never be more than friends because I'm not in love with him. Simple as that. After being loved by you so well, there is no one else who could stand in your place.' Tears continued to slide down my face, no longer noticed by either of us as I lowered my head onto his shoulder and sobbed.

'Promise me you'll give him a chance when the time comes. He's like a brother to me, an' I trust him completely in every way an' with everythin' I have, includin' you, mo anamchara.' He lifted my face to his and kissed the tears from my cheeks, while I stroked his brow with my fingers, committing to memory every detail.

'Aaron, please stop. This feels no different from when Aunt Isabelle arranged for us to be betrothed, and you were chosen for me without my consent.' I continued to cry as he placed my face between his enormous hands.

'And look how that turned out, me beautiful girl. I've enjoyed thirteen-years of pure happiness with ya by me side. Me life has been better than I ever could have imagined, an' if I was asked to swap those years for a full life without ya, I'd choose what I've been given an' not change a bloody thing.' He leaned forward and placed his lips on mine, our tears mingling together. 'Remember when we spent New Year's Eve at Heavenly Hideaway, an' ya asked me what I wanted for the twentieth century?' I nodded, feeling utterly and completely miserable. 'I told ya I wished that when the day should come for us to part, we would be as happy as we were then. Well, I'm happier havin' been with ya than I've ever been, an' we part with deep love between us, but with such love comes deep sorrow when it ends, me darlin' girl.' I watched a tear slowly slide down his face, and I raised my hand to rub it away with my thumb.

'This is unfair, and not just on me. I will not be able to go on without you, Aaron. You are my life, and the only man I will ever love. My heart belongs to you whether you are here or wherever you go when you die. I know in my heart the soul lives on; however, I don't know where it goes. I have always been taught that if you are a good catholic, then you go to heaven, but I don't know if I believe that part. A God of love wouldn't send a good person to hell just because they didn't go to church on a Sunday. It doesn't make sense to me, but I do know wherever you are going, it will be beautiful and you will be happy. Deep within me somehow, but don't understand why; I have such complete faith there is a place where your soul is taken soon after you die. I have dreamt of it, and cannot describe the place in words, it's so glorious. How I knew it was heaven, I do not know or understand, but I did and it was. There were people there who knew me, and they had the same golden aura you have, only I couldn't recognise them. They had bodies no different to ours, and they ate and drank a great deal, only they didn't have to prepare any of it.' He threw back his head and laughed, a smile touching my own lips.

'No different from you back home, mo anamchara.' I kissed his cheek, grateful he could still feel joy under the circumstances.

'They really were strange, not the usual dreams that wander through my mind without warning. There were many things in that place I have never seen, and didn't understand. It was a planet, no different from this, only so far away that man could never reach it, despite your science fiction stories of steel ships flying to the moon and other planets in the solar system.' I smiled at him, his grin widening as he brushed away his tears with the back of his hand.

'When did ya have this dream? I've never heard ya talk of anythin' like this before.'

'Once after Maslow told me all that scaffy about past lives, and again just the other night. It was the same place I saw the first time, and even then I felt I had been there before. I was comfortable there, even in my dream I explored the place, and the one mountain over-shadowing the sea, and spoke to the souls who chose to remain there. They told me once you die, you can choose to stay on this planet or reincarnate back here. A young man who was familiar, although I couldn't place him, told me the majority chose to stay there because it is so wonderful. All they know is love and pure peace, from what he said, and what I saw with my own eyes confirmed it. The only ones who do come back apparently have unfinished business they must resolve. I'm of the firm opinion Maslow got into my head and now my imagination has run wild. Maybe Leo's right and you should have signed me into Ararat years ago when you had the chance. I've confirmed everything he's ever said about my stability with that dream, and I'm now officially a lunatic.' He chuckled again as I tried to smile.

'Maybe, maybe not. I'd like to think there's a place like that where I'll be goin'. I'll make sure wherever I end up, Abi, I'll come back an' give ya a sign to ease ya mind an' let ya know I'm all right. I dunno how 'cause I'm not a spiritual person, but I'm baptised, an' that should help. I dunno what I believe, but I'll find a way back to ya an' the nippers. I know ya haven't accepted any of it yet, but I have, me darlin' girl. You've done everythin' ya could to save me. I know it's selfish of me, but I don't regret attackin' him for a moment after what he made ya endure. He murdered our children, an' I was obligated to seek vengeance on behalf of all of ya. I'm sorry for what I'm about to put ya through, mo anamchara. I know me death will hit ya hard. We've been side-by-side for nearly thirteen-years now, confidin' everythin' in each other. You're me best friend, an' I love ya with every part of me bein'. As I was tryin' to say to ya before, I need to know you'll be happy again in the future. That ya must promise me. You're too lovely to sleep alone, Abi. You're not betrayin' me in the future when ya do take another man to ya bed. I want ya to listen to me about Hamish. I know how much he still loves ya, even if he won't admit it, even to himself. He's the one that'll make ya happy again one day. I want ya to promise me you'll give him a chance when that time comes, Abi. I'm being very serious. I don't want just any bloke around ya or me nippers. It must be someone I trust an' respect. If ya wanna make me happy, you'll consider what I'm sayin' seriously instead of dismissin' me. That's what I want. That is me dyin' wish, mo anamchara. When you're ready to love again, I want ya to give Hamish a chance.' He held my face between his hands, staring down into my eyes as I shook my head, wrinkling my nose then jutting out my chin.

'How can you ask such a thing? No. I cannot promise you that, and I will never be ready to love again. How could I when my heart is filled with only you? You have been my husband and best friend for so long now, there is no one else for me. I cannot consider replacing you, because you are irreplaceable to me. I will not survive without you by my side. I certainly do not wish to be with anyone else, including Hamish, despite how much I care for him as our friend. That's all it will ever be, Aaron. Friendship. I know he will be there to support us once you're gone, and that is enough.' I broke down again as he held me to his chest and stroked my hair.

'There's one more thing. I want ya to take the voyage we always planned for your birthday. Go with the nippers, an' take Hamish as ya friend, only if ya wish. Ya must promise me you'll go an' see all the things we talked about with Thomas an' little Emmy. Promise me you'll take Hamish as ya escort, even if ya won't consider anythin' more than friendship. At least I know you'll be safe walkin' the streets of London, Paris an' New York with him as ya chaperone. I want ya to give me ya word on this, Abi.' I nodded once, only slightly as he stared down into my eyes, a smile touching his lips.

'Fine, I will promise you that. I won't let the children down, and I am comfortable with Hamish accompanying us. I'm only twenty-seven, Aaron. I have years to think about it. It's the last thing on my mind at this moment.' I shook my head in irrigation, wanting to speak of other things.

'Abi, ya turn twenty-eight in just over three-months. Ya have two-years to prepare for this journey, an' now I have ya word it's eased me mind.' He took me in his arms before kissing my lips'; however, I soon pulled away, tears streaming down my face.

'Aaron, I don't think I can do this. I cannot live my life without you in it.' I sobbed as I clung to him, the warmth of his body heating my own, while trying to stop a thousand thoughts, none of them good, racing through my head, reminding me come tomorrow, he would be stone cold and gone forever.

'You're strong, Abi, an' ya have a lot of people around who love ya an' the nippers, so ya have no other choice but to go on, mo anamchara. It would bring me great comfort to know before I die you'll eventually move on an' find happiness again. I know if I don't make ya promise, you'll grieve me 'till the day you yourself go to God.'

'I cannot look at Hamish in that way, Aaron. What we had all those years ago is gone, replaced by friendship. There will never be more than that between us, but if it will give you peace, then yes, I promise. If I am ever ready to love again, I will consider Hamish, but if it's not meant to be, you must understand. I cannot force myself to love another, especially when I love and adore you with all my heart, and always will.' I sobbed, my body shaking, as Aaron sighed, appearing relieved. Although I'd relented and given him my word, I had only done so for his peace of mind. I had no intention of ever marrying again. I would raise my children and concentrate on my friends; however, my heart would never belong to any other man but him. Aaron nodded his head, a grin on his face, but his eyes gave him away. It was clear just how deep his pain, his attempts to hide his anguish failing. He leaned back on the chair, holding me close to his chest as he stroked my back.

'The first time I saw ya standin' in front of me wearin' this dress, I knew ya were mine. I was struck by ya beauty. An' then when ya argued with Mr McPhee an' stomped ya foot—well, from that moment, I was in love.' He smiled as he ran his hand down the fabric. 'I told ya it'd still fit ya. The orange suits ya so well. Like an ember in the hearth late in the evenin',' he remarked, unable to hide his pride. I shifted on his lap, turning to face him while discreetly lifting my skirt and straddling my legs around his. Slipping my arms around his neck, I kissed his ear and a small sob escaped his lips.

'Aaron, I love you more than I have ever loved any man, and ever will. You have loved me, protected me, and cared for me for so many years now, and made my life happier than I ever imagined it could be. I thank you for loving me so well. You melt my heart as a father, and I will never let Thomas and Emmy forget you. I will remind them every day of moments you shared, and words spoken between you. I will remember every moment we spent together, and go there in my mind often, keeping you alive until the day we are reunited. I will always adore you, my love, and will only ever belong to you.' I broke down, placing my head on his shoulder as I sobbed, and he started to cry. Stuart appeared uncomfortable as he placed his magazine down on the floor and stood, shifting from foot to foot while avoiding our gaze.

'I'm just going outside the door, mate. Only to have a smoke. I'll be back in about half-hour,' he said, his voice gruff, before hurrying out of the room, gently closing the door behind him. I was forever grateful for his kindness, even though he would never admit to doing anyone a good turn.

'Now, I'm gunna make love to ya one last time so we both have somethin' to keep forever.' He grinned at me, tears in his eyes, while lifting the front of my dress further. We made love in silence, tears streaming down my face and his own, a desperation I had never felt before engulfing us both. The thought that this was the last time we would ever touch was like a knife through my heart. I cried throughout, wanting to remember the feel of him on my body forever.

Afterwards, he gently kissed me, pulling away only when Stuart loudly stepped back into the room.

'I'm sorry, mate, but your time is finished. I wish there was more I could do, but your wife has to leave. I've left you as long as I could, but the officers are starting to ask questions. I'll take the basket and put it in his cell when I escort him back once you leave. He won't be alone tonight, Missus, unless he wants to be. The men on duty tonight have brought in a few bottles of spirits for him, whisky I think, and some cards. They'll keep him company throughout the night if he so wishes. I am sorry we didn't meet under better circumstances, and I wish only the best in the world for you and your children. I hope you realise how many people really do care about what happens to the three of you after tomorrow.' He bent down to pick up the large basket, then straightened up and waited in silence.

I stood as requested, my legs unsteady, then brushed down the skirt of my dress with my hand, Aaron gracefully rising to his feet beside me. He towered over me as I lifted my arms and wrapped them around his neck, while he slipped his around my waist, lifting me from my feet, my face only centimetres from his own. He stared deeply into my eyes as he held me tightly.

'Even though ya won't be able to see me, if I can find some way to show ya I'm around ya an' the nippers an' I'm all right, nothin' will stop me. I promise ya that, me darlin' Abi,' he whispered in my ear, and I clung to him even tighter and sobbed. Aaron placed me back down on my feet; however, I couldn't take my arms from him. An officer, who I had never seen before, came to take my arm and escort me out. I turned and snarled like a wild animal, roughly shaking him off while glaring hatefully at him.

'I can walk,' I snapped bitterly, pushing him away before kissing Aaron's lips for the longest time, his tears mingling with mine, our anguished sobs filling the room as one.

Aaron walked me to the door of the cell, and we embraced for what would be the final time before I turned to leave. After only a few steps, I stopped and turned around. He smiled down at me, then lifted his hand to his mouth and blew me a kiss, his blue eyes twinkling as he gazed into mine, reminding me of the ocean on a sunny day. I raised my hand to my lips and blew him one back, then gave him the brightest smile I could muster, staring into those beautiful eyes one last time.

I inhaled deeply, then took a mental picture of him and hid it away in my mind. I told him how much I truly loved him, and he did the same. I turned again and slowly walked away, as straight and as calmly as I could manage. Once I rounded the corner and was gone from his sight, I crumpled into a heap against the wall, my backside on the dirty floor, then sobbed my heart out, until an officer found me much later and helped me out to the carriage.

That night, I dreamed of a place called Hiriarni, a pale blue blanket, and a bottle of whisky.

Chapter Fifteen

I LAY BESIDE AARON in the large bed, cosy and warm within the walls of the honeymoon cottage, gazing out the window at the stormy skies whipping the ocean into a frenzy, while eating crème brulee and discussing the children and a recent misadventure they had been involved in. Aaron finished eating and slipped his arms around me, his kiss passionate as I clung to him, his mouth over mine, gently exploring with his tongue. To hold him in my arms and have him here safe beside me was such a relief after all we had been through. He pulled me closer, holding me as if he would never let go—not willingly now he was free and recently returned to the bosom of his family after such a long absence.

I felt myself rising to the surface of slumber, and raised my fingers, touching my tingling lips. My stomach knotted up and I gasped, the reality of what was to occur today flooding my mind. I couldn't be parted from my Aaron, and there had to be someone who understood, who would intervene and stop such an unjust punishment being carried out on my darling man. I held onto the hope that by some miracle, Aaron would be returned to me. I turned towards the door as it opened and Bessie stepped inside, shuffling quietly across the room as she approached the side of the bed. She bent down and stroked my brow, smiling sadly at me.

'Mistress, would you like me to help you dress?' She kissed my cheek then straightened up, tears in her eyes she quickly brushed away.

'Yes, Bessie. Thank you.' I swallowed hard, willing myself not to cry as she pulled the covers back. I sat up and dangled my long legs over the side of the bed, sighing deeply before placing my feet on the carpeted floor and standing up. Bessie held my matching dressing gown up to slip over my nightgown, and I thanked her again before crossing the room to the dressing table. She followed, coming up from behind once I was seated, gently placing her hands on my shoulders while gazing down at me in the mirror.

'For the first time in my life, I don't know what to say. My heart grieves for Mister Aaron, you, and the children this morning. I will never forget what has been so unjustly done to you and your family. I hold such hatred for the police. If they had done their job in the beginning and brought that piece of shite Maslow, to justice, excuse my language, Mister Aaron wouldn't have been forced to do as he did. I am still praying, despite my disappointment in those above, for something to change in the next few hours and for him to be returned home to us, safe and sound.' Tears ran down her face, and I passed her a clean handkerchief as I wiped my own tears away. I felt numb inside and out, and I could no longer speak, even to thank her for her kind words.

She quickly composed herself, picking up the silver brush in an attempt to tame my unruly locks, then once she had mastered every strand, braided it all tightly then pinned it to the nape of my neck. Touching the back of my head gently, she nodded as I stood. Assisting me into a dark blue dress, conservative and formal, she had decided was best, given the newspaper photographers waiting outside The Delmont to catch a glimpse of me, only wanting me to look my best. I couldn't have cared less if I walked naked down the street with my hair in a mess. My mind and heart were with Aaron every waking moment, and it was only him who filled my dreams at night.

I wondered if they had given him the hot breakfast I had arranged to have sent over early this morning, accompanied by strong, hot coffee and his favourite juices. I had also slipped a love letter into the basket, saying my final goodbyes and telling him how much I loved him and always would, and I would be beside him, my arms invisibly wrapped around him as he took his final breath this morning. I had ensured he was supplied with a large breakfast with all the trimmings, just like he received on his birthdays at home with us. My eyes filled with tears at the thought of him while watching Bessie in the mirror buttoning the back of my dress, then smoothing down my skirt with her work worn hand. The sun had barely risen when I kissed Bessie, leaving her to continue packing my things as I walked out into the sitting room.

I shuffled into the dim room, slightly relieved to find it empty. Sighing deeply as I lowered myself onto the lounge to wait for Thomas and Emmy to wake, my mind filled with images of their father. Shortly after, a knock startled me, and I stood to go and open the door. I found Hamish standing in front of me, appearing as if he hadn't slept at all. He nodded sadly as we greeted each other, stepping inside at my invitation before crossing the room and making himself comfortable on the lounge. As I closed the door, a maid thrust her foot inside to stop me, her tray filled with jugs of juice and two pots of freshly brewed coffee. I apologised and opened the door wide, smiling as she nodded cheerfully before carrying on with her business and placing the tray on the low table. I returned to the sitting room, taking a seat opposite Hamish.

'Where's Thomas an' Emmy? I've come tae have breakfast with 'em.' He gazed across at me, shaking his head while closing his red-rimmed eyes for a moment. He was dressed for the day, his dark brown pants and cream coloured shirt complimented with a brown necktie, his black curly hair bound at the nape of his neck, not a hair out of place.

'They're still asleep, surprisingly. It took me a long time to settle them last night. They are still in my bed sleeping deeply. I wasn't quiet when I got up and readied myself, nor was Bessie, and their eyes didn't even flutter.' He nodded, his steady hand pouring us both a cup of coffee, adding sugar and milk to mine. Inside, my heart was broken, and I had no more tears to shed. I sat in silence, despair overshadowing my every thought, and I no longer knew what to say or do. Hamish leaned back and made himself comfortable, a sad smile touching his lips.

'Abigail, nothin' I say will make the burden ye carry any lighter. I wish I could take it from ye, but know there's a crowd o' people surroundin' ye who love an' care fer ye an' the bairns. We'll do everythin' we can tae help ye through this.' His voice faltered, and he stopped to sip his coffee. I nodded, afraid that if I spoke, I would break down again and never regain control of myself. We sat companionably, changing the subject to Willow Grove and the goings on in my absence; however, my thoughts turned back to my darling man, sitting alone in a cell and waiting to die.

I heard voices, and within moments, the twins came running out of my bedchamber, throwing themselves into my arms and knocking the wind out of me, before covering me in kisses. Once they decided it was enough, they went to Hamish and hugged him. He placed his large arms around the both of them, kissing them on the forehead. They climbed onto his lap, and talk turned to their father. He listened patiently, answering their questions as honestly as he could, causing me to burst into tears as I listened to him gently tell my children their father was going to heaven today. I couldn't bear the thought they would soon hang my love by the neck until he was dead. Lifeless. I couldn't imagine Aaron as gone. He was so full of life, with another sixty-years ahead of him to look forward to.

'Are we eatin' our breakfast here or downstairs this mornin'?' Hamish asked, distracting them from their tears for a moment.

'What are ya plans, Mummy?' Thomas enquired, making his way back to my lap, cuddling into me as I wrapped my arms around him.

'I'm staying here, but you can go with Uncle Hamish to the restaurant if you like. I will be fine, I promise. I don't want to go downstairs with the way everyone stares at me. Because our pictures have been in the paper, Thomas, everyone seems to recognise us and want to discuss your father. Today, I don't feel like talking to anyone other than you and Emmy, and the people who love us.' I stroked his shaggy blonde hair, so much like his father's.

'I want to have breakfast here, then. Why would I want to be recognised and have strangers try to talk to me like they do to Mummy every time we leave our room? I don't want Mummy to be alone,' Emmy said sweetly, coming to hug me. I embraced them both on my lap, despite how big and heavy they were becoming. Hamish stared over at us, silent, deep pity in his eyes he was unable to disguise.

'Then 'tis settled. We eat here with yer Mummy.' He grinned widely, leaning forward to pour them a glass of tropical fruit juice. New on the Delmont menu, it contained nine different fruits and had become a favourite of many. My children had become addicted to the sweet, tangy juice, forcing Leo to promise he would make them at home. The maid entered the room to take our breakfast order, and when I requested only more coffee, Hamish intervened and ordered on my behalf, then narrowed his gaze at me. 'Ye know ye have tae eat? Aaron made Leo swear on everythin' that sparkles an' promise he'll ensure yer fed at least three-times a day. I dinnae want tae bring this up, Abigail, but would ye like tae return home today? After we know fer certain?' Hamish asked gently as I closed my eyes, exhaling loudly. Thomas and Emmy had run off to their rooms to dress and ready themselves to eat. I watched as little Mary followed Emmy into her bedchamber, leaving Thomas with the privacy he had started to insist on.

'Yes. As soon as this is over I want to get as far away from this place as I can. Bessie is packing my things as we speak, and little Mary intends to do the same for the twins. We will be catching the train home as soon as I know for certain the undertakers have Aaron with them and are on their way. Only then will I leave here. If I could travel with him, I would; however, they won't let me. I can't bear the thought of Aaron being alone after they have murdered him. I must get him home where he belongs, among those who love him,' I said bitterly as tears poured down my face.

I had greased the palms of many in the judicial system to gain permission to have Aaron's body released to me immediately after the execution, and I didn't want him there with them one minute longer than he needed to be. I had organised for our own doctor to be present alongside the prison doctor to ensure they treated his body respectfully. I had heard stories of what they did to prisoners after they died, either naturally, by their own hand, by accident or execution, including taking their organs. I had asked Doctor Richards to ensure no one but he touched Aaron's body once the prison doctor confirmed death. I had also told the Governor of the Melbourne

Gaol exactly what I expected, and if anyone dared touch a hair on my husband's head—before and after he was dead—I would ensure every single person who had accepted my bribes would be exposed in the newspapers the next day, including him.

I had been told by my in-laws that when Ned Kelly had been executed in the November of 1880 at the same gaol, on the same gallows, much in the same way as what they intended to do to my Aaron, they had made death masks from plaster after he died before slicing off his head. Opening up his body in the days after his death, they removed his organs and placed them in jars, while many interested doctors and medical students watched on. The five death masks that had been made now sat on the desks of several high-ranking members within the judicial system who were involved in hunting Ned down. They had buried his body in an unmarked grave, minus his head, on the grounds of Pentridge prison, refusing to return him even in death to his family, who had grieved him deeply.

It had been twenty-three-years since Ned had been killed, and many who were there and remembered compared the public outcry for Aaron to what was expressed for Ned—only now they had come out even stronger and doubled in size in their support for Aaron. They had the same passion and fury within them when Ned was awaiting his execution, signing a mass petition for Aaron's freedom that held tens of thousands of signatures. This petition, and everything else the people of Victoria had tried to do to help us, had been ignored by the government and those who made decisions regarding the average man, who was forced to live under their corrupt laws with no right of response. People could often be heard grumbling about one law for the rich, and another for the poor. In our case, it did not seem to matter how much money we had. It hadn't saved him, only making his time in gaol more bearable. For which I was grateful.

Mr and Mrs Cavanaugh knew the Kelly family intimately, and were still in touch with Mrs Kelly and Ned's siblings to this day. They had met them when they first arrived in Australia, crossing paths when the Cavanaugh's travelled to Woolshed Falls near Beechworth for a month to visit friends from the old country. They soon became dear family friends to Mrs Kelly and her children—including Ned—several years before the gang were outlawed and went into hiding. They had attended Ned's trial and execution when Aaron was ten-years of age, an event he still remembered clearly, imprinting on his young mind. He had told me his family had travelled overnight to Melbourne to sit in a hotel in the city with members of Ned's family and his friends, all waiting for ten o'clock to come. He and his brothers had looked up to Ned, Joe, Steve and Dan, who formed what they were to call The Kelly Gang. He had told our children many stories of them over the years, which had fascinated me. Ned Kelly was considered an Australian hero by many, despite being convicted as a bushranger and murderer, while others openly referred to him as a cold-blooded killer. I had met the Kelly family when they came to stay with the Cavanaugh's over the last twelve-years, several times since I arrived; however, the famous Edward 'Ned' Kelly was ten-years before my arrival in Australia.

'I'll make sure he's treated with respect, an' plan tae attend the gaol meself tae meet with the undertakers. I've already obtained permission, which cost me a bloody fortune. These prison guards an' their boss cockies must be richer than the King himself.' He grimaced as I sighed deeply, wiping my face.

Richard had arranged for the undertakers, Neilson and Sons from Geelong, to be waiting at the gaol this morning to collect Aaron, taking him home to Willow Grove for burial in the days to follow. I was still waiting for Richard to come bursting through the door to say he had been successful in his appeal, and Aaron would be released back to us; however, he hadn't burst through the door as yet, and as time went on my hope was fading.

Breakfast arrived and we sat together at the dining room table with the twins, Bessie, and little Mary. I drank my coffee while I watched them all eat, a heavy silence hanging over the room.

'Come on, Abigail. Ye must eat somethin'. I promised Aaron, an' I cannot break me word tae a mate,' Hamish said, narrowing his gaze at me. I felt my stomach had shut down and my throat had closed.

'I'm sorry. I cannot even bear the thought of it. Please let me be. I will eat when I can. Just let me sit here and listen to the children talk with you all. It eases my heart to hear them,' I said, giving him a half-hearted smile and he smiled back, his eyes shining with tears.

'Aye, as ye wish, but I'll be watchin' ye, Abigail. Yer a dear friend, an' the mother o' me godchildren. I owe it tae Thomas an' Emmy tae ensure they've a healthy mother who is strong enough tae care fer 'em. If ye stop eatin', I'll force feed ye,' he teased, and I tried to smile. I heard someone at the door, and turned to see Richard strolling into the dining room, followed by Jas, who both stopped to greet me. They made themselves comfortable at the table, serving themselves from a few of the extra platters Hamish had ordered in case others decided to join us. Richard stared at me, unable to hide his pity as he poured himself a coffee.

'I'm sorry, Abigail. I truly am. I tried everything. I'll tell you only the briefest of details, given where we are.' He glanced out of the window, the sky above threatening and grey, before turning back to me, his face pale, only making the dark bags under his eyes more prominent. 'I spent the afternoon and well into the early hours of this morning trying to ascertain who I could bribe for Aaron's freedom. I let everyone in my circles know the amount of money available to anyone who could stop the execution would be significant and they could name their own price. I had several false leads. I paid one man a large sum of money; however, I never saw him again. It is unstoppable now, my dear sister. The execution will go ahead at ten o'clock. I am so sorry, and you have our deepest sympathy. Maybe one day you will forgive me; however, I will never be able to forgive myself.' He broke down, lowering his head into his hands. Jas put her arm around his broad shoulders as his body shook, his anguished sobs filling the room.

I sat back in my chair as if someone had punched me in the stomach, the wind knocked out of me. I was certain he could have stopped the sun from shining with the amount of money I was offering. I felt my lip tremble and my body start to shake, a cold sweat breaking out on my skin, while my heart raced away from me. I broke down and sobbed like I would never stop. Hamish held Emmy and Thomas in his arms, fresh tears running down their cheeks as they listened to the news their Daddy would die within a few hours. I placed my head in my hands, gasping for breath, while Bessie let out a strangled sob as she rose to her feet, then rushed to me, her hands on my shoulders, her body sheltering me from behind.

'There, there, my sweet, sweet girl. We're all here for you. Shhh, shhh, Mistress.' She stroked my cheek with her fingers, her voice soft and comforting. 'I wish I could take away your pain, but unfortunately, it is yours to bear for the moment, darlin'. No one can take this weight from you. It will take time for you to come to terms with it all, but know we will all do what we can to lighten that burden for you.' She stood me up, supporting me by the waist as she led me back into the sitting room, tucking me up on the couch under a lovely teal coloured blanket the children had chosen for me.

I lay motionless staring up at the ornate pressed tin ceiling, thoughts of Aaron and how he was spending his last hours on earth wandering through my mind. I closed my eyes and willed him to hear what I wanted to say, from my heart to his. I concentrated on his face, imprinted on my mind for eternity, as I silently sent my thoughts and deepest love to him, hoping in some way he could feel it. As I pictured him in my mind, I raised my hand and stroked his face, and he grinned widely at me. I swore I could feel the rough stubble on his face as I touched him, staring into his eyes for what I knew would be the final time. It felt so real as I stepped forward and placed my arms up around his neck while he gazed down at me adoringly, kissing for the longest time. All went dark as I jumped, opening my eyes, expecting him to be next to me. I could still smell him, and raised the hand I had caressed his face with to my nose, musk and sandalwood filling my nostrils. I sat up and smelt them again, my eyes darting around the room to find him, his presence still heavy in the room. I considered for a moment if grief had pushed me over the edge into insanity; however, it all felt so real, despite how ridiculous.

Aaron would be thinking of us before he took his final steps onto the gallows. And during. And after, should he have any choice in the matter. He would soon walk the same path many men and a handful of women before him sentenced to death had trod, and would hang within the hour. Friends and family started to arrive at our suite to be with me and the children when the time came, Dana and Catherine immediately making their way to my side to sit with me. Jenny, Margaret and Polly, along with Tamara and Elizabeth, surrounded me with love, all sitting close on the lounges chatting quietly between themselves.

'We are here with you, dear Abigail, and always will be. There are no words to be said at a time like this. One thing I do know for certain is he isn't frightened. Not for himself, anyway,' Dana said soothingly, leaning forward to place her now empty cup of tea with a large splash of brandy on the low table next to her. 'I saw him the other day, and he spoke of many things. One being he would not swap this lifetime for another because you made him so happy. He hasn't had one bad day with you in his life he couldn't cope with, because he had you by his side. He was in very good spirits, Abigail, and told me he will die a happy and contented man. The only thing that breaks his heart is leaving you and the twins.' Dana held my hand as I burst into uncontrollable sobs. Catherine slipped her arms around me, but was unable to speak, and comforted me in her own quiet way, laying my head on her shoulder, stroking my head, while I cried as if my heart had been ripped from my chest.

Mr and Mrs Cavanaugh sat side-by-side, ashen-faced, with Thomas and Emmy on their laps, comforting them as best they could as they cried for their father.

'There, there, me darlin' children. I know you don't understand why this is happenin', an' it's okay, 'cause me an' your Granny don't either. You just need to know you have your Daddy's family all around you who'll continue to love you an' see you every day. We'll all stick together, thick as thieves through this, I promise you,' Mr Cavanaugh murmured, stroking Thomas's brow. Mrs Cavanaugh cried softly, caressing Emmy's long, shiny hair as it fell in waves around her as she clung to her Grandmother.

'Why is it our Daddy the police are killing, Grandpa? He is a good man, and everyone loves him. Uncle Hamish told me all those millions of people on the streets when we go outside are here for Daddy. Is that true? Why are strangers here for Daddy?' Emmy asked, so very confused.

'Well, little one, they all believe your Daddy has been unfairly treated. What you have to remember is your father is a good man, an' always has been. If he were bad, no one would care what happened to him. Be proud of your Daddy just like he is of both of you. He loves you more than anythin' in the world. He asked me to promise to tell you some of his stories when you come to stay with us.' Mr

Cavanaugh grinned down at them through his tears, and I saw their faces brighten.

'How do ya know our Daddy's stories?' Thomas asked, his grandfather smiling down at him fondly.

'Because I was the one who told 'em to him when he was a young lad, just like you.' He tousled Thomas's hair, wiping a stray tear away with the back of his work weathered hand.

I gazed around the crowded room, stopping to watch Aaron's brothers, all stony faced and pale, their wives and children by their sides. Patrick had carried all the chairs from the dining room and placed them around the spacious sitting room, providing ample seating for all. It was quiet, quieter than they had ever been when together, some talking softly between themselves, while others sat alone and silent, reflecting on their own private thoughts and memories of Aaron.

Leo sat comfortably in between Polly and Jenny, much to their chagrin. He had been loudly sobbing into a handkerchief ever since he woke this morning, his eyes puffy and red, while he was highly emotional, more so than usual, and he'd hardly slept a wink over the past few nights.

'Oh, I must break this wretched silence! How can you stand this? I feel like running to that gaol with a rifle to break him out of there myself. Why didn't any of us do that before now? You all say I'm soft in the head, but look at yourselves. Not one of you thought to rescue him until I spoke my thoughts aloud. It's far too late for me to even find a gun now. What am I going to do without my Goliath? I don't care if I make a fool of myself. I have loved that man since he first sauntered into our lives the day we arrived in Geelong. He has been my friend ever since, and protected me from his mad wife, who I also adore, so back off with judgements and opinions.' He glared at them, waving his finger. 'Abigail knows how much I love her, but facts are facts. She has injured me more times than I can count, and truly would have killed me without Goliath. He rescued me from the stable roof once when Abigail lost her mind over a bowl of vegetables.' Leo again, waving both hands in the air dramatically, before fixing me with a stare. 'I know, I know, it's hard to believe something so trivial could cause such a reaction, but that is our Abigail. The resident lunatic of Willow Grove. Every family has one, and she is ours.' I summoned all my strength to lean forward, my attempts to reach across and grab him by the ear thwarted by Catherine, her hand on my arm, the other clamped firmly around my shoulder. 'I do love him for other qualities too. If they do go ahead and kill him, there will be an enormous hole left in my heart, and at Willow Grove. There are few people in this world who measure up to my standards and gain the privilege and pleasure of my friendship, but he is one of the few. A perfect man in every sense of the word. He is the loveliest person I know, and doesn't deserve to die. I love him so much,' he wailed as Jenny swiftly placed her arms around him, allowing him to sob on her shoulder. He had turned the situation from me wanting to inflict harm on his person, to an overwhelming desire to embrace him, all with just a few words, making me cry again as I knew it came from his heart. Leo did count Aaron among his best friends, and he loved him deeply and always had.

I sobbed as Dana moved over so Polly could sit with me. She put her arms around me, holding my trembling body while whispering words of comfort.

'I don't know what to say either, my dear Abi. It's not fair, it's wrong, it shouldn't have happened are only some of what's inside me. I am here for you in any way you need me to be, day or night. I love you, and my heart is aching for you, my darling sister,' Polly said, gently stroking my back.

I glanced at the clock on the mantle to find it was half-past nine, and I stood, excusing myself and telling them I needed to be alone. I ignored the sympathetic glances as I tried to stand straight and not stumble, crossing the room while worrying my legs would go from underneath me at any moment. I quietly closed the door behind me, then lay on the bed, fully clothed, my hands behind my head as Aaron always did. I allowed all the wonderful memories I had with him to run through my mind, all the while silently sending him my love. I closed my eyes and tried again to visualise him as I had earlier, but it wasn't the same. I saw his face, but I couldn't feel his presence or his touch, nor hear him breathing like I had this morning. It was different, and I felt disappointed.

All the precious moments we had shared, what he had taught me, and the family he had given to me, including his own parents and brothers as my own, brought me to tears. This man had changed my life in every way and taken my heart as his own, and now he was leaving me forever. I wouldn't be able to go on without him, nor did I want to. I could not see a future for myself without him in it. He was the love of my life, my heart and soul, and I was confident I would never meet another like him.

We had spent every spare moment together throughout our marriage, and I remembered every detail of it, all stored in my memory like a book. I could open it to read a chapter at will and recall that moment vividly—what I smelt around me, what I thought, and how I felt at the time. I would live inside my own head for the rest of my life, reliving every moment we had ever shared. He was everything, and my everything was being taken by force, and there was nought I could do about it.

I glanced across at the clock on the mantle, similar to the one in our bedchambers at home, finding there was only a few minutes left until the clock struck ten. I stood to go and look out the window towards the gaol, and I gasped. The streets were filled with people, more now than I had ever seen in one place. Richard had told me there were tens of thousands of people in Russell Street protesting, but I had assumed he was exaggerating. I stared down at all the strangers Aaron had touched in some way, igniting such passion rarely seen or sustained in a trial like his. I held onto the windowsill, supporting myself as my body shook uncontrollably, tears streaming down my face while gazing in the direction of where my darling would be walking towards the gallows, his wrists bound and ready to meet his maker.

I heard the gaol bell ring, indicating it was ten o'clock, and I doubled over, gasping for breath, feeling no different than if I had been punched in the stomach at the local gin house. I gripped the ledge of the window, and felt my heart shatter into a million pieces, knowing in my soul at that very moment, my Aaron was gone forever. I attempted to walk back to the bed, a strangled scream piercing the silence as my vision turned to grey and my legs went from under me. Crumpling to the ground, loud screaming now deafening me, I soon realised, it was my own. My darling man was gone. Taken from me in circumstances that should never have happened. He had so much life and love in him, now wasted. The light that burned so brightly inside him would never shine again.

Now hysterical on the floor, screaming and sobbing as I rocked back and forward in despair, I wanted to die alongside him, knowing in my soul I wouldn't survive without him. The life I had before me I no longer wanted without him in it. The beautiful man sent to me by great-aunt Isabelle had turned out to be the most treasured gift I had ever received, and because of him, I knew what unconditional love was. He had taught me how to express love and affection, something I hadn't known how to do when we had married. Because of him, I was able to express to all those I loved just how much I really cared for them. Now he had left me here, all by myself, to raise our children without him. Because of him.

I would never experience the love I had with Aaron with anyone else again, of that I was certain. That part of my life was now gone, along with my beloved husband. My heart pounded in my ears and panic overwhelmed me, leaving me unable to gain an ounce of control as my screams continued to ring out.

Hamish rushed into the room, tears in his eyes when he saw me on the floor rocking back and forward hysterically. He lowered himself down behind me and placed his arms around my torso, attempting to hold me still.

'I cannot live without him! What am I going to do? I need him here. The children need their Daddy!'

Hamish remained silent, my back against his chest and his arms around my waist, trying to hold me still without harming me as I continued to scream and thrash about on the floor. I couldn't see his face, but I could hear his strangled sobs. He had just lost his closest friend, and had still chosen to be here despite his own grief. Margaret and Catherine, and soon after, Polly and Jenny, stood motionless in my bedchamber, watching us on the floor, unable to stop their own tears, all brokenhearted for me.

He gently lifted me up, then placed me on the bed. He hurried off to get a chair, and sat it down beside me when he returned, while my friends surrounded me on the bed as I screamed and sobbed. Hamish held my hand while I cursed God for taking Aaron from me and yelled obscenities that would have made a sailor blush.

'Those fuckin' evil, corrupt, funts of things. If they had done their job that night at the hospital, I would have my man beside me, and the children would have their father. I fuckin' hate them, and I will do everything in my power to make each and every one of them suffer. I just know deep down Judge Murray was bribed to impose the death penalty, but no one will listen to me.' I struggled to sit up, attempting to raise my fist in the air. 'It's the only thing that makes sense. Richard told me he and Maslow went to university together and are members of the same gentlemen's club.' Catherine nodded thoughtfully, sitting herself down on the bed beside me and taking my hand in hers. 'I wish for disease and death to strike down anyone involved who did what they could to see my Aaron dead. Most of all, I curse Judge Murry, and I wish him a slow and torturous death from a painful disease that strikes him down in the very near future,' I spat angrily through my tears. I continued ranting, upsetting my friends no end with my threats to seek revenge on every corrupt copper involved.

My screams had turned to sobs by the time Hamish went to check on the twins, my friends left to comfort me, while Polly stroked my head and tried to calm me. Within minutes, Hamish returned with Thomas and Emmy in his arms, then gently placed the distressed little darlings on each side of me. I held them both close, closing my eyes while thoughts of my beautiful man filled my head, the three of us soon crying ourselves to sleep.

Chapter Sixteen

WHEN I WOKE SHORTLY after, we were alone and they were both cuddled close to my body. I kissed their tear-stained faces until they woke. Their big eyes stared back at me with such sadness, I felt my own prick with tears once again. My chest felt hollow, as if someone had removed my heart while I slept. I felt no pain and was completely numb, my body no longer my own. I wrapped my arms around them and spoke of Aaron, telling them several stories about their father they hadn't heard. They laughed and cried with me as I held them tight and smothered them in kisses. They clung to me and talked of their Daddy, and their love for him. I heard the door open and looked over to find Bessie rushing into the room. She appeared devastated as she stood by the bed, gazing down at us snuggled closely together.

'We're almost ready to depart, Mistress. I left you and the kiddies to sleep for as long as I could while we organised everything. The luggage is packed, and the trunks already taken to the train. Most have left to ready themselves for the journey, apart from Hamish.' She smiled sadly, her hands resting on her hips. 'He's waiting in the sitting room for you, as are your friends from Melbourne who want to see you before they return to their own homes.' Tears poured down her face as she reached for the back of the chair to support herself, lowering her head as she sobbed.

'Thank you, Bessie. I don't know what I would do without you. My brain has shut down and I cannot think straight no matter how hard I try. I cannot explain how I feel, other than empty and cold. I have nothing inside me anymore. Whatever was there before has gone with Aaron. He has taken everything I have with him,' I told her sadly as she sobbed harder.

Thomas and Emmy quickly got up, hearing their godfather was here, kissing me on the cheek before hurrying out to the sitting room. I slowly rose to my feet and straightened my dress, before going to Bessie and embracing her.

'He loved you, you know? He felt like he had his own personal maid, which then gave him a swollen head and caused him to believe he was king of the castle. Bessie, you made him feel very special, and very loved, and he adored you,' I told her, trying to smile.

'He was a cheeky wee devil of a man, and I will miss him dreadfully. I went to see him a few days ago, and he was confident he was leaving you in good hands. It eased his mind knowing you had me to care for you after he was gone. You were the only worry on his mind. He had settled all his affairs other than you, and made me promise to always look after you and guide you like a mother. He also said he knew no other man would be able to get near you with me ready to pounce on them. A frightening hurricane of a woman with a heart of gold, he called me.' A smile touched her lips at the thought of what had passed between them.

'He knew what he was talking about. You have always looked after me, dear Bessie, and I know I have you to depend on now he has been taken from me,' I replied, bursting into fresh tears. I made my way to the bathroom and washed my face, glancing in the mirror to see dark shadows under my swollen eyes. I dried my face, then hurried to the sitting room to find Hamish, the twins cuddled into him, one under each enormous arm.

'Go an' find little Mary an' ask her tae take ye down fer an ice cream before we leave,' Hamish gently ordered as I sat down opposite him. They came to me, embracing me tightly before Thomas took Emmy's hand and they raced down to the restaurant—I assumed to eat as much ice cream as they could fit. They loved the cold, creamy substance and would eat it until they were sick and I took it away from them. Mary had overheard Hamish, and came out of the bedchamber when the door of the suite closed.

'And where have those two tykes gone? I heard the mention of ice cream, so I suspect they're headed downstairs to the restaurant?' She smiled at us, and Hamish laughed aloud.

'I did tell 'em tae find ye first, but as soon as they heard the word ice cream, everythin' else went out o' their heads. They're so much like their parents when it comes tae eatin'.' Hamish smiled at her, and she giggled softly to herself.

'It'd be best I follow along behind them, then, before they have the table filled with all sorts of flavours they'll never fit into their stomachs. Their eyes are bigger than their bellies, and they'll order everythin' if I'm not there to stop the wee fiends. They think because their mother owns the hotel, they can order anythin' and everythin' all at once and no one will challenge them. Well, they've got that wrong this mornin',' she called out as she hurried out the door, Hamish's loud laughter filling the room. After he had poured me a cup of coffee and passed it over, he settled back into his chair.

'I went tae the gaol to ensure the undertakers collected Aaron an' took all his personal belongin's, includin' the blue blanket the twins gave him yesterday. It'll all be returned tae ye in the next few days. I saw him, Abigail, an' he looked at peace. Even had a slight smile on his face. I'd say he was thinkin' o' ye the whole time, right 'till the end.' He smiled sadly as tears slid down my face.

'Thank you, Hamish. Aaron would really appreciate you doing that for him. I need to know his body was treated with respect after he was hanged.'

'I wanted tae ease yer mind an' reassure ye that Doctor Richards never left his side once he was pronounced dead. Naw one touched him, nor were any o' those death masks made. The undertakers took him an' are now on their way back home. It surprised me tae see the people followin' the hearse tae Geelong. They're on horseback an' in carriages, some fancy, while others are carts filled with people sittin' on the back. There must be thousands o' 'em, Abigail. An' all because they believe Aaron did the right thing. He was a good an' decent man an' the people o' Australia know that.' A tinge of pride in his voice, and despite his intent, his words brought me no comfort. All

I wanted was my husband here beside me, not dead in the back of a carriage.

He passed me a handkerchief to wipe my tears, reminding me of what happened earlier when in my bedchamber. He had held my hand as he sat by my bed, his arms around me as he tried to calm me when on the floor. I realised I had felt no hot pins running through my body, nor any attraction towards him. He no longer set my body on fire, spreading warmth to every part of me—the reason I had avoided his touch throughout my entire marriage, worried I would weaken despite how much I loved my husband.

I was relieved what was between us had passed, as we were such close friends. I hated feeling I had to be on guard when he was around, never allowing myself to even touch his hand in comfort when he had needed it in the past. He had kept his word and never touched me since he kissed me all those years ago. I was unaware of when things had changed; however, I was extremely glad of it. I needed his support more than anyone's, having been Aaron's best mate and godfather to the twins. He knew more than anyone what Aaron's innermost feelings and thoughts were, and had spent so much time with him over the years. He knew everything there was to know about him. I wanted to be surrounded by people who would keep Aaron's memory alive for Thomas and Emmy, and I knew I could rely on Hamish.

'I really do appreciate the people of Australia, and everything they have tried to do. Because of them, and for only that reason, I have agreed to give Cain an interview for the Geelong Advertiser after Aaron's funeral. I want to thank the public, and that is the only way I can reach everyone,' I told him as I sighed deeply.

'But, Abigail. Yer such a private person. Do ye really think yer up tae sharin' yer grief with a nation?' His brow creased in concern as I wiped my face with a fresh handkerchief.

'Yes, Hamish, I do. Even if I'm not up to it, as you say, I think it's important that people have closure now—and it is closure. It's all finished, and my darling man is gone.' I burst into tears again. He moved over and sat next to me, putting his arm around my shoulders as I sobbed. Leo strolled into the room unannounced, quickly making himself comfortable on the opposite lounge, his eyes twinkling mischievously.

'Don't tell me you two are bumping uglies before Goliath is even cold. Well, if you are, I want to be the first to know. How terribly inappropriate,' he announced, his hands going up to his cheeks as he gasped in mock horror. I felt Hamish stiffen. His jaw clenched tight as he narrowed his gaze, an angry glint in his eyes.

'When will ye learn tae fuckin' weel mind what ye say? Dinnae be so bloody disgustin'. Ye open that big mouth o' yer's afore ye think, ye bloody moron. Ye've got me so enraged 'tis takin' all me strength tae keep me hands from yer throat.' Hamish stopped for a moment to compose himself, a slight smile touching my lips. 'Surely even ye understand Abigail is grievin' an' needs her friends with her? It would naw hurt fer ye tae put yer arms around her an' shut that hole in yer face.' Leo's eyes widened; however, he remained silent. 'When you speak, even when tryin' tae help, Leonardo, ye make everythin' a hundred-times worse. Comfort her, but do it in silence. Start thinkin' o' others instead o' yerself,' Hamish growled, leaning forward to pour me a glass of apple juice. Leo quickly came to my side, pushing Hamish's arm away from me and placing his own around my shoulders before kissing me on the lips, still remaining silent. Hamish smirked as he returned to the opposite lounge.

Brian and Tamara, along with Eric and Elizabeth, came to sit with me for a time, talking of their love and respect for Aaron, while encouraging me to call on them for anything. They promised they would be down to Willow Grove before Aaron's funeral, and would stay on for a few days afterwards. I thanked them for everything as they embraced me before departing to their homes nearby.

My friends and family had started to gather in our suite, some going downstairs to the restaurant to eat before catching the train.

'Have ya seen all the people on the streets? There must be tens of thousands out there. I can't believe they're here for me boof-headed brother. Bloody Aaron sure knew how to put on a show, didn't he?' Aiden asked fondly as I saw him wipe a tear from his eye.

The time had come to leave and meet little Mary and the children downstairs, then make our way to the train for home. Hamish and I walked together, side-by-side with Bessie, to the restaurant to find them finishing their ice cream as the others waited outside in Swanston Street.

'Are we all ready tae go?' Hamish asked, and the children screamed in affirmation. I looked at the empty bowls of ice cream on the table and sighed deeply, knowing we were probably in for some tummy aches later on today.

We walked together in our large group to Flinders Street Station, crossing at the corner where Young and Jacksons stood. I loved that pub. We always spent time there when we stayed in Melbourne. Or we used to. I kept forgetting Aaron was gone. I looked back over my shoulder at the three-story building standing proudly on the corner, my thoughts filled with all the wonderful times Aaron and I spent in there. We had met so many new people there over the years, some becoming friends, all of them working class, and felt far more comfortable dining there than at the Delmont restaurant with the upper classes.

I followed my loved ones across the road the moment no more carriages or men on horseback threatened to run us down—the street so very busy. Holding Thomas and Emmy's hand tightly as we walked past the ticketing booth, we came across a number of labourers carrying out work on the building. The train station was always busy, and had become even more so since our arrival more than a decade ago. During the 1890s, the need for more substantial facilities was identified, and they built three additional platforms, but halted any further expansion at the time.

I had been told by Eric, my dear friend Elizabeth's husband who was well aware of my interest, that the first terminus contained only a single platform spanning ninety feet when it opened on the 12th of September, 1854, and had been located beside the fish market on the corner of Swanston and Flinders Street. They added another platform in 1877, along with two overhead footbridges to provide passenger access, followed by several timber and corrugated iron buildings, already standing when I laid eyes on the humble train station for the very first time. A telegraph station had been added in 1879 and the first signal boxes opened in 1883, one at each end of the platform. By the 1890's we found it so much easier to travel when they added a third island platform.

In 1899, the parliamentary committee for the railways approved construction for a new station on the site, and a competition was held to design the facade and platform connections. From seventeen entries, the winning design, named Green Light, was submitted by James Fawcett and H. P. C. Ashworth, Fawcett an architect, while Ashworth a civil engineer, both employed by the railways themselves. They received □500 for their efforts, describing their design as French Renaissance in a free manner, the cost to build estimated to be in excess of □260,000.

We were yet to see it, but preparatory work had commenced last year, and the Turret clock was no longer there. Made by Thomas Gaunt in 1882, the clock had been installed later that same year on a tower at the Elizabeth Street entrance to the station, and was one of the first things I admired in my new home. Commonly known as the water tower clock, it had become a landmark and popular meeting place until last year when the clock and tower were relocated to Princes Bridge Station. Aaron adored Melbourne and all of her buildings and had been so looking forward to watching their progress in the years to come. To be here, standing amongst the crowd for the opening of the finished station. But it was not to be. And that would grieve me every time I looked upon the building in the future. Was there even a future for me without him? Oh, my heart would never be the same, of that I was certain.

I sighed deeply while following behind my loved ones, pausing occasionally to shake my head to try to clear my mind of the memories hurting my heart. Dressed in black, they solemnly made their way to the platform where the train to Geelong stood in all its glory, waiting to leave and carry us home. A place I hadn't been for months. I had refused to leave Melbourne since Aaron was transferred here and hadn't returned home since; relying on those who did to bring me back anything I needed or had forgotten. Now I was returning to the place I loved the most without my beloved Aaron. He was such a big part of Willow Grove, and I didn't know how I would stand being there without him.

I held back tears as we boarded the train to settle into our compartments. Hamish soon found ours, then stood back to let us in. Thomas sat down where Aaron always did, next to the window and facing forward. I went and settled myself next to him, Emmy beside me. Hamish sat opposite between Bessie and little Mary, casting his eyes over the three of us with pity, while our companions made themselves comfortable.

He had done everything in his power to make our lives easier, not just today, but ever since Aaron was arrested. He had succeeded in more ways than one by running the farm for Aaron, being a wonderful friend to me, and a loving and attentive godfather to the twins. He had sacrificed his own time with his sweetheart, Nellie, only seeing her on his return at the end of the week, and he was often too busy to spend much time with her before rushing back to Melbourne for the trial. I knew he had met with her father to ask for her hand months ago and had every intention of asking her to marry him shortly after; however, Aaron was arrested and his plans put on hold.

The anguish and grief he felt at losing Aaron was clear on his handsome face for all to see, yet here he was trying to bear our grief for us on top of his own. He had done more than enough, and I was grateful to him and always would be. Now he was free to resume his life. The thought lightened my heavy heart a little to know he was in love and content with his lot, even if I no longer was. Emmy moved over to his lap and cuddled into him, laying her head on his chest before closing her sparkling emerald eyes as the train rocked back and forth. Hamish stroked her long, red hair, loose today and falling in curls to her waist, gently holding her while she slept.

'Abigail, I know ye feel like givin' up, but look at what ye have tae live fer,' Hamish murmured, his dark eyes fixed on Emmy, then a sleeping Thomas cuddled into my side.

'I know, old friend. What I do not know is if I have the strength to live this life without him. It's something I cannot even contemplate or think of, now or six-months from now. Time makes no difference,' I replied, pushing everything to the back of my mind. I stared out the window at the passing farms and, on occasion, the passengers getting on and off at the tiny train stations that serviced the small towns nearby. All while listening to Bessie and little Mary cry quietly. I relaxed my head back onto the backrest and closed my eyes, a million thoughts flooding my mind, all of them of Aaron.

Our carriage waited just outside the Geelong terminus in Railway Terrace, alongside three more to accommodate our friends and family and take them back to Willow Grove—an enormous cart they called a dray waiting behind. Harry rested his tall frame back against the shiny black exterior of my favourite carriage, one my aunt used herself. His pipe between his lips, he raised his work-worn hand in greeting when he caught sight of us. The Cavanaughs, Dana, and Catherine had left their carriages and stabled their horses at Willow Grove during the trial, and would find their way home from there. Those left either lived nearby in the village or in the main house and didn't have far to go.

Angus and Polly, along with Hamish, would soon be back in their cottage with Willy and Bella, who had enjoyed their stay in Melbourne with their parents and cousins, despite the circumstances. The children had missed months of school; however, Mrs McGinty had assured Angus and Patrick the fourteen children would catch up in no time under her guidance. And I did not doubt her for a moment.

Harry pulled away from the carriage and straightened up, extinguishing his pipe and placing it in his pocket, while the grooms and stable boys he had brought with him were busy loading our trunks onto the dray waiting behind. Tears filled his eyes as he watched me slowly walk towards him, leaning heavily on Aaron's father, unable to stop my own tears spilling down my face. He silently helped me into the carriage, Thomas and Emmy quickly joining me, while Jenny, Margaret and Hamish followed. The journey home was quiet, leaving me pondering on the thousands of times Aaron and I had travelled in this very carriage, and reminding me of his touch and warm embrace, only two things out of a million I would miss forever. Tears sprang to my eyes for the hundredth time today, threatening to spill over as Hamish passed me a handkerchief. Jenny took my hand in hers and smiled sadly, brushing away her own tears.

'Abigail, there's nought I can say to ease you, other than we're here and surrounding you and the twins with love, ready to do anything you need. Harry mentioned that all at Willow Grove are in deep mourning, but have still turned up to work today out of respect for Aaron. He was well loved, and so are you and the children. The souls who work for you don't only look upon you as their employer, they see you as friends, some even as family. I'm sorry for your loss of a good and decent man. This should never have happened,' Jenny said sympathetically as she leaned forward to take a clean handkerchief from her handbag, tears still streaming down my face no one seemed to notice anymore.

'Anything you need, Abigail, you only have to ask. We're all here for you and the children. When they play in the village with their friends, I always keep an eye on them, just so you never have to worry. Jenny makes sure they're fed and watered, while I make sure they keep out of mischief, unlike their mother and her best friend, Leonardo,' Margaret said, her mouth twitching as I smiled weakly through my tears. I knew I had the love and support of so many wonderful people. They not only loved me, but loved Thomas and Emmy beyond measure, and would always keep a guiding eye on them now their father was no longer around to do so. The thought of him made me cry harder, while they all remained silent, listening to my deep sobs of grief.

We soon arrived home, and Hamish politely assisted us down from the carriage. Margaret and Jenny embraced me warmly, before making their way home to their own families, and the lives they had so generously put on hold for so long now. Polly and Catherine came to my side and linked arms with me as Hamish lifted Emmy up onto his back, slowly making his way towards the front entrance with his large hand on Thomas's shoulder. We walked companionably to the kitchen, the smell of freshly baked bread filling my nostrils. Hamish and the children joined the Cavanaughs at the table, while Leo cast a critical eye over the staff as they went about their business. Polly and Catherine joined them while I stood in the doorway, watching Sally and Erin carry the platters of food to the table.

'Good afternoon, my sweet little slaves. Your master has returned. What a relief to see you have the food prepared for our return. Very well done treating your betters how they deserve to be treated. I was certain I would be forced to bring my stock whip out and tickle your fancies. Now, while away, I did not miss one of you, nor did I bring any presents; however, I know you have pined for me. How could you not? I'm the sunshine in your day, the rainbow after a storm, the laughter of a bell ringing out its musical song,' Leo announced, bowing to them, while I heard a snort then several giggles.

'Yer the storm cloud filled with thunder hangin' over this house, ye fool,' Hamish remarked as he helped himself to a slice of beef and onion pie. I stared over at them, listening as they spoke amongst themselves while serving the children. Thomas and Emmy helped themselves, filling their plates, before sitting at the end of the table with their rambunctious cousins, the adults far more subdued. Catherine soon noticed I hadn't sat down, her eyes darting around the room, then settling on me, still in the doorway.

'Abigail, please come and sit down with us. You look poorly,' Catherine called out as I gazed around the large room, now filled with so many people I felt I could no longer breathe.

'I'm sorry. I cannot bear it. All I can see is Aaron standing here. Memories of him over the years eating in here and talking to the staff while sitting at the kitchen table are tormenting me. I expect him to walk in any minute now to join us. I cannot do this. He has to be alive, I need him back,' I screamed as I turned and ran towards the stairs, stumbling up them and to my bedchamber, unable to see through my tears.

Hysterical and blinded by my own grief, I climbed up onto the bed and slipped under the quilt on his side, where he had slept beside me for so many years and never would again. I lay my head on his pillow, breathing in his scent, a gaping hole in my chest where my heart once was. My only wish was to have him back by my side, for our lives to be the way they used to be before this sorry business. I cried out his name, begging him to show me a sign as he had promised, but there was nothing. Only the echo of my screams, my empty cries and pleading for someone, anyone, to return him safely to my arms unanswered. Bessie was soon by my side, stroking my brow as she sat on the bed.

'There, there, my sweet girl. Hush now. I'm here to look after you. Just try and breathe slowly, in and out. It will calm you. No one expects you to be strong right now. It's best you get it all out, my poor girl. I'll be here by your side to make sure you get through the grievin',' she soothed, a tear sliding down her face. She held my hand as she murmured reassuringly, a knock on the door startling us both before Hamish strode in, appearing concerned.

'I brought ye this. Margaret mentioned last night if they were tae go ahead with the execution, I should make sure ye have this when ye arrive home. She talked o' how difficult it would be fer ye comin' back tae the house without Aaron here. I agree with her, an' think it'd do ye good tae settle yerself, Abigail. I can send fer Doctor Richards tae give ye somethin' if this is o' naw help.' He raised his eyebrows, waiting for my response while holding a tray from the kitchen.

'No. I don't want the doctor. He gives me injections and tonics that make me feel nauseous. I would rather smoke the green buds.'

He nodded, setting down the tray on my side table, a bowl filled with chopped up buds Margaret had harvested from the island, along with a carved pipe I had never seen before sitting on top. I assumed Leo had prepared it for him, as I wasn't aware there even was a spare pipe, my other still packed away in my trunk. Bessie rose to her feet, saying she would return shortly, while Hamish sat down on a chair next to the bed and lit the pipe. He handed it to me, and I slowly lifted it to my lips, drawing deeply as I closed my eyes.

'Now, Hamish, don't you go getting her out of her mind like Mister Aaron used to do. Hmmm, I suppose he had his own deviant reasons for allowin' it, now that I think of it. It'll probably do her some good, and at least give the poor love some rest. Make sure you come find me when you leave her, as I don't want her left alone in this state. I will come straight back up,' Bessie promised and he nodded obligingly, leaning back to relax in his chair as I inhaled again. A soft grey cloud billowing above the bed.

'I don't usually smoke it during the day, and rarely at night, only when I'm in pain or really cannot find sleep. It's only when Margaret or Leo corrupt me and I smoke it with them it leads me down the devil's path straight to the pits of hell. Or so I'm told.' He chuckled to himself as I tried to smile, and failed miserably.

'Aye, weel, yer in pain now, Abigail. Just naw the kind anyone can see.'

I inhaled again, holding it in my lungs for a few moments, then gently exhaled, watching in fascination as the smoke gently rose, hovering above. Hamish had never smoked it to my knowledge, and was uncertain of what it was, only seeing it ground up ready to smoke. Aaron had told me these green buds were called marijuana and although appeared to be a harmless shrub, it was something you craved the more you used it. No different from ale and spirits. I was now careful not to smoke it too often, not wanting to become like the drunks that hung around the taverns and alleys in Melbourne and Geelong with no bed to go to.

I lay back on Aaron's pillows, raising the pipe to my lips again. Smiling to myself as the grey tendrils of smoke danced in the air, I watched them dissipate for the longest time. It was helping ease the pain in my chest, while my body slowly started to relax as I listened to Hamish talk. Once I had finished, Hamish took it from me, my body now heavy, my eyelids starting to close. Hamish left me to sleep, while Bessie soon returned to help me into a nightgown, then tucked me into bed. Where I stayed until Aaron's body was brought home the following afternoon.

All I dreamed of was Aaron. He showed me a white feather, a gold locket, and a street paved in gold.

Chapter Seventeen

T HEY HAD RETURNED AARON to me three-days ago. He had been dressed in the clothes he wore on our wedding day, and wrapped in a blanket we always used when we would go for picnics together. We had lain on that blanket thousands of times eating and laughing, making love, and spending hours wrapped in each other's arms while we talked of our hopes and dreams. I would have liked to have kept the blanket for myself to hold close at night; however, it eased my heart to know he would be enveloped in our memories for eternity until I was able to join him.

The undertaker, Mr Neilson, was a lovely man. His sons, and sons-in-law, all worked in the family business. They were caring and compassionate, and had been the undertakers who buried Jack and Harrison. Not for a moment did it cross my mind I would be burying my beloved husband beside the boys, two-years and three-months after them. Mr Neilson had treated our sons with dignity and respect, while being sympathetic and caring towards us, carrying out all our requests for their funeral without question.

Richard had sent word to them once he knew Aaron's case was hopeless, and had made arrangements on my behalf, wanting to take the burden from me. I had been relieved that Mr Neilson and his family agreed to take care of my Aaron, confident they would do everything they could to make the process as easy as possible for me. Nothing was too much trouble when it came to my requests, and I was grateful to them for not taking advantage of my financial situation and charging a small fortune.

Bessie had cut the blanket in half that the twins had given him the day before he died. She had sewn a silky, pale blue ribbon around the edge of each blanket and embroidered their father's full name down one side of the ribbon, then stitched Thomas's name on his intertwined with Aaron's, adding a red love heart on each end, then did the same for Emmy. They had turned out beautifully, and I knew it was something the twins would cherish for as long as they lived. Bessie had placed the finished blankets on the end of their beds, explaining their father had slept in it the night before he died and now they could have his memory close when they closed their eyes. They were both touched by her kindness, as was I, and treasured her gift, placing the blanket near their pillows so they could smell him when they slept. I had admired them myself before she had presented them to the children, and cried when his musky scent and the strong smell of sandalwood filled my nose.

Aaron had been placed in the sitting room in his highly polished wooden coffin. Hamish had been right; he did look peaceful and had a slight smile on his face. I sat with him from the time he arrived, often leaning over his coffin to hold his hand or stroke his face while talking to him. Or sobbing over him as I traced the black rope mark around his beautiful neck with my fingers, the only sign of trauma to his body. Hamish and little Mary had taken over the daily care of the twins, encouraging them to spend time with me at night in my room, or in the sitting room where I was most of my time.

It was Hamish who was there for Thomas and Emmy when they woke in the morning, and it was he who ate dinner with them in the dining room at night with Angus, Polly and Leo—all trying to maintain a normal household for them given I could not function due to the deep grief I carried.

I stared out the window over the back garden. The sky had started to change colour as the dawn tried to break through the heavy clouds—the bushman's clock calling out his song across the paddocks glistening in dew, the cattle mooing in the distance—while movement could be heard in the hallway. Murmuring to Aaron through my tears, his hand in mine, Leo stepped into the sitting room, a large tray in his hands holding several covered dishes and a pot of coffee.

'I'm sorry you have wasted your time and energy, my friend. I cannot stomach anything.' I lowered my head onto Aaron's lifeless chest and burst into fresh tears.

'Oh, my precious butterball. You haven't swallowed a thing for days now. You must eat, if not for your own sake, have some for Thomas and Emmy. You are the only parent they have left. They need you, Abigail. I can't do everything. I don't have time to raise your children for you, no matter how much I love them and think them both perfect. Nothing like the gruesome little mongrels from that village. My oath, they get uglier every year. Even the newest wean has a face that's hard to tell apart from a monkey's backside. Anyway, enough of the unfortunate looking bairns who roam the halls and paddocks of Willow Grove. It surprises me how you can breed the most majestic looking horses, but when it comes to children, they're all crockadillapigs. Well, except for my twins. They're the spit of their Uncle Leo. Perfect to look at. Anyway, as I said, enough about the misfortunes we are forced to tolerate. I want you to eat this, and I mean it. Please try, Abigail. I love you more than chocolate, but how can I continue to call you a fatty alongside Pollyanna if you stop eating altogether?.' My mouth twitched slightly, despite my melancholy. He could be sweet as sugar; however, in the same sentence could ruin it all with just a few words he would be best to keep to himself.

'Please, Leo. I just want to be left alone with my husband. I have had no appetite since I lost him. I know you are trying to help, but I cannot fix my mind on anything but him.' He ignored me, placing the tray down on the small table in between the lounges. He made his way over to my side, then took me firmly by the shoulders, gently guiding me across the room towards the lounges.

'I made your favourite,' he said, smiling as he roughly pushed me down on the lounge, causing me to lose my balance and reach out to stop myself falling to the floor. I sat myself back up and stared back up at him, uncertain of what he had said. So many here would speak to me; however, I often didn't hear a word, so focussed on my own pain and helplessness, my heart damaged, raw and bleeding, my will to live no more. Leo sat himself down next to me, leaning forward to remove the wire mesh food covers from the plate and several bowls. 'I probably need to narrow that down.' He waved his hand in the direction of the food. 'This is a recipe from my own homeland that I know you adore. I also brought you dessert for breakfast, again your favourite, but do you appreciate me? No. No one does in this house. I am treated like a slave in this mansion, and I'm sick of it. Polly keeps trying to boss me when it comes to you, and she can bang that up her clacker, let me give you the drum. I am your best friend, therefore, it is my responsibility to get you to eat. You will eat before Polly takes over and I give you my famous bitch slap, as it is now known throughout the district. I'm famous because I have a signature fight move,' he said proudly as he picked up the tray and placed it on my lap. My mouth started to water as I looked down at the fettuccine pasta, the smell of bacon and onion filling my nostrils. I put the tip of my finger in the cheese sauce, tasting garlic as I put it into my mouth. I couldn't remember when I had eaten last, but knew I must try given how worried he was. I was grateful for everything he did, not only in the kitchen every single day. From preparing to cooking the foreign fruits, herbs and vegetables my aunt had planted here so many Australians had never seen or tasted before, he was my confidant and friend, and I valued that more than anything he could feed me.

'All right. Thank you, my dear Leo. I will try.' I lifted the fork to my mouth, chewing carefully before I swallowed. I felt it hit my empty stomach, and for a moment thought it was going to come straight back up. I took a sip of lemonade and tried again. It was easier this time, and I managed to eat half of what he had served me while he watched on like a hawk. There was a gentle knock at the door and I looked across to see Hamish, the twins following behind. They ran to me, both making themselves comfortable beside me.

'Leo made us my favourite, Mummy. Pasta with cheese. We aren't allowed to have ours because we haven't even had breakfast yet. You are so funny eating lunch for breakfast, and breakfast for dinner,' Emmy remarked, touching my nose with her finger for a moment as I smiled. I had eaten a boiled egg on a slice of toast for dinner a few nights ago, which had amused her to no end, loudly stating she had never seen anyone do that before. They would eat a hot lunch in the dining hall when at school, and consume a larger meal for dinner in the evening, or tea as Aaron and his family called it. They only ever had eggs on toast for breakfast, not for any other reason than the food prepared for us was always elaborate, and if we wanted anything simple, we would have to ask or make it ourselves. She rose to her feet and went to her father, leaning into the coffin to kiss him on the cheek.

'I love you, my Daddy. I hope they have a horse just like Goliath for you wherever you are,' she whispered, then quickly returned to sit with us. Hamish put his arm around her tiny shoulders, and she smiled up at him, tears in her eyes. Both Thomas and Emmy were being so very brave, and appeared to have accepted their father's death better than I had. They were sad and cried at times; however, with everyone around to distract them, they had settled back into Willow Grove and started playing with their friends again.

I felt empty and numb, and despite seeing Aaron in his coffin, I still expected him to walk through the door. No matter where I went in the house, each room was filled with his presence. Leo poured another cup of coffee as Hamish sat back on the lounge opposite, while I struggled to my feet to return to Aaron, leaving them to talk. After some time, they all stood, Thomas and Emmy coming to my side.

'We're gunna have brekkie with Uncle Hamish. We'll come back an' see ya before we leave,' Thomas said, embracing me before turning to touch his father's face. I watched them leave with Hamish and Leo, exhaling loudly as they closed the door behind them.

Thomas and Emmy had asked to return to school the morning we had arrived home. I felt it could only help, and would keep them occupied and distracted through this heartbreaking time. I knew the death of their father was affecting them more than they let on, but I also knew the sooner they could get back to their normal routine, the better.

I had refused to leave his side for three-days, spending the first night home in my bed alone; however, I had not been back in it since. They had returned Aaron to me the following day as promised, and I hadn't been able to remain in my room other than to bathe and change my clothes. Death hadn't changed the fact I needed to be by his side. It was the same as it had always been. I could not stand being apart from him and did not know how my life would continue without him in it. I lay my head on his unmoving chest and sobbed like I would never stop.

I felt someone place their hands on my shoulders from behind, startling me. I gasped aloud and turned to see who had snuck up on me, finding Richard, a sad smile touching his lips.

'I'm sorry, Abigail. I thought you heard me speak when I entered. I've just come to take you for lunch.' He gazed down at Aaron for the longest time, then looked at the coffin begrudgingly. Made from a lovely mahogany wood, the outside so highly polished you could see your face in it. Or so Leo told me. The lid of the coffin leaned against the wall near the fireplace waiting for the undertakers to seal the coffin on the day of his funeral—Aaron's name and the date he was born and died engraved on a small silver plate attached on top. Mr Neilson hadn't forgotten the size of Aaron, despite the years that had passed, and had set about organising his casket the day he was murdered by the state of Victoria, his carpenter son working through the night to ensure Aaron could come home to us the very next morning. Mr Neilson was aware how important it was to me to have my loved ones at home after witnessing my grief when our boys were killed. I remained seated, Richard silently standing behind me, his hands still resting on my shoulders.

'Take me where, Richard? The only place I want to be is here beside Aaron. I haven't gone mad, and tell the others to stop questioning my sanity. I know he isn't in there anymore, but I do know he's around me. I can feel him. Being in here allows me to talk to him while he is still physically present. I know none of you understand, and I do not expect you to. He is here, Richard. I could always feel when he was watching me. I always knew when he was close, even when not in my sight. It's not his body laying here making me feel this way. It's his soul, and he's here.' I felt ridiculous once the words were spoken aloud, my cheeks becoming warm as he squeezed my shoulders in comfort.

'I do not know what to say to that, Abigail. I'm unsure if I believe in life after death. I was taught when you die you sleep until judgment day. As for his soul being here, nothing would surprise me with Aaron. I know he believed in an afterlife, and had every intention of contacting you if he was able.' I heard the smile in his voice as he stood me up, then walked me over to sit on the lounge.

'It matters not what anyone believes. I know what I feel, and although he hasn't found a way to show me he is safe yet, I know he will.' I wished I felt as confident as I sounded, and attempted to smile back as Richard gazed at me sympathetically, my hand in his.

'Now, I'm not going to take no for an answer. I understand you find it difficult to be in the kitchen, so I am taking you out into the back garden for some fresh air and good food. I will carry you if you give me any problems, Mistress Abigail,' he said firmly, and I let out the breath I didn't know I was holding.

'All right. I can see I will not win this battle. Some fresh air may do me some good, clear my head and all that,' I remarked as I went and kissed Aaron on the cheek before Richard took my hand, led me through the front door, and out to the garden.

We made ourselves comfortable at the outdoor table and chairs on the back verandah. I adored this setting, the seats designed in a manner that supported the entire body as they curved around you. The large cushions, made of soft cowhide and filled with goose feathers, were most comfortable when reading a book or eating something extra between meals. It was informal and comfortable, two of the more important things that mattered to me when it came to furniture.

All the lounges in the sitting room, along with all the others in my office and the drawing room, had been replaced just before Aaron had been arrested. He had designed them, drawing large couches wide and deep to seat up to five people. He had a local man make them, and chose the fabric himself, which Catherine had managed to ship over from England.

He also designed the outdoor table and chairs, hand carved from solid pieces of redgum by one of our farmhands, who was talented in the art of crafting furniture. Catherine had made all the cushions for them, taking the measurements while ensuring they were sturdy enough to survive the harsh Australian climate.

I heard singing and looked up to find Leo strolling around the corner of the house towards us, a wide grin on his handsome face, a tray in his hands.

'Ahhh, you did manage to drag her out of the sitting room. I owe you five-pound now, damn it. Good to see you out in the daylight, Abigail, although you look dreadful. You will never catch another husband walking around like that. I will be forced to intervene, and I don't care what Bessie says. I am the only one who knows how to style your hair properly. Now, I know I've been told by every man and his dog around here to not bother you with trivial matters, but I don't see this as trivial. Polly must be thrown out of the cottage. I don't care where you send her, but I've had enough.' He sat down opposite us, making himself comfortable, then grunted indignantly. 'She had the nerve to hover around in my kitchen this morning bossing me, which everyone knows not to do, then grabbed me by my python.' His eyes widened as I tried to smother a smile. 'I cannot believe what the tavern trollop did. I see you yourself are quite surprised, even though you always defend her bad behaviour. I had no idea her hands are as big as a man's. She came close to getting her fingers halfway around it, and threatened to rip it off with her bare hands and make me cook it. Then eat it, Abigail. That is who your sister is. The most horrible person in the entire world, and I have been forced to put up with her bad manners ever since I met you. You let her get away with everything; however, now she has crossed the line, with her enormous backside following along behind her several minutes later. If you don't get rid of her, I will.' I narrowed my gaze at him as Richard snorted beside me, then threw back his head and howled with laughter—just as my Aaron used to do.

'What did you do to her?' I felt calmer than I had for days as I sipped the pear juice he had brought out for us.

'Nought, I promise you. Well, I may have pulled her hair a wee bit when she was at the table eating. It would not have hurt a five-year-old bairn, and what I did certainly didn't deserve what she did.' Richard continued to laugh, while I did not.

'I was present in the room when the incident occurred,' Richard interrupted, composing himself then clearing his throat. 'It wasn't that you may have pulled her hair, Leo. You grabbed a fistful, and yanked it so hard some came out in your hand. And would you like to know why?' he asked, turning to me, and I nodded. 'All because she said her eggs were runny, and she prefers Sally's cooking to Leo's.' He turned back to my wayward friend as I shook my head in disbelief. 'I've never seen Polly move as fast as she did when chasing you into the scullery. And she's quick with her hands. I could hear your squealing from where I sat.' Richard laughed again, Leo's face now flushed.

'It wasn't funny at all. She had no right to say those lies about me. Everyone knows I am the only chef here, and the rest of them are just cooks. I will not be compared to a mere cook. Polly deserved what I dished out to her instead of breakfast. She only said it to vex me.' He wrinkled his nose in disdain, while I glared across at him.

'Did Richard drag me out here for a relaxing lunch, or to hear your complaints, you selfish wee shite? I cannot cope with anything more than what I already carry at this very moment so you will have to sort out your own problems. I'm not getting involved,' I told him firmly as he abruptly rose to his feet.

'Oh, fine then. I now know for certain Polly is your favourite and you don't love me anymore,' he shrieked, his high-pitched whining causing me to stick my fingers in my ears until he stomped away. He made his way inside, his hands waving about, his screams still filling my ears long after he was gone from my sight. Richard shook his head while he listened to Leo's tantrum, sipping his drink as he chuckled softly to himself. He soon started to talk of his parents and family as I tried to listen, completely distracted and unable to concentrate.

It was nice sitting out here on the verandah. I did not have a single memory at this table with Aaron. He was living under the house when it was finished and the couches were delivered. It made it just a little bit more bearable when I was obliged to go to the sitting room or outside. I had missed my garden, especially when my roses were in full bloom, covering the backyard in a sea of white. Planted when aunt Isabelle was residing here, Harry confided that it had always been her wish to have a garden full of white roses, just as she had in the home she grew up in—so he ensured her wish was granted as a surprise from him to the great love of his life.

Although the back garden was filled with white flowers, Sean had planted lavender around every rosebush, resulting in a lovely contrast of colour and fragrance, while Tommy spent six-days a week from dawn 'till dusk toiling the near ten-acres of gardens surrounding the mansion to ensure it was immaculate. He was responsible for the house gardens, while Sean worked the vegetable gardens and orchards, along with four farm-hands employed to assist him. Tommy supervised three men, all dedicated to the land with some talent for growing, while two of them had been head gardeners at grand estates back in England and brought a great deal of experience to Willow Grove. Between Sean and Tommy, they kept the gardens so well-manicured, the grounds of Willow Grove appeared to have come from a story book. There wasn't a weed out there I could find, and I had cast my eyes many a time over the lawns and flowers, always finding them healthy and blooming.

The vegetable garden and orchards had become well known and very much admired for its unique produce, thanks to all who ate at Willow Grove commenting on the variety and freshness of the fruits and vegetables served to anyone in the district who would listen. I had seen for myself how much time and energy went into growing the large vegetables and herbs, along with the fruits and nuts in the orchards. I was incredibly impressed with the team of gardeners we now had on staff.

'I dragged you out here to enjoy my company, and now I don't know what to speak of to distract you from your grief,' Richard remarked, shifting in his seat, his face deepening.

'There is only one thing you could say that upsets me. Please don't ask me how I am. I know it's the only thing they can think to say, but how do people expect me to be? I've just lost my husband, the only man who I will ever love, and who loved me back just as thoroughly. As the days, the hours, the minutes pass by, it puts even more distance between us and when I last spoke to him or was in his embrace. I will not survive without him, Richard. You all say I am strong and brave, but I'm not.' I watched the magpies on the lawn, jumping to and fro as they ate scraps from the kitchen brought out by Erin. She giggled to herself before turning to wave, then hurried back around the side of the house towards the kitchen. 'I relied so much on him. Not to do anything for me. I depended on his love and friendship. We were always together, except when he had to work. He wasn't like other men who would go off with their mates for days at a time, or go drinking all night at the taverns and neglect his family. He was an extension of me, Richard, and the connection we share is strong. Even now. I can still feel him, as I told you. I know you think me mad with grief, but it's more than that. I fear my soul has been taken with his, and all that is left of me is an empty shell.' My voice faltered as he took my hand in his across the table, his lovely kind eyes filled with tears.

'I don't think you mad at all, Abigail. We all know and witnessed with our own eyes how close you and Aaron were. I'm confident that if there is an afterlife, he is certainly here and around you.' He patted my hand sympathetically as Leo brought out our lunch and placed it in front of me. He had made veal ravioli in a cream sauce, created from his Nona's recipe handed down over seven generations, and one of my favourites he had first cooked for us the week we arrived at Willow Grove. I slowly picked up a fork and began to eat. I was starting to feel better in myself since eating breakfast this morning, but my appetite had not returned. Leo glared down at me before turning on his heel and marching back to the door leading to the kitchen, not uttering one word to us throughout the entire time he had graced us with his presence. He turned back towards us, lifted his hand and made a rude gesture, then disappeared through the door, leaving Richard and I alone.

'Abigail, I must ask you this, even though it's not the right time. There won't be a right time. Before Aaron died, he dealt with every aspect of your business. Now he is no longer with us, and you have no father to care for you or your finances, it's important I know if you want me to consult with you directly?' I sighed deeply, closing my eyes for a moment as he gazed out over the lawn, several rosellas picking at a bowl of minced meat left outside for Dingo.

'I cannot cope with the burden I already carry, Richard. I'm unable to care for my children without assistance, which hurts my heart even more. I walk around here feeling like a ghost myself, as if I'm watching everything from above and am no longer connected to my body. My mind is fragmented, and I cannot concentrate on a thing, so talking about business with me will only waste your time.' He nodded, smiling sadly at half a dozen yellow-crested cockatoos screeching at each other as they fought for the scraps from our table only a few yards from us. 'I will leave my business dealings for you to manage, if you would be so kind as to agree to the arrangement, my dear friend. I trust you completely, and I know whatever decisions you make in the future would be in my best interest. Mr Cavanaugh is always available if you need someone to consult with, and Hamish will be managing Willow Grove. You can meet with him in relation to anything to do with the running of the property. As for all my other business interests, I leave them with you and my father-in-law.' I swallowed hard, not caring if I made another penny or lost everything I owned.

It all meant nothing to me. I had never been interested in accumulating wealth, only ever wanting a warm bed to lay my head and food in my stomach. As long as I was surrounded by people I loved and who loved me back just as fiercely, and now I had no interest in anything at all. All I wanted was my darling man back in my arms. For Thomas and Emmy to have their Daddy back to tell them their morning stories. To take them down to the kitchen for breakfast each morning and be there to greet them when they arrived home for school. I wanted my husband to wrap his arms around me and tell me everything was going to be alright. To have him here beside us to go on adventures around the property in the afternoons with his children, as we so often did, and to sit at the table in the evening to eat tea together, wanting to hear every last detail of their day only because he took such delight in them. They needed him here to lay beside them in bed each night while I read to the three of them from books I had collected over the years, many of them selected just for them. No amount of money in the world could ever replace him or what he meant to us. Our wealth hadn't saved him—not money, gold or diamonds could buy the love and happiness he brought to me and those around him. We needed him here, not lifeless in a wooden box laid out in our sitting room where we had spent thousands of hours together as a family.

'I know you are not in a fit state to even think of such matters; however, I was obligated to ask. I'm sorry, dear Abigail. It eases my mind that you have Aaron's parents acting as your own and you trust them. Have you read the letter Aaron wrote to you the morning of his execution? I made sure it was returned to you, along with his possessions.' Aaron had written me a ten-page letter that was beautiful, heartbreaking, loving, honest and generous, and it grieved me he would never receive my reply .

'I've read it a hundred-times at least since Mr Neilson returned Aaron's belongings the night he was murdered. The kind man made a special trip here when he could have brought the bag the next morning when they returned him to us. I have put it with all the letters he has ever written me since we were courting. They are all in my bedside table, wrapped in a silk cloth and bound together so I can take them out and read them at will. They make me feel close to him. Despite making me cry, I cannot stop reading them. They are so Aaron. Everything he was and is as a man. He worried dreadfully for me being left here without him. He knew me so well, and predicted how I would be feeling at this moment. He believes I will fall in a heap for a while. What he doesn't realise is I already have, and will never recover. My life has shattered into a million pieces, no different from a crystal vase thrown onto the floor. Neither could ever be put back together like it once was. That's what our lives were like, Richard. A beautiful vase full of magnificent flowers, but it's all gone now. Broken and shattered on the floor, never to be put back together.'

'I do not believe or accept that for a moment, Abigail. That's not what Aaron wanted for you or the children. He knew you would grieve deeply, and asked everyone to take great care of you, but he wanted your life to go on. You are right and cannot have the life you once had. That is now gone forever. When you move past the deepest part of your grieving, you will need to start thinking about the new life you are obligated to create, if not for yourself, for Thomas and Emmy. Aaron knew they would be the only thing that would motivate you to go on living. He loved and adored you, and you must go on for him. I don't know what you will choose to do in the future, Abigail; however, I am confident whatever that may be, it will be in the best interest of your children.' His voice was low and gentle as he continued to hold my hand, silent tears trickling down my face. He handed me a handkerchief as Leo danced himself outside, singing a song from a performance he had recently seen at The Princess Theatre in Melbourne by Dame Nellie herself, a tray holding two bowls in his hands. He wiggled his backside as he placed an entire cake down in front of us, our disagreement and resulting tantrum now forgotten.

'What's this? It looks different to anything I have seen you make before.' I ran my finger along the side, scraping up a creamy substance, then popped it in my mouth. I could taste caramel; however, there was a subtle hint of flavour I was unable to identify.

'This dessert is the result of the gift bestowed on me in the area of culinary art.' He looked up towards the sky, nodding in thanks before continuing. 'It's my own creation. Sent from the angels above but came to me by accident, and I mean that more than you know. I mistook the sugar for salt, thanks to Sally, but the results speak for themselves,' he announced proudly as he cut us both a slice, spooning a generous dollop of thick cream beside each wedge before placing them in front of us. 'Surely you are aware I trained under the chef of kings, and the king of chefs for a short time, Georges-Auguste Escoffier?' I nodded my mouth full. It was something he never let any of us forget. Chef Escoffier had changed the way food was served in France, then around the world. A la francaise, or service in the French style, where all the dishes were brought to the table at once and laid out as a banquet was quite magnificent, but highly impractical when serving at a restaurant. Chef Escoffier insisted the courses be brought out to the table one after another in sequence, the same way Leo insisted the meals were served at Willow Grove.

'It sounds awful, Leo. Salt and caramel together set my teeth on edge. It seems what you are really saying is that you are feeding us your mistake?' Richard remarked, his suspicious gaze fixed on the generous wedge of creamy cake in his bowl. He picked up his fork and hesitantly put a small spoon of it in his mouth, then chewed thoughtfully, his face brightening as he took another mouthful, larger this time.

'See, Richard? I told you I'm magical. I am so talented, I can make a feast for a king out of anything supplied to me and it always tastes delicious. Even my mistakes are requested constantly, and many are now on the menu. This one has a pound of curds whipped into the batter; therefore, I christen thee, Salted Caramel Cheesecake.' He waved the knife over the cake as if casting a spell, a smug smirk on his face as he danced back inside without another word, while whistling a tune I recognised from somewhere.

I had no appetite when I first stepped outside into the fresh air, the smell of eucalyptus making me lightheaded, and happier. My stomach growled so loudly Richard turned to me and grinned. I finished my dessert, then cut myself another slice. It was absolutely delicious and like nothing I had ever tasted. I would ensure Leo did remember to put it on the menu and pass on his mistaken recipe to Jenny, so the workers could enjoy it too.

Richard and I chatted about stuff and nonsense for a time, until the tug at my heart became unbearable, pulling me back to Aaron. I excused myself and made my way back to him. Where I intended to stay until we were forced to part, and I said my final goodbye.

Chapter Eighteen

I HAD EATEN DINNER with Thomas, Emmy and Hamish in the sitting room, the twins sitting on the floor around the coffee table, while Hamish and I ate from a tray on our laps. I had left the children with Hamish playing cards, returning to Aaron's side where I listened to them talk from across the room, then their indignant howls when their godfather was caught cheating.

Their bedtime soon arrived, and they came to me, embracing me tightly. Thomas touched his father's face gently in farewell, while Emmy kissed his cheek. Hamish took them both by the hand and led them upstairs to little Mary. He spent some time up there with them, reading a few chapters of a book to them before returning to the sitting room. He sat down on a lounge opposite Leo, while keeping a watchful eye on me.

He and Leo talked amiably in hushed tones, while I stayed where I was, close to my love. I gazed at his lifeless face, the cheeky grin gone forever, his cold and lifeless hand in mine. Intertwined and resting on his broad chest, I ran my free hand over his fingers, thick and long like the sausages Leo would make that he loved so much. Leo yawned loudly before struggling to his feet, his eyes half closed as he came to my side to kiss me goodnight. He leaned down and gently kissed Aaron on the lips before embracing me.

'Sleep well, Goliath, wherever you are. We all love you, if you can hear me,' he shouted up to the ceiling, my arms still around him.

'Goodnight, darling Leo. I'm confident there is no need to shout for him to hear you. You're fortunate souls can do you no harm. If he were physically here, he would smack you for kissing him on the lips. You know he hated it when he was alive.' A smile touched my lips for a moment, while Leo's face lit up, his eyes sparkling with mischief.

'Well, isn't it a blessing he hasn't the experience or knowledge to haunt me yet? I know he would if he could, just to torture me like he was always complaining I did to him. I think he loved me in secret, and enjoyed me allowing you to let me grace you with my presence. There is no denying he loved me and will miss me dreadfully. Wherever his sweet little soul is. Goodnight, Goliath.' Gently stroking my husband's face, Leo turned to embrace me once again, calling out his farewells as he crossed the room before stepping into the hallway to find his bed—leaving Hamish sitting on the lounge, shaking his head in disbelief.

'I cannae believe Aaron put up with him fer all those years. What's this allowing ye tae let me grace ye with me presence scaffy? I would've killed him meself by now. Jesus, Abigail. I warned ye years ago about gettin' tae close tae yer servants. He says the most disgustin' things tae ye an' ye simply ignore it, only pickin' out the words ye like an' overlookin' the rest. Dinnae misunderstand me. I'm fond enough o' the man. He does amuse me, at times, but some o' the things that come out o' his mouth are offensive, naw matter what yer station. I dinnae know whether tae call him a bigot, or assume Charlie Darwin is a close relative on his father's side.' He smiled to himself as I half-heartedly smiled back. 'Ye really should get some sleep, Abigail,' he called out, yawning widely as I murmured in Aaron's ear, my head on his chest, his hand still wrapped in mine.

'No. Sleep will never find me tonight, anyway, even if I go to my bed. I would rather be here where I feel close to him. You go, Hamish. I will be fine,' I promised, his yawn wider this time.

'Naw. I'll stay a wee bit longer tae keep ye company.' He took a blanket from the back of the lounge and lay down, his snores filling the room only moments later. I placed my head back down on Aaron's chest, just like I had done so many times before, and wondered where he was now. Was there a beautiful place you went to when you passed over, or only darkness? Just a black hole of nothingness somewhere past the stars. Even if this place existed, could you leave to come back and be around those you loved? I had not a clue, but I hoped it to be true and silently sent my love to him, wherever he was.

I felt hands on my shoulders, and I sat up, finding Leo standing behind me. I had fallen asleep, my head on Aaron's lifeless chest most of the night. Hamish slept soundly on the lounge, another blanket thrown over him, no doubt by Leo. He could be quite thoughtful. When not too involved with himself. I smiled weakly, watching him cross the room, a cup of freshly brewed coffee in his hand.

'Why don't you go up to bed and rest properly for a few hours, Abigail?' He kissed my cheek, handing me the cup before sitting down beside me and slipping his arm around my shoulders in comfort.

'I cannot leave him, Leo. After tomorrow, he will be gone and buried. I need this time with him. I know you think me insane since he was taken from us, and I can give you no rational explanation as to why I need to be by his side.' I started to cry, waking Hamish. He sat up bleary-eyed, shaking his head as if he didn't know where he was. Leo took him a cup of coffee, which he accepted gratefully while watching me sob over the coffin.

'Oh, sweetheart. It hasn't been since he was taken. I thought you mad long before that,' Leo called out before disappearing back into the hallway.

Hamish rose to his feet and stretched before coming to my side. He took me by the shoulders and led me over to the lounge where he made me lie down, then returned to his own to drink his coffee without another word. The twins ran into the room shortly after to get Hamish for breakfast, both embracing me with great affection. Once Leo, Hamish and the children had left for the kitchen, I returned to Aaron's side and stayed there the entire day, the afternoon passing quickly surrounded by his family and our friends visiting to pay their respects and comfort me. I could no longer speak, a lump lodged in my throat I was unable to dislodge. All I could do was cry as our loved ones said what they could, attempting to express their sincerest feelings in words lost to them in their own grief. An endless sea of faces came and went throughout the day in a blur of tears and pain, and I had no recollection if I had spoken a word to anyone, or them me.

I breathed a sigh of relief once I was alone again, the night silent once they all retired to their beds, leaving me to my privacy with Aaron. I talked to him of the memories I held dear, and the life we had shared, the fire in the hearth burning warmly while providing comfort to my broken soul. Hamish silently entered the room carrying a tray, smiling sadly as he crossed the room, then made himself comfortable on the lounge. Listening to me reminisce with Aaron about our time together, talking of how our life would have been had he lived, Hamish quietly came to my side. Gently guiding me over to the lounge, he had mugs of hot chocolate and carrot cake waiting on the table.

'I know how much ye cannae resist cake, so I brought ye some,' he said encouragingly, returning to his chair with his own cup of hot chocolate.

'Thank you, Hamish. I appreciate everything you are doing for us. You are a dear friend.' I felt tears sting my eyes, and quickly brushed them away before bringing the mug up to my lips.

'Abigail, go rest in yer bed tonight. It's goin' tae be a big day tomorrow an' ye'll need all yer strength.' His voice soothing and sympathetic, I shook my head, exhaustion weighing heavily on me.

'No. It's my last night with him, Hamish. I don't expect anyone to understand but please accept this is something I must do. I need to memorise every detail of him before he is taken from me. The feel of his hair, the skin on his face under my fingers, his hands that always caressed me whenever he was close. Things I never want to forget about him, and he can hear me in here. I know he can. He hasn't shown me a sign yet, but I know he will. He promised me, and he has never broken his word to me. Please, stop haranguing me. Surely you, out of everyone, understand?' I pleaded, taking the piece of cake he kindly offered. He sighed deeply, gazing across at me with such deep pity.

'Aye, but I'm stayin' in here then. I'll be sleepin', but yell out if ye need anythin'.'

He took a blanket from the walnut cupboard, making himself comfortable on the lounge as I finished my cake, then picked up the mug of hot chocolate, taking it with me as I stood. I returned to Aaron, resuming where I left off before I was interrupted. I could hear Hamish sobbing quietly as he listened to me pour my heart out to my beautiful man, who would never again answer back.

I lay my head on his cold chest, no longer hearing or feeling the familiar, regular beat that would resonate in my ear and against my cheek, just as it had for so many years. I was confident I hadn't gone mad, despite the common opinion around me. I knew he was gone, but I was holding on to the last piece I had of him in the hope he was around me and listening. It gave me some comfort, and I allowed myself to give in to sleep, drifting off to another place and time while dreaming of a ship, a prison officer's uniform, and the honeymoon cottage.

I woke to the smell of coffee and sat up to find Leo pouring a cup for Hamish and myself as they sat side-by-side on a lounge. I stood, then crossed the room to join them, stretching my body while attempting to get the kink out of my neck before sitting down next to Leo.

'Did ye get any rest, Abigail?' Hamish asked as I picked up my coffee, made just as I liked it by my dear friend. Leo smiled sympathetically in my direction, his eyes fixed on the paintings on the walls of people we were not acquainted with, nor ever would be given the age of some of the portraits.

'Some,' I replied, sipping my coffee while snuggling under a blanket. I placed my cup on the table, then lay back listening to them speak softly between themselves. Soon after, I opened my eyes to find Bessie shaking me awake.

'Come along now, Mistress. I have let you sleep for as long as I can, but the time has come to ready yourself,' she said sadly. I struggled to my feet and hurried to Aaron's side, leaning down over the coffin to kiss him one last time. Placing the photographs next to him, memories flooded my mind of how I had given them to him at the gaol. How he had treasured them, keeping them close in his breast pocket. He carried them to the gallows next to his heart—along with a single chocolate cupcake. I had asked Leo to make a batch the same as Aaron brought me each month throughout our entire marriage. And to never, ever make them again from that day forward. Leo kindly reassured me he planned to retire the recipe due to that fact, but would always keep it in his book to remember him.

I looked at the items the children had placed in with their father. A picture of him holding them, a stuffed rabbit Emmy had loved since she was born, a toy boat Aaron used to play together with Thomas, several letters they had written to him, along with drawings and paintings they had created at school. Thomas had added the painting he had done of the Australian flag—a picture Aaron had been so proud of when he hung it next to his bed under the house. I kissed him again as I placed my own letter next to his heart, then placed my hands on his broad shoulders one last time, my forehead against his, while whispering goodbye to the only man I would ever love.

I straightened up, feeling exhausted as I sobbed my heart out while staring down at Aaron for the last time, then taking a mental photograph of my beautiful man I would keep close. Bessie came up beside me and slipped her arm around my waist, supporting me while guiding me up to my bedchambers. She sat me down on the bed, then hurried off to my wardrobe to get one of the three mourning dresses Catherine had made for me, along with a matching black hat.

'Come now, sweetheart. It's time to get ready,' she said sadly, then led me over to my dressing table. She had insisted on washing my hair last night when I had come to bathe to ensure it was clean and fresh, my locks now smelling of vanilla. I sat at the dressing table while she silently did my hair, twisting it up onto the top of my head. Aaron would have wanted me to wear it down today, but I didn't have the strength to fight my headstrong maid, allowing her to do as she wished. Thomas and Emmy came in running to me soon after, standing on each side of me while gazing into the large mirror.

'Where's Daddy's body goin' today, Mummy?' Thomas asked, kissing my forehead before crossing the room to sit on the bed.

'We are burying him on the island with your baby brothers. We can visit to leave flowers for them,' I replied, and they smiled, Emmy hugging me tightly before sitting on my lap and cuddling into me.

'Remember what Daddy said, Thomas? He is in us, and that means he will never die, only his body. His soul is somewhere around us, only he is invisible now. Remember when he used to tell us stories about men and women who could become invisible when they were trying to stop a world war? Well, he is like that now. Still the same, only we can't see him. He is definitely in you. You are the spit of him,' Emmy remarked. A truer word had never been spoken. Thomas was exactly like Aaron, and although Emmy looked like me and had my spirit, she also had a lot of her father in her.

Bessie finished my hair, tears slipping silently down her face, then helped me into the new gown. Catherine had made several of them the day we had arrived home, bringing them to me the following morning. All were house dresses and very comfortable. Except for one. The dress I was forced to wear today, made especially for the funeral. If it weren't black, I would have thought it beautiful with its delicate lace and beading over the simple skirt, a fine lace overskirt with matching long sleeves, along with intricate black beading covering the bodice through to the back. I briefly glanced in the mirror, not caring how I looked, before I thanked Bessie and took the twins' hands in mine to guide them downstairs.

We walked into the sitting room to find our friends and family waiting, many standing to embrace us when we entered. Aaron's coffin had already been taken out to the hearse, and now we were to leave and follow them to the church. I slowly made my way outside with Thomas and Emmy by my side and found my carriage, Harry waiting beside it. All who lived and worked at Willow Grove were attending the service in Geelong, leaving Harry and the stable hands to prepare every working carriage on the property, along with saddling up a number of horses broken to ride for those without any means of getting to the church. Hamish leaned back on the carriage in deep discussion with Harry as we approached before they turned towards us, Harry assisting us in before Leo joined us, soon followed by Polly. Hamish climbed up after them, closing the door behind him.

'We mustn't leave yet. Angus is coming with us too,' Polly said. Hamish called out to Harry, asking him to wait.

'How? Where is he going to fit? Have you not noticed the size of Angus and Hamish? Just the two of them by themselves take up half this carriage, let alone putting another fatty between them. I refuse to be smothered to death by you, Pollyanna. I will sit between Angus and Adonis, and you go over there to Abigail and the children. On the other hand, I do not mind being squashed between the twin warriors. They are unlikely to notice when my hand wanders up their thighs. Accidentally on purpose, of course.' Polly raised her hand, pointing her finger in his face, their bodies touching as they sat side-by-side. Hamish remained silent next to Polly, his eyes twinkling in amusement.

'I've warned you a thousand-times about touching my husband. He is mine, so keep your filthy mitts off him. I mean it, Leonardo. Not only will I cut off your hands with an axe, I will tie you down and slice something else off,' she warned him as Leo smiled down at her.

'You're just feeling threatened and jealous because your husband likes me more than he likes you. He spends far more time in my company, and I cook for him every day, unlike you. Immediately makes me a better wife than you have ever been to him,' he told her indignantly as Angus opened the carriage door. Hamish stood, moving over to us while picking Emmy up and placing her on his lap. He settled himself next to Thomas, while I sat on the other side of my son. Polly refused to budge from the opposite seat, despite Leo's attempts to push her to the floor. Angus made himself comfortable next to her, much to Leo's disappointment. I listened in silence as Polly and Leo bickered the entire way to the church. Angus was of no help and laughed at them, infuriating Poly further. Hamish was quiet throughout the journey, choosing to talk in whispers to Thomas and Emmy while I stared out the window at the passing farms and the occasional general store.

Our carriage stopped outside Saint Mary of the Angels, and Hamish helped us down onto the cobblestones. I turned and gasped aloud. There must have been thousands of people spilling out of the already full church and onto the streets. The hearse had arrived long before us, and Aaron's coffin had already been taken inside. I made my way through the crowd, holding Thomas and Emmy's hands tightly while pulling them along, my head down, following Hamish as he walked in front of us, attempting to clear a path. I could hear people crying, some sobbing so loudly I couldn't think, others praying quietly while strangers called out their condolences to us.

As we walked towards the church, a photographer stepped out in front of us and took a picture, the flash blinding me. We kept walking, and as I entered the grand bluestone building, all the memories of our wedding day came flooding back, tears stinging my eyes for the thousandth time since he had gone. I slowly made my way down the aisle, and instead of seeing Aaron standing at the front waiting for me as he once had, all I could see was his coffin.

We sat in the front row with Aaron's family, and I stared at his coffin by the elaborate altar, a sacred place to me where we once stood and declared our love for each other. We had been so young and full of dreams and believed nothing bad would ever touch us. And it hadn't. For many years. His life had been cruelly cut short sixty-years too soon. I thought about how much happiness I had experienced with him, and knew I would never find a love to compare twice in a lifetime. I would have to keep him in my heart until I joined him and draw whatever future happiness I could from memories of our time together. Father Donnelly cleared his throat, preparing to start the service, then welcomed everyone while acknowledging what a sad day it was for all involved.

'A place of worship is not a place tae discuss politics or personal views, but I feel strongly that an injustice has occurred, an' Aaron's untimely death was unnecessary, an' unfair,' Father Donnelly said, his voice shaking with emotion as an eruption of clapping and cheering exploded behind me, deafening me. He began the service with a hymn, and all around me rose to their feet, except me for all I could do was stare at Aaron's coffin and sob. Aaron's brothers delivered his eulogy. And did him proud. I listened to them, one after another say beautiful words about their brother, all so alike and the spit of my Aaron. I held Thomas and Emmy close while they listened to the lovely words spoken about their father, wiping away their tears with my handkerchief.

The service continued in a blur of tears, while I gazed at Aaron's coffin, the native floral arrangement draped over the top, his favourite blossom from the wattle tree predominating. An Australian flag covered him completely underneath the willow branches, eucalyptus leaves and bright yellow wattle entwined into a floral masterpiece, complimenting the kangaroo paw, banksia, bottlebrush and lilly-pilly picked from the ground of Willow Grove. A native man currently camping on the property had kindly offered to make the arrangement for his casket, and I had gratefully accepted. Aaron loved everything about Australia, including her original owners. He had managed to develop deep friendships with many over the years, and it grieved him how they were treated. He admired the native flora and fauna, and I felt it a fitting tribute to include as much as I could as my way of telling him how much he was loved.

My love, my heart. I would never recover from his loss, of that I was certain. The pain was unbearable, and like no other I had ever experienced. I couldn't think about anything but him every minute of every day since he left, and my grief was all consuming. I wanted God to strike me down, take me in my sleep or by some terrible accident. I no longer cared what became of me. I knew I was selfish, having Thomas and Emmy to think of; however, my grief was blinding me.

The service drew to a close, and Mr Masters walked to the front and stood near the altar, as did Patrick, Aiden, and Luke, while Angus and Hamish followed behind, Leo joining them moments later. They stood solemnly beside Aaron's coffin, ready to carry their brother and mate to the waiting hearse, glancing across at Mr Masters as the music started and he began to sing.

'And I will love you until the sun no longer shines, the earth no longer turns, and the seas no longer rise. Our hearts will be together beyond the end of time, our souls will never die, and I will love you to eternity and for all time.'

It was the song we had made ours all those years ago when I was carrying the twins and dancing in the pub. Since that night, Mr Masters had always sung the sweet melody for us whenever we were there.

They lifted the coffin onto their shoulders, and I was thankful they were large men and able to carry Aaron's weight. I stood to follow them down the aisle, holding Thomas and Emmy's hands as we walked slowly behind, then stopped outside the church to watch them place their Daddy in the hearse. I broke down and sobbed, barely able to stand by the time Mr Cavanaugh came to my side. He picked me up in his arms and carried me to the carriage, followed by the twins and Mrs Cavanaugh. They settled me into my seat and placed a soft blanket over my knees as the carriage started to move.

We followed the hearse towards home. I noticed all the people lining the streets, clapping and cheering. Some threw flowers at the hearse as it passed, leaving the road strewn with colour. I felt a sense of pride so many believed Aaron to be a good man who didn't deserve to be murdered. I sat back and watched Emmy and Thomas, both cuddled into their grandparents' lap.

'Abigail, I want you to know even though Aaron is no longer with us... ' His voice broke, and he coughed before continuing. 'It changes nought how we feel towards you. You're our first daughter, an' nothin' will change the love we have for you. We're your family, an' will help you get through this sorry business. There will come a time in the future you'll marry again, an' our family will embrace him as our own. We'll always trust your choices when it comes to how you an' the little ones choose to live. We'll never interfere. Nothin' will ever change our love for you, our precious daughter,' Mr Cavanaugh said gently, my hand in his. I kissed him on the cheek and squeezed Mrs Cavanaugh's hand, her soft sobs filling the carriage as she cried into her handkerchief.

'Thank you. I love you all very much. You are the only family I have, and ever will have. I cannot contemplate marrying again. I will never have the love I shared with your son.' I burst into tears, resting my head on his chest as Mr Cavanaugh put his arm around my shoulders.

We arrived home, but the horses did not stop in the driveway, continuing on past the stables and following the hearse to the island. The men carried Aaron to the boat and placed his coffin inside, then rowed him across. I watched as they carried him from the bank up to the graveyard while we waited near the landing. We needed ten boats to carry the mourners across, and it still wouldn't have been enough. There were so many here today I had never met who knew Aaron, most calling him a mate. There were farmers he used to trade with, friends from school and all around the district, and several small groups who had never met him, but somehow managed to sneak through and join the funeral procession back to Willow Grove.

Patrick rowed back and forth, collecting the guests and transporting them across to the island. It took some time until everyone was present and ready for the burial to proceed. His coffin sat over a gaping hole, held there by tightly strung ropes. I couldn't help but go straight to him. I knelt beside his coffin, sobbing as Father Donnelly conducted a graveside service. All eyes were fixed on me as I knelt beside him, my arms outstretched over his coffin. I sobbed loudly, screaming for him. I could hear those around me breaking down at my distress, aware I was hysterical and unable to be comforted no matter what they tried. I screamed as loudly as I could when Father Donnelly committed Aaron's body to the ground and white roses were placed on top of his coffin one by one by the mourners. I howled in pain as they lowered him into the ground, inconsolable and blinded by grief, those around me sobbing louder. Angus stood behind me, his large hands on my shoulders to ensure I didn't fall into the grave—or throw myself in after him—I wasn't certain.

A number of mourners started to leave to make their way to the house for the wake. Finally, I was left alone and leaned back against the gumtree where Aaron usually sat. Gazing down next to me at our sons, then next to them at my husband's grave—the freshly dug soil filled back in over him. He was now under a mound of dirt and lost to me forever. It was over and he was gone. I would never see him again on this earth, and the thought caused me to scream in anger, asking why he had been taken from me far too soon. I was unable to contemplate how my life could go on without him. Patrick returned to my side, standing silently by his brother's grave, his head bowed, while the birds in the tree above sang a cheerful chorus.

'Abigail, let me take you back to the house,' he said gently, his hand on my arm.

'I cannot leave him, Patrick, and I cannot go on without him,' I replied, lowering my head into my hands and sobbing as if I would never stop.

'Listen to me, Abigail. Aaron's gone, an' there's nothin' that'll bring him back. I know the love ya had for each other was strong. Ya sufferin' somethin' terrible right now but Aaron wouldn't want this for ya. He was me brother, an' we were as close as two brothers could be. I know how much he loved ya, an' how happy ya made him when he was here. I also know he didn't want ya to get stuck in ya grief. He'd hate to see ya in such despair. I dunno how to help ya. Come with me, sister, an' let me take ya' home.' He wiped tears from his handsome face, then mine.

I tried to stand, but my legs would no longer support me under my own strength. Patrick picked me up in his arms, murmuring soothingly to me as he carried me to the boat. Once on the other side, he walked back to the house, still carrying me while I sobbed into his chest. Hundreds of mourners stood in the back garden having refreshments when they saw us coming towards the house, many of them strangers to me. Several of my friends quickly followed Patrick to my room, stepping inside to find him placing me down on the bed, before kissing my cheek and returning to the garden to join the others. They surrounded me on my bed as I sobbed and screamed, cursing the world.

'I know what you're going through feels like it will kill you, the pain is so, so awful. It does lessen in time, I promise, sweetheart. It never goes away, but you won't always feel like this,' Dana said reassuringly, her hand stroking my brow. Catherine sat beside me, my hand wrapped tightly in her own.

'He was a good man, and we are sorry for it,' Tamara said sadly. Polly unpinned my hair, running the brush through it as we sat together on the bed, then plaited it like she used to when we were at the orphanage, knowing it had a way of soothing me. There was a knock on the door, and I turned to see Hamish in the doorway; however, he would not come in.

'I'm sorry tae disturb ye, Abigail, but there's a bloke here who says he was a guard at the gaol an' knew Aaron well. He'd like tae talk tae ye if yer up fer it.' I raised my eyebrows in surprise. I had seen a number of prison officers at the church; however, I hadn't noticed any at the burial.

'If you stay, Hamish, I will see him here. I don't give a fat rat's arse it's not considered proper to have men visit with me in my bedchamber. There is no other room I want to be in at the moment. I am fully dressed and respectable,' I said, quickly wiping my face as my friends struggled to the feet.

'We will come back to keep you company when you have finished. Come and get us, Hamish. We will be in the back garden having something to eat, and will bring a plate back for you, Abi,' Polly assured me as they made their way out of the room and towards the grand staircase. Hamish brought the man in and invited him to sit at the table, soon making themselves comfortable. I gazed across and smiled weakly at Stuart, Aaron's almost constant companion and guard. I was touched that he made the effort to come, given he lived on the other side of Melbourne in a new house just purchased from only a small portion of the money we paid him.

He had been good to us, despite coming at a cost. I didn't resent for a moment having paid to have Aaron made as comfortable as possible. It had made such an incredible amount of difference in so many ways, from the approval of visits from family and friends, down to bringing in small comforts to make his days a little more bearable.

'Good afternoon, Mrs Cavanaugh. You have me deepest sympathy. Your husband was a good man. I came to know him well,' he told me kindly. I nodded silently, waiting for him to go on. 'I understand you're beside yourself with grief, but I do need to talk to you. I will only keep you for a few minutes. I wanted to ease your mind about Aaron's last hours.' His eyes filled with sympathy, he stared across at me, his hands clasped tightly on the table.

'That is extremely kind of you, Mr Milne,' I replied, bursting into tears. I lay back on my pillows, sobbing quietly. A heavy veil of silence hung over the room. Hamish and Stuart glanced around the room awkwardly as I attempted to compose myself, sitting up to blow my nose.

'After you left in the evenin', I took him to his cell where I stayed with him while he ate the meal you supplied. He talked constantly while eatin', tellin' me how each was his favourite food. He could eat like a horse that husband of yours.' I smiled weakly across at him, Hamish unmoving beside him as he gazed out of the window, paying us no mind.

'Thank you for taking the time to go so far out of your way to come and tell me. I'm grateful he had you there for company and to listen. It does ease my mind a little to know he was amongst friends. Travel safe,' I replied through my tears, waiting for him to stand.

'Oh, no, Missus. That's not all.' He waved his hand, then smiled kindly. 'I'm here 'cause he asked me to come once he... ' His voice faltered for a moment, and he coughed while Hamish poured a glass of water from the jug on the table and swiftly passed it to him. 'He wanted you to know every last detail of how he spent his final hours. He told me you possess a vivid imagination an' could have been a writer of fantasy novels. He didn't want you thinkin' the worst.' Hamish threw back his head and laughed aloud, and I turned to narrow my gaze at him. 'Once the big fella finished eatin' he wrapped himself in that blanket your children gave him, an' he sat on his bed an' talked for hours while we shared a bottle of whisky. He loved you more than life itself, an' he truly believed the sun only rose for his nippers, as he called them. He spent a pleasant night, but didn't sleep a wink of it, choosin' to play cards with the guards an' talk. He wrote some letters he asked me to pass on to you. He was brave until the end, Missus. I walked with him to the gallows, an' stood beside him 'till the end.' He reached up and touched his own throat for a moment, swallowing hard before turning his attention back to me. 'I gave him the bottle of whisky to drink after he told me the message he asked me to give you. I know his mind wasn't fuddled with the grog, even though he sounded like it. I wanted you to know that.' He shook his head in disbelief, tapping his finger against his chin, his gaze fixed on a small finch sitting on my window sill. 'He also told me when they slipped the rope around his neck, he was a happy man 'cause his mind was filled with thoughts of you an' your children. He went quickly an' didn't suffer, Missus. The hangman did a good job an' broke his neck almost as soon as he dropped. I know I shouldn't be sayin' it so forward like, but it's the reason I'm here. To reassure you. Many will say it's a terrible death, an' that can be true, if it isn't got right the first time. I didn't want you imaginin' it was that way for your man, or allow others to mislead you. Seems every bastard has an opinion these days, an' opinions an' arseholes are very similar. Every bastard has one. Oh, beg me pardon, Missus.' He stopped for a moment and composed himself, his face flushed. 'That's why you needed to know he died quick an' brave, so no one can fill your head with somethin' different.' I nodded again, feeling slightly confused and ready for a nap.

'Thank you for passing on his last message. It eases me to know his mind was filled with memories of us.' I nodded politely as he thrust his hand up in the air, cutting me off.

'That wasn't the message he asked me to pass on to you, an' he made me give him me word I would nay forget.' He smiled weakly, appearing self conscious, his left eye twitching several times before he continued. 'Just before it was time to walk to the gallows, he was layin' on his bed with his eyes closed. He felt you next to him. Even felt your fingers touchin' his face. He heard everythin' you said to him while holdin' you in his arms in his mind. His answer is yes. He said only you would know what that meant.' Now it was his turn to appear confused, while chills ran up my spine and down my arms.

'What time was that?' I asked, excitement welling up in me as I struggled to sit up, knocking a pillow from the bed in the process.

'Just after half-past eight in the mornin'. About an hour an' a half before he died.' He glanced across at Hamish, who appeared just as confused, and I smiled to myself.

'Thank you, Stuart. It does make sense to me, and it means more than you know. I appreciate what you have done for us, and I wish you well in your future.' He rose to his feet, then came to my bedside and shook my hand politely before turning on his heel to leave. Hamish glanced across at me quizzically as he escorted him out, closing the door behind them before making their way downstairs.

Not a soul was aware of my vision that morning, nor that it was the exact time I had lain on the lounge after breakfast and closed my eyes, willing Aaron to hear me. I had felt as if I were standing in front of him as he took me in his arms and kissed me. Then he was gone. I had asked him a specific question, and he had now given me my answer.

I still remembered it vividly, and how I failed to replicate it when I returned to my room an hour later and tried again.

Within a few minutes, Polly and Catherine returned to my room, followed by Dana and Elizabeth. Soon after, Tamara and Victoria joined us, all soon squashed up together on the bed beside me. We talked of our memories of Aaron, some making me laugh, while others made me sob aloud, but they stayed beside me and held my hand, reassuring me I was not alone through this dark time, or on the sad journey I must take to healing. A dainty hand—whose, I was uncertain—stroked my head as I drifted off to sleep, dreaming of a silver possum, the Eiffel tower, and a woman named Charlotte.

Chapter Nineteen

M Y DARK LASHES FLICKERED before I slowly opened my eyes, the night air moving the lace curtains, their elegant dance the only life in the room. I was alone, and still wearing my mourning dress, the afternoon sun now replaced by the moon hanging low in the sky, the dark clouds covering all but a sliver of pale grey light, the majestic light show of stars and planets usually on display above covered by blackness. No different from my broken heart. I glanced at the clock on the mantel, and groaned aloud. I was unlikely to find sleep again tonight after snoring all afternoon and into the night. I threw the quilt off and placed my bare feet on the floor, sighing loudly before struggling to my feet. Stripping off the dress I would never wear again, I threw it in the corner of my bedchamber on the floor, then slipped on my nightgown and dressing gown. I made my way downstairs, my pipe and tobacco in hand, soon stepping out the back door to the verandah to find a seat at the table, the night so dark and gloomy.

'Are ye feelin' all right, Abigail? 'Tis well past midnight,' I heard someone say, startling me. I turned to see a darkened figure a few yards from where I sat, gazing up at the slip of a moon. I took my matchbook from my pocket and lit the pipe, the flame illuminating my face as I drew the smoke deep inside, then slowly exhaled.

'No, I'm not all right, Hamish, and I doubt I ever will be again in this lifetime,' I murmured. 'I haven't asked you, more so because

I have been melancholy and only thinking of myself, but how are you? Are you all right?' I drew on my pipe again, and heard him sigh deeply, pausing for the longest time before he answered me.

'Aye, but I miss the bloke. More than I knew I could. Tae watch ye an' the twins in so much pain an' naw be able tae help tears at me heart.' I could hear the pain in his voice; however, I couldn't see him—the night so very black. 'I gave Aaron me word the last time we ever met on this earth that I'd take care o' ye, Thomas, an' wee Emmy just as he would. I dinnae feel I'm doin' a very good job at keepin' me promise,' he remarked, his voice low and full of emotion.

'Come and sit with me, Hamish,' I said gently, moving a chair out for him with my foot, pushing it away from the table. He slowly made his way to my side, lowering himself onto the seat next to me, grunting as he tried to get comfortable. 'You've helped us more than you know. You are running the farm, just as Aaron did, and you are there every morning in the kitchen to eat with the twins and see them off to school. You return to care for them when school finishes until bedtime. Something I'm unable to do for the moment. My world has fallen apart, and as a result it's become clear I'm a terrible mother. All I want is to be alone with my memories. Aaron and I trust you more than anyone in this world when it comes to our children. You have kept every promise you made to him, and he'd be grateful for it. He wouldn't have asked you if he wasn't confident you could, or would.' I took his hand in mine as we sat in comfortable silence, side-by-side, relieved I no longer reacted to his touch. 'How are things between you and Nellie? I have been expecting an announcement for a while now.'

'Aye, things have changed in recent times. I was serious about marryin' her 'till she became upset an' gave me an ultimatum. When she didn't get the answer she was seekin', she threw me over.' His voice flat and without emotion, he lifted a bottle of ale to his lips and took a deep drink.

'I'm sorry for it, Hamish. I really believed she was the one for you.' I squeezed his hand in sympathy, an owl hooting somewhere above us in the old gumtree. 'What was the ultimatum she gave you?' He remained silent for the longest time, grunting as he swiped at a bogong moth that flew into his face.

'Either her, or ye an' the twins. She said she was naw longer prepared tae share me with every man an' his dog. An' if I spent more time with her, we'd have our own bairns. An' I could dote on 'em instead o' wastin' me time with other people's brats.'

'Ouch, that hurts.' I saw his head move as he nodded in agreement, chuckling quietly to himself.

'Aye, it does.'

'Hamish, if you need to cut back the time you spend here to save your relationship with Nellie, you can, and we would understand. The children and I will cope fine as we have so many people around us. I truly think you would find happiness with her. Don't ruin your future over a silly promise.' My eyes had adjusted to the dark and I could see the outline of his body, his curly hair loose and falling around his shoulders.

'Naw promise is silly, Abigail. Somethin' ye need tae remember. As fer Nellie, I'll naw be beggin' her tae take me back. Naw after what she said. She's shown me she has naw compassion fer others, even innocent bairns. Once she said such terrible things about people I care fer, 'twas the end o' it fer me. I cannae see meself makin' a life with someone who thinks that way.' He reached over and took the pipe from my hand, raised it to his lips and inhaled deeply, remaining beside me as we passed it back and forth until it was finished. 'At least ye'll sleep in yer own bed tonight, an' hopefully rest well after this.' He passed the pipe back to me, and I slipped it into my pocket.

'My body is exhausted, but my mind won't rest. It has settled a little now, but I will wake through the night, no doubt.' I stared up into the dark sky, my mind slow, my body heavy. 'Hamish, do you ever wonder what life here on earth really means? What's the point of it all?'

'Aye, all the bloody time. If I figure it out ye'll be the first tae know.' He chuckled to himself again, both settling back to enjoy the sounds of the Australian bush, before he let out a high-pitched shriek, his hand sending a bogong moth to the great beyond within moments.

I woke with a start, bathed in cold sweat but unable to remember the dreams that had tormented me since laying my head only two-hours before. I turned to stare out the window, the sky starting to brighten, our resident kookaburra singing his morning song to all who inhabited Willow Grove, man and beast. I had never felt more alone in my life despite being surrounded by people who loved me. Aaron filled every room with sunshine and now he was gone, the house felt different. I could not cope spending time in any part of the main house, other than our bedchamber, I felt close to him here, and could allow my tears to flow in private without the worry of upsetting those around me, while in any other room of the house, everything reminded me of him and set me off without warning in front of witnesses.

Today was our monthiversary, yet I would receive no chocolate cupcake. I thought of him, and how he would be down in the kitchen now eating them as fast as Leo could take the trays from the oven, while always reserving the best one for me. I pulled back the quilt and placed my feet on the floor, then stood and crossed the room to close the window, the clouds dark and threatening. Pulling on my dressing gown, I hurried down the hallway and into Thomas's bedchamber to check on my babies, both sleeping soundly in Thomas's bed. Bending down to kiss their sleeping faces, I whispered I would see them in a few days. Then straightened up to leave.

'Where are you going, Mummy,' Emmy asked, struggling to sit up as I turned back to her then sat down on the bed, kissing her again.

'Somewhere that was very special to your Daddy. I need some time alone there to gather my thoughts, if it's all right with you?' I said, Thomas opening his eyes and yawning. I repeated myself, and he nodded thoughtfully.

'Ya really gunna leave us to fend for ourselves when ya the only parent we have now?' I cringed as Emmy turned to him, her face starting to flush.

'Stop being so selfish, Thomas. We have Uncle Hamish and Mary to look after us, while Mummy doesn't have anyone anymore. If it makes her feel better to go and be close to Daddy, then you and I will be perfectly all right,' Emmy said sweetly, running her fingers through my loose hair.

'All right, Mummy. Maybe ya do need time alone if it'll make ya return to how ya were before this sorry business. I love ya, an' I didn't mean to make ya feel worse than ya do. Emmy's right, we'll be all right. I'll see ya when ya decide to come back.' Thomas sat up to embrace me, tears stinging my eyes as Emmy wrapped her little arms around both of us. 'Don't be too sad, Mummy. The old man is still lookin' after us,' he called out as I stepped into the hallway, pulling a dirty handkerchief from my dressing gown pocket and blowing my nose into it anyway.

I returned to my room and quickly packed a leather overnight bag of Aaron's, before pulling on a housedress and cloak, then sneaking out to the stables. It was still early, but there were people up and about and I did not feel strong enough to face anyone at the moment. I hurried into Delly's stall and quickly saddled her, attaching my bag to the back of the saddle, then walked her out from the stables, mounting her before making my way through the back paddock towards the sea.

I arrived at the honeymoon cottage, thoughts of the last time I had been here with Aaron overwhelming me, my mind unable to focus on anything but the memory of him waking me during the night to come here one last time not long before he was captured. I dismounted then swiftly unsaddled Delly, leading her to the small paddock and securing the gate before picking up my bag and entering the cottage. It was as we had left it, even down to the rumpled quilts. I had forgotten to tell anyone we had been here, so no one had known to come and straighten up, which I was glad of now.

I ran my hand down the side of the bed where Aaron had slept so many times, lowering myself heavily onto his side before bursting into tears. I had only buried him yesterday, and I wasn't coping. I missed him dreadfully already and couldn't bear the fact I would never see him again. Couldn't bear it and could not accept it. I felt I was going insane, losing my mind, just as Leo predicted day in and day out since moving here, and I was unable to think of anything other than my lost love. I curled up under the quilt where his body had lay what felt like a lifetime ago, and sobbed myself to sleep.

It was late afternoon when I woke, and I remained where I was under the heavy quilt, thinking of Aaron and all the memories we created in this little cottage. I went to get a glass of water, but returned to my bed soon after, my head on his pillow as I sobbed silently, wiping tears from my face with the back of my hand. I heard a horse, then the front door opened and closed, the heavy footsteps getting closer. I looked up to find Leo standing in the doorway of my bedchamber, his hands on his hips.

'Abigail, we have all been so worried. We thought you had gone for an early walk this morning, so no one thought much about it until the children came home from school and you hadn't returned. It was only when they told Hamish you were going to a place that was special to you and Aaron that I thought you could be here, and I came straight away. Come home, Abigail. It's not good for you to be alone here,' he said gently, making his way to my side before sitting down on the bed next to me.

'No. I need some time alone with Aaron's memory, and I do not want anyone coming here intruding and trampling on our memories that are mine and his alone. No one understands, but I need to be somewhere where I can feel him around me. He is going to show me a sign he's all right and safe. If I stay here alone and think about him, I know he will come and I will get the sign I'm seeking to ease my own mind,' I cried, pleading for him to understand as he put his arms around my shoulders, and I laid my head on his chest.

'All right, butterface. I understand, even though I believe you to be quite insane these days, my dear friend. You must agree to let me come each day and bring your food and drink and check in on you. If you consent, I will tell everyone else to stay away,' he said softly, stroking my hair. I nodded and he stood to leave, gazing down at me while still holding my limp hand, sighing in defeat.

'I'll be back soon with your dinner, and I'm staying until you eat every bit of it. No arguments or I will drag you home by the hair. The hair on your head, not your short and curlies. Although that could be very effective. At least a bit more interesting for those watching on,' remarked, his eyes twinkling wickedly as he smirked, and I couldn't help but smile back.

Leo and I sat outside eating the tender roast beef and mashed potato, the dark brown gravy covering both—a favourite of mine, and he knew it. The sun sat just above the horizon, the evening breeze coming off Bass Strait chilly. He had brought me crème brulee for dessert, going out of his way to make dishes I couldn't help but be tempted by.

'Abigail, everyone is so worried about you. They send their love, by the way.' I shifted on the bench seat, placing my fork down and chewing slowly as I gazed out over the ocean. 'I thought you would like to know the children are coping better than expected, despite everything, and I have to say I believe it is due to Hamish. He keeps them in a regular routine and is there with them when he says he will be. He and I have never been close, but I do have a newfound respect for him since Aaron was incarcerated,' he said thoughtfully. 'Do you think he would be interested in a handsome Italian chef who would take care of him better than any of the women he's been with, including you?' He collapsed into giggles, and I shook my head.

'That I doubt very much, Leonardo. He would do you an injury if you said anything of the sort to him. You can only dream, my sweet boy, and do it silently so he doesn't strike you in the face.' I raised the glass to my lips and sipped the raspberry lemonade he had brought along.

'Well, if you do not ask, the answer will always be no. He is a very handsome man, with those broad shoulders and that far too beautiful face, his long shiny black hair, and that backside he has. I could go on for days talking about it. I haven't called him Adonis all these years for nothing, you know?' he said, stars in his eyes, and I smiled. Hamish was the last person who would take kindly to romantic attention from another man, and I pitied the poor soul that ever tried.

'Hamish isn't like Aaron when it comes to your flirting and touching him in inappropriate places. He will hit you,' I warned, and his face lit up in a smile.

'He would never do that. He loves me too much. I feed him every day, so why would he want to put his potential wife out of action? Who else would fill his belly? Polly can't cook to save herself and he adores my cooking. It may take a little time before he realises he is attracted to me,' he teased, making me smile. We finished dinner and I thanked him, immediately making my way back to bed, the only place I wanted to be. After cleaning the dirty dishes and tidying the kitchen, Leo came to my side and said goodnight, kissing me lovingly on the cheek. 'Now, I will be back in the morning with your food, and more importantly, to see how you are. Please relax and try not to think too much, something I'm well aware is impossible for you right now. Why am I even saying it? I will shut up now.'

He giggled to himself as he kissed me, before waving goodbye, soon disappearing into the small hallway and hurrying through the kitchen and sitting room. I heard him close the front door behind him, and settled myself into Aaron's side of the bed. I breathed in his scent, musk and sandalwood making me heady, while I felt his presence next to me again as I fell into a disturbed sleep, filled with deep holes, a long rope and an axe.

Five-days and four-nights had passed since I arrived at the honeymoon cottage, and I had spent my days alone, crying and sobbing, screaming and begging God to give Aaron back to me. Most of the time I had remained in my bed, or could be found sitting in the places we had sat together over the years. Except when Leo would come in the morning to bring my food for the day. We would sit and talk, passing several hours before he would reluctantly return to the house. He was finding it difficult to keep my friends from coming here, as they were becoming more concerned, the longer I stayed away. Hamish wanted to visit several times to check how I was faring; however, Leo talked him out of it, explaining the cottage was the one place no one was welcome as they would intrude on Aaron's memory for me, invading the only private place I had that belonged to Aaron and me alone.

I heard Leo in the kitchen and rose from my bed, slipping on my dressing gown before making my way out to him. He kissed me good morning, then embraced me warmly.

'I have only brought breakfast as you are coming home with me today. I can't keep people away any longer, and unless you want them here trampling over your memories with their big fat feet, connected to big fat legs, with a giant bum on top and an empty head filled with air, you had better get home. I am talking about Pollyanna, by the way, which I will fill you in on at a later time. Anyway, back to me. If you don't want them here, you better organise yourself to leave.' He smirked across at me while preparing breakfast. He brought me out a mug of freshly brewed coffee, and I accepted, smiling back appreciatively. After serving me first then himself, he sat down beside me and we ate in companionable silence for a time. 'So, are you coming home?' he asked, and I nodded. 'Well, praise you, Lord God, and thank you, Jesus, for listening this time,' he called out to the ceiling as I grimaced.

'There is no Lord or God or Jesus up there that is loving, kind or fair. No God would have taken my darling man from me in the circumstances he left in. It was wrong and I cannot accept that he is gone. I feel him beside me, but I can no longer see him. He refuses to give me a sign, though.' I lowered my head onto my arms resting on the table and sobbed. 'I cannot go on without him, Leo. I know I am the most selfish mother in the world, but I cannot even think of Thomas and Emmy because my mind is completely filled with Aaron. I really do believe I've gone mad. The tears will not stop until he is here beside me once more, and if not, I want to go to sleep and never wake again. I need to be with my husband. I cannot cope with any of this.' I continued to sob as he gently stroked my back.

'I know you feel like this now, but you won't in six-months even though you will still be grieving. Then in a year, it will have become a little easier without you even noticing. It won't always be like this, my dear friend. This too shall pass. You must always remember that.' He embraced me tightly, wiping away my tears with his fingers. 'In two-years' time, you'll be shagging everything that moves, and others that don't,' he teased. I gently smacked his arm before he pulled me to my feet, then helped me gather my belongings and tidied the kitchen before we left.

I sat behind him as he guided Delly through the paddocks and back towards the house—the further away we got from the cottage, the further away I felt from Aaron. The time passed quickly, and we soon arrived back at the house where I left instructions with Mr Masters, briefly explaining that the honeymoon cottage was off limits, and unless I gave specific instructions, no one was to go there. I took the key back from his large key chain to ensure my instructions were obeyed and no one entered without my knowledge or permission.

I made my way upstairs to my bedchamber, stripped off my clothes and changed into my nightgown before returning to my bed, where I stayed until Thomas and Emmy came home from school. They slept with me that night, and it was wonderful to have my babies back in my arms, holding them close to my heart while dreams of Aaron, a rusted anchor and an enormous English Manor filled my tormented mind.

A Word from the Author

THANK YOU FOR TAKING the time to read my series 'Samsara-The First Season'.' It's been nearly a decade since I wrote the first sentence of Abigail's story, and it is a privilege to share it with you.

If you have a few moments, I would be deeply grateful if you left a review on your chosen platform or website. It will help other readers find books that they may never have discovered otherwise. Your feedback means the world to authors and we cannot thank you enough for your support! Thank you for investing your valuable time and money in this story and I hope you enjoyed reading it.

If this series was not for you, that's perfectly okay. We all have different tastes as readers and we can't please everyone all the time. Thank you again for your support and I wish you well in finding novels that bring you joy. Much love to all xx

To find out more,
go to www.jlmartinauthor.com

SAMSARA

THE FIRST SEASON

Returning Home
Volume One Book Six

What if you could remember a past life?
Or worse, what if you couldn't?

Abigail buries her soulmate and embarks on a journey to her home-land, desperate to return to the arms of her beloved Sister Josephine. Unfortunately, she is left feeling confused when the handsome Lord Harrington III makes her acquaintance on the journey, while Hamish has become a thorn in her side, demanding her attention and love, which she is unable to give.

Will Abigail be torn between two men yet again, and will she return to Australia with the twins after all that has happened and the memories Willow Grove holds? Only she can reconcile the unbearable pain she carries as she decides just where her heart belongs.

Continue your journey with Abigail in the epic new Australian historical fiction series spanning a lifetime. Based in Geelong, this debut series by J L Martin spans a lifetime, from 1890 to 1968. Join thousands of readers accompanying this cast of characters through each decade, sharing their joy and sorrow, their triumphs and tragedies, while trying to find out the meaning of the golden glow. The first series of twelve full-length novels are available in ebook, audiobook and paperback from all good bookstores and on-line platforms, and the author's website.